Don't Leave

By

Pru Heathcote

Don't Leave

Pru Heathcote 2020

All Rights Reserved

The author respectfully recognises the use of any and all trademarks.
Published by Red Dragon Publishing LTD 2022
ISBN; 978-1-7396062-2-0

Don't Leave

CHAPTER 1

'Oh, all right, Whisky. I know you're hungry.'

The sleek tabby cat sidled round the woman's ankles as she made her way to the kitchen. She glanced out of the window. The sea was calm and deep blue-black today. Forty years of living here had taught Peggy Mortimer how to forecast the weather by the ever-changing colours of the sea. There were grey banks of cloud on the horizon, so it would be cool and misty by the afternoon.

At the kitchen door, she paused. 'Better check on the bairns first.' She pushed open the nursery door and looked with satisfaction at the three white cots neatly arranged around the room. 'Arabella today, I think,' she said, lifting the bundle from the cot and cradling it in her arms. She rocked it gently, making quiet shushing noises. 'I think I'll put you in your new blue outfit.'

The cat meowed impatiently in the doorway. 'Oh.' Peggy Mortimer stiffened. 'I forgot. That couple are coming at eleven and there's still things need tidying next door. Sorry, Arabella, first things first.'

She tossed the bundle back in the cot, and the white crochet shawl unravelled. One chubby little arm flopped out through the bars.

****

Jane had been dozing. The car was stuffy and hot, and she woke up with a jolt. She looked out of the window. They were well out of the city now and driving between a wide landscape of soft yellow-brown and green fields rolling on towards the distant Cheviot Hills.

1

'You OK, love?' Peter leant over and squeezed her fingers as they tensed on her lap. She knew he meant to reassure her, but she wished he wouldn't do that.

'Nearly there. About another twenty minutes I think.'

Jane stretched her arms, flexing her wrists, and glanced at her watch. They had been driving for nearly an hour now, and she realised it was an hour since she'd had even a passing thought about Angela. The longest time ever. The thought of Angela thumped back into her solar plexus like a heavy blow and the pain came back again as it always did, only this time she felt a wretched, sickening guilt. How could she forget for an hour, for a whole, long hour? The bereavement counsellor told her there would be longer and longer periods between the waves of pain, but she didn't want that to happen. She didn't want to lose the pain. It was the one tangible thing, the only real, solid thing that kept her connection with Angela alive.

She tried to focus on the scenery, to appreciate the beauty of the huge, cloudless late summer sky, the swallows swooping low over the wide-open fields, and the dusty gold of the horse chestnut trees lining the road. They had turned off the A1 and its endless stream of traffic now and were on quiet, winding country lanes. Jane shivered. As they came closer to their destination, the bright sun faded quite suddenly to a faint blur of light in a dismal, misty sky. 'Look, there's the sea,' said Peter. 'We can't be far.'

The sea lay grey as the sky, in a low-level strip beyond a field dotted with bedraggled-looking sheep and a wall of dark, craggy rocks. They were passing through a village, a small collection of low stone cottages, holiday bungalows, and a more recent development of a dozen or so new builds.

'The turning's about half a mile up here, on the left.' Peter was talking in his unnaturally cheery, mock-excited voice that he always used when Jane was in one of her silent moods. 'You wait till you see it, the cottage. The location is out of this world. I think you're going to love it.'

They came to a farm building and next to it turned into a bumpy track deeply rutted by tractor tyres with a muddy strip of grass down the centre. 'Look, there it is. Two Chimneys.'

The two tall and narrow chimneys, each with two even taller chimney pots, stuck up like pillars beyond a dip in the field, at either end of the just visible line of the roof. Jane's body ached from tensing herself against the lurching of the car. The track seemed to go on forever. She looked out at the field with its clumps of brambles and yellowing grass. More sheep. And something – someone – else.

There was a small girl running a little way ahead of them in the field, just near enough for Jane to see her long fair hair blowing behind her. She was wearing something red. A tracksuit? As the car drew level with her, the figure stopped quite suddenly and she turned to stare at the car, directly at Jane. She was too far away for Jane to notice any expression on her face, but there was something about her – the forlorn droop of her shoulders that sent an icy wave of melancholy sweeping over her.

'Peter, look at that little girl,' she said. It was the first time she'd spoken since they left Newcastle. Peter braked gently and peered out.

'Where?' he said. 'I can't see anyone.'

Jane glanced at Peter. He was looking in the wrong direction. 'No, not there. She—'

When she looked back, there was no sign of the child.

'Perhaps she lives on the farm,' Peter said. 'I wonder why she isn't at school. Don't they go back this week?'

Yes, thought Jane, and I should have been taking Angela for her first day in Reception.

The cottage lay in a deep dip at the end of the track. It was built of solid grey stone, with an entry porch at each end. There had obviously been some recent work done to update the property. Some of the stones had been replaced with lighter sand-coloured stone and new windows gleamed under the eaves of the slate roof.

Peter leapt out of the car and stretched his arms. 'What do you think then, Jane?'

Jane didn't answer. It felt like there was a heavy boulder in her chest, pinning her to the car seat.

Peter had found this place on the internet and been to see it a week or so earlier. He'd hardly talked of anything else. Of course, he'd researched the history. The original cottage dated from the early 1800s, when it had been a bathing house for the aristocratic family who lived in the big house near the village. It had been derelict for years until the 1940s when a retired doctor from Berwick had bought it, extended and renovated it as his retirement home, and his grandson was the current owner. Now it was divided in two, the larger section used as a holiday and sometimes longer-term let, and the small section on the end was occupied by a woman who oversaw the letting and upkeep of the property.

'We'll have to get the key off Mrs Mortimer,' Peter said, opening the passenger door for Jane. He lowered his voice. 'She's a funny old stick, looks a dead ringer for Morticia Addams, but don't worry. I think she's the type that keeps her herself to herself.'

Jane sat quite still. She didn't want to get out.

'You know, Jane, if you really don't like it, you don't have to move here. But at least give it a look over, eh?'

Mrs Mortimer took some time to answer. They saw a dark shape behind the frosted glass panes on the top half of the door. It opened just a crack, and a face peered out at them – a long, pale, bony face. Jet black eyes, beaky nose, black hair – probably dyed, Jane thought – scraped back into a tight knot. She could have been any age between fifty and seventy, it was hard to tell, especially as she had whitish powdery make-up on her face, and eyebrows that had been painted on with a thick black pencil. She looked at them without a trace of a smile.

'Ah, Mrs Mortimer, good morning.' Peter beamed at her, her blank expression making him uneasy. 'Er – good to see you again. This is my wife, Jane. She's come to have a look at the cottage?"

'Yes.' She nodded. 'I was expecting you. I have the key ready.' She had a strong local accent, but spoke slowly, and with an old-fashioned clipped pronunciation, as if she were trying to sound correct and proper, or 'talk posh', as Jane's nan used to say.

Mrs Mortimer didn't look at Peter or Jane as she led them to the door. Peter had been hoping she would just let them in and leave them to look round on their own, but she unlocked the door and walked in ahead of them. It was pleasantly light and clean inside, with a smell of fresh paint and furniture polish. Pale grey paint, spotless wooden floors, pine furniture, and tasteful seascapes on the walls – it all looked perfect. Mrs Mortimer, wearing a black cardigan buttoned to the neck and a black knee-length skirt, ushered them in to the gleaming kitchen. 'It's a fully equipped kitchen – microwave, fridge-freezer, double oven – all the usual requirements,' she said, with something like a smile twitching the side of her mouth as she ran her hand over the new granite worktop.

'And this is the living room.' She marched ahead of them. 'Quite comfortable, I think you'll find.'

Jane looked around. She hadn't realised from the other side of the house just how close it was to the sea. A wide low window looked out on a little strip of mown grass, enclosed by a dry-stone wall, and beyond that was a sheer drop down to the sea, now a pearly grey expanse flecked with white and stretching out to the distant horizon.

'Excellent. Excellent.' Peter bounded over to the window. 'Just what we've been looking for, isn't it, Jane? Oh, and will you look at that view? The sea's so close it feels just like we're sitting on a ship, but without all that queasy bobbing up and down.'

Jane felt her stomach clench with irritation. She hated it when he talked in that hearty way, trying to sound upbeat – what he called 'jollying you along'. It never worked.

To the right, the coastline curved a little, revealing a steep cliff with jagged black rocks below.

'I think there's a little sandy beach just below the garden wall there,' Peter said. 'But it's almost high tide now, so we can't see it. There are some steps down, aren't there, Mrs Mortimer?'

She nodded. 'Yes. Slippery, mind. You have to watch how you go. But it's private, you'll find. No one can get to it unless they use the steps from here.'

'Just think, Jane, if we get a nice warm autumn, you'd be able to sit there and do your writing and sketching and have the beach all to yourself.' Peter put his hand on the window catch. 'May I open it for a moment?'

'If you like,' said Mrs Mortimer. She was standing very still and upright, with her hands clasped in front of her. A blast of cold air and the quiet hiss of the waves came in as Peter opened the window. He leant out and breathed in noisily.

'Come on Jane, breathe in this air. Marvellous. This'll blow the city cobwebs away, all that salty spray too. You can smell it in the air.'

Jane shivered: 'It's rather cold. Shut the window, Peter.'

'Cold? Nonsense. Bracing, not cold. Anyway, we love it, Mrs Mortimer. I think we'll take it, won't we, Jane?'

Jane stood up; her apathy replaced by annoyance. 'Just a minute, Peter. We haven't even had a chance to discuss it yet.'

'What's to discuss? Come on, love. We'll not find another little gem to rent at this price. What a position. It's perfect.'

'I'm just thinking – it's a little bit remote, perhaps, so far from the road? It'd be OK when you're here, Peter, but what about when you're at work – or away?'

Peter turned to Mrs Mortimer. 'Ah but Mrs Mortimer, you'll be just the other side of the wall in the adjoining cottage, won't you?'

She nodded, unclasping her hands. Jane noticed that her fingernails were painted a vivid shade of crimson. 'Of course. I'll keep an eye on her, don't you worry.'

Jane felt she might scream but kept it in check. 'I am here in the room, you know,' she said. 'And I don't need anybody keeping an eye on me, thank you. It is a lovely house, yes, but I really don't want to be stranded in the back of beyond. I'll only agree to come here if I can come off the medication and have my own car.'

Peter put his arm round her. 'It's OK, darling. We'll talk about that later.'

'I've had interest from another couple.' Mrs Mortimer was looking at her watch. 'You'll not have to delay too much in making a decision.'

'Right,' said Peter, raising a questioning eyebrow at Jane. 'Shall we have a quick look upstairs?'

Peter bounded ahead of Jane up the stairs leading to two bedrooms and a tiny all-white bathroom, spotless and newly furnished, with deeply sloping ceilings. Peter had to bend his tall frame to peer out of the window under the eaves. 'Jane, come and look at this. This is what we'll wake up to every morning.'

Under the huge sky the sea stretched out to the long low horizon.

'Isn't this what you need, darling? Peace and quiet, complete rest and tranquillity?'

'How long for?' said Jane, sitting on the bed with its neat white bedspread.

'Well, how about we take it till December to start with? Then we can take stock, see how you're feeling. '

There was a long silence. All her instincts were screaming NO! The isolation, the weird woman…it didn't feel right. But she found herself nodding. 'Yes, all right then.'

She came and stood beside Peter at the window, still gazing at the view. 'I'd better pop down and tell Mrs M we're having it,' he whispered.

When he'd gone Jane stood a while and looked out of the window. She could hear Peter and Mrs Mortimer's murmured conversation downstairs. She wondered if he was telling her about Angela, what he was saying.

Just as she was turning to go back downstairs, Jane caught a flash of red at the bottom of the cliff, down among the rocks. It was the little girl. She saw clearly the child's blonde head bobbing about between the large boulders that littered the shore. The tide was coming in fast, the waves rippling over the rocks, swirling and crashing dangerously close to the child. She wore a red top, and her thin arms stretched wide as she balanced herself, jumping from rock to rock. Jane's heart was thumping. She'd have to alert someone before the little girl was cut off. Where on earth were her parents? She couldn't be much older than seven or eight.

'Peter?' She turned to call down the stairs. 'Peter?' When she looked out again there was no sign of the little girl.

Jane ran down the stairs. Peter, always anxious and alert, was at her side. 'What's up?'

'I thought I saw – no, I did see – oh it's nothing,' She felt awkward and foolish. Peter was looking at her quizzically.

'Well, I've told Mrs Mortimer we'll be here at least until Christmas. Maybe longer.'

'It can be bleak here, in the winter,' said Mrs Mortimer, still holding herself stiff and aloof. 'As you know, it's a quarter of a mile to the road, three to the village.'

'Not a problem.' Peter beamed, rubbing his hands together. 'We'll make it cosy, won't we, Jane? Can't wait to get that log burner blazing away.'

Mrs Mortimer was at the door, holding it open for them.

'I'll be in touch about when we plan to move in,' Peter said. 'Probably Friday week, if that suits you?'

'I daresay it will.'

In the doorway Jane paused. 'Mrs Mortimer, do you live here on your own?'

'I do. Unless you count my cat.'

'It's just – well, I saw a little girl just now, playing on the rocks. I thought it might be your granddaughter visiting, perhaps?'

'No. I don't have grandchildren.'

'Oh. Holidaymakers on a walk I expect. Although I didn't see adults with her – or anyone. I was worried about her.'

Mrs Mortimer's mouth tightened into a thin line. 'I doubt it. We don't get that many walkers along this particular stretch of coast. The old coastal path long since eroded away, and now there's far too many rocks and dangerous drops. Not good for walking.'

'Oh, OK. Perhaps I just imagined it,' Jane said, although she knew she hadn't.

'Yes.' Mrs Mortimer shut the door behind them and locked it with a firm click. She didn't say goodbye or turn to watch them as Peter started the engine and manoeuvred the car round from the gravelly patch outside the cottage. Jane glanced in the wing mirror and saw her marching back to her side of the house.

'What a peculiar woman,' she said as they bumped back up the track to the road.

Peter laughed. 'Isn't she. Don't think she cracked her face into a smile once. And she's got a cat. Definitely a witch, Jane. '

'Don't say that,' snapped Jane. 'Not every eccentric woman with a thin face and a cat has to be a witch, Peter. It was people like you who got so many harmless old women burnt at the stake in the past, you know.'

'I know, I know. Just having a joke. You remember what those are don't you, jokes?'

She tried to ignore the put-down, but it stung. There was a hard lump in her throat as she felt the tears pricking her eyes and she wanted to say, Oh, sorry that losing my child has destroyed my sense of humour. But she was in no mood to start an argument.

They drove on in silence. The sky had darkened and rain began to pelt against the windscreen. Peter turned on the wipers and they stared out at the empty road ahead.

It was nearly ten minutes before she spoke again.

'I did see her, Peter. The little girl in red. She was there.'

CHAPTER 2

The young people were noisy in the street below as they tumbled out of the club round the corner. The girls screeching, the boys bellowing and laughing. Freshers' week, of course. *Away from their parents for the first time they all went a bit mad*, Jane thought, sighing as she reached for her phone. Peter snored gently away next to her. It was three in the morning, and in a few hours, they would be leaving their flat in a side road not far from Gosforth High Street and heading up to Northumberland.

The constant noise of the city was the main reason Peter decided they must move away for a while. It wasn't helping Jane's insomnia, he said. One night he found her in the early hours, curled up in a ball on the floor in Angela's room, with her fists over her ears, screaming there was a strange baby in the cot calling to her, a little boy with red hair, not Angela.

'That settles it. We've got to get you away from here,' Peter said. So the decision was made. They were letting their flat out to a Chinese couple, both doctors, that Peter had met through the university, a quietly spoken, smiling pair. They didn't look the types to throw wild parties and wreck the place.

'But tell them not to use Angela's room,' Jane told Peter. 'I don't want anyone but us going in there, touching things, moving things.'

'They won't. I'll put a lock on the door if you insist, but honestly, Jane, there's no need to worry.' There was a pause and Jane knew what he was going to say next. 'And, darling, I hate to say this, but isn't it time we sorted it out, that room? It's been nearly three years and—'

'No. And it's not been nearly three years, Peter. It's been two years, five months, and six days.'

Jane often sat in Angela's nursery, with its pale lemon walls, the Peter Rabbit frieze and the matching mobile hanging over the white painted cot. Even though the pain it caused was almost too much to bear, Jane loved to hold the soft cot blanket close to her face and try to catch a remnant of Angela's sweet baby smell on it. All the soft toys sat in a neat row on the chest of drawers, as if waiting for her return.

The shrieks and singing of the partygoers faded into the distance, and only the faint rumble of occasional night traffic broke the silence.

Jane fell into a restless sleep. She was standing still in the field beside the track that led to the cottage with only its two tall chimneys in view. She was still wearing the oversized T-shirt she always slept in, and her feet were bare. Coming up the field ran the little blonde girl, stretching her arms out towards Jane. She came so close that Jane could see the sprinkling of freckles across her nose, and the Minnie Mouse cartoon on the front of her red top. She smiled, and Jane noticed her two front teeth were missing.

Jane smiled back and said, 'I'm coming to live here for a while. I hope we can be friends.' Then somehow, they were sitting together on the doorstep of Nan's house in Durham and the little girl had changed into Nan's old black dog, Rex. He was licking her hand, and coming up the garden path was Peter, carrying Angela in his arms. She was smiling and clapping her chubby little hands, her dark curls bobbing as Peter hurried towards them.

He called out to Jane. 'It's all right, here she is. It was only a dream you know, all just a bad dream.'

Not for the first time, Jane woke up with a lurch, wonderful, blissful relief sweeping over her. It had all been a horrible dream, and Angela was still in the room next door, lying safe and alive in her cot. Only she wasn't, and the unbearable living nightmare of reality quickly flooded back.

****

In the cottage by the sea, the phone rang. Mrs Mortimer put Aidan back in his cot, tutting. She had only just got him changed and brushed his soft dark hair. There was always some interruption.

'Hello?'

'Nigel Blackwood here, Mrs Mortimer. Just wondered whether the new tenants are still arriving today?'

'They are, Mr Blackwood. Mr and Mrs Eagle. All the paperwork is complete, and I have their deposit here.'

'Excellent. Efficient as ever. I'll pop by later this week to see if everything's OK. They seem like a nice couple, do they?'

'Pleasant enough. They'll be no trouble I'm sure, Mr Blackwood.'

'Please, I keep telling you, call me Nigel.' He laughed. Mrs Mortimer didn't reply. 'Yes, well, see you later this week then.'

Mrs Mortimer went back to the nursery and drew the curtains closed. She didn't want the new couple peering through the window, not that they would have any reason to come round this side of the house.

They wouldn't understand about the babies. They were a strange pair, she thought. He was obviously much older than her, in his fifties at least, and her – well, she was probably older than she looked. How he fussed over her too, like she was a simple-minded child. She was a plumpish, sulky sort of lass, with all that thick rusty-red hair, and a fresh face with not a lick of make-up on. The way she was going on about seeing a child playing on the rocks.

'Well,' she said to the cat, who sat on the windowsill staring unblinkingly at her. 'We'll have to keep our eye on that one, won't we, Whisky?'

****

That first night in the cottage, Peter and Jane made love to the sound of the waves as they ebbed and flowed outside the open window. She found consolation and comfort in his arms, safety, and solace, but pleasure and the old passion? No, it was still too soon for that.

It had been one of those hazy golden early autumn days, and even though their cases and cardboard boxes still cluttered the living room downstairs, Peter decided they must go for a walk while the weather was fine, and they drove to Craster and walked across the fields to the jagged ruins of Dunstanburgh Castle. The sea was flat and still, a sheet of dazzling silver flashing in the bright sun. The fresh air brought a flush of colour to Jane's cheeks. They bought some smoky-smelling kippers for their supper. Jane felt something close to happiness again, although she still carried her sorrow around with her all the time, like a heavy stone.

Now, with Peter's head snuggled into her neck, she felt drowsy and ready to sleep.

'Darling,' Peter whispered into her hair, 'you do know I've got to go back to work next Monday, don't you? I should have been back three weeks ago, but Richard's been covering my lectures for me far too long and I've got to get the new intake settled in.'

'Of course, I realise that. It'll be OK.'

'You won't be lonely all day? Bored?'

'It would be nice if you could leave me the car. Then at least I could take myself off to Alnwick or Berwick, maybe.'

Peter sighed. 'Jane, I'd love to but, well, I can't. You know you were told not to drive while you were on the medication. And even if you drove me up to the bus stop in the village, it would take at least a couple of hours to get to Newcastle. And the same coming home. I suppose I could let you have it occasionally, and I could get the train if you drove me to Alnmouth station, but—'

'Oh, forget it.' Jane rolled over with her back to him. 'Stupid idea.'

'Maybe we could think about getting you your own car? When you're well enough not to need medication?'

'We can't afford it. Not now I'm not working. Anyway, I'm tired now, Peter. I just want to go to sleep.'

'Yes, me too.'

Jane lay still, listening to the quiet rhythmic hiss of the sea. It was a mild night, so she'd left the bedroom window slightly ajar. Then there was another sound. It came from somewhere below the window. It sounded like someone crying. A whimpering sob. A child's crying.

For a brief moment the crying stopped, and just as Jane was thinking it must be an animal of some kind, perhaps Mrs Mortimer's cat, it started again. Peter was already breathing the slow heavy breath of sleep as Jane slipped out of bed and went to the window. The crying grew a little louder as she opened the window wide and looked out at the patch of grass below with its two garden chairs and picnic table, everything clear as day in the moonlight. She looked and looked. There was nothing – no one – there. The crying stopped, and the only noise to break the silence of night was the sound of the sea. Jane closed the window and went back to bed, wondering if she was going out of her mind again.

When she woke in the early hours, she tried to tell herself what she'd heard had been part of a dream. Later, as she sat in bed sipping the tea Peter had brought up to her and looking out at the golden sun rising over the sea, she contemplated telling him what had happened, but decided against it. Too often she'd seen that look in his eyes, that look of pity and concern mingled with exasperation, and more often than not followed by his soothing reassurances these imaginings were just another symptom of her illness, and would pass in time.

****

She'd been in the cottage over two weeks now and Peter was back at work. Ever since she heard the crying, she'd suffered insomnia every night, lying awake till dawn, straining her ears, expecting to hear it again, but she didn't. And then when she did fall asleep there were the dreams, the dreams where Angela was still alive and well. The days were better. At first, she was getting to like the solitude; she liked opening the bedroom curtains every morning and looking out at the sea and sky. She liked the seaweed smell at low tide, reminding her of seaside holidays with Nan when she was a child. But now the weather was turning murky and damp and time began to drag. This morning she couldn't even see beyond the stone wall for the wet blanket of mist. There was nothing but greyness. Getting into a routine, that was the important thing, Peter said. Find things to do.

She made herself a coffee, carried it into the living room, opened the curtains. She flipped open her laptop and went to her emails, hoping to find a response from Suzy. Good, the connection was OK today. Peter told her Mrs Mortimer had warned him how the internet connection was sometimes dodgy, as was the mobile phone signal. It was something to do with where the cottage was situated, in a dip.

'Would you believe old Morticia next door is a bit of a techie? We had quite a little discussion about stuff. She gets everything online,' he said.

'I know. I've seen the delivery vans bumping down the track a few times already,' Jane said. 'And it's not just groceries, either. Goodness knows what she's buying.'

So far, Mrs Mortimer had kept her distance. They'd opted to do their own cleaning and laundry, a service that Mrs Mortimer would normally come in and perform once a week. But as they were going to be staying much longer than the usual holidaymakers, and there were plenty of cleaning materials, a washing machine, and spare bed linen and towels, Jane was more than happy to do it herself and avoid a weekly intrusion.

She'd sent Suzy three or four chatty emails, and tried to ring her twice, but there was no response. Of course, they would be busy in the office, with it being the start of the academic year and all the new students' data to be processed. But she did miss Suzy. Suzy was the sister Jane never had but always wanted. She worked alongside Jane in the university admin office. She was nearly ten years older than Jane, but one of those strong, wise women, motherly but not smothering, a woman who was warm and listened rather than talked. When Jane's world fell apart, when she lost Angela, Suzy was there for her, not offering advice or platitudes, just there.

By the afternoon there was still no reply to her emails. Jane got out her phone, tapped the office number, and asked for Suzy's extension.

'Hello, Suzy Shaw. Can I help you?'

Excited to hear her voice, Jane plumped herself down on the sofa, hugging the phone to her ear. 'Suzy, thank God, I've got you at last. It's me, Jane.'

'Oh, hi, Jane. Is everything all right?'

She sounded a bit different, Jane thought, a bit strained.

'Oh yes, fine. You know we've moved up to Northumberland for a month or two, don't you?'

'Yes, you told me. How's it going? How are you?'

'Oh, getting better, I think. Just a bit bored. Missing work. Missing you. Is it busy there?'

'Frantic. But listen, you need to forget about work and concentrate on getting well. Enjoy the peace and quiet. I bet it's lovely there.'

'Yes, it's lovely. It's right on the coast, practically on the beach. Nothing to look out on but the North Sea in all its grey hugeness.'

'Right. What are you doing all day? Done any painting? Started writing that novel yet?'

Jane laughed. 'No. I can't seem to settle for anything. I go for long walks, read books, that sort of thing. And now the weather's getting worse...We get this mist, this damp sea fret, and it gets cold sometimes, so cold, I can't seem to warm myself up.'

'So, Jane, was there anything in particular you wanted to...?'

'No, no, not really. I just wanted to talk to someone. Someone friendly.'

'Is it really that remote there? No neighbours you can talk to?'

'Well, there's this odd woman next door.'

'Odd? How?'

'I can't say exactly, just odd. Think Mrs Danvers in Rebecca. Really creepy.'

'Oh dear. I haven't seen much of Peter at work lately. How is he?'

'Still treating me like a baby. He's back at work now. You'll probably bump into him some time. And, Suzy, I've not been sleeping that well. It's these dreams. I dream that Angela is… Look, Suzy, you couldn't come up for a visit sometime, could you? I'd love to see you. Hear all the work gossip.'

There was a bit of a pause on the line. Jane wondered for a moment if the phone had gone dead. 'Jane, I'd love to, but like I told you it's so busy here. Mike and I hardly see each other all week and the weekends are a bit precious. I'm absolutely knackered by Friday. You know how it is.'

'Yes, I understand. I remember what it was like, pressure, pressure.'

'Maybe when things calm down a bit, yeah?'

'Sure, no problem, it's OK. Ring me when you're not so busy, though.'

'Will do. Sorry. Got to go. There's a queue of students waiting…'

'OK. Thanks. Bye… Oh, and, Suzy—'

There was a click as Suzy hung up. Jane hugged her phone to her chest. Something had changed between her and Suzy and she felt a sinking sensation inside.

Someone behind her coughed. Jane gasped and her phone clattered to the wooden floor. She swung round to see Mrs Mortimer standing at the living room door, still as a statue, ramrod straight with her hands folded together in front of her.

'Oh my God, Mrs Mortimer. You gave me such a fright. How long have you been standing there?'

'Long enough.' Her face was blank as a white mask. Jane's heart lurched with horror when she recalled her conversation with Suzy. Mrs Mortimer must have heard every word.

'Oh no, how embarrassing. Look, the stuff I said about Mrs Danvers—'

'I've never heard of the woman. Friend of yours, is she?'

'Um, yes. That's right, a friend. Did you want something?'

'No. Your husband asked me to call in on you. He's concerned that you've not been sleeping well.'

'I haven't. Honestly, Mrs Mortimer, I'm very grateful for your concern. But I really don't need checking up on and I would prefer it if you didn't just creep in like that or eavesdrop on my private conversations.'

Mrs Mortimer pulled up her shoulders. 'I can assure you, Mrs Eagle, I don't creep anywhere. I came in through the door. And I have better things to do than listen to your chit-chat.' Despite her frosty tone, her voice was low and calm.

'I didn't know you had a key.'

'Of course I have a key. I'm the appointed caretaker of this property.'

'Well, another time I would prefer it if you knocked first, please.'

'If you say so.' She walked over to the window. 'I'll close the curtains for you, shall I? There's a thick fog rolling in. Makes the place dark as night.'

'No, leave them please.' Jane jumped up and stood beside Mrs Mortimer. She didn't want her touching anything. 'I am capable of drawing the curtains myself.'

There was an icy silence as the two women stood together by the window. Jane heard a little gulping sob coming from somewhere outside in the fog. Then another.

'Oh. Listen. That sound.'

Mrs Mortimer put her head on one side, listening. 'Sound? What sound?'

'It's a child. A child crying. Surely you can hear it?' She stared out of the window but could see nothing out there but a ragged grey mist.

'You'll not be used to the sounds of nature here,' Mrs Mortimer said. 'That'll be the wind. Or the gulls. They make a noise people tell me sounds just like a baby crying.'

'No. I do know the difference between a seagull and a child's cry. And that is a child's voice, not a baby's. Listen.'

Mrs Mortimer frowned. 'I can't hear anything. But then, I've never had children myself, so I'm not familiar with how they sound.'

Jane stepped towards Mrs Mortimer, suddenly feeling guilty that she'd spoken to her so sharply.

'But I am familiar with a baby's cry, Mrs Mortimer,' she said, softening her voice. 'My daughter, Angela—'

'Oh?' The older woman raised a quizzical eyebrow. 'Your husband gave me to understand you were a childless couple.'

'We are – yes – childless. She…we…lost her. Two years ago. She wasn't quite two. It was sepsis…very sudden.'

There was an awkward silence. The crying sound had stopped. Jane waited for the response she'd come to expect when she told strangers about Angela: the rearranging of their face into an appropriate expression of sadness and concern, perhaps a gentle pat on the hand, a few fumbling words of sympathy. But from Mrs Mortimer, there was nothing, nothing at all.

'I'm sorry to hear that I'm sure,' was all she said. 'Anyway, if you're quite certain there's nothing you need?' she added briskly.

'No, thank you, no.'

Mrs Mortimer left as swiftly and silently as she'd arrived. Shivering, Jane sat for a while on the sofa, hugging the big red cushion for comfort and trying to make sense of what had just happened. She ought to be laying the fire, it had turned so cold.

Someone was tapping at the window. A soft but persistent tap. *Tap–tap-tap*. A pause. *Tap–tap-tap*. Had Peter come home early, forgotten his door key? Oh no, not Mrs Mortimer again…

She turned and jumped to her feet. A little girl's small white face pressed up against the glass, staring straight at Jane.

CHAPTER 3

Cats, Mrs Mortimer decided, were easier to understand than people. You knew where you were with cats. Whisky always made it quite plain when he wanted to go out, or come in, or be fed. There were times of course when he took her by surprise. He could be purring on her lap one moment, and then, for no accountable reason, would suddenly turn and bite or scratch her hand before stalking off with his tail in the air. But on the whole, she preferred his company to the effort of trying to make sense of the puzzling behaviour of humans.

Her Next Door for instance. What had she meant, describing her as *odd*? And *creepy*? It didn't make any sense. And then that business about hearing a child crying. Oh well, the husband seemed a straightforward sort, and he'd told her his wife had been ill. Mental health issues, he said. Well, that was what they called it these days. Not right in the head was what she would have called it.

She glanced at her watch. She liked her day to follow a regular timetable. Routine made her feel safe, comfortable. Now it was four o'clock, time for a cup of tea and a sit down in front of the TV. A nice quiz show perhaps, or one of those programmes where they take people house hunting and have a good nose around. She would put the kettle on then pop into the nursery and decide which of the bairns she would have on her lap while she watched TV. It was one of her favourite times of the day. Cuddling a baby, rocking its soft body and feeling its weight in her arms, was soothing to the spirit.

But as she went into the kitchen for the kettle and glanced out of the window, she heard a woman's voice shouting 'Come back, come back.' and a figure flashed past and vanished into the mist. She recognised the flying red hair and the stripy jumper – it was Her Next Door. Whatever could be the matter now?

Peggy Mortimer banged the kettle back down and went to the kitchen door. 'Mrs Eagle? Is there something wrong? Are you all right?' she called out.

Jane appeared, her hair wild, her face flushed. 'She knocked at the window. Mrs Mortimer, I saw her. That little girl again, the same one I saw on the rocks. I wanted to see where she went but she's just vanished. Could she…do you think…be from the farm at the top of the track? Do they have children?'

'Mr and Mrs Armstrong at the farm have no children. Well, they have two sons, but both the lads are in their early twenties, I'd say.'

'Could they perhaps have visitors with a child?'

'I really couldn't say, I'm sure.'

Jane waved her hands in frustration. 'But, Mrs Mortimer, she really shouldn't be wandering around here on her own. I'm quite worried. She seemed to be wanting to get my attention, but then she ran away. Should we not tell someone? Do you have the phone number for the farm?'

A light but persistent drizzle began to fall out of the grey sky.

'No, I do not,' said Mrs Mortimer. 'I suggest you get back into the house, Mrs Eagle, or you'll get wet.'

She shut the door with a firm click and turned her back. 'Not right, that one,' she muttered to Whisky, who was waiting by his food bowl. 'I'll feed you in a minute. I'll just put the kettle on, then see to the bairns. I think it's Lily's turn today.' She tutted, still irritated by the interruption. 'Now she's made me miss ten minutes of Escape to the Country.'

****

In the cottage, Jane paced up and down, her hands tucked under her armpits. They were cold as ice, and she couldn't seem to get warm, even with the central heating switched up to maximum. Outside, the mist wrapped around everything, like a damp grey shroud. Jane felt as if the house could be floating in space, in nothingness, with no landmarks visible. She picked up her phone to ring Peter, then put it down again. He was probably driving home right now. What would she tell him first? About Suzy being distant with her on the phone? Mrs Mortimer coming in the house? Her cold reaction when she told her about Angela? The child tapping at the window?

He was late arriving, held up by a staff meeting and heavy traffic and then the fog as he came closer to the cottage. It was already growing dark as summer finally faded into autumn. It was obvious he'd had a trying day, so Jane resisted the urge to fly into his arms. She stayed calm and went into the kitchen to make him a cup of tea.

She called to him, 'Peter, could you light the log burner? It's so cold.'

'Really?' he said. 'It's like an oven in here.'

As Peter screwed up the twists of newspaper to start the fire, Jane sat on the sofa, hugging the big red cushion, and told him about the day's events.

Peter, being a scientist, always tried to find a logical explanation to everything. 'I'm not surprised Suzy sounded stressed. I had to go in the admin office today and it was totally mad. They've got two people off sick and the paperwork is getting ridiculous these days. I didn't see Suzy though.'

And when she told him about Mrs Mortimer, and her "Friend of yours, is she?" remark when Jane mentioned Mrs Danvers, he chuckled heartily.

'Hilarious. I can see what you mean. I remember that film was one of my mother's favourites. Hitchcock, wasn't it? Laurence Olivier was Maxim de Winter—'

'Yes, yes, but when I told Mrs Mortimer about Angela, she was…well…she didn't react at all. I've never met anyone so devoid of any human emotion. It's scary.'

Peter, squatting in front of the stove, held a match to the paper and kindling and the flames roared up, licking round the logs as he wedged them in. 'There you are now, Jane,' he said, beaming with satisfaction. 'Haven't lost my old boy scouting skills. Come and warm yourself.'

Jane stood in front of the fire, holding out her hands, but the warmth didn't seem to touch the chill deep inside her.

'You know, I think I've worked out what it is with old Morticia next door. The signs are all there, it's obvious. She's an Aspie,' Peter said.

'What?'

'Asperger's syndrome. High functioning autism. Although these days I believe we're supposed to call it neurologically atypical. It's a bit of a cliché that Asperger's people are good at maths and physics, but I've had more than a few students with it, so I do recognise it…the problems with social interaction, the apparent difficulty with empathy and understanding the social norms.'

'Or she could just be a cold-hearted buttoned-up bitch,' Jane said. Peter smiled and sat down on the sofa, sipping his tea.

'Shall I do the supper, if you're feeling tired?' he said. 'Macaroni cheese, OK? I think we'll have to do a big shop on Saturday. There's not much in the fridge.'

'Peter, I saw her again. The little girl. This time she tapped at the window, right there. I saw her face pressed up against the glass, staring at me. She looked scared…desperate. I tried to run out after her, but she vanished.'

'Ah,' he said.

'What do you mean, Ah?'

'Darling, have you considered the possibility that—'

'What possibility?'

'That there is no little girl. The things you've seen and heard are part of your illness. You're having another acute episode, perhaps?'

'No. No. it was real.'

'To you, yes, I'm not denying that. But the voices, the hallucinations, they're not new to you, are they? Remember that little boy you swore you saw in Angela's cot?'

'I don't want to talk about that,' she said stiffly, and walked off to the kitchen.

After their supper, Peter said he was shattered and went up to bed, leaving Jane sitting beside the glowing remains of the logs. It was quiet as the grave outside, even the constant sound of the sea just a muffled rumble. Peter came stamping downstairs in his dressing gown, stopping halfway. He was holding something.

'Jane,' he said, waving a small packet in his hand. 'I just found these in the bathroom waste bin. Explain.'

'My Risperdal tablets,' she said. 'What about it?'

'They're all still in here, the tablets. You haven't been taking them, have you?'

'No. I don't want to take them anymore, Peter.'

He sighed and flung the packet down at her feet. 'Well, that explains it then, doesn't it? The hallucinations. Honestly, Jane, you can't just take yourself off anti-psychotic medication like that. You at least should have discussed it with the doctor.'

'Why? They make me feel half dead, sleepy, lethargic. I can't be bothered to do anything. And I've gained too much weight. I don't feel like me anymore. Anyway, I am an adult. I can make my own decisions.'

'Jane, you had a diagnosis of paranoid schizophrenia. It's serious stuff.'

'You know I didn't agree with that diagnosis. They said the brain scans were inconclusive, if you remember. I am not schizophrenic, Peter. And I don't need medication – or lectures from you.'

'Oh, please yourself,' he said, turning back upstairs. At the top he called back down to her, 'Just don't blame me when you find yourself back in St. Nicks.'

Jane lay awake that night, her heart pounding, her stomach churning. Was she really sliding back down into that dark place again? She was trying to remember what happened in those terrible days leading up to her being admitted to hospital last summer, but it was all a blur. And it wasn't the first time. It started about eight months after losing Angela. She had tried going back to work but was constantly bursting into tears and being sent home. Then there was the sleepwalking. Peter said he would find her in Angela's bedroom, wandering round and round, touching things, opening and closing drawers. He would guide her back to bed and in the morning, she remembered nothing about it. Or she suddenly woke in the dark depths of the night, hearing Angela calling for her. Once, she lashed out and punched Peter hard on the jaw when he tried to stop her getting up to go to the nursery. She didn't remember that either, or much about the day that led up to the first time she landed up in hospital.

It was their lunch hour, and she and Suzy were walking through the Eldon Centre. It was three weeks before Christmas and everywhere was packed with shoppers. Suzy went into Boots, and Jane said she'd have a sit down outside and wait for her as she was feeling a bit wobbly. Jane did remember that bit, feeling dizzy amidst all the sparkling decorations, the surging crowds, and a brass band booming out carols nearby. And then she heard Angela's voice, loud and clear, shouting, *Mummy! Mummy!* She knew without a doubt it was Angela calling for her from that buggy being pushed by a young woman with a scraped-up ponytail, just in front of where she sat. Of course. It was obvious that Angela wasn't dead at all, she'd been kidnapped. And that was the last thing she recalled.

Apparently, according to Suzy's account, Jane lunged through the crowd after the woman, screaming, 'That's my baby, my Angela. Give her back.' She'd tried to grab the child out of the buggy. Suzy came out of the shop to see Jane on the ground being held down, thrashing and shouting, by a huddle of people.

What happened after that she didn't know, only that she'd struggled back through a nightmarish fog of confusion to wake up in a hospital bed not knowing who she was, or where she was, or why she was there, or why there were bars on the window. She didn't even know who that middle-aged man was, sitting next to her bed, holding her hand, and telling her it was all going to be all right.

Now as she lay staring at the low sloping ceiling of their bedroom, she heard Peter stir beside her, and his arm reached out for her. 'I'm sorry, darling,' he mumbled sleepily. 'I just worry about you so much. I just want you to be well, you do know that, don't you?'

'Of course I do,' she said, nestling against the comfort of his warm body.

For the next few days, the mist dissolved, and the skies cleared, the sea smooth and silver under a watery sun. Jane didn't see Mrs Mortimer, and there was no more sign of the child, no more tapping on the window. All the same, Jane took to sitting in the kitchen, well away from the large sitting-room window, flipping through magazines without taking in a word, drinking coffee. And she was still cold.

Saturday arrived, sunny but breezy, and although Peter had a load of paperwork and his big research paper to edit, he and Jane drove to the nearest town, Alnwick. They did a supermarket shop, wandered round the busy main street, browsed the market stalls in the square, had lunch in an old-fashioned cafe. Jane began to feel almost happy and relaxed, and for the first time since they left Newcastle, warm. The icy feeling in her bones began to melt as she sipped her soup, and she felt her mood lighten with the movement and nearness of people, the sound of voices. She liked the awareness of normal life going on around her and in the street normal people, going about their ordinary business.

Peter said, 'Jane, when are you going to start doing your painting and drawing again? I think it would do you the world of good.'

'I was thinking of that. I left all my paints and brushes and stuff back at the flat though.'

'Well, I'll give Dr Tan a ring, shall I, ask if I can drop by the flat on the way home next week and pick up whatever you need? I was thinking of calling in anyway, to collect my telescope. I can't think why I didn't pack it in the first place. The Northumberland skies are so much clearer and better for looking at the stars than in town.'

'Yes, good idea. I'd love to try to capture the colours of the sea. It's amazing how it changes from hour to hour – almost black one moment, gunmetal grey the next, then pearly turquoise. It's almost mystical – like the sea has moods and emotions of its own.'

'*Hm*, it's just reflecting the sky colour, you know.'

'You scientists.' Jane laughed. Peter put his hand over hers. It was the first time he'd seen her smile in a while, and he loved it, even though she was teasing him.

A couple, a young man and woman, came in the cafe and sat at the table next to them. The woman was carrying a child, a little girl, a toddler. Peter threw Jane an anxious glance as they settled their child in a highchair. The girl was babbling happily and pointing her chubby finger at the mock antique horse brasses and pans and blue and white china plates on the wall.

'Darling,' Peter whispered. 'Shall we pay up and go?'

'It's all right,' she said, pushing the half-finished soup away. In the first year after losing Angela, Jane couldn't bear the sight of other little children. It wasn't just sorrow, it was plain raw anger and jealousy. Why did those people have their child, and she didn't? But she was getting better at coping with it. The counsellor had talked to her about not trying to fight those feelings, not blaming or hating herself for having them, but just acknowledging them and letting them pass. 'I can't go on forever avoiding children,' she said. 'I'm learning to live with it.'

Peter nodded. 'That's good. Shall we head back?'

'No. Let's make a day of it. Go somewhere else?' Just thinking of being back in the cottage made Jane shiver.

They headed for the second-hand book shop housed in the town's former railway station, and somewhere they'd often driven out to visit in their early married days. Jane loved books. They were like friends. They had always been her escape and comfort in troubled times. She felt relaxed and calm wandering between the packed shelves, gentle classical music playing in the background. While Peter pottered in the science section, Jane browsed the classic literature; Jane Austen, the Brontes, all her favourites. She had most of them already, but her Wuthering Heights had fallen apart, so she found a new copy, bought it, and settled herself in front of the cosy coal fire at the front of the shop.

'You look comfy there,' said Peter, holding an arm full of astronomy books. 'I've just got to pop back into town a minute, a couple of things I need. I'll bring the car back up here in half an hour, OK?'

Jane nodded, engrossed all over again in Cathy and Heathcliff and the wild, windy moors.

When he came back, Peter handed her a bag. 'Present to keep you going till I fetch your paints,' he said.

Jane waited until they were driving back up the coast before opening the bag. Inside was a sketch pad and a large box of oil pastels.

'I think I shall like experimenting with these,' Jane said, running her fingers over the neat rows of coloured sticks. 'I've never really tried, but I know you can get some wonderful effects with pastels. And not half as messy as paints. No brushes to clean either.'

'Great.' Peter smiled. Seeing Jane happy made his spirits soar. Things were going to get better from now on, he was sure.

CHAPTER 4

It was going to be a wild, windy day. The sea was heaving and frothing and flecked with white spray. But that Sunday morning, Peggy Mortimer was feeling quite comfortable. Nothing untoward had so far disturbed her morning rituals; the washing and dressing – always in something clean and always something plain and black – applying the make-up to obliterate the old woman's face that the mirror reflected, brushing and twisting her hair into its tight knot, making tea and toast, seeing to the bairns, feeding Whisky. As long as everything was in its place, in the right order and as it should be, she was content.

She hadn't much liked the cottage when Eric brought her here, back in 1980. She felt then – and still did – that the world outside the window was too big, too wild, that she was living on the edge of the universe, and if she ventured too far, she might fall off into a terrifying void. But if she was safe inside, the door closed and her familiar things around her, all was well. It was so much easier now. With technology, she never needed to go out. She could get everything she wanted online. In fact, she'd been very busy on eBay and was expecting a parcel to arrive tomorrow.

She would carefully wash up her breakfast things and put them away, then she would go out and put some washing on the line. She hoped she wouldn't have to bump into Her Next Door. That was the only fly in the ointment. Her life would be more or less perfect, she thought, if it wasn't for the people who came to the other side of the cottage. Since Miss Blackwood left and it became a holiday rental, she'd seen all sorts. Rowdy parties, nosy parkers forever knocking on her door, wanting to know this and that, people with teenage children shouting and drinking and carrying on at all hours. But mostly they were quiet types, walkers, birdwatchers, just there for a few days, then gone. And the Americans who came every summer. She didn't mind them too much. But most of all she wished Miss Blackwood was still there, Miss Blackwood as she was before the dementia set in. She had been the ideal neighbour in those early days; they understood each other, looked out for each other. That was until she started to go round the bend. Mrs Mortimer often felt she was the only sane person in the world.

As she came out of the porch with her washing basket on her hip, Him Next Door came out. Nine o'clock and still in his dressing gown. He was holding an empty milk carton in one hand and gave her one of his bright and breezy waves.

'Ah, good morning, Mrs Mortimer. We seem to have run out of milk. You haven't got any to spare, by any chance? Just enough for two cups of tea?'

'I haven't,' she replied briskly as she struggled with the wind to peg out the flapping sheets on the rotary drier. 'If you go up to the farm, they'll have milk there to sell you. And eggs, you'll find.'

'Ah, right, yes, we'll do that. Nice morning for a bracing walk. A bit on the windy side today, isn't it?'

But she'd already gone back inside. That was the trouble with people, always wanting something from you, always wanting a chat. She didn't know how to chat, unless it was to Whisky. Or the bairns. And thank the Lord, they never bothered her by chatting back.

****

Peter said he would drive up the track to the farm, but Jane said no, she needed the walk, and she wanted to talk to the people who lived there.

Now with a bitter east wind roaring in off the sea, tugging at her duffel coat and whipping her hair into an untamed mess, she wished they'd taken the car. The rutted track was an uphill slope, and the straggly little trees by the side were permanently bent inland from the wind's relentless battering, their last few withered leaves torn away.

'I bet that mean old crone had plenty of milk,' Jane muttered, but the noise of the wind carried her voice away, and Peter was striding on ahead. She really hoped he wouldn't make his usual remark about 'blowing the cobwebs away'.

It was a square, plain old farmhouse, built of solid grey stone, unadorned by trees or plants and surrounded by a jumble of barns and outbuildings. They picked their way across the yard, which was, as Jane's nan used to say, all claggy with clarts – big lumps of wet mud and manure.

They were wondering whether to knock at the front door or go round the back when a figure with a spanner in his hand emerged from behind a tractor, a young man wearing mud-spattered overalls and a beanie hat pulled down to his brow.

He was friendly enough as Peter enquired about the milk. 'Mam will sort you out,' he said, and led them round the back of the house.

Mrs Armstrong was a weather-beaten woman in mud-encrusted wellingtons and a green padded gilet. She was busy in the back yard, wrestling with a roll of chicken wire. 'Got to repair the fence,' she said. 'There was a fox prowling round the henhouse last night. Tom got it with his shotgun though, didn't you Tom?'

Her son nodded in the direction of a tangle of matted blood and auburn fur spread out on top of the coal bunker. Jane shivered. Mrs Armstrong wiped her hands on her jeans.

'It'll be raw milk we sell here,' she said. 'Is that all right? Better for you than the pasteurised stuff, they reckon.'

Peter said it was fine, and they'd have a dozen eggs too. 'I'll make you one of my special omelettes Jane,' he said, and followed Tom Armstrong into a nearby outhouse to collect the goods and pay. Once

31

he was out of earshot Jane said, 'Mrs Armstrong, I was wondering – well, we're staying at the cottage down the lane and—'

'Oh aye, Two Chimneys. Mind, some of the locals still call it Miss Blackwood's house. She used to live there, years ago. Mad as a box of frogs, she was. It's been done up lovely, I've heard.'

'Yes, it is. Lovely. But I just wanted to ask you something. I've noticed a little girl, about six or seven, with blonde hair, running around on the rocks, and even in the field behind. She tapped at the window the other day, then ran away. I was worried about her. You don't know who she is or where she comes from do you? Are there any children living nearby?'

Mrs Armstrong frowned. 'No, I'm afraid I don't know who that could be. There are a few children living in the village, but that's a couple of miles away. We do a bit of b and b in the summer, and sometimes they have kids with them, but not often. And we haven't had any children here this year at all. Sorry, I can't help you there.'

'Oh, OK. Maybe it was someone visiting Mrs Mortimer, although I did ask her, and she said no.'

There was a bit of a pause. Mrs Armstrong gave a wry little smile. 'Mrs Mortimer having visitors? I don't think so.'

'OK, well, never mind,' Jane said. Peter came out of the barn, a bulging plastic bag in his arms.

'Oh, before you go,' said Mrs Armstrong, 'I nearly forgot. The postie left a parcel here yesterday for Mrs Mortimer. He doesn't like going down that track if he can help it – says it knackers the van's suspension. I was going to ask Tom to drop it off, but—'

'That's fine, no problem, we'll take it down for her,' Peter said.

Mrs Armstrong went back in the house and came out with a brown paper package in her arms.

'It's a bit on the bulky side I'm afraid,' she said. 'And the postie said to apologise to Mrs Mortimer. The wrapping's got a bit torn in the post.'

'I'll carry it,' Jane said. 'Peter, you've got enough to handle with the milk and stuff.'

It was a large parcel, filling Jane's arms. It felt soft and squishy. The brown paper wrapping crackled as she squeezed it gently.

'Well, that was all a bit *Cold Comfort Farm*, wasn't it?' Peter said, closing the five-bar gate behind them. 'Dead foxes, shotguns, and mud. Probably something nasty in the woodshed too.'

This time the wind was blowing fiercely against them as they struggled back down the track, Peter hugging the milk and eggs in their plastic bag close, but at least it was downhill.

The tear in the corner of the parcel seemed to be getting worse. Jane lifted the flap of paper, telling herself she was just trying to tuck it in, but really, she couldn't resist having a quick peep at the contents. It seemed to be something knitted, pale pink. She gave it a gentle tug, and a tiny cardigan sleeve peeped out. Jane probed a bit more, being careful not to make the tear any bigger. They were all baby clothes, dozens of items. Sleep suits, bonnets, a frilly summer dress with butterflies on. And more, which she couldn't see without ripping the parcel even more.

Peter had marched on ahead, not noticing that Jane had stopped in her tracks.

'Peter.' she called. 'Will you come and have a look at this?'

He stomped back to her, annoyed. 'Jane, what are you doing? You can't go poking around in somebody else's parcel.'

'I couldn't help it. It was sort of spilling out of the package. Peter, it's baby clothes. Why on earth do you think Morticia is buying this stuff?'

'I don't know. She's probably got a relative who's just had a baby. There's really no need to make such a mystery out of everything. And we should mind our own business.'

'You mean I should mind *my* own business,' she muttered.

As the two tall chimney pots reared up over the horizon, Jane couldn't stop thinking about the parcel and its contents. And then there was the little girl. She had been hoping Mrs Armstrong would say, 'Oh yes, that's little so-and-so, she's always playing around here.'

Now she felt a shiver of apprehension that something was not right, not right at all.

And most terrifying of all, what if there was no girl at all, and she really was losing her mind all over again?

Peter patched up the torn wrapping with sticky tape when they got in and took it straight round to Mrs Mortimer's. 'I don't think there's any need for me to tell her about it getting damaged,' he told Jane.

He wasn't gone long.

'I don't suppose you got a thank you, let alone an invitation to come in and have a cup of tea,' Jane said.

'No, you're right, she snatched it out of my hands pretty quickly. But she did thank me – I think. "Much obliged I'm sure",' he said, chuckling at his own impersonation of the woman's clipped way of speaking.

The low roar of the wind and the restless crashing of waves on the rocks below the house were making Jane unsettled all that afternoon. She picked up the pastels and put them down again after a half-hearted attempt to capture the sea's colour and movement. She flicked through the pages of her book, the familiar story, but couldn't take in a word. Peter was working on a presentation upstairs in the spare bedroom, which he now used as his office.

The daylight was already starting to fade as Jane went into the kitchen, thinking she might make tea. Although she didn't really want any it would give her something to do. She looked up the track. The wind was still bending the grass in the field almost flat, and little groups of forlorn sheep huddled against the hedgerows.

She took a mug of tea up to Peter, sitting at his laptop, lost in his work amid a chaos of books and papers. The noise of the wind seemed to be softening as she perched on the stool at the breakfast bar, sipping her tea. It was so quiet she could hear the ticking of the kitchen clock – and then another sound. A scrabbling, scratchy noise outside the kitchen window. Must be that cat on the windowsill again, she thought. But it wasn't. There was something, no, two things, small and pink, moving about on the window ledge outside. It looked like two rows of little blobs. It was hard to make out in the dim light. She got up and went to the window, leaning over the sink to look.

They were fingertips, two small hands clinging to the ledge. She could see the pearly fingernails, turning white with the effort of holding on. Her mind raced, trying to make sense of what she was seeing. She leant closer, her nose almost touching the windowpane.

And just as she did so, a face reared up in front of her, just inches behind the glass.

It was the little girl, her face deathly white, eyes like two sunken hollows, mouth wide open in a silent scream, ropes of fair hair fluttering and whirling around her head.

Jane shrieked. She reeled back from the window, crashing into the stool, sending it clattering to the floor. She steadied herself, looked back at the window, her heart banging in her chest. The face had gone. Peter was there in an instant, holding her, soothing her, trying to understand her garbled words. 'She was there, at the window, I swear it.'

'There's no one at the window, Jane. I'll go and have a look round outside if you like. If there was anyone there, they won't have got far.'

'What do you mean, *if* there was anyone there? I saw her, plain as I'm seeing you now.'

Peter was back within a minute. 'There's not a soul around out there.'

She sat on the sofa, hugging the cushion, trembling violently. Her breath came in fast, shallow gasps.

'You're in shock, darling,' said Peter. He'd fetched the duvet from upstairs and wrapped it round her. 'I'll make you some more tea, with sugar in.'

'I don't want tea. I feel sick. Light the fire, Peter, I'm frozen.'

It took a while to get the fire going, but its comforting blaze helped a little, and she began to breathe more easily.

'I just don't understand what's happening,' she said, her head in her hands.

Peter took her icy hands in his. 'OK, let's just think about this logically, shall we? The first explanation is that she isn't there at all. She is a hallucination, a very real hallucination, but nonetheless, a product of your imagination.'

'We've been through this before,' Jane said wearily. 'I am not going back to the doctor. I do not have schizophrenia and I won't be turned into a drug-addled zombie.'

'I accept that. But you have to admit you do have an amazing imagination, Jane. It's one of the things I love about you.'

'Didn't you once tell me Einstein said that imagination was more important than knowledge?'

'*Hm*, yes, well-remembered, darling,' Peter said.

'So even scientists should sometimes consider things that seem impossible?'

Peter smiled. 'That's a very profound thought. I might just use that in my next lecture.'

Jane felt as if she'd been given a patronising pat on the head.

'But, you know,' Peter continued. 'I think I may have sussed out what lies behind this particular vision – or whatever you want to call it.'

'Tell me.'

'There's a condition called hypnagogia. It happens when you're a bit sleepy, but not actually asleep, and you have a dream. Dreaming while you're awake, in other words. Sometimes it's as if you're getting vivid flashbacks of dreams you've had before.'

'That's weird. I wasn't aware of feeling sleepy any of the times I've seen her.'

'No, well, the brain is a complex and wonderful thing. There's so much about its functioning we still don't understand. And there's something else I've thought of too.' Peter picked up the book Jane had bought the day before and waved it in front of her. 'You've been reading this again, right? Wuthering Heights? Ghostly Cathy at the window, tapping away, wanting Heathcliff to let her in? Maybe that's what triggered your dream.'

'Yes, yes, I get what you're saying. I suppose you could be right.'

'And, of course, there's Angela.'

Jane stiffened. 'What do you mean, there's Angela? This has nothing to do with Angela, nothing at all.'

'Well, the little girl – God knows never a day goes by when I don't think of Angela, wonder what she would be like now, if she was still with us.'

'No. The girl I see is not Angela. Do you think I wouldn't recognise my own child if I saw her again? Angela would have been four years old now. This child is older than that, six or seven at least. And she has straight blonde hair. Angela's hair was curly, and dark brown. Don't you remember her lovely hair, how it bounced when she ran, the chestnut glints in it when the sun shone?'

Peter took her in his arms and held her close as she sobbed.

'Jane, I think perhaps we should leave here, look for somewhere else to stay. Somewhere with people and shops and more things for you to do. There's obviously something not right about this place.'

Through her tears, Jane nodded. 'Yes. Let's leave. Soon.'

'We can't go back to the flat yet, but we could find somewhere else to stay.'

Next morning Jane woke later than usual. She had slept surprisingly well, deeply and without dreams. Peter was just beginning to stir next to her.

'Peter. Oh God, we've overslept. Shouldn't you be at work?'

'It's OK,' he mumbled, turning over to face her, gently moving a strand of hair from her cheek. 'I forgot to tell you, I'm taking today off. I don't want to leave you on your own after yesterday. I haven't got any lectures and I can work from home. Just as well – I had a bit of a restless night. Didn't get much sleep.'

'OK, I'll go down and make the tea, shall I?' She opened the curtains. The wind had dropped, and the sea was flat and still, a deep dark blue streaked with turquoise.

As she went downstairs Jane noticed something was different in the sitting room. The pastel sticks which she'd left neatly lined up back in their box yesterday lay scattered all over the floor.

That was odd, she thought. She went over to pick them up.

'Peter,' she called up the stairs. 'Did you come down here during the night at all?'

'No. Why?'

'The pastels are—' She stopped suddenly, noticing the sketchpad lying open on the coffee table.

In big childish capital letters that filled the blank page someone had written two words:

DONT LEAVE

CHAPTER 5

She liked the baby girls best, and Lily was her favourite. Lily was tiny and delicate, with downy soft golden hair. Peggy loved dressing her in particular. There were so many beautiful outfits for baby girls these days, and this latest parcel had some especially lovely ones. She never took the bairns out of course; although she did have a pram, one of those neat little three-wheeled things. Sometimes she put one of the babies in it and wheeled them round the house, but she never used it outside. As she carefully brushed Lily's hair, she thought she might take some pictures of her in the adorable butterfly dress, or maybe make a video.

Getting a parcel of clothes was always the highlight of Peggy Mortimer's week, nearly as exciting as the arrival of the babies themselves. They usually came with a selection of clothes, feeding bottles, and dummies. Soon she was going to need another chest of drawers for the nursery, just to keep everything nice and tidy.

****

Jane was triumphant. 'You see, Peter, the child isn't a figment of my imagination. She's real. She's been in the house and written this message – for us.'

Peter, still in his dressing gown, paced up and down in front of the window.

'Come now, that's hardly likely, is it? I think you were sleepwalking. You wrote it in your sleep.'

'But you said yourself you'd not slept well. Surely, you'd have woken up if I'd been wandering around? Those times back in the flat when I used to sleepwalk you always woke. Anyway, how do you know it wasn't you who sleepwalked, you who wrote it?'

'Well, if I had I wouldn't have left the apostrophe out of don't,' he said. 'Even in my sleep.'

'Nor would I. A child wrote this, a real child.'

'OK, supposing – just for a minute – that this girl exists. Where does she come from? How did she get into the house? I checked the door last night, I know, and it was definitely locked. And why this message, don't leave? Why doesn't she want us to leave?'

Jane was quiet for a moment. She got up from the sofa and stood beside Peter, putting a hand on his arm to stop him from pacing the floor.

'The answer is obvious. Can't you see? She must come from next door, from Mrs Mortimer's.' Peter started to interrupt, but she raised a hand. 'No, listen a minute. I know she said there were no children there, but I think she's lying. And I think she's keeping that poor little kid in her house against her will. She keeps trying to get away. That's why I heard her crying and that's why she looks so desperate. She got into our house last night because she managed to get hold of Mrs Mortimer's key. She slipped away while Mrs Mortimer was asleep and let herself in. I don't know why she wrote us that message. Maybe she feels she stands a chance of being rescued while we're here. She wants our help.'

'Are you saying she's been kidnapped?'

'Perhaps, yes. If Mrs Mortimer was just looking after a child for a friend or relative, why not just say so? She's keeping her secret for a reason. She never seems to let anyone into her house, does she? That's peculiar too.'

'I don't know Jane. It all sounds a bit far-fetched to me. If a child had been kidnapped, we'd have heard about it, surely. Look how the news was full of nothing but stuff about Madeleine McCann's disappearance for months on end.'

'I don't know about that either. I just know something's not right and we can't go anywhere until we get to the bottom of it. We need to contact the police, or social services.'

Peter held up his hands. 'Whoa. Let's not go there yet. How's it going to sound, me explaining that my wife, who has – well, let's say serious mental health issues – thinks our next-door neighbour is keeping a child captive, but she's the only one who's actually seen the child? It's a serious accusation to make.'

'So, what do you suggest we do?' Jane flapped the paper with the message on it in front of Peter's face. 'Just ignore this?'

'Tell you what. I'll go round and speak to Mrs M,' Peter said. 'I won't accuse her of anything. I'll just explain what you've seen, show her the message, ask her if she can shed any light on it.'

'She'll just deny it. You know what she's like. A witch.'

'You bit my head off when I jokingly said that before,' Peter said, a slight edge of bitterness in his voice.

'Well, maybe you were right. Maybe she tempted the child in, like Hansel and Gretel.'

'Ha. She hasn't been round offering you poison apples, has she?'

'That was Snow White,' said Jane.

It was clear to Jane that the last thing in the world Peter wanted to do at that moment was to go round next door and talk to that woman about a child he was convinced was a figment of his sick, deluded wife's imagination. She watched him make his way to the door, his shoulders hunched, clutching the sketch pad page in his hand. But when he got to the door, he suddenly stopped.

'Jane, come here a minute,' he said.

'What? What is it?' She stood beside him.

He pointed up to the top of the door. 'I thought I had, and I was right. The door's bolted. I pulled the latch across before I went up to bed. Look at it, it's a big heavy old-fashioned latch. I remember now, it was rather stiff when I tried to slide it in place, and I made a mental note to put a bit of oil on it sometime.'

'So you're saying…?'

'I'm saying with the door bolted like that from inside there's no way anyone could have let themselves in with the door key during the night. Unless you came down and undid it, and then came back down later to bolt it again.'

'Of course, I didn't.' Jane's mind was racing. There had to be some other explanation. 'Were the windows all shut?'

'Yes. I double checked that, because of the wind.'

'Maybe there's some other way in. The cottage may be divided by a wall, but both sections share a roof space. Could she have come down through a loft hatch in the ceiling, do you think? Or we could check the back of the cupboards and behind the wardrobe – there might be a secret connecting door we don't know about.'

Peter took her shoulders firmly in both hands and swung her round to face him. 'Jane, no. You've got to face facts, darling. This child is a hallucination. You wrote this message while you were sleepwalking. It's nothing to feel guilty or ashamed about. It's part of your illness. But tomorrow morning I want you to ring the GP and get him to make a referral back to the psychiatrist. We need to get this sorted.'

Jane felt she might crumple to the floor, but she steeled herself, summoning all the strength she had. She must stay in control, she must. She couldn't let this thing defeat her, this wretched illness. Maybe Peter was right, and she was just having a psychotic episode, nothing a course of medication couldn't sort out.

'All right,' she said at last. 'I'll ring the doctor.'

Peter kissed her on the forehead. 'Good. But, darling, I still think we need to leave this place, find somewhere else. I thought you'd find what you needed here, complete peace and tranquillity, but it hasn't turned out that way. Having Morticia lurking around hasn't helped you, I can see that. As I said, we can't go back to town yet. I promised the Chinese doctors they could stay at the flat till December. So maybe I should ring Blackwood's today and ask if they've got anything else to let? '

'No, I can speak to Blackwood's tomorrow, when I've had more time to think things over.'

'What's to think about? But OK, if you like, leave it till tomorrow. And as for today, we're going out somewhere for lunch and then we'll have a good long beach walk, to blow—'

'The cobwebs away. Yes, yes, I know.' Jane sighed, fetching her coat. She had a sudden image of a mass of sticky grey cobwebs clogging the inside of her head, and somewhere deep in the centre, a crouching black spider, waiting to pounce.

Although yesterday's wind had dropped and there was a weak sun filtering through the clouds, autumn was creeping in now, a thin mist hovering over the fields of rough yellowing grass, coppery leaves fluttering down ahead of them as they drove up the coast. They parked the car by the side of the road and walked down towards a pub tucked away in a little settlement of cottages close to a wide sandy bay. Inside, it was surprisingly busy for a Monday and noisy with late tourists, walkers, and dogs, but they found a little corner near the inglenook and ordered drinks – wine for Peter, tonic and lemon for Jane – and crab sandwiches. Their conversation was strained and sporadic, trying to avoid discussing the events of the morning.

And afterwards, along the small horse-shoe beach, they walked a little way apart from each other, Jane stooping now and then to pick up shells, Peter marching on ahead, hands deep in his coat pockets. A golden retriever with a ball in its mouth bounded up to them wagging its tail, and Jane smiled and patted its head before it followed its owner's call.

'You love dogs, it's a shame we can't have pets in the cottage,' Peter said. 'It would be company for you.'

'I would like that. But it wouldn't be right to keep a dog in the flat either, especially when I go back to work. I really do want to go back after Christmas.'

'We'll see how things go, shall we?'

'No, not we, *I'll* see how things go,' Jane said, her irritation flaring up. 'It'll be my decision. Mine alone.'

Peter said nothing. The mood had changed, and they walked on in silence.

Jane felt the chill as soon as they stepped back inside the cottage. It's colder inside than it was out, she thought. Nights were drawing in and it was already nearly dark. Peter said he'd light the log burner. While Jane closed the living room curtains, he began to lay the scrunched-up twists of newspaper to start the fire. He picked up the sketch pad page with the message on it.

'I'll burn this I think,' he said. Jane lunged forward and grabbed it from his hand.

'No.'

'Why do you want to keep it? I thought you realised now you must have written it in your sleep.'

Because I know in my heart of hearts I didn't, she thought.

But she said, 'I need to keep it, that's all.' Peter shrugged but let her take it. She folded it carefully and put it away in the dresser drawer. The fire alight, Peter headed upstairs to get on with his work, and Jane went into the kitchen to wash up a few things in the sink and pull down the blind. She dreaded seeing the girl at the window again. Then she went and sat by the fire and tried to read, but all the while she was tense, waiting to hear that *tap-tap-tap* on the glass. But everything was quiet, and all she could hear was the murmur of voices coming from Mrs Mortimer's television next door.

Tuesday dawned still and dismal. Peter left for work, reminding Jane to ring the doctor and contact Blackwood's about finding another cottage. Jane looked out on the great expanse of sea, the horizon merging into the same pale grey as the sky above. A big stretch of blank nothingness, thought Jane. In summer, on a sunny day, it would be so different, the sea and sky vibrant, bright blue, full of promise. But today it was as flat and dreary as she felt, with the added knot of anxiety in her stomach.

It was in the empty spaces of days like this all the *if only* thoughts crept in again. If only she'd taken Angela to the doctor's as soon as she developed the sore throat. If only she hadn't gone to work that day, hadn't ignored her listlessness, hadn't taken her to nursery. If only the nursery had called her sooner. If only she'd taken her to the hospital then instead of taking her home. If only she'd noticed the first signs of the mottled rash on her body, checked on her earlier in the night. If only Peter had driven a bit faster as they rushed to the hospital.

If only.

If only.

The two saddest words in the world.

She pushed those agonising and useless thoughts to the back of her mind, looked at her phone, checked her texts and emails, hoping for a message from Suzy. There was nothing.

She didn't feel like painting today, or writing, or ringing the doctor for an appointment. That could wait. Her mind still in turmoil, all she knew she wanted to do was get out of the house. She fetched her coat, put on her walking shoes, and headed off to the right, in the direction of the steep cliff.

As she rounded the corner, she saw a small huddle of people up on the cliff top, five or six of them in woolly hats and anoraks, binoculars round their necks. One man seemed to be lying down flat on his front at the very cliff edge, fiddling with a camera.

Jane felt strangely elated to see people – any people. She quickened her step, nearly stumbling on the rocky pathway. A fine drizzle was falling now, but she strode on to the top.

'Hi,' she called. 'Is there something exciting going on?'

A cheery-faced woman in a green bobble hat raised her hand in greeting as she approached. 'There could be. A gull-billed tern. But we haven't seen it yet.'

'Ah, you're birdwatchers,' said Jane. 'So that's rare, is it?'

'Very rare, yes,' the woman said. 'If we get a sighting today and a twitch goes out, there'll be birders all over here by tomorrow.'

A man came over to them, big, bearded, jolly looking, with smiling blue eyes. He nodded a quick greeting to Jane, then spoke to the woman. 'Think it may just have been a sandwich tern, Moira. It's easy to confuse them; they're quite similar.'

'Oh, that's a pity,' said Jane. 'Have you come far?'

'Ponteland,' the woman said. 'Never mind. We'll stay around for a bit, just in case. We've made that mistake before, leaving too soon, haven't we Bob?'

Jane had a sudden urge for company, for people to fill the cottage. Normal, friendly people who didn't know anything about her, about Angela, about her illness. 'Look, I'm staying at the cottage just down there. You're all very welcome to come in and I could make you coffee, or tea. I'd love to hear more about the bird life round here.'

'Well, that's very kind,' the woman said. 'But we've all got our flasks and sandwiches here. Thanks though.'

'That's fine, just a thought.' Jane was disappointed. It must have showed in her face, because the man called Bob smiled and held out his binoculars to her.

'Would you like to have a look down the cliff with these? I could point out one or two interesting birds.'

Jane was amazed. She'd never looked through such powerful binoculars before. It took her a while to focus and hold the binoculars steady, but when she did, she could make out every feather on a bird, every pebble on the shore, as if they were right in front of her eyes. She was aware that Bob was talking to her, pointing things out, but she was mesmerised and transfixed by the strange sensation of seeing so much detail from such a distance. She lifted the binoculars towards the sea's edge, to the waves lapping and splashing their white froth over the rocks. And then she saw it. A dark shape bobbing in the shallows, a shape like a small body, arms outstretched, fine strands of yellow hair fanned out, swaying, and rippling with the current.

She gasped and dropped the binoculars, Bob managing to grab them just in time before they tumbled down the cliff face. 'What did you see?' He looked worried.

Jane couldn't speak at first. She pointed. 'There. Look. It's – it's something – somebody – in the water. Oh God, no.'

Bob was looking through the binoculars now, scanning the water. 'Oh yes, I see it. It could be a bit of debris though. Don't worry, bit too small for a body, I think.'

'But it's a child.' Jane could hear the edge of hysteria in her voice, but she couldn't control the rising panic. She knew she was babbling but the words came out in a tumble. 'I've seen her before – a little girl. Running around and playing here. I knew she was real. I knew it. I knew I wasn't seeing things – and now – she's drowned. Oh no, oh no! I should have done something. Oh dear God, what should we do?'

The birdwatchers were huddling round her now, concerned, reassuring. The woman called Moira put her arm around her shoulders.

'Now, don't panic, dear. Take some deep breaths, that's right. I'm pretty sure it's nothing sinister, but Bob will go down and see if he can get a closer look.'

Bob was scrabbling his way down a less steep part of the cliff, his feet skidding on the stones, so that he had to cling on to clumps of grass to stop himself slithering down to the bottom. The shape was some way beyond the shore, being knocked by the waves against a rocky outcrop covered in slippery greeny-brown seaweed. Bob hopped precariously from rock to rock towards it, nearly losing his footing a couple of times. Jane couldn't look. She buried her head in her hands, expecting to see the man toppling into the water at any moment. When she did dare look again, he was crouching down on the rock, reaching out to pull the object closer.

Jane shut her eyes again. She didn't want to see him lifting up the little girl's lifeless body. Why hadn't she done more to save her? Why hadn't she alerted the authorities the first time she saw the child, that first day they came to see the cottage? Why did nobody take her seriously?

'It's all right,' Moira was saying, 'Nothing to worry about. You can open your eyes now.'

Bob was still on the rock, standing up now, grinning, with both thumbs in the air. She couldn't understand it. Why hadn't he pulled her out of the water? She began to tremble violently. Moira was pouring her some coffee from her flask.

'Here, drink this, love. You've had a bit of a shock, but it's fine.'

'How can it be fine?'

'It's an easy mistake to make,' she heard one of the others say. 'Just like mistaking a sandwich tern for a gull-billed tern.' And they were all laughing.

Bob had climbed his way back up now and was standing beside her, his trousers black and dripping with water up to the knees. But he was smiling. 'It was just a log, a piece of tree. The two bits of branch sticking out each side did look a bit like arms, I'll grant you.'

'But the hair…I saw the hair—'

'Seaweed. That stringy stuff. Eel grass, I think it's called. Very hair like.'

Tears sprang into Jane's eyes and spilt down her cheeks. And she felt bad that she wasn't crying with relief but with utter shame and embarrassment. All she could think was how glad she was Peter wasn't there to see, giving her one of his sad-eyed, pitying looks. Once again, she'd made a complete fool of herself, got hysterical, and it had all been a stupid, stupid mistake. She'd intruded on these nice people, made one of them risk life and limb going down the cliff and scrambling over slippery rocks, getting his trousers soaking wet.

Now all she wanted was to get away as fast as she could, back to the cottage. 'Sorry, so sorry…' she muttered, and turned away towards the cottage, running down the path and not looking back.

Outside the cottage, parked on the gravel patch, was an expensive-looking silver-grey car. It couldn't be anyone visiting her, could it? And surely not a visitor to Mrs Mortimer. But as Jane hurried past, Mrs Mortimer's door opened, and she stood in the doorway next to a big, solidly built man in a smart navy-blue suit. He had a briefcase under his arm.

'That all seems in grand order then, Mrs M.' He had a deep reassuring voice, a slight Northumbrian burr. Just as Jane reached her door, fumbling for her key, he spotted her. 'Ah, hello.' he called out cheerily. 'You must be Mrs Eagle. Nigel Blackwood – so pleased to meet you.' He came towards her, hand outstretched. Jane was horribly aware of her unbrushed hair, frizzy from the rain, and the tear streaks on her cheeks. She really wasn't in the mood for company anymore;

the longing to be with people had evaporated, and she just wanted to be alone. But his handshake was firm and warm, and anyway she'd promised Peter she'd contact Blackwood's today about moving to another cottage, so this would save her a phone call.

'Would you have time to come in for a coffee?' she said. 'I need to talk to you about something.'

CHAPTER 6

Mrs Mortimer was pleased. Mr Blackwood's visit had been quite satisfactory. He had praised her for her meticulous attention to detail. 'You're an absolute star, Mrs M,' he said. She didn't know exactly what he meant by that. She'd only done what he asked her to. Gone through the bookings, made a note of which confirmation emails she needed to send out. The enquiries were coming in for next spring and summer, right up to the end of September next year, so she would be busy. Less time to spend with the bairns, but that couldn't be helped.

Blackwood's owned twenty-one holiday cottages scattered along the north Northumberland coast, Beadnell, Embleton, Bamburgh, Seahouses, Warkworth, Amble – and various little remote locations in between. But this cottage was special, and not just because of its location and history; it had been in the Blackwood family since just after the war, and Mrs Mortimer's home since 1980. She liked the arrangement that she could live here rent-free in return for keeping the place ship-shape and sorting the admin. While the office in Alnwick handled that for all the other properties, Mrs Mortimer dealt with everything here, even the financial side. Mr Blackwood had bought her the computer which she taught herself to use and made life so much easier. She liked computers – much easier to deal with than people. She'd become quite an expert at spreadsheets. She no longer had to get on the bus to go to the office; she didn't have to talk to people on the phone. Everything was forwarded on, all communications sent and received online. Really, Mr Blackwood did not need to call in at all, but he always said he liked to 'touch base' from time to time, whatever that meant.

She could just as easily have emailed him this information she'd given him today, but she'd printed him out a paper copy, as requested.

'You'll see Mr and Mrs Eagle have booked it till December seventeenth,' she told him, 'But Mr Eagle told me when they first came, they may well decide to stay on over Christmas, longer even. I've had an enquiry for a booking for the week leading up to Christmas, but I can't confirm that till I know if Mr and Mrs Eagle will be staying on for certain.'

'Not to worry, Mrs M, I'll pop in and have a word. Will they be in, do you know?'

'He'll be at work. His car's not there. And I saw her heading off for a walk an hour or so back.'

It was just as well Her Next Door came back before he left, Mrs Mortimer thought, heading for the nursery. She lifted Arabella from her cot, admiring her new pink and white outfit with the rabbits on. She would give her a bottle, sit with her in the rocking chair for a while, she decided. She always found it soothing, feeding the bairns. Visitors of any kind were unsettling, even Mr Blackwood. Still, she was glad he would sort out the booking question. She didn't like uncertainty.

'Mind, Her Next Door looked in a bit of a state just now, so he'll maybe not get much sense out of her.' She liked to talk to the bairns, knowing they wouldn't understand, let alone answer back, but that didn't matter. Cradling Arabella's soft little body, supporting her tiny head in the palm of her hand, she eased herself into the rocking chair. 'Not right in the head, that one,' she said, gently stroking the fine brown baby hair, ''Not right at all.'

****

Nigel Blackwood looked in his late forties, maybe even early fifties, but still an attractive man; well-built, not in bad shape.

51

Probably been a rugby player, Jane thought. His broad frame filled the armchair, and he looked at ease, sipping the mug of fresh coffee Jane had just brewed up. The smell of coffee was comforting, reminding Jane of the happy times spent after work in Starbucks or Cafe Nero in town, with Suzy and sometimes other girls in the office. She'd been missing that.

'So, Mrs Eagle, what do you think of this place? Pretty special, isn't it?'

'It's lovely,' said Jane. 'And please, call me Jane.'

'OK, Jane. And I'm Nigel.' Jane liked his twinkly blue eyes, and the way his face crinkled when he smiled. 'I've been trying for years to get Mrs M next door to call me Nigel. But she won't have it. And I wouldn't dare call her Peggy.'

'Is that her first name? We always call her Morticia. Not to her face of course.'

Nigel's shoulders shook with laughter, nearly spilling his coffee. 'Ah, she's really not as sinister as she looks. It's just her way. Anyway, Jane, I needed to speak to you too, to ask you about your future plans so we can sort out the bookings. And you said you wanted to speak to me about something. Everything all right with the cottage, I hope?'

Jane looked down at her hands. It was so awkward. How could she explain?

'There's no problem with the cottage. It's more the problem's with us – well, me. We were wondering if there was another vacant property we could move to right away, not quite so remote?'

He looked surprised. 'Well, we can certainly look into that, if you like. But I really am curious to know why you want to change. It's not about Mrs Mortimer, is it?'

'No, although…kind of.'

'Is the rent a problem? We could possibly sort something out about that, although I have to say you've been really lucky to get it at such a reasonable amount, and we can't offer you anything much cheaper, I'm afraid. And for this cottage, over the spring and summer months, we'll be charging double what you're paying now.'

'No, it's not that. The rent is fine, the cottage is fine. In fact, it's absolutely perfect.'

Nigel Blackwood looked round the room and smiled. 'It is, isn't it? I chose the decor myself. We do a complete refurbishment of all our properties every three years, new furniture, fittings, the lot. This was done up about a year ago, and it's still looking good, I think. Of course, we gave the paintwork a bit of a going-over before you came, and Mrs Mortimer gives everything a thorough clean.'

'Yes, it's spotless,' Jane said. She really didn't want to talk about the decor or Mrs Mortimer's cleaning skills. There was an uncomfortable silence while Jane wondered how much she should reveal to this man she'd only just met. But there was something about him, something open and approachable, that made her want to confide in him as honestly as she could.

'Mr Blackwood – Nigel – the problem is I'm finding I feel a bit cut off here, isolated. My husband takes the car to work so I can't go anywhere much when he's not here. I've not been well on and off for the last two and a half years, you see. In fact, I've had a couple of quite serious breakdowns. I thought I was getting better, but the last one was in July this year. I've been off work since then. My husband thought I needed to be away from crowds, from people, somewhere quiet and peaceful. But since I got here, I've been seeing – things. Strange things have happened. And I don't know whether it's because of my illness, or...'

Her voice trailed off as she wondered what on earth to say next that wouldn't make him think he was talking to a completely crazy woman. Or was that what she really was, a completely crazy woman?

Nigel put down his coffee cup and leant forward, his hands clasped together.

'Jane, you poor lass. That sounds bad. I am sorry. Do you mind if I ask you what strange things have happened while you've been here?'

It all came spilling out of her then; the sound of a child crying, sightings of the girl around the cottage, the tapping and the face at the window, and then the scrawled message saying Don't Leave. She went to the dresser drawer and took out the sheet of paper, the words a little smudged but still clear enough. Nigel Blackwood frowned as he examined it.

'I'm not surprised you're freaked out. Anyone would be. What does your husband think?'

'Oh, he's quite convinced I must have written it while I was sleepwalking. I've sleepwalked before, but I'm pretty sure I wasn't this time.'

'And what does he think about this child you've been seeing?'

'He thinks it's in my mind. Hallucinations.'

'Is that what you think?'

Jane paused. What did she think? She wasn't sure she knew.

'I don't think it's hallucinations. I think – perhaps – the little girl is real and is being kept somewhere close by against her will. She seems to want my help. She doesn't want me to leave. And the only place close by is Mrs Mortimer's.'

Nigel leant back, rubbing his chin thoughtfully.

Oh no, Jane thought, does he think I'm crazy?

'Jane, I believe you, I really do. But I don't think Mrs Mortimer can be anything to do with it. I know she can come across a bit frosty, but she's a canny old thing underneath. I've known her since I was a lad, when she and her husband moved in next to my aunty Irene.'

'Is that Miss Blackwood? Mrs Armstrong at the farm mentioned she used to live here.'

'Yes, that's right. And I've been into Peggy Mortimer's house many times over the years. I was in there today. I can honestly say in all that time I've never seen a child, or evidence of a child, in that place. I haven't been in every room of course – Mrs M likes her privacy – but I'm sure I would have noticed or heard something. I've had four kids of my own, and they're not exactly easy to keep quiet.'

'I know,' Jane said. Suddenly, it was important for her to tell him everything. She wanted him to know about Angela. 'We had a child too. She died suddenly of sepsis two years ago last April, a month before her second birthday. She was so beautiful, Nigel. Oh, I know every mother thinks that, but she really was. Look.'

She opened her phone. She kept hundreds of photographs of Angela, but this one was her favourite, Angela on her last Christmas Day, toddling towards the camera with chubby arms outstretched, holding her new pink rabbit toy, and beaming with joy and excitement. Nigel took the phone gently from Jane's hand and studied it carefully.

That was unusual, Jane thought.

Usually, when she had been telling people about Angela and shown them the photo, they would make some suitably sad 'Ah' sound and hand it back hastily, embarrassed and not knowing what to say.

But not Nigel. He cradled the phone in his big hands, gazing at the photo. His eyes closed and he shook his head slowly from side to side. 'Oh, Jane, that's just so...' He paused, as if searching for the right word. 'Wrong!' The word exploded from his mouth. 'A lovely little lass like that...why? So wrong.'

Jane nodded, the tears starting up again. At last, somebody really understood. This man she'd only just met, who she didn't know, had just described in one word the feeling she hadn't been able to put a name to before now. After Angela died, people were always asking Jane how she felt, urging her to talk; Peter, the doctors, the psychiatrist, the bereavement counsellor – always saying, So tell me what you're feeling, Jane. But she couldn't, because she didn't know what that awful, overwhelming feeling was, what label to put on it. There was numbness and disbelief, grief, of course, sadness, desolation, and anger, yes, certainly anger. But there was something else that she carried with her all the time, long after the first shock and pain had subsided. And now she knew it for what it was: a sense of the wrongness of such a loss, that this wasn't what was meant to happen, as if someone had torn up the script of the life plan she'd written for herself and her daughter, and if she could only rewind time she could set it right again.

'Thank you,' she whispered. 'Thank you for saying that.'

Nigel Blackwood and Jane sat in silence for a while, and it no longer felt uncomfortable. She was aware of the clock on the mantelpiece ticking and noticed the time. 'Oh look, I've kept you here far too long. You'll need to get back to the office.'

'Yes, I suppose so. I'll look into the possibilities of another cottage, but can I just leave you with a thought?'

'Yes, of course.'

'Is it really going to change anything, moving somewhere else? From what you told me, if your husband is right, the things you've experienced aren't necessarily to do with this cottage. Why don't you give it a day or two, think it over?'

'So, you think I'm imagining it too?' she said, disappointed.

He held up his hands. 'I don't think anything. I've no idea what could be happening. I wish I could shed some light on it for you, but I can't. But look, Jane, you probably already have my office number, but here's my card. It's got my mobile number. Any time you want to talk, any time at all, drop me a text or give me a bell, OK?'

She nodded, taking the card. 'Thank you, I will.'

In the doorway, he took her hand, closing his other hand over hers. The gesture felt comforting and reassuring, her small cold hand enfolded in both his large warm hands. She didn't want him to leave. As he was easing his bulky frame into his car seat he said, 'It's a pity my old aunty Irene isn't around to talk to you. She was a great one for seeing and hearing things nobody else could. What a character.'

'Your aunt? Who lived here?'

'Yes, she was a devout spiritualist, called herself a medium, used to hold séances, that sort of thing, so I believe. Anyway, I'd best be off now, so you take care.' He turned on the ignition and she watched his car bounce away up the rutted track.

Jane's mind was in turmoil. She was still trying to process the deep and immediate emotional connection she'd made with this man – not just a physical attraction, but something on a much deeper level, not unlike the connection she used to have with Suzy. But then he'd thrown in that aside about his aunt, Miss Blackwood. Nigel had said

Jane's visions might not be connected to the cottage, and yet his aunt had once held séances, communicated with spirits, here, right here.

She was almost certain now that the little girl wasn't a hallucination, nor was she a real living child being held and hidden next door by Mrs Mortimer.

She must be a ghost.

CHAPTER 7

Peter wasn't in a good mood when he got back. He'd had a bad day. He snapped at a student who kept challenging him during a tutorial, and he'd accidentally lost quite a large body of text on his computer, which he'd have to re-write tonight. There'd been heavy traffic and delays on the long drive home, and it had started to rain quite hard, with lorries and buses sending up great waves of spray that obscured his view of the road ahead. His neck and shoulders were knotted with tension.

Jane was sitting on the sofa, staring blankly ahead, when he came in. The fire was unlit, the supper uncooked, killing his hope that he could just sit down and relax.

'Is something wrong?' he asked her. 'You can't have had a worse day than me.'

'No, it's been OK,' she said. She'd decided not to tell him about the incident with the birdwatchers. 'I saw Nigel Blackwood today. He stayed for coffee, and we had a really good talk. He's such a nice man, Peter, so understanding.'

'Hmm. So, you've been entertaining gentlemen while I've been at work, eh? He should be nice, the amount of cash we're putting in his pocket.' He said it in a jokey way, but she could detect some irritation in his tone. Was it jealousy? she wondered.

'So, what did he say about moving to another cottage?'

'He's looking into it. And Peter, he told me his aunt, Miss Blackwood, who used to live here – she was a spiritualist medium. He said she used to hold séances.'

'Oh, a crackpot,' he said. 'So, is that significant in any way?'

Jane could sense that an argument was brewing, but she had to tell him what she was thinking, what she'd been sitting here going over and over in her mind since Nigel Blackwood left. 'I know you think it's all rubbish. And I know what you're going to say if I suggest this cottage could be haunted. That what I saw – the writer of that message – might be a spirit. A ghost child.'

Peter gave a long sigh. 'Oh, Jane, I think you've been reading one too many Stephen King novels. You'll be telling me next this house is built on an ancient pagan burial site or something. Well, I tell you now, I'm not pulling up the floorboards.'

'You may be old enough to be my father, Peter, but don't treat me like a stupid child.' she said, clenching her fists. 'I know I've been ill, that I may have imagined some things or made mistakes because of it, but I am not an idiot.'

Peter bristled, as he always did when Jane reminded him of his age. 'Of course you're not. And why do you always have to bring up the age difference thing? I know you're a rational, intelligent adult. Impressionable, emotional, yes, but you know as well as I do there's no such thing as ghosts.'

'Do I? You're the one who's always telling me we don't know even a tiny fraction of how the universe works.'

'And that's what we theoretical physicists are trying to do – find out how it works but using the laws of science, logic, mathematical equations.'

'Yes, yes, I know. But just for once, Peter, open your mind to the possibility that there might just be some things that can't be explained by physics, proved or disproved by science and logic. Psychic energy perhaps – that manifests itself as a ghost? Energy can't be destroyed, right? So where does it go, what happens to it, when the body dies?'

Peter sighed again. 'A load of bollocks,' he said, going towards the kitchen. 'I don't want to carry on this conversation, Jane. I'm tired. I'm hungry. I'll fix our supper tonight; your head is obviously not in the right place to concentrate on real life just now. And I bet you didn't ring the doctor, like I told you to do.'

'No, I didn't. I've changed my mind. I don't want a doctor. I don't want medication or therapy. I just want somebody to listen, to understand.'

'Like your nice Mr Blackwood I suppose,' she heard him mutter as he rummaged in the fridge for some supper.

Later that night, Jane lay awake in bed. Peter was still up, working in his little office room, and would be until the early hours. The wind had got up again, wild and roaring. Even the new double-glazed windows couldn't shut out the sound of it, or the hiss of huge waves smashing against rocks.

Like the waves, her thoughts tumbled in, one after another, swirling round inside her head. She couldn't stop thinking of Nigel Blackwood, his warm crinkly smile, his big firm hands touching hers. And most of all, she kept going over the way he'd reacted when he saw Angela's picture. Empathy, yes, that was it, real empathy. He understood what that loss had done to her. He knew the emotions that were eating away at her, destroying her peace of mind.

People's reactions when she talked about losing Angela were varied, and few of them had been helpful. She hated to be told that Angela was safe in the arms of Jesus, was up in heaven or had become an angel, or a star in the sky. She realised that was a comfort to some people, but she knew as well as anybody that stars were definitely not dead people, and, as yet, exploration of the universe had not thrown up any sign of angel babies floating by on clouds, of Jesus, or heaven. Then there were the ones who said that Angela's death was 'meant to be' or 'everything happens for a reason.' No! What possible reason could there be for destroying a healthy, happy little child who was so loved, so wanted? Angela's death was meaningless, random, and utterly pointless. In many ways, hurtful though it was, she preferred the people she knew who crossed the road to avoid her, pretending they hadn't seen her. She understood they didn't know what to say, feared they would say the wrong thing.

And of course, people sometimes did say the wrong thing. The worst had been that incident in Asda last summer, an incident which triggered off what the doctors called her last acute episode. She had been pushing her trolley, doing the weekly shop, and somehow she found herself walking down the aisle with all the baby food and nappies in it. Not really thinking of anything, she reached for a pack of nappies, the ones she always bought for Angela. Then she remembered she didn't need to buy nappies because Angela was gone. She couldn't be reached because she was nowhere, just as she'd been nowhere before she was conceived. She had disappeared to nothing, like a beautiful bubble floating briefly through the world that popped and vanished. Tears ran down Jane's cheeks. She stood there in the crowded supermarket and sobbed, only vaguely aware of the furtive glances from other shoppers swerving nervously round her.

Then out of nowhere an elderly woman was advancing towards her. Curly white perm, big spectacles, and despite the warm weather wearing one of those padded nylon coats in the dingy maroon colour that old women seemed to favour.

'Aw, hinny,' she said, grabbing Jane's arm. 'Whatever's the matter? Do you need a hanky?' She began rooting around in her handbag.

'No, no, really, it's OK,' Jane said, recovering her senses and trying to pull away and make a hasty exit. But the woman still clutched her arm.

'I can see you're in a right bad fettle,' she went on. 'Now just you come and have a nice cup of tea with me, and you can tell me all about it. Trouble with a fella, is it? It usually is.'

Jane said, 'No. My little girl died. Sometimes things happen that make me think of her, and I can't stop myself from crying. Thank you, but I shall be all right now.'

The woman's grip tightened, and she shuffled even closer. 'Aw, that's terrible. I know just how you feel, hinny. I lost my cat Mitzi over a year ago, and I still have a little cry over her now and again.'

Jane stared at her. 'Your cat? You lost your fucking cat?' she heard herself screeching. 'You don't know how I feel, so just fuck off and leave me alone will you? Leave me alone.'

She abandoned her trolley and ran out of the supermarket. It was late Friday afternoon, crowds of people and traffic everywhere, deafening noise, everything whirling around and closing in on her. She began to run down the street, bumping into people, not knowing where she was going, just wanting to escape from everything. She didn't remember anything after that. Apparently, she'd been found wandering around Jesmond Dene with no shoes on, and threatening to jump in the river, but all she recalled was being back in St Nick's again and Peter at her bedside gazing at her with that sad, haggard look on his face.

She remembered saying to him, 'I swore at that old lady, Peter, and she was only trying to be kind. I never swear. Nan hated it. "No excuse for language", she used to say. She'd be furious with me.'

Now, lying in bed and listening to the rain dashing against the window, she re-lived that horrible day and felt her cheeks burning with shame all over again.

She must have drifted off to sleep soon afterwards and slept for an hour or two. Something woke her, and she stirred. There was someone, or something, tugging gently at the duvet covering her shoulders. She could hear breathing very close to her ear. She felt hot little puffs of breath on her cheek. 'Peter? Is that you?' she whispered. No answer, just quiet breaths, in and out. She turned over towards the sound. The room was dark and still but there was enough light from the radio alarm clock on the bedside table for her to see that there was nobody lying on the pillow beside her and through the slightly open bedroom door she saw the light on across the landing. Peter must be up working still. She heard him cough and the rustling of papers. The clock said it was twenty past two.

She turned over again. She must have been dreaming. But there it was again. Little breaths, right against her ear. And then a whisper, quite clear.

It was a child's voice, urgent, pleading: Don't leave. Don't leave.

CHAPTER 8

She wasn't going to say anything to Peter. It would only start another argument. He must have been aware that something was wrong when he finally came to bed at about three in the morning, because the bedside light was on and she was curled up in a tight ball with her head under the duvet. But he crawled in beside her without a word, and fell asleep straight away.

The breathing and the whispers had stopped abruptly the moment she sat up in bed, heart thumping, and snapped on the bedside light. There was nobody, nothing, there. More than ever now she was convinced of one thing: the cottage was haunted by the spirit of this child, a spirit only she could see. And that spirit wanted only one thing, that she must not leave. But why?

She lay awake until morning, every muscle in her body tense, waiting for the whispers to return. They didn't. Peter groaned when the alarm went off, and later brought her up some tea, kissing her briefly on the forehead. He opened the curtains. Outside, a grey dawn was only just breaking, the sea frisky in the blustery wind which was still hurling sheets of hard rain inland.

'I might be a bit late back tonight,' he said, straightening his tie in the wardrobe mirror. 'I'm popping back to the flat after work. I'll pick up your art stuff and my telescope, maybe stop and have a chat with the doctors, see how they're getting on.'

'Oh, OK.' She felt a sudden pang, thinking of other people in her flat, sleeping in her bed, cooking in her kitchen. 'You will check that they haven't, you know, changed anything?'

'I've told you, Jane, they won't go in Angela's room, I promise.' He picked up his car keys. 'Oh, and get on to Blackwood again, will you. Find out if he's come up with another place for us. We don't want to spend any more time than we have to in this spooky haunted house, do we?' He waggled his fingers in the air as he said the word 'spooky'. He probably thought he was teasing her in a light-hearted kind of way, but it made Jane cringe. She felt she was being mocked, belittled. She got out of bed, edged past Peter without a word, and headed for the shower.

She heard him shout 'See you later' as she stepped under the comforting embrace of the hot water. She didn't answer. What was happening to them? He'd always been her rock, her anchor. The age thing never mattered to her because he made her feel safe, cared for, his strength protecting and supporting her through their bereavement and her breakdowns. But now it was all falling apart. They seemed to be slipping deeper into controlling parent/dependent child roles, and at the same time drifting further and further away from each other and she couldn't think of a way to stop it.

The day stretched ahead as bleak and empty as the view from the window. How was she going to fill the long hours, she wondered? She didn't feel in the mood to draw or paint or write or read anything. The weather was too wet and windy to go for a walk. She decided to do some baking, make cheese scones. Peter loved those, and it might help heal the rift between them. And it might take her mind off the whispers of the night still echoing round and round in her head.

She put down the packet of flour and other bits she'd begun to assemble to make the scones. It was no good, she had to do this, what she'd been wanting to do since yesterday. She found Nigel Blackwood's card in the back pocket of her jeans, picked up her phone, and keyed in his number.

'Hello?' Hearing his deep voice made her heart flip.

'Nigel, it's me. Jane Eagle. I'm sorry to be bothering you, but I really need to talk to you about something, and I don't want to do it over the phone. I know you must be really busy and I'm probably being a nuisance, but could you call in some time, do you think?'

'You're not a nuisance at all. Is everything all right?'

'Well, not really. I heard her again last night, the little girl. She was whispering in my ear, *Don't leave*. I'll tell you more when I see you, but I must get to the bottom of this. I think the house is haunted, Nigel, and I need to find out what this child is trying to tell me, what she wants of me.'

'OK.' He sounded wary, doubtful, drawing out the second syllable. 'I'm not sure what you want me to do though.'

'I don't want you to do anything, it's just that I need to talk it through with someone who will listen, someone who doesn't immediately think I'm having a schizophrenic episode and it's all in my head. You were so understanding yesterday, I thought, well, you did say I could ring any time.'

'I did say that, and I'm glad you took me up on it.'

'I'd like to ask you a few things about the cottage, its history, and about your aunt and things that might have gone on here. It could give me a few clues as to what might be happening.'

There was a silence, and Jane thought for an awful moment he had hung up on her. Then he said, 'I'll tell you what, I'm tied up today but why don't I pick you up tomorrow, about twelve, and we'll have lunch somewhere? How does that sound?'

'It sounds – yes, yes please. That would be great.'

When they'd said their goodbyes, Jane felt something she hadn't experienced since the day Peter asked if he could take her out. A bubble of happy excitement rose up inside her. She almost danced back into the kitchen. It hadn't stopped raining, but a watery sun was attempting to shine through the clouds. She looked out of the window and saw a rainbow forming over the distant coastline. Perhaps it was a sign that things would turn out all right.

66

The hours dragged by. The house was too quiet, too still. All she could hear was the low rumble of the sea and the raindrops pattering against the window. And all she could think about was how long she had to wait until noon tomorrow and seeing Nigel again. She baked the scones, she wandered restlessly round the house, did a bit of vacuuming and wiping round with a damp cloth. The early years of her childhood in a dirty, chaotic flat had made her obsessive about keeping things clean.

Jane tried not to think back to those days, but sometimes the memories flashed into her mind; once again she was that chubby little kid with hair that was too bushy, too frizzy, too ginger. Walking out through the playground, being pushed and poked and jeered at by the bigger kids, but not wanting to go home either. Her door key on a string round her neck and climbing up the dark stairs smelling of boiled cabbage and cat pee to the dingy third floor flat. The post piled up on the mat, final demands in angry red print, piles of unwashed clothes strewn over the floor and the kitchen stacked with dirty dishes and empty bottles. 'Mum?' There she was sprawled on the sofa, cigarette butts strewn across the stained carpet. Shaking her but getting no response but a slurred mumble. Well, at least when she was asleep, she wasn't shouting at her, slapping her. Going into the kitchen to make her own tea again – a slice or two of stale white bread.

Jane pushed those thoughts away. Nan was right. They were in the past and going over that time wouldn't change anything. 'Pull your socks up, bonny lass,' she heard Nan's voice in her head. 'Get yerself smartened up.' On a sudden impulse, she went to the bedroom and searched in the back of a drawer for her make-up bag. She rarely bothered with make-up and hadn't at all since she last went to work. What was the point when she never went anywhere? She dabbed a bit of lipstick on her mouth, smiling and making kissing movements at her reflection in the mirror. She found some mascara, a little dried up through not being opened in a couple of years, but she applied it and suddenly her invisibly pale lashes were transformed, making her eyes look large and bright. A bit of blusher brushed over her cheekbones, and the sad, wan face had already been replaced with a reflection that looked like the old Jane, the Jane before she lost Angela. She experimented with her hair, turning her head this way and that, trying it tied back, pulled into a high ponytail, pinning it up in a clip, then tumbling loose around her shoulders.

There was a cold blast of air on the back of her neck. In the mirror, something moved behind her. She heard a rustling sound and saw a quick flash of red, something, someone, flitting past, gone in a split second. She gasped, dropped her brush, swivelled round. There was nothing there, but the window was wide open, and the curtain was flapping in the wind. Still weak-kneed with the shock, she got up and closed it. She – or Peter – obviously hadn't shut it properly. It was just the curtain moving, of course. But she was sure she saw something red. And the curtains weren't red – they were pale grey.

'First the log in the sea, now this,' she muttered to herself. 'My nerves may be in shreds, but I'm not making that mistake again. It was just the curtains blowing about. Just the curtains.'

Later, she made herself a sandwich and some tea, and switched on the TV. She settled herself on the sofa, half watched *Come Dine With Me,* but she couldn't concentrate. The lack of sleep last night finally caught up with her, her eyelids drooped, and she fell deeply asleep, her head resting on the big red cushion that she'd become so attached to. There was something about the soft material of its cover, its warm colour and its plump bulkiness that she found especially comforting.

When she woke, the room was dark. The rain was still pelting down, dashing against the window as she closed the curtains. The TV was still burbling away, the news and the weather forecast; easterly winds, heavy showers possibly turning to sleet later. She must have been asleep for three or four hours. Her phone jangled. It was Peter, 'Darling, are you OK? I'll be home in an hour or so. I've had a bite to eat here, the Tans insisted, so don't bother to cook anything for me.'

'Oh OK,' she said. 'I'll get the fire started. It's turned so cold.'

'Right. See you soon.' She found the TV remote and clicked it off.

Peter had left some twists of paper and kindling by the stove, but the log basket was empty. She laid the fire ready, picked up the basket and went to get the logs. They were stored in a little brick outhouse next to the porch. The porch light came on automatically as she stepped out, wishing she'd put her coat on. The rain was hammering down. God, what a filthy night.

She staggered back into the house, her arms clutching the laden basket, and kicked the door shut with the back of her heel. Peter usually did this job. She hadn't realised how heavy logs were. The light in the sitting room was dim, with just a small table lamp on the dresser illuminating a small corner but leaving most of the room in shadow.

Jane turned her head towards a noise, a slight snuffling sound.

The little girl stood very still in the far corner of the room. Her head was down, wet ropes of hair hanging over her face, arms dangling by her side, and water dripping from her hands, from her hair.

The basket dropped from Jane's arms, the logs rolling out and tumbling noisily across the wooden floor.

'You!' Jane's voice was shrill with shock. In the shadows, the girl stood motionless, water still dripping down her and pooling on the floor round her bare feet. The Minnie Mouse red top and red trousers, which Jane now realised were pyjamas, were soaking wet and clung to her small frame. She looked real, solid, not ghostly.

Jane tried to move, but her body had turned to stone. Her words came out as a rasping whisper: 'Who are you? Where did you come from?'

There was no answer. No movement. The wind and rain rattled against the window, and the muffled sound of Mrs Mortimer's television came faintly through the wall. 'Please,' Jane spoke softly, moved by a terrible wave of sorrow and pity. She wasn't afraid anymore; she wanted to put her arms round the child, make her feel safe. 'Tell me what you want me to do, sweetheart. I want to help you.'

The girl raised her head, looking directly at Jane with her sad blue eyes. 'Don't leave,' she said, her high, child's voice had a hollow, echoing quality about it, as if she was in a cave.

'What do you mean, don't leave?'

'Don't leave,' she repeated.

'Of course I won't leave. Oh, you poor little love. You're soaking wet. Are you lost? Where's your mummy? Your daddy? Are you real? Do you come from next door? Mrs Mortimer's? What's your name? Tell me, tell me, what you want me to do? Please, please, speak to me.'

The lamp in the corner of the room began to flicker violently. It blinked rapidly on and off, making everything look speeded up, jerky, like a strobe light or a very old silent film. Then, snap. The room was in darkness, nothing but blackness. Jane could see nothing. She fumbled around, her hands seeking out the back of the sofa. If she edged her way towards the shelf above the mantelpiece, she knew there was a box of matches there, and a thick church candle. She stumbled forward, nearly tripping over the spilt logs, knocking her shin sharply against the coffee table. She yelped in pain and confusion. She had to find light, quickly, see the child again. 'Are you still there?' she called out. 'Stay here, don't go, I can help.'

She groped her way along the mantelpiece, knocking something over – the carriage clock? It clattered on the hearth tiles with a crash of shattering metal and glass. At last, her frantic fingers closed around the box of matches and found the candle next to it. Her hand was trembling so much she dropped the first match, and cursing, lit another, lit the wick and the flame flared up, casting its dim glow over the room, and throwing huge looming shadows on the walls and ceiling. She stared. There was no sign of the child. She seized the candle, looked in all the corners, behind the curtains, the chairs, ran to the kitchen, screaming at the top of her voice, 'Where are you? Where are you?'

She ran up the stairs, hot wax dripping on to her hand, checked every room, every cupboard, stumbling, crying, shouting, desperate to find her. Downstairs again, she rushed towards the door. Someone was knocking.

Rap-rap-rap.

Not Peter, he's got the key, she thought. Oh please, let it be her, the poor little girl, soaked to the skin. If she was real and alive, not a ghost, she would bring her in, wrap a warm towel round her, keep her safe, call for help.

She flung open the door. *Oh.* It was Mrs Mortimer. She stood ramrod straight, as usual, her white expressionless face looming up out of the dark, like a Halloween mask. The porch light had not come on. 'It's just a power cut, Mrs Eagle,' Mrs Mortimer said. 'Nothing to be concerned about. I've brought you a torch. I heard you shouting. You are all right, I hope?'

'I…er…yes, I mean no, not really.' She took the torch from Mrs Mortimer's outstretched hand. 'I had a bit of shock. It was so…dark.'

'You won't be used to the dark, being from the town,' she said. 'The wind's probably brought down a power line. They'll get it fixed in no time, I'm sure.'

'Yes, yes, I shall be fine now.' Jane just wanted her to go away. She certainly wasn't going to tell the woman what had happened. She could just imagine her reaction – a slight twitch of the mouth and quizzical raising of one black-pencilled eyebrow.

Car headlights came jolting down the track, the downpour caught in their beam. Thank God, Peter was home.

He leapt out of the car, holding his raincoat over his head, and dashed to the shelter of the porch. 'Mrs Mortimer. What's happening?'

'There's been a power cut. I heard your wife screaming. I came round with a torch.'

'Thank you so much Mrs Mortimer,' he said, going to put a hand on her shoulder, but thinking better of it. 'That was very thoughtful of you.'

He turned to Jane. 'You were screaming darling? What on earth was the matter? I didn't think you were scared of the dark.'

Jane grabbed Peter's arm and pulled him inside, snapped a brisk goodnight to Mrs Mortimer, shut the door on her, then bolted it firmly.

'I am not scared of the dark,' she said, turning to face him. 'It's what's in the dark that scared me.'

'What are you talking about?'' He was shaking out showers of raindrops from his wet coat.

'Mind you don't trip,' Jane said, pointing the torch to the floor. 'The logs—'

'What are they doing all over the floor? And what happened to the clock? We'll have to replace that. Come on, let's get this fire lit, then at least we'll have a bit more light and warmth. I need to dry out and then you can tell me what's been going on here.'

CHAPTER 9

Mrs Mortimer was not happy. Things were not going to plan. She had just got herself nicely settled for *Coronation Street*, Arabella in the crook of one arm, Lily in the other, and Whisky curled up asleep at her feet, when she heard a rattling, thumping noise next door, like something rolling over the floor. Then the sitting-room light started to dip on and off, and everything snapped off; the telly, the electric fire, every light in the house. She had to let the babies drop on to the sofa and nearly fell over Whisky as she shuffled in the dark over to the sideboard where she kept a torch. Power cuts weren't unusual round these parts, so she had a torch ready in every room. Hadn't Mr Blackwood always praised her for being so well-organised?

Better check the fuse box, just in case something's blown, she thought. But just as she was heading for the kitchen, there was a racket coming through the wall from next door. A noise of something smashing, then all this screaming and yelling. It must be Her Next Door, up a height again about something. And hubby's car wasn't there, so she was on her own. She sighed. She would have to investigate. She didn't want to, but it was part of her job to keep an eye on what was going on.

'It's all right, Whisky, Mammy's just popping round to see what's up with wifey next door.' She fetched the spare torch from the kitchen. 'Better take her this. These town folk get in a right fettle when they can't see lights.'

She'd remembered to knock. The lass made it clear she didn't like it that time when she walked in. And when the door opened, Mrs Eagle stared at her like she was from outer space and grabbed the torch out of her hand. Not so much as a thank you either. Then her hubby turned up. Very civil, he was, thanked her quite politely. And so he should, coming out in the rain like she had done to see his missus was all right. And then she'd just slammed the door shut in her face. Some people had no manners.

'I won't bother to go round if I hear her yelling again like that,' she told Whisky. 'I thought she was being murdered, the noise she was making. "Where are you?" she was shouting, over and over. Who could she have been talking to? There was nobody there.'

****

'So, let me get this straight,' Peter said. 'You just came in the door, and you saw her, this child, here, in this room, standing in the corner, by the bookshelves?'

Jane sat on the sofa, clutching the torch. Peter was kneeling at the hearth, sweeping up the shattered remains of the carriage clock with a dustpan and brush.

'Yes, yes, that's right. I've already told you.'

'I need to get this sorted in my head. You say she just vanished?'

'It was pitch-dark for at least a minute before I managed to light the candle, so I suppose she could have run away.'

'So, if she was real, where did she go?'

Jane shrugged. 'I don't know.'

'*Hm*. So…'

'So, what?'

'So you're back to thinking she is a real, live child now? Not a ghost, not a waking dream or a hallucination? Or a mistake?' Peter stood up, pacing up and down, stroking his chin.

'A mistake? How can I have made a mistake?'

Peter seized the red cushion Jane was hugging. 'Look, you said she was wearing red pyjamas. From a distance, in a dim light, this red cushion might just look like—'

'For God's sake Peter.' Jane snatched the cushion from his hand and threw it to the floor. 'I'm not completely stupid. I do know the difference between a cushion and a little fair-haired girl, wearing Minnie Mouse pyjamas.'

'OK…OK. I'm just saying, it's easy to get things wrong. Especially when you've got a fantastic imagination. Do you remember that time we were both convinced we saw a swan trapped in the hedge in the park? You were on the point of calling the RSPCA, but I went for a closer look and discovered it was just a white plastic bag caught on a branch and flapping about in the breeze.'

'Yes, yes, I do remember that,' Jane said. 'It wasn't just me though. You thought it was a swan too.'

'That's what I said. We were both sure it was. Just shows how easy it is for anyone to misinterpret what we think we see.'

An image of that log in the water flashed into her mind. She shuddered, pushing the memory away.

'But this wasn't a mistake. I saw her as clearly as I see you now. And look, come over here.' She took Peter's arm, pulling him towards the corner of the room where she'd seen the child. 'There.' Jane pointed the torch at a little puddle of water on the wooden floorboards. 'I saw the rain dripping off her. She was soaked, wet through. Just like she'd been in the sea.'

'Ah.' He laughed. 'A mermaid then. Did she have a fish tail instead of legs?'

Why did he make a fool of her? Why couldn't he take her seriously for once? Jane wanted to cry but swallowed down the lump in her throat. Crying would make her seem even more of a stupid baby than Peter already made her feel. She wouldn't do it. She used to be strong, she used to be able to stand up for herself, stand her ground, so she could do it again. If only she didn't feel so alone.

Peter had seen her blinking, struggling against the tears. He put his arms round her, and she didn't pull away, although his face in the torch's beam looked sinister, like a stranger's, gaunt and hollow eyed.

'I'm sorry, darling,' he said. 'I can see there's water on the floor, and I've no idea how it got there. I'm as mystified as you are, and I do believe you saw something, if you say you did. But look, we can't put up with this another day. Have you spoken to Blackwood yet? Or the doctor?'

'I've told you till I'm blue in the face, I'm not going back on medication,' she said, despite everything finding herself comforted by the familiar smell and firm tweedy roughness of his jacket against her cheek. 'And no, I haven't spoken to Nigel Blackwood again.' It was a lie, of course, but it was true she hadn't raised the question of them moving when she phoned him that morning.

'Well, make sure you do tomorrow. Or if not the doctor, see if you can get an appointment with the therapist. We've got to get you some help and getting you away from here's a start.'

'No. No…' She shook her head. 'How can I leave? That's the one thing she doesn't want me to do. She keeps begging me, you see, *Don't leave* – over and over again. She doesn't say Don't leave *me*. She says *Don't leave*. Don't leave this house. For some reason I don't know she wants me to stay here.'

'Well, if you don't know the reason, how can you possibly help? I've said this before I know, but you've got to accept the facts, Jane. And the facts are that we don't even know if she's real, or a manifestation produced by your brain because of your illness.'

Or she's a ghost, Jane thought, dreading the same old tedious arguments it would lead to if she said it out loud. She was tired, so tired. She couldn't bear to prolong this futile discussion any longer.

As suddenly as they'd gone, the lights snapped back to life, flooding the room with brightness. The power had come back. Everything seemed normal again, the shadows banished.

'Ah great.' Peter said. 'I'll get the kettle on and make us a hot drink. Then I think we should get to bed. We can talk about all this again when we're both feeling more settled.'

Peter brewed up tea, and Jane carried her mug up to bed. When she'd gone, Peter got the kitchen roll and began to mop up the water on the floor. There was a half full bottle of tonic water on the shelf nearby, leftover from when he poured himself a gin and tonic the other night. Ah, so that's it, it must have got knocked over. He sniffed the wet kitchen paper. It didn't smell of tonic water. He dipped his finger in one of the few little drops left on the floor, tentatively dabbed it on his tongue. It tasted salty. That's odd, he thought. It was sea water.

CHAPTER 10

Jane's stomach was rolling over with nausea and excitement as she waited at the kitchen window, staring up the track for Nigel Blackwood's silver grey Mercedes. She hadn't felt like this since she was seventeen and waiting outside the Odeon for Alex, the first boy who had ever asked her out, the first of a few short-lived and unsatisfactory relationships she'd had until she realised she had nothing in common with boys her own age. It was ten past twelve. She began to wonder if he was going to come at all, if he had forgotten. Or changed his mind.

It was the first time in a long while she'd worn a skirt, black tights with knee high boots and her best suede jacket, not her usual stay at home uniform of joggers, fleece and trainers. She'd shampooed and conditioned her hair and fastened it back with a clip, put on the dangly silver earrings Peter gave her last Christmas and which she'd never taken out of their little velvet box.

Perhaps she was being ridiculous, reading more into this than she should. Nigel was just a nice, kind man who was good at listening and probably felt sorry for her. He surely had a lovely wife at home and wasn't thinking of anything other than a friendly, professional relationship with any woman, let alone a married, crazy woman who saw things nobody else did.

A quarter past twelve, and still no Nigel. Jane turned her back on the window, her shoulders drooping. She would take her jacket off, get back in her fleece and joggers, forget about Nigel. It was a bad idea, anyway, really quite a relief that nothing was going to happen. She would go for a long walk now the rain had stopped and there was a bright burst of sunshine piercing the dark clouds. Then she heard the crunch of the car tyres. He was here.

The autumn colours were blazing red and gold and yellow as Nigel drove down the country roads, under the winding tunnels of trees. They were heading south towards a little seaside town set in a wide, sandy bay. With its church spire, rooftops, and cluster of pastel-coloured houses, from a distance it made Jane think of the Enid Blyton stories she'd read avidly as a child, *Five Go to Smugglers Bay,* perhaps?

'This place used to be bristling with pirates and the like,' Nigel told her. 'Supposed to have a canny few ghosts as well.'

Now they sat opposite each other at a fireside table in the corner of a low-ceilinged bar with its ancient beams and horse brasses. It wasn't busy, but there was a quiet hum of conversation in the background, and a crackling fire in the grate next to them. Jane said she'd have tonic water with lemon.

'Are you sure? Not a glass of wine?' Nigel said.

'No thanks. I know it makes me sound a bit prim and proper, but I just don't like the smell of alcohol, never have. Oh, but I don't mind the smell of beer though,' she added hastily, watching Nigel set down his pint glass.

They ordered fish and chips. Nigel sat back. 'So, Jane, you wanted to talk to me about the house? Its history?'

'Yes. I told you about the face at the window, didn't I? And the whispering in my ear at night?' He nodded. She went on, 'Well, you probably won't believe this, but last night she was in the house. Standing in the corner, as close as you are now. I tried to ask her questions, but she didn't answer. All she said was *Don't leave.* Then there was a power cut, and she disappeared. Nigel, she looked so real, but I think it's possible she might be a ghost. I think the house is haunted. So I wondered, have any other people staying there reported anything like that?'

'Hmm. No. I can honestly tell you nobody's ever said anything like that before. In fact, most people have commented on what a nice atmosphere it has, cosy, welcoming.'

Jane felt deflated. So she was the only one, the oddball, because for all its quietly contemporary fresh decor, the house had felt cold and forbidding from the moment she first saw those two chimneys on the horizon. It was, to her, as if even the old stone walls themselves held some secret sorrow she couldn't understand.

'Do you know anything about the background of the cottage? How did your aunt come to live there? What about these séances she held?'

Nigel took a long swig of his beer and tapped his fingertips together. 'Well, it does have quite an interesting history. Lord Townley from the Hall had it built in about 1810, I think. He had a huge family – fourteen children – and the cottage was a kind of glorified beach hut for them when they came down to bathe, have picnics and so on. There was probably more of a beach then, and the house was not so close to the sea. The coastline's eroded quite a bit over the last couple of hundred years.'

'At high tide it can't be more than two or three metres from the edge now. So, if it carries on eroding, the whole house could eventually disappear into the sea?' said Jane.

'Eventually, yes.'

'So, were there any tragic events from that time, do you know, children drowning, things like that?'

'Not that I've heard. Are you thinking your little ghost might be one of Lord Townley's brood?'

'No, perhaps not. I don't think she'd have been wearing Minnie Mouse pyjamas in 1810.'

'That's true. Anyway, the Townley family died out a couple of generations later and the Hall and the bathing house both fell into disrepair. I think the army occupied the Hall in both world wars. And I know in the last war the cottage was used as an invasion look-out spot for the Home Guard, like one of those coastal pillbox things. The Hall was restored by the National Trust after the war. But the cottage stayed an empty shell with a caved in roof until my grandfather – that was Arthur Blackwood – bought it for a song. That would have been a few years after the war, about '47 or '48. He was a doctor from Berwick. I don't think he was that keen on the prospect of working for the new NHS, so he decided to retire early, do the place up, extend it, and move the family there.'

Their lunch arrived, two plates heaped with huge golden-battered fish and fat chips.

'That must have taken some doing, restoring a ruin,' Jane said, suddenly very hungry. Her knife cut into the crisp batter with a satisfying crunch.

'I believe so. Of course, that was over twenty years before I was born, but my dad was a lad around ten or eleven, so he remembered moving there. Apparently, the builders had to shift a whole lorry load of bird muck from inside before they could start work.'

'So, your aunt – Miss Blackwood – was she your dad's only sibling? Was she younger or older?'

'Yes, there were just the two children, my dad, and my aunty Irene. She would have been about eight years older than Dad.'

'And Irene never married, and stayed on and lived there after your grandfather died?'

'Yes, that's right. Granddad died in 1978, Grandma Mabel about a year later, so my dad divided the cottage in two. Irene stayed on in the part where you are now, and he let out the smaller part to the head groundsman at the Hall, Eric Mortimer. He'd just got married to Peggy, needed somewhere bigger than his one room over the stables.'

'Ah, Mrs Mortimer.' said Jane, trying to imagine that grim-faced figure in black as a blushing young bride. 'What happened to Eric Mortimer? Did he die?'

'Ah, no. They were there about five years before Eric ran off with a woman from the village. Quite a scandal that caused. We never saw him again, but Dad let Peggy stay on, mainly because she looked after Irene for him. My dad was busy all through the early eighties, buying up cheap properties to restore as holiday homes. He employed Peggy Mortimer as a cleaner for them.'

'Poor old Morticia,' said Jane. 'I feel quite sorry for her now. It must have turned her bitter. She told me she'd never had children.'

'No, she never did. I overheard my dad saying to Mam once that it must have been like making love to a broomstick, so maybe that was why.' He laughed. 'Mrs M was always on the thin and bony side, even in her younger days. And the young lady he left her for was quite buxom – and pregnant, so the rumours went.'

'This is all very fascinating, but it doesn't get me any nearer finding out who my little ghost girl could be. I was wondering – I know it sounds far-fetched – if she could be a spirit summoned up by one of your aunt Irene's séances, and she just kind of hung around the place? But you say there's never been any reports of a ghost haunting the cottage before?'

'No. And I can't tell you very much about Irene and her séances. After Granddad and Grandma died Mam and Dad used to take me and my brothers to visit her sometimes when we were kids. But we always thought she was a bit of a weird old bird, so we used to go off exploring the rock pools, plodging in the sea, mucking about on the little beach when the tide was out. We knew people regularly used to turn up and pay her a few pounds to tell their fortunes or try to put them through for a chat with some relative or other who'd passed on. But Dad never approved of it. He used to say Irene had always been nuts, *round the bend,* as they used to call it. So he wouldn't talk about what went on, at least not to us kids.'

'So when did she die, your aunt?' Jane said, laying down her knife and fork, finally defeated by the last three chips.

'Oh,' said Nigel. 'She's not dead. Well, not physically anyway.'

'What do you mean?'

'Dementia, I'm afraid. She was more and more away with the fairies as she got older. Peggy Mortimer got on with her quite well – as far as she gets on with anybody – so she used to look after her, but it reached a point where Aunty Irene was wandering about on the cliff top stark naked in the middle of the night, that sort of thing, so it wasn't right to expect Mrs M to deal with her. She's been in a nursing home, oh, must be twenty-six, twenty-seven years now. It's amazing she's lived that long, almost unheard of for dementia sufferers. I visited her quite often after my dad died four years ago, but she didn't know who I was, so what was the point? Now I only pop in to see how she is once or twice a year.'

'So when she went to the nursing home, that's when your father turned Irene's part of the house into a holiday let?'

'Yes, and very popular it's been too. Do you know there's an American couple book it for five weeks every summer? They just love it, the solitude, the sea view. And of course, all the nearby old castles and history the Americans go for.'

'And these Americans, do they...?' Jane began.

'I know what you're going to ask. Do they have children, maybe a little girl? A little girl who happened to meet with some tragic accident at the cottage, perhaps?'

'I was wondering that, yes,'

'The answer to that is no. They're in their seventies, their children are grown up and they come on their own. Sorry, Jane.'

'Nothing to be sorry about. I'm glad. I wouldn't wish losing a child on anybody. It's the worst thing in the world.'

'Of course,' Nigel said. He put his big, firm hand over Jane's. 'Forgive me, I was being thoughtless.'

'That's OK,' she said. She would forgive him anything with the warmth of his hand enveloping hers. She didn't ever want him to take it away. 'Just one more question, Nigel, I promise. You say Eric Mortimer's girlfriend was pregnant when he ran off with her. Do you know if the baby was a boy or a girl?'

'I don't know, I'm afraid. I heard they'd gone somewhere down south to live, or possibly gone abroad, that's all, and I was a young teenage lad at the time, so my parents didn't think it was a suitable topic to discuss in front of me. Do you think your ghost girl might be

Eric Mortimer's love child? Come back to haunt poor childless Peggy?'

'Just a thought. I'm exploring every possible angle at the moment,' Jane said, thinking to herself she sounded like the detective in a murder mystery.

'Well, if it was a girl, and she has come back, she must be a ghost. That child would be in her late thirties by now.'

They ordered two coffees. Jane longed to ask more questions, but she didn't want him to feel as if he was being interrogated. In particular, she wanted to ask Nigel about his wife, if he had one. He said he had children, but he wasn't wearing a wedding ring. Instead, they chatted about inconsequential things – the weather, Newcastle United's prospects in next weekend's match – although Nigel was, as Jane had guessed – more of a rugby man, an avid Falcons supporter.

Nigel paid the bill. Outside, the day had turned mild, almost unseasonably warm, the sun's rays drawing a steamy mist of evaporating rain up from the pavement. 'I haven't got to go back to the office this afternoon,' Nigel said. 'Do you fancy a little leg-stretch along the beach?'

They walked side by side along the path through the dunes and down on to the wide sweep of sand. Jane wished she'd worn her sandals so she could splash barefoot through the shallow water's edge, letting the foamy waves trickle through her toes. Peter always said there were two types of people: those who loved to kick off their shoes, walk barefoot on grass, paddle in the sea, or dangle their feet in a cool, trickling stream – and those who kept their shoes and socks firmly on wherever they were, however hot the day. Peter was a shoes off type, and so was she. Mrs Mortimer was definitely a shoes on person. But she wasn't sure about Nigel.

'My turn to ask you a question,' Nigel said.

'Of course, ask me anything.' Every nerve in Jane's body was tingling and tight with anticipation. Their arms brushed each other as they walked along. Was he going to stop, put his arms around her, kiss her?

'What does your husband think about what you saw last night?'

'Oh, to put it bluntly, he thinks it's a load of bollocks,' Jane said, disappointed. She really did not want to talk about Peter. 'He's a scientist. When he's confronted with something that can't be explained or worked out with logic, he dismisses it completely. There always has to be a logical reason for everything.'

'And what does he think the reason is for these things you've been seeing?'

'My mental health issues. Psychosis. Waking dreams.'

'So what sort of scientist is Mr Eagle?'

'He's a lecturer in theoretical physics. And he's actually Professor Eagle, although he only uses that title professionally. He reckons everyone not in academic circles pictures some eccentric wild-haired person wearing odd socks and a funny bowtie when they hear the word professor.'

'Ah yes, I know what he means. Einstein pulling crazy faces in front of a blackboard covered in complicated mathematical squiggles.'

'Exactly. Only it's a whiteboard these days. And he's not crazy. Although his hair can get a bit Einsteiny sometimes.'

'What is theoretical physics anyway? Do you understand any of that stuff? I'm sure I don't.' He chuckled.

'Not really,' said Jane, wishing they could change the subject. 'I do try, and I can grasp some of it. And as for what it is – Peter once tried to sum it up by explaining it's basically about trying to work out what stuff is and what stuff does.'

'And as yet we haven't worked out who your ghostly girl is, or why she's doing what she does,' Nigel said. 'I haven't been able to help much, have I?'

The sun had moved behind a low purple-black cloud, rolling in from the horizon.

The temperature dropped as the sunlight vanished. Jane shivered. 'I guess I'll just have to accept I'll never know the answers. And please don't feel bad about the things you've told me not being helpful. I've learnt a lot today.'

'It's gone cool,' he said. 'Looks like it might rain again, let's get back to the car.'

They didn't talk much on the drive back. It started to rain, fat drops splattering the car windows. Jane wished they could just drive on and on and never go back to the cottage. But soon they were back, parked on the gravel patch. Nigel left his engine running, jumped out and went round to open the passenger door. So it was to be a quick goodbye then; there was to be no embrace, no kiss. She thanked him for the lunch, said how nice it had been.

'Pleasure's all mine,' he said. 'We'll do it again some time. And call me if you think of anything else I can help with. Give my regards to the Professor.'

She nodded, got her door key out of her shoulder bag.

'Oh – and Jane,' he called, one leg back in the car. 'I nearly forgot. Can you confirm with Mr – Professor – Eagle you will be vacating the cottage on December seventeenth, and let Mrs Mortimer know? She's got someone who wants to book for the week after that, so she'll need to sort that out a.s.a.p'.

'Yes, will do.' She smiled back at him. And he was away.

As Jane put her key in the lock, she saw a hand moving aside the net curtain at Mrs Mortimer's kitchen window, and Mrs Mortimer stared straight at her, her expression even grimmer than usual. Jane smiled and waved, and the curtain immediately dropped back.

Poor old Morticia, Jane thought. What a sad, lonely life she's had.

CHAPTER 11

'Well, I wonder what's going on there?' Peggy Mortimer had seen Mr Blackwood's car drawing up outside. She was boiling herself an egg for her lunch. How inconvenient of him to call on her without warning. He never usually did that.

It must be something important, she'd thought, taking off her apron, checking her hair in the little mirror by the door. But he wasn't getting out of the car, and when she looked again, she saw Her Next Door running out towards him. She'd tidied herself up a bit, put on a skirt, sorted out that messy hair. And there was Mr Blackwood, beaming all over his face, holding open the passenger door for her, and off they went.

It was a good few hours before she saw them come back. Surely there couldn't be anything going between them? He'd been round at hers just a couple of days ago, now here he was again, whisking her off somewhere. That didn't usually happen with other occupants of the cottage. If there was a problem, he more often than not asked her to sort it out for him. Everything was kept on a very professional basis, as it should be. She tutted. She was disappointed in Mr Blackwood. She would have thought better of him. But then, he was a man, so what did she expect? Of course, she could be wrong. She hoped she was. Mr Eagle seemed decent enough for a man and she didn't like to think of that sort of sordid carry-on happening right under his nose.

'We'd better keep a close watch on those two, Whisky.' The cat blinked his amber eyes at her, stretched, and curled up back to sleep in his basket.

87

****

'Everything nice and peaceful today, was it?' Peter asked, turning the salad to go with the pasta bake Jane had made for their supper. 'Nothing untoward happened?'

'No, it's all been quiet,' Jane said, setting the plates on the breakfast bar. 'I went for a walk before the rain started. Did a bit of reading.'

'Ah, good.' He smiled, but he seemed tense.

'Oh, and I did speak to Nigel Blackwood. He needs to know if we are definitely leaving on December seventeenth. They've got a possible booking for the following week.'

'OK. Well, what do you think? It's really up to you, darling. Do you want to stay on longer?'

'I'm…not sure. I don't particularly want to spend the depths of winter here. But, Peter, I know you'll not like me saying this – I don't want to go back until I've found out what that little girl wants, why she wants me to stay. Because if I leave before I know I'll always wonder about it, whether it's just my messed-up mind, whether she was real. Or dare I say it, a spirit.'

'Well, we don't want to go over the same old ground again,' Peter said. 'You know what I think about so-called ghosts.'

Jane put down her fork. The big lunch she'd had with Nigel had killed her appetite – or was it the decision she was being forced to make?

'All right. Let's go home on December seventeenth. But, Peter, will you go round and tell Mrs Mortimer? She still gives me the creeps, even though I feel a bit sorry for her, knowing what happened.'

'Oh? Has she been telling you her life story?'

'No, she never speaks to me unless she has to. I don't think she likes me, and I have to say the feeling's mutual. But Nigel Blackwood told me her husband ran off with someone a few years after they were married, and he was never seen again. Maybe that's what turned her sour.'

'Been having a good old gossip with nice Mr B, have you?' He was smiling, but there was an edge to his voice. She ignored his remark and scraped her uneaten food into the bin.

That night, she lay thinking about Nigel, wondering what it was that attracted her. He wasn't particularly good looking, and he certainly wasn't young, although a few years younger than Peter. There was just something about him, his warmth and good humour, his complete acceptance, without judgement, of everything she told him. He treated her like an adult, and she felt she could confide in him, and it wouldn't lead to an argument, as it always seemed to with Peter.

Peter came to bed and reached for her. 'Sorry I got a bit tetchy about you chatting to Blackwood. I'm just a grumpy old sod, I guess. A grumpy old sod who's terrified he's going to lose his lovely young wife.'

'Don't be silly, you're not going to lose me,' she murmured. Although she'd rather have gone to sleep, she turned towards him. But she couldn't stop herself imagining it was Nigel kissing her neck, stroking her body.

The morning dawned calm and mild and the sea lay smooth and pearly blue under a clear sky. Jane opened the window and breathed in the scent of the grass, fresh and glistening from yesterday's rain. And there was that evocative salty, slightly rotten smell that wafted up at low tide, reminding her of seaside holidays with Nan in Whitby or Scarborough or Whitley Bay. Nan always said 'Oooh, Flower, will you breathe in that ozone? Does you a power of good.' But Peter explained later that ozone had nothing to do with it and ozone was in fact a toxic gas that smells of burning wire, and what you can actually smell is dimethyl sulphide released by microbes in decaying seaweed.

'The trouble is you scientists have no poetry in your soul,' Jane had teased him, shushing him when he began to tell her there was no scientific evidence to support the concept of a soul.

Before he left for work, Peter said, 'I'm not going to have time to speak to Morticia this morning, and I know you don't want to, so can you write her a quick note and pop it through her door? Just to confirm we are going on that date.'

Jane said she would and watched at the kitchen window as he drove away. Now the day was hers to do with as she chose. But first she had to write that note. She kept it brief and formal:

Mrs Mortimer,

As requested by Mr Blackwood, I am confirming that we will be vacating this property on the morning of December 17th.

Regards

Jane Eagle

She folded the paper, stuffed it in an envelope, and as she went towards the door, she felt a sudden overwhelming compulsion to tear it up and throw it in the bin. The child's voice echoed loudly in her head, Don't leave. Don't leave. It took every bit of strength she possessed to hold on to that envelope. She clenched it in her hand. 'But I must. I have to,' she said out loud.

To reach her door she had to pass Mrs Mortimer's kitchen window, and as she approached, she saw that Mrs M had pulled aside the neat white net curtain and was leaning over her sink, vigorously cleaning the inside of the window with a duster. Mrs M didn't seem to have spotted her approaching, so Jane hung back, wanting to avoid her coming out to ask what she wanted and then having to engage in one of their uncomfortable exchanges. She waited out of sight for a while, until Mrs M put down the duster and turned away. Jane crept towards the door quickly, crouching down below the level of the window as she went and hoping Mrs M wouldn't notice the top of her head bobbing past.

She glanced quickly at the window. Mrs M was bending down to pick something up, her back to the window, then straightened up, lifting something to her shoulder.

'A baby.' Jane gasped. 'She's holding a baby.' It was only a split second but that was surely the top of a newborn's wobbly little head she saw, sticking out of a white shawl as Mrs M held it against her. A moment later Mrs M left the kitchen, still carrying the bundle, still with her back to the window.

Jane rushed to the door and pushed the note through the letter box, then pelted back to the safety of her own door. What the hell was that? Was it a baby – or am I imagining things again? Yes, she was sure it was a baby. But then she'd been absolutely sure it was a swan trapped in the hedge, that it was a child's body floating in the sea, that the flapping curtain was someone dashing behind her when she was looking in the mirror. What else could it have been? A bundle of washing, a rolled-up blanket?

The other possibility was that Mrs Mortimer was looking after someone's baby for them, someone from the village, perhaps? She'd not noticed anyone coming to the cottage by car last night or this morning, but they could have wheeled the baby down the track in a pram. It must have been some kind of emergency if so. Surely only a desperate parent would leave their tiny baby with an old crow like Mrs Mortimer, a woman who seemed to Jane the absolute antithesis of a maternal type?

It was a sunny, windless autumn day; she would go for a long walk and think this through – yet another strange thing to try to make sense of. And on her way, she would call in on Mrs Armstrong at the farm and see if she could give her any answers.

As she walked up the long track, Jane remembered the parcel they'd brought down from the farm for Mrs Mortimer – the parcel that contained baby clothes. It seemed certain to Jane now that there was a baby in Mrs M's life, one she looked after from time to time, one she cared for, one that had been born very recently to someone Mrs M knew.

She was in half a mind whether an intrusion on the Armstrongs would be welcome, but she needn't have worried. As she approached the farmyard gate there was Tom Armstrong, busy forking a pungent mountain of manure on to the back of a trailer. He saw her, gave her a grin and a wave and walked towards her, wiping his hands on his overall.

'Hello again. The postie's left a package for you. You are Mrs Jane Eagle, aren't you?'

'Yes, that's me. I can't think who's sending me a package.'

'Oh, and there's a big parcel for Mrs Mortimer too. But it'll be too big for you to carry back. I'll drop it down later on the tractor.'

An older man in a flat cap emerged from a barn. Tom called out, 'Dad, come and meet Jane. She's staying down at Two Chimneys.'

Mr Armstrong was a big-bellied man with the ruddy, leathery face of someone who's spent most of his life out in the open.

'Brian Armstrong, pleased to meet you.' He gave her a little half salute with his forefinger to his cap. 'Won't shake your hand, I've been mucking out the cow shed. Do you fancy a cuppa? It's our morning break. Been up since five. Our lass is brewing up a pot of coffee, if you want to come round to the kitchen.'

So Jane found herself sitting in the Armstrong's big messy kitchen, while Mrs Armstrong, wearing her wellingtons, poured the coffee. She cleared to one side lopsided piles of paper and what looked like the assorted oily innards of farm machinery that littered the table and set a chipped mug down for Jane. Another young man she'd not seen before entered, nodded at Jane.

'This is Adam, our other lad,' Mrs Armstrong said. 'Adam, fetch the little parcel the postie left for Mrs Eagle. It's on the hall table somewhere, I think.'

Two dogs were sleeping in front of the Aga, an old grey-muzzled black Labrador, and a young sheepdog. The Labrador stirred itself, then lumbered over and rested its chin on Jane's lap. She fondled its friendly head, enjoying the feel of its silky ears.

'Dogs always seem to make a beeline for me. They must know I like them,' Jane said. 'I wish I had a dog to keep me company, but pets aren't allowed at the cottage.'

'I bet it was Peggy Mortimer insisted on that. She wouldn't want dogs around the place, chasing the cats,' said Brian Armstrong. 'How many cats does she have down there these days?'

'Only the one, I think. Why, did she used to have a lot of cats?'

'A lot? The bloody place was overrun with them.'

'You're exaggerating, Dad.' Tom had come in and was washing his hands in the sink. 'But I think she did have about twelve at one point.'

'Yes, until John Blackwood – Miss Blackwood's brother – intervened,' said Mrs Armstrong. 'He had to. She was struggling to keep the place clean, and it was costing her a fortune feeding them all. The RSPCA came and took them, found them all good homes, I hope. They did leave her one. That must have been – oh, a good twelve years ago, so that cat she's got now must be a descendant. She must have got it neutered if she's just got the one.'

'How come she had so many?'

'Ah, well, I'll tell you, lass. It's a long story.' Brian Armstrong settled down with his coffee mug in the chair opposite Jane. He was clearly a man who enjoyed a good gossip. 'Peggy Mortimer loved her cats. Preferred them to people, I reckon. She brought this cat with her when she and Eric moved in. But he hated cats, and that one in particular. He really liked his little garden out the back, and he used to throw stones at the cat when it started scratching up his seed bed. Anyway, this cat was female, and Eric was too mean to pay the vet's bill to get it seen to, so of course, it kept producing litter after litter of kittens, at least two or three lots a year.'

'Aw, don't tell her this bit, Brian, it's horrible,' said Mrs Armstrong.

He ignored her. 'Well, I was just a lad at the time. My dad had the farm then, and he sent me down the track to mend the fence where the sheep kept getting out at the bottom of the field, near the cottage. And when I was down there, I saw him, Eric Mortimer, coming out of his house with a sack. He picks up the biggest stones and rocks he could find lying around, chucks them in the sack and ties up the top with string. Then she comes out, his missus, wailing and shouting, *No Eric, please, not again, please don't do it. I'll find them homes, don't Eric, don't.* But he just pushes her away and marches up to the cliff top, and hoys the sack into the sea.'

'There were kittens in the sack? He drowned them?' Jane said, aghast.

'Oh aye, and that's what he did, apparently, every time the cat had another litter. And old Miss Blackwood told me – before she went completely doolally – that sometimes he couldn't be bothered with the sack and the rocks and just threw the kittens on the open fire as soon as they were born. I reckon the only reason he didn't kill that cat was 'cos he used it to keep Peggy under his thumb. He was heard boasting in the pub he'd shoot it if she ever stepped out of line.'

'He sounds a horrible man,' Jane said.

'Aye, he was. Another thing I heard, he used to shoot rabbits, do a bit of illegal poaching too, I expect. Anyway, he bought in this rabbit he'd shot for Peggy to prepare for a stew, but it wasn't quite dead, so when she refused to skin it alive, he forced her to stamp on its head till it was dead, knowing how she had such a soft spot for animals. Good looking young fella mind. He could turn on the charm with the ladies when it suited him.'

'I heard about him running off with a woman from the village,' Jane said, feeling slightly sick. 'I should imagine Mrs Mortimer was glad to see the back of him.'

'Aye, you're not wrong. After he'd gone, the cat kept on producing kittens and this time of course she kept them all. Well, most of them. Some escaped and went feral, and Mam and Dad took a few off her hands to keep the rats down in the barns.'

'Tell her about the bonfire, Brian,' his wife urged. 'I couldn't believe it when you told me that story.'

'Well, it was only a few days after Eric and his young girlfriend disappeared, our Mam came running in and said she'd seen a big cloud of smoke down the track. Me and Dad jumps in the Land Rover and rushes down there, thinking the cottage must be on fire. But there, in the field, just where Eric used to have his garden, was this huge bonfire, and on top of it was a bed. It was blazing away, mattress and all, so that just the metal bedsprings were left. And out comes Peggy, and Miss Blackwood, both holding big armfuls of bedding, all Eric's stuff, his clothes, even his shoes, and they hoyed them all into the flames. It was like she was trying to destroy every trace of him.'

'I don't blame her,' said Jane. 'It does seem a bit extreme to burn a bed though.'

'My dad calls out to Peggy, asks her why she's burning it, and she doesn't answer. But Miss Blackwood chips in: *It's defiled, Mr Armstrong, tainted with sin.* She was very religious, was old Miss Blackwood. I reckon it was her told Peggy about Eric and Katie Harris sneaking down to the cottage for their secret trysts while she was out doing her cleaning job. Miss Blackwood must have had a good idea what was going on, being right next door.'

'Katie Harris – that was the woman he ran off with?' Jane asked. 'I heard she was pregnant.'

'Yes, that was the rumour. I guess that was what made them decide to do a runner. She was only a teenager, no more than eighteen, a bonny lass, and old man Harris would've murdered Eric, given the chance. Her dad was landlord at the Dog and Duck – that was the village pub – long since gone of course. He found the note she left, saying she and Eric were leaving and couldn't say if or when they'd ever be back. He was mad as hell, but I think it destroyed him in the end, and his missus. Katie was their only child. They always hoped she'd turn up one day, but she never did. After a few years they let the pub go downhill, never recovered.'

'Eric and Katie – they went to London, didn't they?'

'Well, that's what her note said, but Mam and Dad always reckoned that was just to throw Jim Harris off the scent and they'd really gone abroad somewhere. Eric drove one of those old beat-up Morris Minor Travellers. You'd be too young to remember them. Looked like a garden shed on wheels. It was found abandoned in a field near Newcastle Airport. No, I think they jumped on a plane and went abroad, probably opened a bar in Benidorm or somewhere like that. Wouldn't surprise me if they're still there today.'

Tom came over and sat at the table. 'Yeah, and you oldies are still going on about it nearly forty years later.' He sighed. 'It was the only exciting bit of scandal that's ever happened round here, I suppose.'

'Well, it sounds to me like Mrs Mortimer was well rid of him,' Jane said.

'Yes, but you wouldn't want to get on the wrong side of Peggy.' Brian Armstrong leant back in his chair. He was enjoying re-telling the story. 'She must have been that angry and bitter after he'd gone because she even ripped up his beloved little garden. My dad let him have a bit of land behind the cottage for it. It's not a good field for crops, too flinty. But Eric dug in some quality topsoil, put up a fence round it to keep the sheep out, spent every minute working there, when he wasn't up at the Hall – or enjoying a spot of rumpy-pumpy with Katie.' He chuckled, only stopping when Mrs Armstrong turned and gave him an old-fashioned look. 'Aye, anyway, after he'd scarpered, she pulled up all his leeks and stuff, tore down the little greenhouse, even filled in the pond he'd spent hours making, and got rid of the rockery next to it with the water feature and everything. He was clever like that, Eric. A work of art it was—'

'Brian, give it a rest will you. She doesn't want to hear about all that,' Mrs Armstrong interrupted. 'Tom's right, it's ancient history now. Let the lass get away.'

'Actually, I think it's all fascinating,' Jane said. 'I really couldn't make head nor tail of Mrs Mortimer before, but now I understand a bit more why she's the way she is. Thank you. And for the coffee.'

'You're welcome, call in any time,' Mrs Armstrong said. 'Oh, and don't forget your parcel.'

Jane had been so engrossed in Brian Armstrong's story, she hadn't even noticed Adam putting the padded envelope down on the table in front of her.

'Oh, and by the way,' said Mrs Armstrong, 'Did you ever find out who that little girl was you were asking us about last time? Have you seen her again?'

Jane didn't know what to say. To tell them everything would have involved another long conversation, and they were busy people with a farm to run. 'I…er …have seen a glimpse of her a couple of times. You've still no idea, I suppose, who she could be?'

'No, sorry. We haven't seen any kids playing around here, have we?'

Brian and the boys all shook their heads. 'Nope, nothing like that.'

Jane was halfway out of the kitchen door when she remembered the one question she'd intended to ask. 'Mrs Armstrong – you wouldn't happen to know if Mrs Mortimer ever does childminding, looks after a baby? For a friend, or someone in her family, perhaps?'

'Peggy Mortimer? I wouldn't think so. She does have a sister, I believe, and a couple of nephews, but they're grown up and never visit. Why do you ask?'

'Oh, I just thought I saw – no, it's all right, I must have made a mistake. Right. Thanks. I'm off to the village now. It's such a nice day.'

'Aye, canny weather for the time of year.'

Once back on the track, Jane perched on a dry-stone wall and tore open her parcel. It was a paperback book, *Rebecca*. Attached to the front cover by a paper clip was a hand-written note. With a joyful little heart-skip, Jane recognised Suzy's familiar big loopy handwriting.

Hi Jane,

Found this at the back of my bookcase today, and just in case you haven't read it, or you've lost your own copy, I thought it might help you deal with that 'Mrs Danvers' neighbour you told me about.

Sorry I've not been in touch for a while. I'm due a few days off so thought, if it's OK with you, I'd come up and keep you company in the sticks sometime soon. I'll drop you an email and we'll sort out dates.

Lots of love, Suzy

PS, got some mega exciting news, but you'll have to wait till I see you!

CHAPTER 12

The walk to the village took longer than Jane had expected, but she was enjoying it. The autumn air was dry and still, with a nostalgic scent of wood smoke drifting from a field somewhere near, and the trees a brilliant blaze of red and gold. Her feet fell into a satisfying rhythm on the road, and only the occasional passing car required her to step back onto the grassy verge. Suzy's note and the book had lifted her spirits. Being out and away from the cottage, the heavy stone of grief she carried inside felt lighter; the brightness and colour that had drained from her life when Angela died was beginning to creep back, slowly.

The village had no centre, no village green or duck pond, just a collection of old stone houses straggling along the road, mostly with drawn blinds at the windows, and a small modern estate, still being built amidst a sea of mud, with a big noticeboard at the entrance announcing the opportunity to acquire one of thirty-six stunning new executive homes. And further along the road Jane found an ivy-covered red-brick, house which she guessed must have been the Dog and Duck, because there was an empty post outside which looked as if it had once held a pub sign. The place had been converted into a holiday let, as there was a plaque outside showing that it had been awarded five-star accommodation status. Jane could picture the teenage Katie Harris creeping out of the side door, giggling with excitement, suitcase in hand, climbing in beside the handsome Eric

Mortimer, waiting for her in his ancient Morris Traveller, engine running for a quick getaway.

A little way further on was a Victorian building with a bell tower, named The Old School House, now long closed and converted into another holiday home. Next to it a tiny teashop called Polly's Parlour, closed, the chairs all upturned on the tables. Then a shuttered gift shop – also closed. And then an even smaller shop and post office, miraculously not closed, with a rack of dog-eared looking postcards outside. The bell clanged as Jane pushed the door open, but the place seemed deserted. She looked around. It was crammed from floor to ceiling with all sorts of random stuff, shelves packed with groceries, a freezer cabinet full of ice cream, dusty buckets and spades and fishing nets, books about Northumberland history and local walks. She picked up a packet of Polo mints from the sweet selection on the counter and called out a tentative 'Hello?'

A little beady-eyed woman, who reminded Jane of a Beatrix Potter mouse, suddenly popped out from behind a stack of toilet rolls. She was the first person Jane had seen since she left the Armstrong's farm.

'Goodness, this is like a ghost village,' Jane said. 'Where is everybody?'

'Oh it's always quiet this time of year,' the woman replied. Her voice was mouse-like too. 'It's a different story come the summertime.'

'Have you lived here long?'

'Oh yes, all my life. One of the few left. It's nearly all holiday homes now. Not like a proper community anymore. This place'll be closed soon too, not turning a profit these days, and I'm retiring next year. Got my eye on a nice little bungalow down in Amble.'

Jane paid for the mints and browsed the book selection. Her attention was drawn to one with a blurry picture of Elsdon gibbet – thankfully without a body hanging on it – on the cover. *Ghosts and Haunted Highways of Northumberland* by Norman Bell. She picked it up. £4.99. She had a fiver in her backpack. 'Oh, this looks interesting. Are there any ghost stories from around here, do you know?'

'Ooh, I'm not sure. I think there might be a Grey Lady, or something supposed to haunt the Hall, but I don't really take any notice of all that stuff. Gives me the heebie-jeebies.'

'I'm staying at Two Chimneys cottage. One or two creepy things have happened. You don't happen to know if there's any stories about it, do you? '

The woman twitched her mousy little nose and lowered her voice, although there was nobody there to overhear. 'No. But I'll tell you this. When we had a dog, me and my husband, we used to walk down there a lot when the old coastal path was still there, before they made the new path higher up near the road. The dog always used to freeze when he got to the cottage. Just sat down whining, and wouldn't budge. He didn't like it one bit. We had to pick him up and carry him. Right as rain again once we'd got past. '

'They say dogs can sense things we can't.' said Jane, handing over the five-pound note.

'Aye, or it could have been something to do with all those cats that used to be running about the place. Does the cat woman still live there? Haven't seen her in the village for years.'

'Mrs Mortimer? Yes, she's still there. She's only got one cat now though.'

The woman was ferreting about behind the counter looking for a paper bag for the book. While she waited, Jane glanced at the posters pinned to the noticeboard leaning against the counter. There weren't many. A card advertising a cleaning job for a holiday cottage. Something about the next WI meeting, St Michael's Church Christmas Fayre committee meeting, an art exhibition in the village hall. Art exhibition! Jane felt quite excited – and it was still on, not closing till tomorrow.

'Where's the village hall?' she asked.

'Turn left out of here, dear, and a little way along you'll see the church. It's next to that, just down the lane.'

Jane put the book in her backpack next to *Rebecca*. Plenty of reading matter for the next couple of days. She called out a cheerful

'Bye', but the woman had already scurried away to some dark hole at the back of the shop.

The village hall next to the little church was a low wooden building, what her nan would have called a glorified potting shed, with some sad-looking bunting fluttering at the entrance and a sandwich board outside: Art Exhibition. Tea. Cakes. Entrance £1.

A spindly elderly man was inside the door, taking things off the trestle table and packing them in cardboard boxes. He gave Jane a surprised smile as she came in. 'Oh, we were just thinking of shutting up shop for the day. We've not had anyone in for hours.'

Jane said, 'Oh, sorry. Could I just have a quick look round? I do a bit of painting myself.'

'Do you? Yes, of course, take all the time you want. You're most welcome. I'm Tim Wetherall by the way, chairman of the art group, for my sins. I'll see if Sheila can rustle you up a cup of tea and some cake. I think there's a bit of coffee and walnut left, maybe some gingerbread. All home-made.'

Jane rooted around in her coat pocket for enough small change to cover the entrance fee. She threw a pound's worth of ten and twenty pence pieces in the biscuit tin. 'No, it's fine. I haven't got any cash left for tea and cake I'm afraid.'

'No, no, refreshments are all included. Just pop into the side room when you've finished looking round. You'll find Sheila in there, presiding over the tea urn.'

This day was turning out better than Jane had expected, and she'd almost forgotten about what she thought she saw in Mrs Mortimer's kitchen. She wandered along the display boards, looking at the artwork. They were pleasant enough pictures, mostly landscapes, seascapes, watercolours so watery as to be insipid, one or two bright and cheery naive-style pictures inspired by Lowrie, and some impressionistic oil paintings. One of these caught her eye immediately. It was of the cottage. At least, the view from the top of the field with just the familiar two tall chimneys visible, poking up against the backdrop of a dazzling blue strip of sea. It was a summer scene, under a sunny sky. The foreground showed the field behind the cottage, not a scrubby piece of land full of thistles and clumps of yellowing grass and dotted with sheep as it was now, but a lush meadow, bright with a carpet of red poppies. Jane went right up close, her nose almost touching the canvas, studying the brushstrokes. She loved the impressionists, the magical way that what looked close-up like a series of seemingly random blobs and dabs of paint, when viewed from a distance, came into focus and became wonderfully rich and real. And then, as she stepped back, she noticed something else in the picture.

There was the little girl. Standing amid the poppies, near the cottage, just where Jane had seen her for the first time. There was her blonde hair, her little white face, her red pyjamas. Jane peered at the figure, hardly able to believe her eyes. It was tiny, less than a centimetre high, and looked at closely was composed of three or four minute dabs of red, white and pale-yellow paint, yet when she moved away, it was quite obviously a child.

Breathless with shock, Jane found Tim. 'Excuse me, that painting of the cottage roof and the field of poppies – do you know who painted it?'

He grinned. 'Do you like it? It's lovely, isn't it? You're in luck – it's one of my wife's efforts.' He looked towards the adjoining room and the sound of clattering teacups. 'Sheila. Come here a minute, dear, there's a young lady here likes your picture.'

Sheila was an elegant slender lady, late sixties or early seventies, wearing a floaty turquoise blouse and her grey hair pinned up. 'Hello.' She smiled eagerly. 'Are you interested in that picture? It was marked up as seventy pounds, but I'd be happy to let you have it for sixty.'

This was awkward. Jane could just imagine what Peter would say if she said she'd spent sixty pounds on a good, but nonetheless, amateur painting, and anyway she didn't have her bank card on her.

'Well, I'm not sure...I...need to think about it. It is a lovely picture, of course, but I'm mainly interested in it because I'm staying at that cottage at the moment. And what intrigues me...what I wanted to ask you...is about the figure of the little girl.'

Sheila frowned. 'Little girl? There isn't a little girl in the picture. I do sometimes put a human or animal figure in my paintings, but I didn't with this one. It's actually copied from a photo Tim took of the poppies last summer.'

Tim nodded. 'Yes, and if there was a human figure in the photo, I don't remember seeing it.'

They walked round together to examine the picture. Jane pointed to the figure. 'It's tiny, but look, you can definitely see it's a child.'

Sheila lifted the spectacles that hung on a chain round her neck and peered at her painting. 'Oh yes, I see what you mean. How very odd. I'm sure I didn't paint that. It's got a bit of yellow in it. I don't think I even used any yellow when I was doing it.'

The three of them stood, staring at the picture, at a loss for what to say, what explanation to offer.

Jane broke the uneasy silence. 'Could someone have added it, without you knowing it?'

'Why on earth would anyone do a thing like that?' Tim said, rubbing his chin.

'This probably isn't any help, but…' Jane hesitated. 'Do you know of any children round here, a visitor, who looks like that? A little girl with long blonde hair?'

'I can't think of any,' said Sheila. 'To tell you the truth, there aren't many young families left in the village now. They all want to be nearer to schools and entertainment, and there's not many can afford the new houses being built. As for holiday visitors, people with children generally like to be closer to a decent beach.'

'Well thank you for pointing it out to us.' Tim patted Jane's shoulder in one of those kindly meant but patronising gestures that reminded her of Peter. 'I think it may have to go down as one of those weird mysteries we'll never solve.' He paused, looking at the picture again. 'Or, of course, it could be an optical illusion. Like those visions of Jesus or the Virgin Mary people see in clouds or pieces of toast. Have you seen those pictures taken on Mars? One of them showed a figure that looked just like a woman in a long dress, and all the alien-life fanatics got very excited, but of course it was just a strange-shaped rock or a shadow or something.'

'Yes, of course,' Jane said. The swan, the log in the sea, the flapping curtain, the baby next door. Here you go again, Jane, she silently scolded herself, making a total idiot of yourself.

Her sunny mood had faded, and she just wanted to get away now. 'Look, don't worry about the tea and cake, I think I'd better be on my way.'

'Well, I'll tell you what, why don't you pop down your name and phone number?' Tim handed her a piece of paper and a pen. 'You said you were an artist? You'd be very welcome to join our little group. We have a session on the second Thursday of every month, sometimes with a speaker or a demonstration, or even a visiting critic to point us in the right direction. But mostly we just sit and paint and have a good chat if we feel like it. How long are you staying in the area?'

'We go back to Newcastle in the middle of December.' Jane reluctantly scribbled down her phone number. She couldn't think of an excuse not to.

'Oh, that's splendid, quite a while then. We'll give you a call to let you know what's happening at the next meeting.'

Jane thought how rude it would sound if she told him that when it came to painting, the only company she wanted was her own. So, she said, 'Yes, thank you. But it is rather a trek out here and I don't have a car.'

'Oh, we have members come from all over, not just the village. I'm sure we could sort out a lift for you.'

Sheila handed her a small card. 'And here's my number, if you decide you do want to buy the painting. It would make such a nice souvenir of your stay there, wouldn't it?'

The walk back seemed much longer, and it started to spot with rain. Jane wished she'd brought her phone with her. Nigel may have been trying to call her. It was only quarter to four in the afternoon, and already the light was fading.

****

Peggy Mortimer was feeling out of sorts. She must have pulled a muscle cleaning the windows because there was a nagging pain in her back and under her right shoulder blade and apart from a slice of toast at breakfast time, she hadn't felt like eating a thing all day. Thinking about Her Next Door carrying on with Mr Blackwood had upset her more than it should have.

She saw to the bairns, although her heart wasn't in it today. Especially not with Aidan. She really hadn't taken to him like the others. She didn't like the way his head flopped and wobbled, and his arms quivered so much when she picked him up, the clammy feel of his bare skin, and she didn't care for the way his startlingly blue eyes stared up at her, as if he was terrified of her. And most of all she didn't like having to look at him naked, with the ugly little boy parts every time she changed or bathed him. If she didn't warm to him, she could see she was going to have to get rid of him, or at least shut him in the cupboard where she wouldn't have to see him.

She was just thinking of having a lie-down to rest her painful shoulder when young Tom Armstrong from the farm came chugging down on his tractor and lifted a box off the back of the trailer. He banged on her window, shouted, 'Another of them parcels for you, Mrs M.' before dumping it on her doorstep and heading back up the track. She brought it in. She would open it later, when she felt a bit better. The box smelt of manure. She wrinkled her nose. Really, that new postie was a lazy bugger, not bothering to come down to the house anymore. She didn't want nebby busy bodies like them up at the farm poking and prodding and speculating about what was in her private post, let alone getting it soiled with their filthy muck.

It was dark when she woke up from her rest. The shoulder still hurt, so she took two paracetamol and put the kettle on. And here was Him Next Door, getting out of his car, home from a long day at work, while his missus had been out gallivanting who knows where. He smiled at her as she looked out of the window and waved. On an impulse, she opened the back door.

'Mr Eagle,' she said, 'Please thank your wife for the note she put through my door this morning, about your leaving date. It has certainly clarified the situation.'

'No problem, Mrs M.'

'I was a little surprised to hear that you will be staying on until December.'

'Were you? Why's that? It's the date we agreed on when I booked us in.'

'Indeed, yes. But I was under the impression that your wife was – unsettled – here? I couldn't help but notice she was out nearly all yesterday with Mr Blackwood, and I assumed she must be looking at alternative accommodation.'

He didn't say anything, just grunted, picked up his briefcase and went through his door.

Mrs Mortimer returned to her kitchen. The kettle was boiling, and she was feeling much better.

****

'Had a good day, darling?' Peter kissed Jane's cheek as she stood in the kitchen, peeling potatoes. 'Go anywhere interesting? Speak to anyone?'

Jane thought it was odd, the way he was looking at her so intently. 'Well, yes, actually. I called in at the farm and had coffee with them. Mr Armstrong told me all sorts of interesting stuff about Morticia. Then I walked to the village. It was a bit – well – dead.'

'Ah, no rosy-cheeked children dancing round a maypole? No peasants leaning on five bar gates chewing straws?'

'Oh, stop teasing. Of course I wasn't expecting that sort of thing. But I did get to talk to some locals. A funny little woman who runs the post office, and there was an art exhibition in the village hall which was quite interesting, and I met a couple called Tim and Sheila who were very friendly, trying to get me to join their art group.'

'Well, you should, it would do you good to have some company.'

Jane wondered whether to tell him about the weird business of the figure in the painting. After all, this time it wasn't just her who saw it; Tim and Sheila did too. On the other hand, telling him would probably trigger off another lecture bringing up that bloody swan that wasn't a swan in the hedge again, and other examples along the lines of Tim's woman on Mars story. And she definitely wouldn't mention Mrs Mortimer and the baby either.

They ate their sausage and mash in the kitchen. Jane gave him an account of the things Brian Armstrong had told her about Mrs Mortimer, the hordes of cats, Eric and Katie Harris, the kitten-killing, the bed-burning, and the garden-destroying.

'Good grief,' he said. 'Sounds like you wandered into the plot of a Thomas Hardy novel. Extraordinary.'

But after this, Peter lapsed into a thoughtful silence. Probably tired, Jane thought. And he kept looking at her, with a slight frown on his face. He'd left quite a bit of his meal uneaten when he put down his knife and fork.

Then he said, 'Jane, I had a phone call a couple of days ago, asking me to do a presentation at a big conference. A bit of a last-minute thing. The guy who was meant to be delivering the main presentation has had a stroke or a heart attack or something, so they wanted me to step in. Of course, I told them I couldn't.'

'Why ever not? Where is this conference?'

'The Netherlands. University of Utrecht. There's some pretty exciting new stuff coming out of research now, and they seem very interested in my last paper.'

'But you must go, Peter. Why ever did you turn it down?'

'Well, to be honest, because it would mean being away for at least four days. Away from you.'

'So?'

'Darling, I can't leave you here on your own. Not with the way things have been with you lately. I'd be driving myself to the airport, so you wouldn't even have the car in an emergency.'

'Oh, really. I shall be fine. You have to do it, the amount of work you've put into your research.'

'No, Jane, it's impossible. Unless you came with me, of course?'

Jane thought about it. A trip to Holland might be good. While Peter was at his conference, she could wander around Utrecht, which she'd heard was an interesting old city. But if she was here on her own...she thought of Nigel. And then there was Suzy's promised visit. Suzy. Of course.

She grasped Peter's hand. 'Listen. I've just had a brilliant idea. I heard from Suzy today. She wants to come and visit. Why don't I ask her to come up here on the days you're going to be away? You wouldn't have to worry about me being on my own then, and we could get out and about in Suzy's car, have lots of long walks together. It would be perfect.'

'Really?' The frown he'd worn since he came home melted from his brow. 'You're right, that would be the ideal solution. Do you want to OK the dates with Suzy, then I can get on to the Utrecht people first thing tomorrow, tell them I can do it?'

'Yes, give me the dates and I'll text her straight away.'

'I'd be flying out there a week on Friday,' he said. 'Probably be back by the following Thursday. I'll have to see what flights are available of course.'

Jane picked up her phone. She'd checked it as soon as she got in, but there was no voicemail or text from Nigel. She checked again – nothing. She tried not to feel disappointed, concentrating on the prospect of Suzy's visit, and finding out about the mega exciting news she'd mentioned. She couldn't think what that might be. A new job, maybe? Selfish perhaps, but she hoped not. It wouldn't be the same if she went back to work and Suzy wasn't there. She tapped out a text message and sent it.

They took their mugs of coffee into the sitting room, turned on the television. Jane settled herself on the sofa, reached for her big red cushion. It wasn't there.

'Peter, where's the cushion?'

'Hmm? I've no idea. I've not moved it.'

'Well, somebody has, and it definitely wasn't me.'

Jane searched round the back of the sofa, under the sofa and chairs, all round the living room. Not a sign of it. She even ran upstairs to check the bedrooms.

'Are you sure you haven't put it somewhere? Try to think.'

'No, Jane, why are you making such a fuss about a cushion?'

'Because I'm fed up with all this strange stuff happening, that's why.'

Peter sighed. 'Perhaps Morticia popped in while you were gadding about, decided it needed a wash.'

'She's got no right to *pop in*, as you put it. I told her before not to. I don't want her snooping round the place, moving stuff. And I don't know what you mean by gadding about. I only went for a walk.' She could feel the hysteria rising in her voice.

'Come on, Jane, calm down. Don't get yourself into a state about it. It'll turn up,' he said, patting the sofa next to him. 'Sit down and relax for a bit. Tell me about these books you've acquired today.' He picked up the *Haunted Northumberland* one, gave a scornful chuckle, tossed it back on the coffee table.

'Suzy sent me the *Rebecca* – she said it might help me deal with Mrs Danvers alias Mortimer. The one about ghosts I bought in the village shop.'

'You and your books,' Peter said, smiling as he stirred his coffee. 'This one about the hauntings – does it by any chance mention the infamous cushion-stealing ghost of Two Chimneys Cottage?'

She ignored him.

Her phone pinged. A text from Suzy, prefaced by a smiley emoji. Yay. Those dates are fine with me. See you a week on Friday then. Xxx

CHAPTER 13

It was another mild sunny day, almost an Indian summer, the sea sparkling in the sun. Jane took her morning coffee outside and leant on the stone wall that separated the tiny strip of grass from the beach below. She breathed in the sea air, the seaweed smell that wasn't ozone.

The phone in her pocket jangled. Nigel? No, not Nigel.

'Ah, is that Jane? Sheila Wetherall here. We met at the village hall yesterday. It's about the picture you were interested in.'

Oh no, Jane thought, how on earth do I tell her politely I don't want to buy her painting? 'Er, yes?'

'It's the strangest thing, Jane. We've just this minute arrived at the hall. It's the last day of the exhibition today. Anyway, when I looked at the poppies painting just now, that little figure – or what looked to us like a figure – well, it had completely disappeared. Not there at all. Tim said I must ring and tell you.'

A cold feeling swept over Jane, although the weather was warm. 'Oh. How peculiar.'

'Isn't it? But Tim thinks it might have been a squashed insect that got stuck to the paint when it hadn't quite dried, and from a distance it did indeed look like the figure of a child. Though it's funny I never noticed it when I was putting it in its frame or hanging it for the exhibition. Another of Tim's suggestions was that it was crumb or two from my strawberry jam and lemon curd tarts that we brought over to the hall with my pictures.' She didn't sound convinced. 'Except the pictures were all well protected with bubble wrap. Anyway, whatever it was, it must have fallen off somehow.'

'Well, thank you for letting me know. I guess we'll never know.'

'No. I wish I'd taken a photo of it now. It would have caused quite a bit of interest on my Facebook page. All good publicity for my work. Oh, and I've reduced the price of the picture to £50. An absolute bargain for an original.'

'Yes, it is. I'm just sorry I can't afford it at the moment,' Jane said quickly. 'Sorry, Sheila, got to go I'm afraid. Thanks again for ringing.'

She tapped the 'hang up' button quickly. Nigel might be trying to get through.

Jane drained her coffee, and left the mug on top of the wall. It was such a beautiful morning, and as the tide was out, she would make her way down the narrow stone steps to the little beach that was only exposed at low tide. She would take a few photos on her phone, and maybe use one of them to embark on a painting. The art exhibition in the village had inspired her to take up her brushes again, and it would distract her attention from everything that had happened. Just as Mrs Mortimer had warned them on that first visit to the cottage, the steps were slimy and slippery with seaweed, so she edged her way down gingerly. The little stretch of sand and pebbles was only about three or four metres wide to the sea's edge, but there was a handy flat rock to climb on and give her a better view. The sea was clear, lapping up the beach in slow, gentle rolls of white froth. Jane took a picture of the waves, thinking the patterns they made as they crawled over the sand and stones would make a good semi-abstract painting. As she stepped down from the rock to look at the picture she'd just taken, her eye was caught by something red wedged down the side. It was the cushion.

Jane tugged at the corner, pulled it out. It was heavy, soaked through and streaming with seawater. It must have been there for some time, submerged by the sea at high tide. Someone must have taken it off the sofa, out of the cottage and left it on the rocks, maybe thrown it in the sea, but who? And why? Yet again, her brain raced through a series of possible explanations. Could Peter have taken a dislike to the cushion, jealous of the way she liked to hold it? No, that was too ridiculous. Or perhaps one of the farm dogs, or a passing walker's dog, got in the cottage when the door was open and taken it out? That was a possibility, although she hadn't seen a dog around and never left the door open for any length of time. Peter suggested yesterday that Mrs Mortimer might have taken it to wash, but why would she have dumped it in the sea? If she'd washed it and hung it out to dry, there had been no wind to speak of recently, and anyway it was too heavy to have blown off the line.

She carried the dripping cushion carefully up the steps and placed it on the wall. What sort of insane dream was she living in? Not for the first time, Jane thought of a book Nan had given her when she was a child, the story that first sparked her passion for reading, *Alice in Wonderland*. Now, even more than she had then, she felt like Alice, a girl who finds herself wandering in an alternative world inhabited by strange and fantastic creatures and trying to make sense of a series of random and disturbing happenings that defied all logic.

Mrs Mortimer's tabby cat appeared from nowhere, suddenly startling her by jumping up beside her and sitting on the wall. It swished its tail, staring at Jane. She wouldn't have been surprised at that moment if it had suddenly turned itself into the Cheshire Cat, grinning and talking, telling her what it said to Alice, 'We're all mad here. I'm mad. You're mad.'

'Yes, you're right, Cat. Maybe I am mad,' she murmured out loud.

'Jane?' said a voice behind her. She turned round. Nigel was looking at her with a puzzled frown on his face. 'Are you OK?'

'Oh, Nigel.' Embarrassed, flustered, glad, she felt the tears filling her eyes.

Then he was holding her, enfolding her in his big arms. She rested her head against his white shirt. He felt solid, strong, and smelt of cologne, not overpowering, with hints of citrus and spice. She never wanted him to let go, but he gently released her. 'Come on, shall we go inside, and you can tell me what's happened?'

Jane recovered her composure. She made him some coffee. Nigel seated himself in the armchair. She wished he had sat on the sofa so that she could sit next to him. Instead, she sat on the sofa, and in a rush of words, told him about everything; the cushion, about thinking she saw Mrs Mortimer holding a baby, and yesterday's business with the figure in the painting. Talking through all these things now, they seemed trivial and silly. A series of odd incidents, and apart from the cushion on the beach, probably optical illusions.

'But no more sightings of the little girl here?' Nigel asked.

'No. It's been quiet in that respect.'

'Sounds like your nerves are in shreds. Listen, I called in today because I've got a suggestion I thought might help you. But now I'm not so sure it would be a good idea, if you're feeling fragile.'

'Tell me. I can only say no.'

'Have you heard of the name Norman Bell?'

'Norman Bell? I'm sure I've seen that name somewhere recently. But I can't remember where. Why, who is he?'

'I've known Norman for years. He used to be very friendly with my aunty Irene, through the spiritualist church she went to. He was a kind of young protégé of hers. He's quite a well-known psychic now on these shows you see advertised, you know, the ones that fill village halls and theatres with folk wanting to get through to their late Uncle Fred, that sort of thing. I think he's been on a couple of TV shows as well, where they creep around some supposedly haunted place with torches, and nobody ever thinks to switch the light on.'

'Norman Bell.' Jane picked up the ghost book from the coffee table. 'Now I remember. I bought his book yesterday. There's a coincidence.'

'Ha, yes, it must be a sign. Anyway, he's a canny enough fella, doesn't seem like a fraudster or just in it for the money. I'm not saying I believe in it, but I keep an open mind. So when I ran into him the other day we got talking, and I told him a little bit about what you'd been experiencing, and he got quite excited. He knows this house well, you see, because he used to be a regular at Aunty Irene's séances.'

'And did he say it could be haunted?'

'No, but he's interested. Very interested. And I thought, well, if he could somehow get through to this child, if she is a ghost, find out what happened to her, what she wants, why she doesn't want you to leave, that might answer a lot of questions for you.'

'Yes, oh yes,' Jane leant forward, excited, wanting to grasp Nigel's hands, but the coffee table was in the way. 'Nigel, that would be brilliant. When can he come?'

'I'll have to get back to him. I needed to speak to you first, of course, but it may not be for a day or two. He's quite a busy man these days.'

'Not a weekend though, not when Peter's here. He doesn't approve of that sort of thing, thinks they're all charlatans, preying on people's grief. And Lord knows I know how it feels, being so desperate just to feel some connection with someone you've lost.'

Nigel nodded. 'Of course. Even if it is baloney, if it brings comfort to bereaved people, what can be the harm? But you know, you should tell your husband. I don't like to think I'm helping to arrange something like this behind his back. He lives here too. It wouldn't be right.'

An honourable, principled man, Jane thought. Of course he was, and that embrace they'd shared was just to comfort her, nothing more. She wished it had been more, but then again maybe his basic decency was one of the things she liked so much about him.

After he had gone, promising to be in touch after he'd spoken to Norman, Jane went out to fetch the cushion. It had dried off in the sun, but the material was stiff with salt water and a strong seaweed smell clung to it. She stuffed it in the washing machine and turned it on.

****

He was there again. Peggy Mortimer was looking out of her living room window when she heard his car draw up the other side of the house. She'd been watching Her Next Door down on the beach, seen her come up again carrying what looked like the lovely Ikea cushion from the sofa. She must have taken it down to sit on, probably getting it all stained and torn and covered in wet sand. She would have to have a word with the hubby, point out that on no account were any items, and especially not soft furnishings, to be taken out of the house.

Whisky was out there on the wall. Her Next Door stared at him, looking jittery. So she didn't like cats. That was no surprise. Her sort – nervy, excitable – never did. Just as Whisky jumped down and stalked off, Mr Blackwood came round the side of the house, and next thing she saw, he had his arms around her and they were canoodling – there, in broad daylight. They had no shame.

Disgust twisted her stomach and she wanted to retch.

****

The rest of the week passed quietly for Jane. Nothing strange happened. The cushion, now clean, dry and smelling pleasantly of fabric softener, was back on the sofa and stayed there. There were no visions, no voices. Nigel didn't call, Mrs Mortimer stayed out of sight. The Indian summer continued, and Jane went for long walks along the coast, taking pictures, making rough sketches, and later at the cottage settling down with the easel and canvases and paints Peter had fetched from the flat. Hours passed while she worked, totally absorbed, relaxed, calm. Angela was still always there, of course, but the pain inside was becoming duller, less hard and sharp.

When he came home Peter was attentive and loving. One day he surprised her by arriving back in the early afternoon. He'd taken a few days off, he said, so that he could prepare for the Utrecht conference. He drove them out to Bamburgh for a walk along the wide beach, empty apart from the occasional dog walker, under the shadow of the castle. The clocks had gone back now, so the twilight came early, and they watched the sun set behind the castle in a blaze of red sky, and then went for a pub supper.

On the last day of October, the fine weather broke, turning wet and stormy. It was Halloween. Peter said, 'Well at least on a night like this we won't get any kids pestering us with their trick or treating down here.' He'd been making jokes all evening about Mrs Mortimer being out on her broomstick. The logs crackled soothingly in the burner.

'You know, I think I'm beginning to like being here,' Jane said, putting down her book. She'd only got five pages into *Rebecca*. 'I almost wish we were staying for Christmas.'

'Do you? That's a good sign, darling, a sign you're getting better. I suppose we could always say we'll stay if that other booking falls through. Or we could move somewhere else nearby.'

'Christmas in the flat is quite difficult for me,' Jane said. 'You know, the memories.'

She thought of three years ago, the last Christmas with Angela, how special it had been, she and Peter waking even earlier than her and tiptoeing into her room so they could watch her wake and discover the little stocking stuffed with presents at the end of her cot. The way she toddled round the Christmas tree, clapping her hands with delight, chuckling at all the presents under it. The soft toy rabbit she loved from the moment she unwrapped it, clutching it to her face and shouting 'Babbit. Babbit.'. Peter had said, 'Next Christmas she'll be talking properly.' They never dreamed there wouldn't be a next Christmas for their daughter.

'Shall I have a word with Morticia? See if that other booking is still going ahead?'

Jane thought for a while. The wind outside was getting noisy. 'No, let's stick to the plan. I've got to face it, go back some time. And it is our home. We have to get used to Christmases without Angela.'

She opened her book again. There was a long-drawn-out sigh - an *ah* sound - followed by a slow exhale of breath. 'What's the matter, Peter?'

'Nothing. Why do you ask?'

'You sighed.'

'No, I didn't.'

'You did. I heard you.'

'Must have been the wind in the chimney.'

No. Someone sighed. And come to think of it, it wasn't Peter. It sounded like a child.

That night Jane fell asleep to the soothing sound of rain falling above the low sloping ceiling of their bedroom under the eaves. Some hours later, something woke her, some unfamiliar sound intruding on her dream. For a while she lay drowsily listening to Peter's quiet snoring beside her and the pattering of the rain. And then she was wide awake, her heart pounding, because the pattering sound was not coming from the roof. It was footsteps, quick, light footsteps of someone running up the stairs and along the landing, a slap-slap-slap sound of bare feet on the wooden floor.

'Peter.' She sat up, shook his shoulder. He grunted and turned over, snoring again. 'Peter. Wake up. There's someone in the house.'

The bedroom door slowly swung ajar. In the open doorway was the outline of a small figure, only just visible as a dark shape in the dim light cast by the bedside alarm clock. The voice came in a low hiss, each word clear, deliberate, insistent: 'Don't – leave – don't – leave – don't – leave.'

CHAPTER 14

Peter paced up and down the bedroom, combing his fingers through his hair. 'I thought you were getting better, that things were calming down. We can't go on like this, Jane. We've got to get you back to your consultant again, get you back on the Risperdal. If we don't I'm going to end up—'

'As crazy as me?' Jane said.

'You know I'd never use that word. It's an illness, can't you see? Darling, you need help. I need help. I don't know how to cope with this anymore.'

The beginnings of a grey dawn were breaking outside. Jane lay rigid against the pillows. 'I'm sorry if I woke you, Peter. I was shocked, that's all. You don't expect to see someone standing at your bedroom door in the middle of the night.'

'You were shocked? How do you think I felt, hearing your blood-curdling scream? I thought you were being murdered. And having scared me half to death, I turn on the light and there's nobody there. Not a soul.'

'Well, she was there. In the doorway. What more can I say?'

Jane huddled under the duvet, feeling cold, miserable. She could see Peter was at the end of his tether but she knew what she'd seen and she didn't know how to help him.

Peter sat on the end of the bed. 'I shall have to cancel Utrecht. I can't possibly leave you while you're in this state.'

'No, you must go. Suzy's coming, remember, so I won't be alone. And I'm not in a state, I'm quite calm now. And—'. She hesitated, knowing that what she was going to say would not go down well. But Nigel was right, he must know. 'Peter, don't get angry, but I'm arranging for someone to come to the house, someone who might help. He's a psychic, a paranormal investigator. I'm hoping he may be able to—'

'No, Jane, no.' Peter exploded. 'Absolutely not. You know what I think of those people. Mostly frauds, and the ones who aren't are just plain deluded. How much is he asking?'

'I don't think he wants anything. He knew Miss Blackwood, he used to visit when she was living here, so he's interested to help, see if he can get through to the child.'

'Oh for God's sake.' Peter gave an exasperated sigh. 'You are so naive, it's ridiculous for a grown woman, an intelligent woman. You don't want a ghost hunter, you want medication, Jane. Time to grow up, face facts.'

'No, it's you who should face facts.' Jane hurled back at him. 'The fact that we're not living in the Victorian age, that you can't tell me what to do and what not to do. And you can't tell me what to think, what to believe. I'm your wife, not your slave, and you can't control me. If I don't want to take medication I won't and if I want to get Norman Bell here I will.'

He held up his hands. 'OK, OK, have it your own way. I'm going downstairs to make tea, see if there's any spooks hiding in the kitchen cupboards.'

He stomped off. Jane heard the click of him turning on the landing light, his thumping footsteps. But halfway across the landing, he stopped abruptly. There was a pause, then she heard him mutter, 'Jesus Christ!' Now he was back at the doorway, staring at Jane, his face white. 'Darling, come and look at this.'

She followed him out. Just a couple of strides away from the top of the stairs he pointed down to the wooden floor. The floor felt damp, and along it ran the clear outline of footprints, small footprints, half the size of an adult's. There were the curved outlines of the outer side of a foot, the ball of a foot, two neat rows of little round toes and both heels, leading towards the bedroom door, droplets of water sprinkled beside them. But strangely, there was no trail of the little foot marks coming back.

They stood together, silent, staring. Peter reached for Jane's hand and squeezed it. In a low voice he said, 'OK, so I'll admit this is weird. Seriously weird.'

Jane resisted the temptation to shout, 'I told you so.' She kept her voice calm and steady. 'Yes, it is weird. Peter. Let's go and make that tea and think about this.'

But Peter was flying down the stairs. 'If there's been a kid in this house, they won't have got out. I bolted the door last night, and all the windows are locked. I'll find the little bugger, whoever he or she is.'

Jane ran down after him. 'So, if she can't get out, how could she have got in? When – and why?'

'Oh, I don't know.' Peter stormed frantically round the living room, throwing curtains open, peering under the coffee table. 'Unlikely I know, but maybe it was one of those trick-or-treat pests who go out on Halloween, thought it would be fun to sneak in and hide.'

'So why the bare feet?'

'I don't know, I don't know,' he shouted. 'Or maybe you were right about Morticia all along, and the kid comes from next door.' He paused, frowned, looked upwards. 'Jane, do you remember you suggested once that your mystery kid could have come down through a hatch in the ceiling?'

'Yes, but—'

Peter was bounding up the stairs again. 'There's a hatch into the loft up here somewhere. I remember noticing it the other day,' he called. Then a triumphant yell: 'Yes. It's here, at the end of the landing, next to the bathroom. But if the kid did come down from the loft how the hell did she – or he – get back up there? There's no ladder lying around. And more to the point, how am I going to get up there to have a look?'

Jane wanted to say, *Don't waste your time. There's nobody up there. The child is a spirit.* But she couldn't face another argument with him in this mood. He'd headed for the spare bedroom, his study, and was hurriedly shifting piles of books and paper and his laptop off the small table he was using as a work desk.

'Give me a hand with this, Jane. I need to stand on something to get that hatch open.'

Reluctantly, she helped him drag the table out into the passageway under the hatch. Peter leapt up on it.

'Oh Peter, please be careful. You're going to break your leg if you lose your balance,' she said. Peter was pushing with the flat of both hands against the hatch. The table wobbled.

'Shit,' he grunted. 'There's no handle or anything. It's not shifting. Maybe if I try to slide it…'

There was a grating sound as the trapdoor slid open a few inches. A few more hard pushes and grunts and it was halfway open. Jane looked up into the space above Peter's head. She couldn't see anything.

'I'll fetch you a torch,' she said. 'The one Mrs Mortimer lent me.'

The torch found and handed to Peter, Jane watched as with much puffing and pushing the hatch opened fully. Using all his arm strength he heaved himself up into the narrow space, his pyjama-clad legs disappearing into the dark void.

'Well?' called Jane. 'What can you see?'

'Just a minute. I'm looking around,' came his muffled voice. She heard scuffling and banging. 'It's a tiny loft. There's not much space. I'm having to crawl on elbows and knees, and there's obviously been some thick insulation stuff put down, makes it even more cramped.' He coughed. 'God, it's dusty.'

'No children hiding in there then?' He didn't reply. Minutes ticked by. Jane heard the odd thump, more coughing, and eventually, Peter's legs reappeared at the open hatch, and he lowered himself down, slid the hatch closed. His hair, his face, his pyjamas were grey with dust. 'Well,' he said. 'I think we can safely say there's been nobody up there for a while. And as I thought, it hasn't been divided. Both parts of the house share the same roof space.'

'So did you find another hatch, above Mrs Mortimer's?'

'No. At least I couldn't see one. It's either hidden under the loft insulation or this hatch here must be the only one. So that rather blows out of the water the theory of a child coming from next door via the loft.'

Jane took his arm. 'Come on, Peter, let's get that tea. Then I think you'd better have a shower and get dressed.'

Peter was silent as he sipped the tea, obviously thinking hard. After a few minutes he put down the mug and said, 'I did find something quite interesting up there though.'

'What?'

'Well, there were a few cardboard boxes, about half a dozen, taped up, so I didn't open them. And a tea chest, seemed to be full of gardening stuff, spades, forks, trowels, that sort of thing.'

'Ah yes, they must have belonged to Eric Mortimer. Remember, I told you he used to have a garden at the back.'

'Right. But then there was this long flattish metal box. Absolutely thick with dust, so obviously not been touched in a long while. It wasn't locked, so I had a look inside. It was a shotgun. I didn't want to pick it up to check if it was loaded, but there was a half full box of cartridges next to it.'

'Really?' Jane said. 'Wow. But that makes sense, Peter. Brian Armstrong told me Eric used to shoot rabbits, probably game too. Mrs Mortimer must have shoved it away up there after he left her.'

'Well, strictly speaking, it's illegal. I bet she doesn't have a gun licence for it, and she certainly doesn't keep it locked up like you're meant to.'

'Should we report it, do you think?' Jane said.

'Good grief no.' Peter laughed. 'Poor old Morticia. She's probably forgotten it's there. Just don't let's upset her, that's all.'

They were both smiling now, the mood lightened. Yet the mystery of the footprints hung between them, like a dark cloud of doubt and uncertainty. 'It's like the thing with the cushion, just something we're never going to know the truth about,' Jane said.

And the figure in the painting, she thought. She'd not told Peter about that.

'Unless your psychic pal can come up with something,' Peter said. The whole incident had unsettled him, challenged his confidence in his judgement that there was an explanation for everything. But he was in a better frame of mind now and willing to accept Jane's search for an answer. 'I'll wipe that wet floor over, I think. I don't want to have to wait for it to dry, see it every time I go upstairs.'

He took the kitchen mop up the stairs. But when he looked at the landing floor, it was clean and completely dry.

****

Mrs Mortimer was agitated. Really, this was too much. The sooner those two next door left, the better. She was having trouble sleeping anyway, what with the pain, which was getting worse and had now moved into her stomach. She'd just managed to drop off when she was woken by this screaming on the other side of the bedroom wall. It was her again, yelling and shouting.

The woman was quite obviously off her rocker. She tried to get back to sleep, but she could hear the pair of them arguing, him shouting, her shouting back. What a carry-on. In the end she gave up on sleep, got up and popped into the nursery. Picking up one of the babies always helped to calm her when her nerves were on edge.

Whisky padded after her, wanting his breakfast. She was just lifting Arabella from her cot when there was an almighty thump from above. The sudden noise startled Whisky. He shot up the nursery curtains, ripping the nets with his claws, then slithered down, still clinging on, shredding the nets to ribbons, and bringing the curtain pole clattering down with him. As if she hadn't got enough to do. Now she'd have to hang new nets and refix the curtain pole. Not that she blamed the cat. It was them next door caused it, scaring poor Whisky. She could still hear someone shuffling about up there. What were they doing going up in the loft? Were they poking about, going through things that didn't concern them? She would have to speak to Mr Blackwood, and get him to put a lock on the loft hatch. Mind, that might not do any good, seeing as he's carrying on with Her Next Door. *Was that what all the shouting was about?* she wondered.

She'd go and make herself some tea, have a think what to do. But she wouldn't make toast today. Just the thought of food turned her stomach.

CHAPTER 15

Norman Bell wasn't what Jane had expected. From what she'd seen of celebrity psychics, she'd imagined some smooth shiny-suited type, with coiffed silver hair. The sort you could imagine doing carpet adverts on TV if they hadn't been busy chatting to dead people.

Jane had been up since five that morning, having waved Peter off to the airport for his early morning flight to the Netherlands. He was fussing as usual: 'Are you sure you'll be all right? What time is Suzy arriving tonight? I'll ring you when I get there, don't turn your phone off. Ring me to let me know how you are. Don't forget to lock the door.'

As soon as his car had finally disappeared up the track, Jane tidied her hair, put on a little make-up. It was liberating, not having Peter there watching her with that anxious, disapproving expression. He didn't like her wearing make-up. 'What are you plastering that stuff on your face for?' he used to say. She set out the coffee cups and a plate of shortbread biscuits. Nigel texted her yesterday afternoon to say he was bringing Norman Bell at ten o'clock this morning, and if it was all right with her, he'd sit in on the session and take him home afterwards as Norman had a hip replacement three weeks ago and wasn't allowed to drive yet.

And on the dot of ten, there they were. Norman Bell looked like a wizened gnome next to Nigel; he was even shorter than Jane, a skinny little man with a mop of white hair, thick-lens glasses, and a stubbly white beard. He wore baggy brown corduroy trousers and a thick woollen jumper several sizes too large for his thin frame. As he shuffled in, leaning on his walking stick, Jane noticed the incongruous white trainers on his feet, laces undone.

But as he shook Jane's hand and looked around him, she saw how his eyes behind the thick glasses were quite youthful and lively looking and seemed to be almost sparkling with excitement.

'Oh my goodness, I haven't been here in over twenty-five years. I'd never have recognised it. Poor Irene. It was always rather gloomy and rundown when she lived here. Is that awful Mortimer woman still next door?'

'She is.' There was so much Jane wanted to ask him but didn't want to rush things. She offered him tea or coffee.

'Could I trouble you for a glass of water, dear?' he said. 'It's strange. I've got that same feeling I had the last few times I came to see Irene. Just as I turn the bend in the track and see the cottage, I get this cold, oppressive kind of feeling. A sort of heavy pressure here.' He tapped his chest. 'Funnily enough, I don't feel it here inside the cottage. It seems to come from the field behind.'

Jane said, 'Yes, I know. I felt exactly the same.'

She gave him the water. He seated himself in the armchair, so Jane sat next to Nigel on the sofa. She felt a little nervous and being close to him was reassuring. After a bit of inconsequential chat, Norman leant forward. 'So, Jane, Nigel has told me a little bit about the things you've been experiencing here. Can you tell me everything yourself?'

Jane took a deep breath. She talked, going over everything, starting with the first sighting of the child on the day she came to view the cottage, to the incident of the footprints on the landing. The only thing she forgot to mention was the business with the cushion. And she didn't talk about the things that could have been a mistake, like the baby in Mrs Mortimer's arms, the flash of something red in the mirror, or the figure in the painting.

Norman listened carefully, tapping his fingertips together. He stood up. 'Can I ask you both to sit quietly and not speak to me while I see if I can sense anyone here, trying to get through to me?'

He wandered round the room, limping on his stick, every now and then stopping to touch the wall, pressing his palm against it, eyes closed. 'I'm feeling for vibrations,' he explained. 'Some mediums use different methods of course, but with me, I am sensitive to vibrations. And sounds. A kind of hum. Like this.' He made a soft humming noise. Jane felt a sudden urge to giggle. She glanced at Nigel, and saw he was twitching his mouth, trying not to smile. They both looked away from each other quickly. It wouldn't do to get an uncontrollable laughing fit.

Now Norman had his hands on the wall next to the stairs, the dividing wall. 'Oh.' He pulled his hands away. 'There's a faint but definite vibration coming through here. Not a good one.'

'What do you think that could mean?' Jane said, unable to stay silent. 'Is it a little girl? Did something bad happen to her?'

He came and sat down opposite her again. 'All I can tell you, dear lady, is that there are unquiet spirits about this place. Especially in the adjoining part of the cottage, and outside. Of course, I've always known that.'

Jane thought of what the woman in the shop had told her about her dog not wanting to go near the place. Perhaps it felt the vibrations too. 'Spirits, you say. So, there's more than one?'

'Oh yes. But I'm afraid they're not coming through to me. You see, those in the spirit world will only come through if they want to communicate, and these, I sense, although they're unhappy souls, just want to be left alone.'

'Mr Bell, that's all very interesting, but please, could you see if you can connect with a child?' She went to the dresser and took out the folded page of her sketch pad. 'Here's the message she wrote for me. Don't leave. Would it help if you held it? I really need to know what it means.'

He took it, unfolded it, and studied it carefully. Then he shut his eyes, stood up and started limping round the room again.

'Hello, little child? Are you there? Is there something you want to tell Jane?' They were all acutely aware of the silence in the room, the only sound coming from outside, a lone seagull's plaintive cry and the slow rhythmic whisper of the waves breaking over the shore.

Norman stopped next to the sofa where Nigel and Jane sat. His eyes opened, he let the paper drop and snatched up the red cushion that was on the sofa next to Jane. He clutched it to his chest. 'Oh.' He gasped, spluttering, drawing in gulps of air. His breathing became rasping and laboured. 'Oh. Oh.'

'What's up, Norman? Are you all right?' Nigel was on his feet. Norman staggered back against him, dropping the cushion, struggling for breath. Nigel led him back to the chair. 'Here, drink this,' he said, pressing the glass of water into his trembling hand.

'Oh dear. Oh dear.' Norman shook his head from side to side, his breathing slowly returning to normal. 'I'm so sorry.'

'What happened there?' Jane said. 'Do you suffer from asthma?'

'No. I don't. No,' Norman said, between sips of water. 'Please, don't be alarmed, I'm quite all right now. It was the vibrations coming from that cushion. Very powerful.'

'From the cushion?' Jane said. 'Was it a spirit vibration? Was it a child?'

'I don't know. There was no voice coming through to me. But the vibrations from that cushion – I can't explain. They were – unusual. Not what I normally feel. And they gave me a most unpleasant sensation of choking, suffocation.' He shuddered. 'Quite horrible.'

'Well, I can tell you now,' Nigel said, a defensive note in his voice, 'there's nothing peculiar about that cushion. It's only been here about a year, from when we last gave this place a makeover. I bought it myself, along with a lot of other stuff, from IKEA in Gateshead, not a store noted for its supernatural merchandise.'

'But there is something odd about the cushion, Mr Bell,' Jane said. 'I forgot to mention it before. It disappeared from in here a few days ago and I found it dumped on the beach. I don't know how that happened.'

Norman was still looking shaken and white-faced. He looked at Jane. 'I'm so sorry the child you've been seeing has not come through to me today. But there is something – a vibration – telling me that someone, something, wants you to remove that cushion. And what you've just said confirms that. Destroy it, my dear.'

'So you can't feel any vibration that's telling me not to leave?' Jane said, disappointed and disturbed by the turn of events.

'I'm afraid not. But you'd be wise to heed it. It could be a warning.'

'A warning. How can I heed it? We can't stay here forever. I've got to leave some time. Now I'm going to be really terrified that we're going to die in a car crash or something on our way back to Newcastle.' Jane was beginning to wish she'd never asked Norman Bell to come. He'd planted a sense of doom in her mind that hadn't been there before.

'My dear, that won't happen,' he said, smiling at her. 'I can sense with you that all will be well. You carry sadness in your heart, I can feel that, but yes, all will be well, all will be well.'

Jane thought, He would say that, wouldn't he? They always tell you what you want to hear. Nothing bad, or tragic.

Like the gypsy fortune teller at the Hoppings who told her years ago she'd marry a tall handsome older man and have two beautiful children. Well, Peter was older, tall, and handsome for his age, but she had no children. Not anymore.

Norman seemed in a hurry to leave. 'Would you be kind enough to run me up to Chillingham Castle, Nigel?' he said. 'I'm meeting a television producer chap up there about a programme we're planning about the Castle's ghosts. He'll give me a lift back home afterwards.'

'Hope you find plenty of your vibrations up there,' Jane muttered under her breath as she saw them off at the door.

Before he stepped into his car, Nigel leant over to Jane and spoke quietly in her ear, 'Not been much use, has he? Sorry about that. I'll call back here when I've dropped the old fella off.'

Jane was clearing up the coffee cups when her phone pinged. It was a text from Suzy:

'Hi. Jane, is it OK if I arrive first thing tomorrow morning, not tonight? Got a huge backlog of work to get through (people off sick) and won't get away till late. Sorry about that. Can't wait to see you.'

Jane texted her back at once. No problem, see you tomorrow.

So, she was going to be alone tonight. But Nigel was coming back, so perhaps she wouldn't be...

****

It's him again. Mr Blackwood. Mrs Mortimer was at her kitchen sink, taking another paracetamol, when she saw the grey Mercedes arrive. But to her surprise, he wasn't alone. He had a funny-looking little man with him. She stared. Good heavens, it was Norman Bell. Eee, she hadn't seen him in a canny few years. He was always hanging around at Irene Blackwood's at one time. Her protégé, she said. My, but he'd aged, hair gone quite white. He was only a young man when he first started turning up for Miss Blackwood's meetings. He had the gift, according to Miss Blackwood. Well, it was all nonsense of course. The only gift he had was for being a nosy parker. She saw him once, wandering about in the field at the back, bending down to touch the ground, patting it with his hands. She'd gone out and asked him what he was doing, and he started going on about vibrations and restless spirits. Well, she told him straight he was trespassing on land that belonged to Armstrong's farm, land that had livestock on it, and he and his vibrations could just bugger off. And when Miss Blackwood started going seriously funny in the head, she made it plain when he turned up that Miss Blackwood didn't want him coming round anymore. Miss Blackwood hadn't exactly said as much, but it was Mrs Mortimer's job to look out for her, protect her, now she wasn't quite the full shilling.

What on earth could Norman Bell be wanting here, after all these years? Of course, she'd heard Norman was quite a local celebrity now, writing books and talking about the paranormal on telly. She had an awful thought: was he planning on bringing a camera crew down here, looking for ghosts? Just thinking about a load of strangers swarming about the place made her feel ill again. Why couldn't they just let the deceased folk rest in peace? Why did they have to keep probing into the past, things and people that were dead and gone? She didn't like thinking about the past. She pushed those thoughts away whenever they threatened to creep back, like a black poison seeping into her head.

She would focus instead on the new baby. She was a real beauty, the best yet, just perfect. She'd arrived with the name Serenity, but that was a stupid name. She would call her Serena, a pretty name. She would dress her in a nice outfit, brush her hair, put her in Aidan's cot. And as for Aiden, she would shut him away in the cupboard.

CHAPTER 16

'That was all a bit of a waste of time. The old boy didn't help much, did he?' Nigel was back, sitting on the sofa, having another cup of coffee.

'No. I suppose it was silly of me, pinning my hopes on him. I think he's sincere though, not a fraud. I think he really can pick up on feelings. He knew I was sad, he could sense that. Had you told him about me losing Angela?'

'No, I never mentioned it.'

They were quiet for a moment. Jane looked at the red cushion, still lying on the floor where Norman Bell had dropped it. 'It was odd about that cushion though,' she said.

'Yes, I was worried there for a moment. The way his breath was rattling in his throat, I thought we'd have to ring for an ambulance.'

'Nigel, do you think we should destroy it? Like he said?'

Nigel laughed, stopping abruptly when he saw Jane was serious. 'Pity to chuck out a perfectly good cushion. But if it really upsets you, I'll take it away.'

'It's a shame. I actually rather like it,' Jane said. 'There's a cupboard in the spare bedroom with a lock on it. I think I'll shut it out of sight in there and decide what to do with it later.'

Nigel jumped to his feet, clapped his hands together, smiling. 'Jane, I'm taking you out for lunch. And let's make a pact, while we're having lunch, not to discuss anything to do with cushions or ghosts and especially not vibrations.'

The year was on the turn now, a stinging east wind blowing in, so they drove inland and found a quiet pub with a welcoming fire burning. Nigel did most of the talking, telling her about the holiday cottage business his father had built up, how it had blossomed and grown as Northumberland became more and more of a popular tourist destination. All the while Jane was wondering how she could turn the conversation around to more personal matters. Eventually, when there was a pause in the chat, she said, 'Nigel, can I just ask you about your family? You said you had children, so I presume there's a Mrs Blackwood, only you never mention her.'

'It's no secret. There was a Mrs Blackwood, but we're divorced. We parted company six years ago, on good terms. No bitterness. We'd grown apart, wanted different things. At least Laura did. A different partner, to be exact. But that's fine. She lives over Hexham way now, with Sarah, her partner. Nice woman. Two of the kids are with her, the older two away at university, but we all see plenty of each other. And to tell you the truth, Jane, I quite like being on my own, free to do my own thing.'

'Yes, I can understand that,' said Jane.

The wind was blowing in hard, flattening the grass in the field as they drove back down the track. Jane had been thinking all the way since they left the pub how she would ask him not to leave but to come into the cottage, stay with her. The air between them seemed to tingle with tension and expectation. She didn't need to say anything when they arrived, because he locked the car without a word and followed her into the house. As soon as the door closed, he took her shoulders in both hands and gently pressed her back against the wall and they were holding each other close. His mouth found hers, and she felt all the cold numbness inside her melting away.

The long kiss ended, and Jane laid her head on his shoulder. 'Peter's away all week. My friend isn't coming till tomorrow. Please stay with me tonight.'

He sighed, released her from his arms, guided her towards the living room sofa. He took both her hands in his, shook his head sadly.

'Oh Jane, I'm sorry. That shouldn't have happened. Believe me, there's nothing in the world I'd rather do than stay here with you, and if things were different...'

'What things?'

'If you weren't married. If you weren't a vulnerable young woman who hasn't been well. If your husband didn't live here with you. If it wasn't his bed as well as yours we'd by lying in. It would feel so wrong, at least for me it would.'

Jane's spirits sank, but she was relieved too. He was right. Once these things started they were hard to end, like holding a match to a fire that's soon raging out of control. And who knew what destruction and heartache it could lead to. An image flashed into her mind of that fire Brian Armstrong had told her about, Mrs Mortimer's marital bed, defiled by the sinners, consumed in the flames. Better leave things as they were, a beautiful moment and nothing more.

She nodded. 'I understand what you're saying. Peter and I haven't been getting along that well lately. Sometimes we don't seem to be on the same wavelength at all. And he can be really smothering and controlling at times. But I know he loves me and cares about me. I would never want to hurt him.'

'Yes, and I wouldn't ever want to be the one to destroy your marriage. Divorce is a horrible, painful business, Jane, even an amicable one like mine was.'

'It's just, the first time I met you, I felt an immediate connection with you, Nigel.'

'And I felt it too,' he said. 'And what I'd really like is for us to stay friends. Good friends. Is that all right with you?'

'Of course it is. Good friends.' She felt as if she might cry but fought it back. She smiled at him. 'And thanks for lunch.'

He squeezed her hand, kissed her cheek, and left. Jane sat for a long time as the sky outside darkened into late afternoon. She picked up the red cushion and hugged it to her chest. No vibrations. It was just a cushion, a nice big soft squishy cushion. A piece of material filled with stuffing. What possible harm could it do? It would be silly, locking it away. She put it back on the sofa and got up to close the curtains.

It was already six o'clock. She might turn on the TV, watch the news, but her phone played its jangling ringtone. It was Peter.

'Hello darling? Everything all right?' Yes, everything was fine, she said, and he told her about his flight, the hotel, and he'd had a bit of a stroll around Utrecht, and it was gorgeous, but the weather was as crap as in England. He'd got soaked in the rain and was drying out his wet socks on the radiator. 'Wish you were here with me,' he said. 'Has Suzy arrived yet?'

'No, not yet. She's texted me. She'll be here soon.' Not exactly a lie, tomorrow morning was soon. But no point in telling him she would be alone that night; it would only worry him.

They talked a bit more. Jane told Peter about Norman Bell's visit, that it had been a bit of a disappointment and revealed nothing of much interest.

'Hah, no surprise there then,' he said, sounding relieved. 'Darling, I've got to dash. I'm meeting the other physicists down in the lobby in ten minutes and we're off to find somewhere to eat.'

She reassured him again she was fine, nothing out of the ordinary had happened, wished him luck for his conference presentation. 'You'll be brilliant as always. Oh, and Peter, I miss you. Love you.'

'Love you lots too,' he said.

She rang off, put her phone down and whispered to herself words that had suddenly come into her head: 'Love you lots, like jelly tots.' She always said that to Angela when she put her to bed for the night, and Angela would answer her back from the cot: 'Jelly tops.' When they'd gone to choose a headstone for the spot in the cemetery where they'd buried the little jar of ashes, Jane wanted those words, 'Love you lots like jelly tots', engraved on it. But Peter said no. Not appropriate, he said. So instead, it just read: Angela Jane Eagle, beloved daughter of Jane and Peter Eagle, aged one year, eleven months.

Thinking now of that small white marble headstone, the tears she'd been holding back since Nigel left flowed freely. And after she was all cried out, she felt better, quite calm and peaceful. In some ways she was glad she still hadn't stopped crying for her daughter. It would feel like a betrayal of her memory if she did. She made herself a sandwich for tea, channel-hopped on television for a while, then went to bed. It felt strange to be alone, without Peter's familiar head with its tousled hair, dark with grey streaks, on the pillow next to her. But she was tired, so tired, and fell asleep to the sound of the wind moaning. For the first time in months, she slept soundly and dreamlessly through the night.

Thank goodness it hadn't rained last night, or Suzy's twelve-year-old blue Renault would have struggled to make it through the mud and water-filled ruts down the track. And here she came. Jane spotted her familiar smiling face at the wheel, and the fair hair spilling out from under a woolly hat. She ran out to greet her, and they were hugging, laughing, smiling, both talking at once. Now that Suzy was here, Jane had the feeling that everything was going to be all right.

'You weren't wrong when you said this place was out in the sticks.' Suzy laughed. The blustery wind was tugging at her rainbow-coloured poncho. She pulled it tightly round her. 'But, oh my God, what a fantastic spot. You're almost falling into the sea.'

'I know, it's amazing.' Jane pulled Suzy's little case on wheels into the house, and Suzy followed, her arms filled with flowers, chocolates and carrier bags of goodies.

There was so much to tell her, but it could wait. They had plenty of time. Jane filled the kettle, calling from the kitchen. 'Take off your poncho, Suze, make yourself at home. I've lit the fire so it's nice and warm.'

She brought in their mugs of coffee. Suzy said, 'If I take it off, you'll soon see what my news is, so I'd better tell you.'

'Oh of course, your mega exciting news. I'd forgotten all about that. Tell me.'

Suzy lifted her poncho, pointed at the rounded bump of her belly. 'This isn't down to one too many doughnuts. Jane, I'm pregnant.'

Jane squealed, hugged her. 'Why on earth didn't you tell me before? How far gone are you?'

'Nearly thirty weeks. Due late January. And I didn't tell you because I was afraid – well, you know – that you'd be upset. Because of Angela.'

'What sort of friend would I be if I was upset? I know you and Mike have been trying for ages. It's wonderful news.'

'Yes, twelve years. Five failed rounds of IVF, three miscarriages. It's been a bumpy ride, but here I am, pushing forty, and this time we've hit the jackpot.'

'Ah, I understand now,' said Jane. 'That time I rang you, just after we'd come here, you sounded a bit off, almost like you didn't want to talk to me.'

'Yes, I'm sorry about that. I'd just found out we're having a girl, and I thought—'

'You thought if you told me you were going to have a girl, I'd be angry or jealous because I don't have my little girl anymore? Oh, Suzy, I'm thrilled for you, I really am, but I feel awful now. Does everyone really think they have to tiptoe around me all the time in case they say something to upset me?'

'I guess so, but that's not your fault. I'm so happy you're OK about it. That's all I needed to know. Let's not talk about it anymore.'

Suzy said that as they were so close to the sea, they must have fish and chips, so they drove to Seahouses and ate their lunch in the car park at Bamburgh. The idea was to have a bracing walk on the beach, but Suzy said the wind was much too cold. 'I guess I must be a town girl at heart. I can't get used to no street lights and no hard pavements under my feet.'

As they sat in the car Suzy listened quietly while Jane told her all the strange things that had happened. She didn't interrupt, or ask questions, just listened.

'But I haven't seen or heard anything out of the ordinary since the night I saw the figure in the doorway,' Jane said. 'Oh, and there was Norman Bell's stuff with the cushion and the vibrations. Honestly, Suzy, you would have been giggling. If it hadn't been so alarming when he couldn't breathe, it would have been really funny.'

Back at the cottage, Jane poked the log fire back into life, and they settled together on the sofa. Suzy said, 'So tell me about your weird neighbour. Is she connected to any of this, do you think?'

'I thought so at first. But now I'm not certain. There is something that's puzzling me about her though. One morning I saw her in her kitchen, and I could have sworn she was holding a baby, a very little baby. I could have made a mistake, but I know she's been receiving parcels with baby things in. But nobody else seems to think she's got a baby there, and it just doesn't add up. Mrs Mortimer isn't really the type of person anyone would want to leave their baby with.'

'Her name's Mortimer? How very appropriate.'

'How do you mean?'

'Well, mort – that's French for death, isn't it? And mer – that's sea. Her name means sea of death. You can rest assured I won't be asking her to baby sit this one.' She stroked her bump. They both laughed, but Jane felt a cold sensation creeping down her spine.

Suzy offered no opinion on Jane's experiences, and Jane hadn't yet asked for one. She was just relieved that Suzy didn't immediately talk about hallucinations and Jane's schizophrenia diagnosis or try to reassure her it was all in her mind. But now she'd told her everything, she really wanted to know what her friend made of it all.

'Please tell me honestly what you think. Is it just me being insane? Or could it really be a ghost trying to tell me something?'

Suzy was quiet for a few moments. 'I really don't know, ' she said, slowly. 'But when you were telling me about the little girl I did wonder if perhaps—'

'It's not Angela, if that's what you're thinking' Jane said quickly. 'This child is nothing like her.'

140

'I'm not suggesting that. No, what I was thinking is, could the child be you?'

'Me? What on earth do you mean?'

'You've told me before that you had a terrible childhood.'

'Yes, until I was nine and went to live with Nan. Everything was fine after that.'

'Well, would it be possible that your mind has created an image of yourself before the age of nine? A little girl who's lost, unhappy, needing to be loved and nurtured?'

'So you think she's like my neglected inner child and she's trying to make a connection with me, doesn't want me to leave her behind in the past?'

'Yes, something like that. I'm not saying that's what's happening, it's just a thought.'

Jane was silent while she considered the idea. Part of what Suzy was suggesting made a kind of sense.

'I can see what you're saying,' she said. 'But this little girl doesn't look like me. I was plump and ginger, literally a plain Jane. She's slender and pretty, fragile looking, with straight blonde hair. And I never had any Minnie Mouse pyjamas. No, she's definitely not me.'

'Fair enough,' said Suzy, and moved the conversation on to talk about work and colleagues and shared memories that were funny or happy. For supper, Suzy had bought a quiche from the deli in Jesmond, and Jane put potatoes in the oven to bake and made a salad.

They were in the kitchen together, chatting, laughing. It was almost completely dark outside, but in here with Suzy beside her, treating her like a normal rational human being, Jane felt comfortable, relaxed, safe. 'This is where we really ought to be cracking open a bottle of bubbly,' Suzy said. 'Only you don't drink and I'm not allowed.' She pulled a bottle out of one of the bags she'd brought. 'So sparkling apple juice it will have to be.'

The conversation paused for a moment while Jane checked the potatoes. Then, quite suddenly, the security light outside flashed on. A pause. Then there was tapping at the door. A very quiet but persistent *tap-tap-tap-tap*.

Jane froze. 'That was tapping on the door, wasn't it?' she whispered, staring at Suzy. 'Please tell me you heard it too.'

'Yes, I heard it.' Suzy stared back, her eyes wide. 'Mrs Sea of Death from next door perhaps? Do you want me to go and see?'

'Yes, please,' Jane said, heart pounding.

The door was just a few steps away in the lobby next to the kitchen. Jane heard her friend open the door. 'Hello?' Suzy called. 'Hello? Who's there?'

After a few moments Suzy came back into the kitchen. 'There was nobody there,' she said. 'Nobody at all.'

CHAPTER 17

She had to fix the curtain in the nursery tonight. It wouldn't do to have anyone looking in and seeing the bairns. If only she didn't feel so poorly. Perhaps she could leave it till the morning. Her Next Door had company, so they wouldn't be snooping around looking through her windows tonight, she was sure. She could hear their bursts of laughter and loud chatter through the wall. But no, it wouldn't take long to screw the detached curtain pole and curtains back in place and hang the new nets.

She went into the nursery. The bairns were all tucked up neat and tidy in their cots. The room looked so clean and pretty with the lovely blue and white teddy bear wallpaper she had put up herself. She would need the toolbox and the step ladder, at the back of the kitchen broom cupboard. In the kitchen she turned on the light and suddenly felt she must lean against the sink. Her legs felt wobbly, and her head was spinning. No wonder, she thought. She hadn't eaten anything for three, or was it four, days? She hadn't been able to face food, and her stomach felt uncomfortably swollen and full despite being empty.

Pull yourself together, woman, she scolded herself. Get this job done then you can go to bed.

She let go of the sink, tried to straighten up, and then she was falling. There was a crack and an explosion of pain, then everything was black.

****

'Someone was there,' Jane said. She stood in the open doorway, while Suzy looked out into the darkness. 'You heard it too. Someone was tapping on the door. It was exactly the same sound I heard before when she tapped on the window. It was her, the little girl, I know it.'

Suzy said, 'Yes, it was very quiet tapping. Could it have been an animal, perhaps? Oh.' She paused at the door. 'Look, I think this is the answer.' She was holding a spindly leafless branch growing from a climbing rosebush next to the door. 'I'm sure this is a lovely flower-covered bush in the summer, but it looks pretty bedraggled now. And the wind has snapped this branch half off. That's what must have been tapping against the door. It really is very blustery out here.' She shivered, stepped back inside. 'So, panic over. If you've got some scissors handy, I'll cut it off.'

'Oh, right.' Jane didn't say anything, but she knew it wasn't a branch in the wind. It was too regular and rhythmic, a fast, insistent tapping.

'Have you got a torch?' Suzy said. 'If it'll make you feel happier, I'll have a little look around, just to make sure there really is nobody there.'

Jane grabbed the torch from the worktop and linked her arm through Suzy's. 'I'm coming with you,' she said.

The night sky was starless and cloudy as they crept out of the house, huddled together against the gusts of wind. Jane flashed the torch on to the field, then over the gravel patch where Suzy's car was parked. 'There's nothing there. But look, Mrs Mortimer's kitchen light is on,' Jane whispered. 'We'd better keep our heads down or she'll see us. We don't want her coming out asking us what we're doing. Let's go round the side and have a look out the front.'

They crept bent down low beneath the kitchen window and came round to the side of the house. A light shone out of the window in the end wall, illuminating a strip of the narrow stone pathway that led to the front. 'That's odd,' Jane said. 'The curtains were always drawn in that window before. There's no curtains there now at all.'

Before Jane could hold her back, Suzy edged towards the window, her back flattened against the wall. 'Be careful.' Jane hissed. 'She might be in there.'

Suzy was at the edge of the window now, craning her neck to see inside. 'It's all right, the room's empty.' She was quiet for a moment, then her voice came in an excited squeak. 'Jane, come here, quickly. Oh – my – God. Have a look at this.'

Jane hurried to her friend's side, nervously crouching down and peering in over the window ledge. She half expected to see Mrs Mortimer's white face looming into view any moment on the other side of the glass, but what she did see was even more shocking.

They were looking in at a nursery. Teddy bear wallpaper. A pile of soft toys on a white chest of drawers. A table with a changing mat on, and an empty feeding bottle. Three white cots, one under the window, one – a Moses basket on a stand – against the wall to the right, another rocking cradle on the opposite side. A Peter Rabbit mobile just like the one above Angela's cot hung from the light shade. And in the cot nearest the window, lay a sleeping baby with a dummy in its mouth. A baby so tiny and sweet looking, Jane's heart ached. Its little clenched fist was curled up next to its face. And in the Moses basket the tufty hair of another baby was just visible. They couldn't see what was in the rocking cradle, but the humped shape under the cot blanket must surely be another baby.

Suzy and Jane stared at each other. 'What the…?' Suzy whispered.

'I don't know,' Jane said, her face white. 'But let's get back in the house. Quickly, she's left the light on, so she'll be coming back any minute. We'll go back round the front, so we don't have to pass her kitchen window again.'

Back in the house, breathless, Jane said, 'I knew I was right; I knew I hadn't made a mistake when I saw her with that baby before. What on earth do you think is going on?'

'Well, it's obvious she must be doing some sort of fostering. You can't be a foster parent or even a childminder without going through a whole lot of rigmarole, being registered and checked and so on. She must be doing it on the quiet, illegally. That's why she's kept it secret.'

'And that's why the curtains were always drawn at that window. But what I can't understand is how and when these babies arrive – or leave. There's not much traffic down the track. Even the postal deliveries they've started to leave up at the farm now. There's Mrs Mortimer's Asda delivery. And the lads from the farm bring the wheelie bins to and from the road once a week on the back of their tractor for us. Hey, you don't think the babies are being smuggled inside the bins, do you?'

'Hm, doubtful,' said Suzy. 'Not to mention unhygienic. I have to say those babies looked clean and well cared for, from the brief glimpse we had of them.'

'The other thing I can't understand,' said Jane, 'is why I've never heard a baby crying. A child yes, not a baby. As you'll soon discover, newborns cry an awful lot and they're loud. I reckon you could have heard Angela bawling from half a mile away. Yet all we ever hear through next door's wall is her television. Oh, and I remember now, I had a conversation with Mrs Mortimer soon after we came here, when she claimed she didn't know anything about babies, and that if I heard what sounded like a baby it was probably a seagull.'

'That is very suspicious. Like she was trying to put you off the scent.' Suzy took the quiche and the potatoes out of the oven. 'Come on, let's eat. I don't know about you but I'm starving.'

They set the food out and Jane took a couple of mouthfuls, her brain whirring. She put down her fork and stared at Suzy. 'Of course. I've got it. She must be drugging them, to keep them quiet. She's dosing them with some sort of sedative that makes them sleep. Poor little things.'

'But whose children are they? Why are they there? Some kind of illegal adoption racket, do you think? People wanting to adopt but been turned down, or just put off by all the red tape? There's probably big money to be made, selling babies.'

'Yes, maybe. Or something even worse…' Jane said.

'What? You mean paedophile rings? Oh God, no, that's horrific, they're just babies. I don't even want to go there,' Suzy said, instinctively putting a protective hand over her belly.

'So, what on earth are we going to do about this?' Jane said. She pushed her plate away. She had suddenly lost her appetite. 'What can we do?'

'Tell someone? Yes, I think we should,' Suzy said.

'The police? Social services? Would they believe us, do you think?'

'Maybe, maybe not. But other than us forcing our way in and challenging her, which quite frankly I don't fancy from what you've told me about the woman, what else could we do?'

Jane grabbed her phone. 'I know. I'll ring Nigel Blackwood. He owns the property. He'll have a key. And he's a big strong guy. I'm sure he'll help.'

Nigel's phone rang, then switched to voicemail. Where was he, Jane wondered? After the beep she said, 'Nigel, it's Jane. Can you call me back? There's a bit of a problem here, well, at Mrs Mortimer's actually. It's quite urgent. Thanks.'

Jane felt relieved. Nigel would sort it out, she was sure. She made fresh coffee and Suzy cracked open the mint chocolates. They settled themselves on the sofa.

Jane's phone jangled. Nigel? No, it was Peter. 'All well there, darling?'

'Yes, of course. Suzy's here. We're having a nice time.'

Suzy pulled a face, mouthed 'Tell him', pointing her finger towards next door. Jane shook her head. What was the point of worrying him? She could tell him all about the babies once he was home, and Nigel had found out exactly what the situation was.

Peter started to tell her about the conference, the contacts he'd made that could come in useful, the exciting developments in the world of theoretical physics, the big presentation he was going to do tomorrow and was a bit nervous about. Jane listened with half an ear, conscious that Nigel might be trying to get back to her.

'You'll have to tell me all about it tomorrow,' she said eventually. 'I've got to go now, Peter, there's an apple pie in the oven, and I think I can smell it burning.'

Once she'd hung up, Suzy lifted an eyebrow. 'Apple pie? I didn't know that was on the menu tonight.'

'It isn't. I just needed to get rid of him. And while he was droning on, I had an amazing thought. A thought that explains everything.'

'Go on.'

'That tapping on the door – I don't think it was the rosebush branch. It was her, my little spirit girl. She wanted me to come and look through that window. Can't you see? It's obvious to me now. She knew what was happening to those poor babies, and she doesn't want me to leave the cottage until I've discovered Mrs Mortimer's secret, helped to rescue them.'

'So how do you think she knew about it? Why has she picked on you to expose the situation?'

'Those are the sort of questions I can't really answer,' Jane said. Her face was shining with excitement. 'I suppose she could have been an older child looked after by Mrs Mortimer in the past. Something very bad must have happened to her, and she lost her life. But now she wants to save other children. And as for why she's picked on me – well, maybe I'm psychic, I don't know.'

'I'll be honest, I've never believed in an afterlife, ghosts, that sort of thing,' Suzy said. 'I can't imagine meeting up with all those dead relatives I'd really rather not have to see again.'

'I know what you mean. I'd love nothing more than to think I'll get to see Angela again. And Nan of course.' Jane gave a bitter laugh. 'But on the other hand, I wouldn't want my late mother to come lurching out of the clouds towards me in her vomit-stained nightie, clutching a bottle of gin.'

'Awful thought,' Suzy agreed. 'But you do obviously believe in ghosts. Well, this ghost anyway. Have you ever had any experiences like it before this?'

Jane was quiet for a moment, gazing into the crackling fire. 'Yes, I have. I don't believe in heaven and hell, but I'm sure that the spirit lives on in some kind of alternative dimension. The psychiatrist I told said what I saw was obviously the first sign of one of my schizophrenic episodes, but I don't think it was. It was after I'd left Nan's and started my business studies course at Newcastle College. I was sharing a little terraced house in Gateshead with four other girls. I remember that evening. It was summer, warm, a Friday. The other girls were getting ready for a night out on the town, but as usual I was stopping in, reading, listening to the radio. The six o'clock news had just come on. I looked out of the window, and saw her, my nan, on the pavement outside. I can see her there now, wearing her navy-blue summer coat, the smart one she saved for special occasions, but she didn't have her handbag with her. I thought that was odd. I threw open the window, called out to her. "What are you doing here, Nan?" Something must be wrong if she'd come up from Durham on the train or bus just to see me. But she looked up at me and smiled, a lovely beaming smile, so I knew she was all right. I said, "Hang on, Nan, I'll come down and let you in".'

'I think I know what you're going to say,' Suzy said quietly. 'When you came down there was nobody there?'

'That's right. I looked up and down the street, and there wasn't a sign of her. The guy from next door was sitting on his front step, smoking a tab. He said he'd been there twenty minutes and hadn't seen anyone. I couldn't think where she could have gone. I even went up the road, looking. Later on, I rang Nan's number, but there was no answer. But an hour or so after that I got a call from Betty, her next-door neighbour. She'd noticed Nan's milk still on the doorstep from the morning, so went round to check and found her on the bathroom floor. She'd had a stroke. Betty called 999, but Nan passed away in the ambulance on her way to the hospital. I asked Betty what time that would have been—'

'And she said six o'clock?'

'Yes. Apart from the psychiatrist I've never told anyone until now, not even Peter. But I know I saw her, and I know she came to say goodbye to me.'

'And did you ever see her again after that?'

'Not see. Heard. Angela was only a couple of months old, and I drove up to Haltwhistle to show her off to my aunty Mary, Nan's sister. She's died since, but she was my only living relative then. I was driving back down the A69. It was getting dark, and I was deathly tired – I'd been up most of the night with Angela – and I must have fallen asleep at the wheel, because the next thing I remember was hearing Nan's voice from the back seat of the car shouting, "Wake up, Flower". She always called me Flower. I opened my eyes and realised I was veering off to the wrong side of the road, so I swerved back just in time to dodge a big lorry coming towards me. I pulled over; I was trembling from head to foot, looked in the back seat, and of course there was nobody there except Angela, fast asleep in her baby seat.'

'Wow, that's some story. So, your nan saved your life. But you've never seen or heard her since?'

'Not really. Sometimes I hear her voice quite clearly in my head, saying things she would have said if she'd been alive. Usually it's kind and encouraging things, but sometimes she's scolding me, "giving me wrong", as she would have put it, telling me to pull my socks up. That was one of her favourite expressions. Of course, the doctors would say hearing voices is all part of my schizophrenia diagnosis, but I don't care what it is. I like to hear her voice. It reassures me. I did love Nan, and she loved me.'

'I know,' Suzy said. 'You're a very sensitive person. Maybe you're just more in tune with these things than most of us.'

The two women sat together in silent companionship for a while. Jane felt herself beginning to relax, her taut muscles loosening, but she couldn't forget the sight of those tiny babies tucked in their cribs. And why hadn't Nigel got back in touch? There was nothing they could do tonight, but if Nigel hadn't responded by tomorrow morning, they would have to think of another plan. At least she would sleep safe and easy, knowing Suzy was there in the room next to hers.

'Sorry you're having to squash in with all Peter's books and journals and lecture notes,' Jane said as they went upstairs. 'But if you can't sleep, you can always read up on quantum theory and black holes and stuff.'

'Ha.' Suzy laughed. 'I don't think so. I tried reading Stephen Hawking's book once. Got to about page five when my brain collapsed.'

'Stephen Hawking was Peter's big hero. Did you know he said that time travel might be a possibility one day? Peter explained it to me once – something to do with what they call worm holes, tunnels they think could connect two points in space time.'

'So where would you go then, Jane? Back in time or forward?'

Jane knew what she wanted to say – that she would go back in time to when Angela fell ill and put right all those 'if onlys'. But instead she said, 'Jeez, what a question. I don't know.'

Jane fell asleep quickly. The sea was loud and restless tonight, but she'd grown used to it, and the sound of the waves soothed her. But a couple of hours later she was wide awake again and going over the events of last night. Something Suzy said was bothering her: her speculation that Mrs Mortimer might be part of some illegal set-up trafficking babies for adoption. But where could the babies come from? And then came a memory of a documentary she'd watched some time ago about Chinese babies, abandoned and unwanted, particularly baby girls, and European and American couples trying to adopt them. China...two Chinese doctors were in their Gosforth flat at the moment...Peter knew them. Peter was in regular touch with them. Peter was the one who was so keen to move to this particular cottage, who seemed to get on better than she did with Mrs Mortimer. Peter, the one who was sure everything she'd seen, everything she'd heard, was down to her mental illness. The one who was always on at her to take medication that made her drowsy and lethargic. Oh no, not Peter, surely? The man she'd always trusted, relied upon, loved? The father of her child? And – yes, what about the little girl? She didn't know how he'd done it, but he was a very clever man and it could all be some sort of elaborate charade he had concocted to make her think she was really going mad, to make sure nobody would ever believe anything she said. But now Suzy had seen those babies too, so they'd have to believe that.

She was out of bed, across the landing, shaking Suzy awake.

'Suzy! Suzy! I think I know what's happening. I think it's him – it's Peter.'

CHAPTER 18

'So hang on a minute, let's just get to the gist of what you're saying.' Suzy, still bleary with sleep and blinking in the sudden light Jane had snapped on, propped herself up on one elbow. 'You think Peter is somehow involved in some underground racket selling Chinese babies off to British couples, and the woman next door is part of that?'

'Yes, it's only a theory – but the more I think about it the more it fits.'

'But then you're saying that Peter could be gaslighting you, as they say, setting up situations and ghostly happenings to try to get you back on medication that fogs up your brain and makes you more reliant on him?'

Jane was clutching Suzy's arms so tightly her fingernails dug into her skin. 'Yes. Yes. That's exactly it. Oh God, I can see it all now. He was the one who wanted us to come and live out here. He's the one who makes all the decisions. For heaven's sake, he wouldn't even let me choose the inscription on my own daughter's memorial stone. He's a total control freak, Suzy, and I'm only just beginning to realise it. I should have listened to those other girls in the office. They warned me, you know. They said I was just looking for a father figure, he was much too old for me, that's what they said. You must have known it too . You were my closest friend. Why didn't you say anything?'

Suzy sighed. She gently prised Jane's fingers from her arm. 'Jane,' she said. 'You know I usually listen to everything you say, never try to interrupt or argue or be judgemental. But just for this once, I want you to listen to me.'

'You're going to tell me I'm a crazy paranoid bitch, aren't you?'

'No. I'm just going to tell you the truth. And the truth is that Peter would never have anything to do with something like that. He's a good man, and I could see that from the start. Have you forgotten how totally crazy about him you were back then, how you said he was your rock, made you feel totally safe and cared for? I wouldn't have dreamed of trying to put you off him just because he was so much older. You loved him. And he loves the bones of you, I'm sure of that. Yes, he may be too much into controlling parent mode at times, but it's only because he cares so much.'

'How come you know so much about what he thinks and feels?' Jane got up from the bed and paced round the room, her hands combing through her wild hair.

'I wasn't going to say anything,' Suzy said quietly. 'I usually make it a rule not to pass on private conversations. But in this case, I think I have to tell you something.' Suzy turned back the covers and sat on the side of the bed. She patted the bed next to her. 'Please, just sit down here and listen to me.'

Jane's head ached, thoughts and suspicions tumbling in a muddled confusion in her brain. Who could she trust? Was Suzy part of this too? But she sat down. 'All right,' she said.

'I saw Peter at work a couple of weeks ago. I'd popped into the Atrium for a coffee and there he was, sitting on his own in a corner, and Jane, he looked awful. Distraught. He'd taken his glasses off and had his face in his hands. I thought he might be crying. I couldn't ignore him in distress like that, so I went over and asked him if he was all right. He didn't say anything for a while, and when he did look at me it was like he didn't even recognise me for a moment. Then he told me he'd just had to walk out of a lecture. He was in such a state, he couldn't cope. They'd told him to go home and take a few days off.'

'He did take some days off, yes, but he never told me any of this. He said it was so he could prepare for the Utrecht conference, but I did wonder at the time if he was doing it to keep an eye on me. I don't get it. Why was he so upset? Why didn't he tell me if something was wrong?'

'Because he's treading on eggshells all the time, not wanting to do or say anything to upset you, send you spiralling back into another episode. And then he told me about the things you'd been seeing and hearing. He's so worried, and he doesn't know what to do to help you. The strain of it all is getting too much.'

'Oh it's all my fault then, is it?' Jane said bitterly.

'No. That's not what I'm saying at all. I'm not putting any blame on you, I'm just trying to explain, help you understand things from Peter's point of view. And have you ever thought about how losing Angela affected him? He told me he was so wrapped up in dealing with your grief, he hadn't been able to grieve properly himself, and now it was all coming out and he didn't know how to handle it. He felt he couldn't share those feelings with you because you needed him to be the strong one, the one that does all the supporting.'

'Sounds like you had a really good heart-to-heart. I bet he told you all about me and Nigel, how jealous he is.'

Suzy's eyes widened. 'No, he never said anything about that. You mean, you and this Nigel guy are…?'

'No. Well, we nearly…but no. We've agreed to be just friends. But Peter thinks it's something more, I know he does.'

'Poor Peter, no wonder he was in a bad way. And he told me about the conference in the Netherlands, said he couldn't go because he didn't want to leave you on your own.'

Jane leapt up, her eyes blazing with venom at Suzy. 'Oh, I get it now. I see. You never wanted to come and visit me, did you? It's all lies and pretence. You're not really my friend at all. You're only here, aren't you, because poor suffering Saint Peter asked you, no, begged you, to come and keep watch on me while he was away, make sure I behaved, didn't get up to anything with Nigel?'

Tears blurred Suzy's eyes. She said, 'No, that's not it at all. You've got it all wrong. I'm here because you're my friend, I wanted to see you and I thought you trusted me. Peter never asked me to come. He never mentioned Nigel, or that he suspected you of having an affair. And another thing, when I told him I was pregnant it was him who said not to tell you yet in case you got upset. You probably won't believe me, but that is the absolute truth.'

'Why should I believe you? For all I know you're part of this whole crazy conspiracy, or whatever it is, along with Peter and Mrs Mortimer. Maybe—'

'No.' Suzy jumped up, pulled Jane back beside her. 'I can't let you go on talking like this. How could I be involved? It was me who first saw those babies, told you to come and look, remember? I'd hardly have done that if I was something to do with it, would I? I'm really hurt you could even think that about me. Especially, in case you had forgotten, I'm about to have a baby myself.'

Jane paused, staring at her hands, exhaled a long slow breath. Her whole body slumped and crumpled as if shrinking, deflating. Suzy was right; how could she have forgotten about her best friend's pregnancy, about how excited she and Mike must be after trying for a baby all those years? She had never once asked Suzy about her plans, how the pregnancy had gone so far, what names they'd chosen, where she was going to have the baby. It had all been about her, Jane. Me, me, me. Suzy hadn't said as much, she was too kind, but now Jane began to see herself for what she must really seem; self-absorbed, paranoid. And wrong.

'I'm sorry,' she whispered. She laid her head on Suzy's shoulder, and Suzy put her arm round her.

'It's fine,' Suzy said. 'It's all going to be all right. We'll forget we ever had this conversation, shall we?'

'I wish I could. But you can't rub out the past, can you? You can't unsay things you've said or undo things you've done. And I wish now I hadn't said those things about Peter. He may be annoyingly pompous and fussy at times, but I do miss him.'

They both knew there would be no more sleep for them that night. Suzy went to the kitchen to brew up some tea. Jane opened her bedroom window, letting in a blast of icy cold sea air to clear her head. *Blow away the cobwebs*, Peter would have said. Jane smiled, thinking of him. Yes, she even missed his irritating sayings. It would soon be dawn, the sun a faint glimmer on the dark horizon. The turbulent winds of yesterday were dropping now to a light breeze, gently ruffling the surface of the sea.

They sat together on Jane's bed, cradling their mugs, and watched the dawn break in streaks of red and gold under a huge low canopy of purple-grey cloud rolling in towards the land. 'It's so beautiful,' Suzy said. 'Those colours. You should capture this in one of your paintings.'

'I might,' she said, but painting was the last thing on her mind. She picked up her phone. Still no message from Nigel. She tried to call him.

'I can't get through to Nigel,' she said. 'It says emergency calls only. There often seems to be a problem with the signal here, especially if the weather's been dodgy.'

'So there's not much we can do at the moment,' said Suzy. 'We could try the police, but I don't think they'd consider this an emergency. Like I said last night, the babies looked as if they were well cared for.'

'Apart from probably being drugged up to keep them quiet.' Jane stood, gathering up the empty tea mugs.

'I suppose we could try contacting social services?' Suzy said.

'It's a Sunday. Will there be anybody there?'

'There must be an emergency number – when we can get a signal of course. But quite honestly, I think what we need now is a hearty breakfast and then a good long walk in the fresh air. Looks like it's going to be quite a nice day. Then when we get back you can try your friend Nigel again.'

They worked together in the kitchen, making coffee, frying bacon and eggs and tomatoes, buttering big slabs of toast. Jane was still feeling ashamed of her outburst, but the air between them had cleared and she felt calm. Then she heard a scratchy noise at the kitchen window. Her stomach flipped, but she turned to look. It was only Mrs

Mortimer's cat who had jumped on to the windowsill and was staring at her, its mouth stretched wide in a silent miaow. 'What's the matter with you, cat?' Jane said. The cat's eyes, she noticed, were a strange orange colour, flecked with green. Cats' eyes, with their vertical slits for pupils, had always seemed malevolent to her. 'It gives me the creeps, that cat,' she said to Suzy.

'Just ignore it then,' Suzy said. And they sat down to their breakfast. But Jane was aware of the cat's eyes glaring at her all the time, and now it was scraping its paws up and down the glass. 'It definitely wants your attention.' Suzy laughed.

They put on their coats and walking boots. It looked promising weather for a walk, bright and clear, only a little breezy. Jane picked up her phone and checked it again. Still nothing from Nigel.

Suzy said, 'Let's leave our phones here, Jane. You'll only be checking yours every few minutes. Just for once let's just be out and about and free. Nobody can get to us, and we can forget what might be happening next door, just for a little while anyway.'

As they came out, the cat was waiting for them. It sidled round Jane's legs, miaowing loudly. 'Shoo, go away, go back,' she said. 'Whatever's the matter with it? What does it want?'

They set off up the track, the cat trotting after them. 'Oh, don't say the bloody thing's going to follow us all the way.' Suzy laughed. But they'd not gone as far as the bend when gradually the cat fell further behind and it soon it turned around and slipped back through the cat flap in Mrs Mortimer's door.

Near the top of the track, they followed the signpost to the coastal path, which led round the top of the field then down towards the sea again. Jane pointed out the jagged outline of Dunstanburgh castle in the distance.

'It's a bit too far to walk there today,' she said. 'But we could go to Embleton Bay tomorrow, walk along to the castle from there.'

'Or we could take my car,' Suzy said, rubbing her thighs. 'My legs are beginning to ache already. It's these varicose veins. One of the delights of pregnancy.'

They rested a while, sitting on a rock and looking out at the vast expanse of sea and sky. The air smelt fresh and cool and clean.

'Have you thought about getting your own car? It's beautiful here, of course, but what do you do all day when Peter's at work? I know it's peaceful but this time of year it's too wild, too empty. The isolation can't be good for your mental health,' Suzy said.

'Yes, I know. Peter thought the crowds and noise of the city were making me worse, but that's just what I miss.'

'If you had your own car you could drive to town. You could go shopping, pop into the Uni office to see everyone, come out with me for coffee. You could explore all the towns and villages round here too, join things, talk to people, keep busy.'

'Yes, but we're only here for a few more weeks,' Jane said. 'You're right though, I would like my own car, just the independence of it, not having to rely on Peter to take me everywhere. But I don't think we could afford it. Renting the cottage is costing us a fortune, even with the income from letting our Newcastle flat.'

They'd been out for an hour when it began to spot with rain. They pulled their coat hoods up and headed back the way they'd come. Jane didn't say anything, but she was wishing she had her phone, just in case Nigel had got her message and was trying to get through.

As they passed the farm, Brian Armstrong was in the yard, heaving a hay bale into the barn. He spotted them, waved, and called out, hurrying towards the gate. Jane could see he wanted to tell her something. 'Jane,' he said, wagging his finger down the track. 'You'd better know, there's been something going on down there. You just missed the ambulance. It was down here half an hour ago, blue lights going, sirens blaring, set the dogs off barking. Then, just a few minutes later, it came back up. I'd seen you and your friend going off on your walk a while back, so I knew it wasn't you. Hope it's not your husband.'

'No, he's away at the moment. Oh dear, something must be up with Mrs Mortimer.'

'Aye, reckon so. Our Adam saw her when he was down fetching the bins last week, said she looked very poorly, thin as a skeleton,' he said.

'And I've seen nothing of her at all for a week or so,' Jane said. 'Her cat was trying to get our attention this morning. We never thought something might be wrong with her.'

'Well, she must have been well enough to ring for an ambulance, so that's a good sign,' Brian said. 'Poor old Peggy. She never goes out, hates being away from home. She'll not like it, being in a hospital, having strangers prodding and poking and asking questions.'

Jane and Suzy stared at each other as they headed back down the track. 'What on earth do you think has happened?' Jane said.

'I don't know, but maybe the cat was trying to get our attention because it wanted us to feed it, if Mrs Mortimer had an accident or was taken ill,' Suzy said.

Jane clutched her arm. 'Never mind the cat.' she said. 'What about the babies? Do you think the ambulance people found them, took them away? I hope so. But if they didn't know they were there – oh Suzy, there's no one looking after them.'

They began to run.

The tyre marks left by the ambulance were clearly visible in the churned-up mud as they approached. 'Her door's probably locked,' Jane said. 'Hang on, I'll get my phone, try to get hold of Nigel again. If I can't, we'll have to get the police to break the door down.'

She stumbled into the kitchen, grabbed her phone. There was a voicemail, and it was Nigel:

'Hi, Jane. Sorry, only just got your message from last night. I'm on my way over.'

The message was timed at nine thirty – about the time they'd just left on their walk. So, he must have arrived while they were out, decided to drop in on Mrs Mortimer, found her and called the ambulance.

Suzy was waiting by Mrs Mortimer's door. 'It's open. The door. Look, someone forced their way in, the glass panel's been smashed in. There must have been an intruder, someone attacked her. How awful.'

Jane told her about Nigel. 'It was probably him who had to break in, so don't let's jump to conclusions yet. Come on, let's see if those babies are still there, and let's hope to God they're OK.'

The cat glared at them as they came in. It stalked over to its food bowl, and sat by it, watching their every move. They trod carefully over the splinters of broken glass. The floor felt slippery and sticky under their feet. It was blood. Blood drops on the floor, blood smears on the kitchen unit. Jane's heart was pounding. Which room were the babies in? The small kitchen led into the living room. Everything in the little house was neat and immaculate, sterile, bare of ornaments, books, or clutter. There was a door on the right, slightly ajar. 'This must be it,' Jane said. She turned to Suzy. 'You go in there, Suze, I don't think I want to see if something horrible has happened.'

Suzy pushed the door open. She stood hesitantly in the doorway, Jane peering nervously over her shoulder. The light must have been left on all night, illuminating the little nursery with the teddy bear wallpaper, and the three neat cots. And tucked up in the cots were the babies, eyes closed, completely silent and motionless. Jane stepped back.

'Oh my God, my God, they're too still, too quiet,' she whispered.

Her knees felt as if they might buckle. She squeezed her eyes shut. 'I can't bear it. I can't look at them. They're not alive, are they?'

'You're right, they're not alive.'

It was a woman's voice, but not Suzy's, and she was standing right behind them.

CHAPTER 19

The stranger standing behind them was middle-aged and plump, with a florid face, big hoop earrings and yellowy-blonde hair in a short bob.

For a long moment, they all stared at each other. 'Who are you?' Jane said at last.

'Ha, I was just going to ask you the same thing.' Her tone was friendly, unconcerned. She smiled at them. 'I'm Peggy's sister, Beryl. Beryl Clarke. And you are…?'

'Jane Eagle. I live next door,' Jane said. 'This is my friend Suzy. The door wasn't locked so we came in. We were so worried. We saw the babies through the window last night. And quite honestly I can't understand why we're standing here having this conversation next to a room with three babies in it who are—' She couldn't bring herself to say the word *dead*. 'What in heaven's name happened to them?' Her voice rose to a panic-stricken shriek.

The woman burst out laughing.

What is the matter with her? Jane thought. Is she completely mad? Jane wanted to fly at her, slap her fat pink face.

'Oh dear, you have got hold of the wrong end of the stick, haven't you?' Beryl Clarke was still tittering. 'Oh well, it wouldn't be the first time. Don't upset yourself dear, they're not dead.'

'But you said—' Jane began. The woman brushed past them and strode into the nursery. She picked up the baby lying in the cot beneath the windowsill. Jane saw its legs dangling as the shawl it was wrapped in fell away, its little downy head wobbling. And then, shockingly, the

162

woman turned and in one swift move lobbed the baby towards Jane, just as if she was passing a rugby ball. 'Here you are, take a look at it.' She chuckled.

Jane was still frozen in horror, but Suzy lunged forward to catch it, clutched it to her chest. Slowly, she studied its sleeping face, touched its hand, its feet. Her shoulders dropped with relief. She looked up, smiled, almost laughed.

'Ah, I get it. It's not a baby,' she said. 'It's just a doll.'

'No, that's never a doll, it's too real.' Jane gasped, still dazed with shock.

'That's the whole idea. They're meant to look realistic,' Beryl Clarke said, taking the fake baby out of Suzy's arms. She cradled it, unbuttoning the top of its pink sleep suit. 'Look, you can see its body now. That's not a real baby, is it?' The body was made of some sort of softly stuffed pink material, sewn up the middle and attached to the head. 'And by the way, we don't call them dolls. They're Reborns. Beautiful, aren't they? Works of art.'

Jane wanted to say, *No, they're grotesque. Horrific.* But she said nothing.

Beryl Clarke was now busy showing them the other two dolls, pointing out their perfect little finger nails and toenails, the delicately rooted baby hair and eyelashes, the soft pliant mouths that opened so you could see the gums and tongue inside. 'You can put a dummy in its mouth, or a feeding bottle, but of course they can't drink. You have to block the teat and use fake milk.'

Suzy and Jane watched the demonstration, speechless. They exchanged 'are we dreaming this?' looks with each other. Beryl flung open the cupboard door. 'Peggy loves the dressing up bit best,' she said, sweeping her hand towards shelves neatly stacked with piles of baby clothes. 'Oh, and look she's got another one in here. It's a silicone. I don't think she liked it as much as the cloth body ones, and I know what she means. Their bodies may look more real but they don't feel so much like a real baby when you hold them. But you can give them a proper bath, so some people prefer them. I think this model comes with a detachable umbilical cord, but Peggy must have thrown that away. I'll admit that was a bit yukky.'

Out of the cupboard she pulled a naked newborn-sized boy, perfect in every detail. It flopped in her hands, its arms and legs wobbling. Its head lolled to one side. Unlike the others, its eyes were open, glassy blue eyes staring fixedly right at Jane and all she could think was that it looked like something from a mortuary slab. She had a sudden memory of a hospital room, a tangle of monitors, tubes, and wires being gently removed from her precious child on the bed, looking so small, so fragile, so still. A nurse saying quietly 'Would you like to hold her for a while?' Then the limp body, still warm, being placed in her arms and her whole world crashing down around her.

A sob escaped her lips and she ran out of the house – straight into the arms of Nigel Blackwood.

He held her steady. 'Jane, there you are. I've been trying to ring you all morning. And what a morning it's been.'

Jane couldn't speak. She was trembling, gasping in great gulps of breath.

Suzy and Beryl joined them.

'Are you all right?' Suzy said, rushing to her side.

'Never mind about me,' she said, recovering her composure. 'How about Mrs Mortimer? What happened?'

'Perhaps we should all go in your house,' Nigel said. 'We can catch our breath, have a cup of coffee, and I'll explain what's happened.'

Jane couldn't get over Beryl being Mrs Mortimer's sister. She was her exact opposite in every way; not just in looks, but in her chatty, exuberant manner. She was bustling round the kitchen, taking charge of the coffee making. She didn't seem in the least bit subdued, considering her sister had just been rushed to hospital. 'Have you got any biscuits pet? Chocolate ones by any chance? No? Oh, that's a pity, I could do with a treat after the morning I've had.' It was some time before she stopped talking long enough for Nigel to tell his story.

'Sorry, I didn't get your message till this morning,' he explained. 'I've got a stinker of a cold at the moment, so I had a really early night last night, turned my phone off and didn't look at it till this morning. I rang you back straight away, but you weren't picking up.'

'No, we'd gone out on a walk and didn't take our phones.'

'Ah, I see. Anyway, it sounded urgent, so I came straight over. Knocked on your door, but obviously you were out. So, as you said in your phone message there was some problem at Mrs Mortimer's I went over there. Couldn't get an answer, and the kitchen light was still on, but the door was locked. I thought about going over to the office to collect a spare key, but I reckoned something might have happened to Peggy and it could be an emergency, so I managed to smash a glass pane in the door. Luckily, she'd left the key in the lock the other side, and I could just about reach it. Poor Peggy was on the kitchen floor, not conscious, but I checked, and she was still breathing. She had a nasty gash on her head.'

'Had someone attacked her?' Jane asked.

'I thought so at first. But unless she'd let them in herself, how would they have got in with the door locked? And how would they have locked it from the inside when they left?'

'We were in all evening,' Suzy said. 'I'm sure we would have heard if anything like that was going on next door.'

'That's right, so I think she must have passed out, or slipped, and bashed her head on the side of the worktop as she fell. I called an ambulance right away. They took about half an hour to arrive. I can tell you, I was worried all the time I was waiting. She'd gone a very nasty grey colour, wasn't responding to me at all. The paramedics gave her oxygen and patched her up, stopped the bleeding.'

'And then Mr Blackwood followed the ambulance in his car all the way to A&E at Cramlington hospital,' said Beryl. 'By then she'd come round a bit, and they were asking her for the name of next of kin. Apparently, she said she hadn't got any next of kin, but Mr Blackwood remembered she had a sister, and eventually they got my number out of her. Fortunately, I'm only in Blyth, so I was there in a jiffy, and she'd already been stitched up and admitted to the ward. They're going to keep an eye on her for a couple of days at least. The doctor I spoke to said she was very thin. Malnourished, she thought. Anyway, all Peggy seemed to be worried about was that blasted cat of hers, so I promised I'd come up and feed it, maybe collect a few things for her, clean nightie, wash bag and so on.'

'We should be grateful to Jane and her friend for noticing something was up,' said Nigel. 'What was it that made you think something had happened to her?'

Jane was about to say that it was actually something else that they were worrying about. But knowing the truth now and thinking of all her wild supposition about a baby smuggling racket, she felt foolish and embarrassed. She glanced at Suzy. 'I – we – hadn't seen her for a while, had we? It was just a kind of intuition, something not right.'

'I thought it was the babies you were worried about,' Beryl chipped in.

Nigel frowned. 'Babies? What babies?'

Beryl launched into a long description of what she called the Reborn community, the huge popularity all over the world of ultra-realistic baby dolls, as well as toddler dolls, or 'sculpts' as she called them, about the Reborn fairs and exhibitions she'd attended, her own collection of seven or eight Reborns and silicones, how the best ones cost well over a hundred pounds, or even more, how she'd given one to Peggy after she had to let all but one of her many cats go, and Peggy hadn't been interested at first, but then became nearly as keen a collector as she was.

'I suppose that's because she never had any children of her own,' Jane said.

Beryl shrieked with laughter. 'Oh no, not our Peg. I don't think she cared for children, never wanted them. She wasn't that type at all. Never was interested in my two boys either, her own nephews. No, real babies would have been far too noisy and messy for her. But she liked looking after cats, so I suppose the Reborns were the next best thing. Maybe better, less demanding, cleaner. She liked dressing them up, making them look nice. And unlike real babies, if she didn't feel like it, she could leave them be for a day or two.'

'Why did she keep them such a secret, though?' Jane asked.

'Oh, that's Peggy for you. She always was secretive. And people can be very funny, think it's weird and freaky, grown-up women playing with dolls. But it's not like that. We know they're not real babies. We call it role play. Feeding them, dressing them, taking them out. A friend of mine got some very nasty hate mail after it was in the paper how she left her Reborn in the back of her car at the Metro Centre on a hot afternoon and the police were called to smash in her window because a passer-by thought it was a real baby in there. But me, I don't care what people think. I take mine out in a pram, shopping, everywhere. I love it when people mistake them for real babies, and the look on their faces when I tell them.' She let out more ear-splitting hoots of laughter.

'Aye, I suppose it's not that much different from men messing about with their train sets up in the attic,' Nigel said. 'And I know a couple of fellas who spend hours playing war games with model soldiers. Nobody thinks that's odd.'

'Quite right,' nodded Beryl. She was obviously enjoying herself enormously.

Nigel stood up. He looked bleary-eyed and he had a handkerchief clamped to his nose. 'Well, if you don't mind, I'll be making tracks. It's been quite a busy morning. I think I'll go home and catch a bit more bed rest, take some paracetamol. This cold is getting worse. But do call me if you need anything, Jane. And you, Mrs Clarke. Will you be staying here at the cottage while Peggy's in hospital?'

'Oh yes, Peggy wants me here to look after Whisky.'

'I could feed the cat,' said Jane. 'There's no need for you to stay here just for that.'

'Oh it's fine dear. I shall enjoy it, being out here in the sticks. The sea air. And keeping you two ladies company.'

Jane's heart sank. She looked at Suzy and pulled a face.

'That's grand,' Nigel said, and he threw Jane a sympathetic wink. 'I'll arrange for someone to come down and fix that broken glass in the door first thing tomorrow, Mrs Clarke.'

'Call me Beryl, dear. Everyone does. And I'll clean up the blood and mess, no problem,' Beryl said.

Once Nigel had gone, Beryl seemed to be settling herself down on the sofa, and she was rooting in her bag for her phone. 'I'll just get on to YouTube,' she said. 'Show you a few videos.'

Jane and Suzy complied with her demand that they sit next to her and squeezed on the sofa either side of Beryl. They peered over her shoulder as she showed them video after video of Reborn babies being fed, burped, cradled, dressed, having their hair brushed, and their nappies changed, only the hands of their 'mothers' visible.

'They talk about them as if they were real babies.' Suzy was amazed. A woman with an American accent was chirruping on about little Melody having woken three times in the night for a feed and had only drunk half her bottle. 'And now she's just playing with her toys,' said the voice, with a shot of a rattle wedged in a silicone fist being waved by an unseen human hand. The sound effects of crying and gulping bottle-feeding noises had been dubbed on the video for extra realism. There were videos of babies in prams, car seats, on shopping trips, and tours of nurseries stuffed with clothes and expensive-looking nursery equipment.

'This is so weird,' Suzy said.

'And not a little creepy,' Jane added.

'Oh, it's just role play, a harmless hobby,' Beryl said. 'Like Mr Blackwood said, the same as men and their model trains and soldiers.'

'Well,' said Jane, 'don't let us hold you up any longer Beryl. I'm sure you'll be wanting to get stuff together for your sister before you visit her in hospital again. I expect she'll be pleased to see you.'

Beryl's loud cackles were beginning to make Jane's head ache. 'She won't be bothered. We never were on the best of terms, you know. If it weren't for me keeping an eye out for her, she'd have nobody, so I do my best. Not that she appreciates it, mind.'

'I hope you don't mind me mentioning it,' Jane said. 'But I would never have thought you two were sisters. You're nothing at all like each other in any way.'

More bellows of laughter. 'Chalk and cheese we are, pet, chalk and cheese. Hardly surprising though. We're not blood sisters. Mam and Dad thought they couldn't have any children, so they adopted Peggy. Well, her real name is Margaret, but Dad always used to say she was like a square peg in a round hole, so the name Peggy stuck. It was a shame really, they never took to her, she was such a solitary, unresponsive child. Hard to love. She'd had a sad start in life, you know, found as a newborn, in a brown paper carrier bag in the ladies' toilet in Binns department store. And then Mam fell pregnant, and I came along, and I was a completely different kettle of fish, so they doted on me, of course. It's no wonder Peggy didn't care for me, she must have been jealous, I suppose.'

The house seemed suddenly peaceful and blissfully quiet once Beryl Clarke had finally gone.

'I think I'd rather have Morticia next door to me than that woman.' Jane sighed. 'I don't mind a bubbly personality but she's positively boiling over.' She and Jane were making sandwiches for their lunch. 'How are we ever going to put up with her coming in every five minutes?'

'Well, with any luck, Mrs Mortimer will be back before long,' Suzy said. 'And while Mrs Foghorn is next door, I suggest we get out and about as much as possible. I've got my car so we can go exploring all the castles and stuff, not to mention a few nice pubs. Not that I can have a proper drink, alas, but there's always pub grub.'

'Great idea,' Jane said. She felt happy and relieved now that the baby mystery had been cleared up. But there was a sadness too. She couldn't help but feel deeply sorry for Peggy Mortimer, abandoned at birth, unloved as a child, abused and then deserted by her sadistic husband, left alone and bitter with only her cats and her dolls for companionship. Autistic too, probably, so unable to relate to people or make relationships.

And then there was another thought nagging her. If the little spirit girl wasn't alerting her to what was going on next door, what was it that she wanted?

CHAPTER 20

'Your sister's here to see you, Peggy.'

Peggy Mortimer heard the swish of the curtains round her bed as the nurse opened them, but she kept her eyes tightly shut. She did not want to see Beryl. She did not want to hear her loud prattle. She absolutely did not want to talk to her. All she wanted to do was sleep.

'Wakey wakey, dear,' Beryl's voice boomed round the quiet ward. 'I've brought you some bits and bobs from the house. And you're not to worry about Whisky. He's been fed and he's fine.'

When she'd first come round she thought she'd died. So this was heaven – everything bright and white and somebody shining a torch into her eyes. But her head hurt, and she could feel a stinging sensation under the bandage around her brow. So she was alive. She felt slightly disappointed about that. What must she look like – hair down and all over the place, no make-up? And then Beryl appeared.

'Oh dear, what have you been up to, Peggy?' What did she mean by that? Was she trying to suggest she had done something wrong?

'Just go to the house and get my make-up bag,' she managed to say in a hoarse whisper. 'And feed the cat.'

'A please wouldn't go amiss,' Beryl sniffed. 'It's a long drive up there.'

Now three hours later here she was again. And at least she'd done what she'd asked her. Reluctantly, Peggy Mortimer opened one painful eye. 'Thank you,' she grunted.

'Oh well, what are sisters for? I'm sure you'd do the same for me.' Only of course, she knew Peggy wouldn't. She put a big bag of grapes on the bedside table. 'I thought you might like these. Though by the look of you, you could do with something a bit more filling.' She plonked herself down on the chair and helped herself to a grape. 'I met your neighbour and her friend this morning. Very nice people. We had a lovely coffee and chat together, Mr Blackwood as well. They were so pleased I'm going to be staying next door, said I must keep popping in to keep them company. Oh, and they wanted to know all about the Reborns. It was so funny, Peggy, they'd seen yours through the window and thought they were real. Oh, I did laugh.'

Peggy Mortimer turned her head painfully towards her. 'Beryl,' she murmured.

'What dear?'

'Just go away will you? Go away.'

****

Jane was in the driving seat, and loving it. She'd forgotten how good it felt to be in control and free to come and go anywhere she wanted. And what a joy it was, driving here in the Northumberland countryside, the roads all but empty and all around the glorious vistas of open fields and winding lanes with a canopy of trees blazing in their autumn colours.

It was all down to Suzy. That morning she'd said to Jane, 'You know you said you couldn't afford your own car? I could help you out, you know, let you have a loan.'

'Wow, that's a really kind offer. But I have got some savings I could use if I wanted, a bit of money Nan left me. I've been saving it for a rainy day.'

'Well, now's your rainy day,' Suzy said, pointing at the fat drops of rain crawling down the windowpane. 'How much have you got?'

'I think there's just short of seven thousand in an ISA. I'll check – I've got the passbook somewhere upstairs.'

And so, they headed off to Alnwick in Suzy's car. Suzy had researched second-hand car dealers, and they made for one on the industrial estate on the edge of town. Jane walked in and said, 'What have you got for under five thousand pounds that I can drive away today?'

Within a couple of hours, Suzy helped her choose a white Suzuki, six years old, one owner, low mileage. Jane found a branch of her building society and drew out the money, organised the insurance, and filled in the paperwork, and the car was hers. She was exhilarated. She hadn't done anything so impulsive in years and all without consulting Peter. It felt good.

The rain had eased, so they stopped off for a celebratory lunch at a cafe in the town. Out of the window they watched a group of men in yellow hi-viz jackets starting to put up the Christmas lights.

'Christmas is only six and a bit weeks away,' Suzy said. 'You'll be back in town then, and we can spend Christmas Day together, you and Peter, me and Mike.'

Jane said, 'Sure,' but she felt nothing. She used to love Christmas. Now it was a painful and melancholy ordeal without Angela.

Suzy followed Jane in her new car back to the cottage. Halfway down the track they had to pull over to the grassy verge, as a car was coming up the other way. It was Beryl. She waved cheerily at them, leant out of her window, 'Hello, girls. I'm just off to see Peggy again.'

'How was she when you saw her yesterday?' Jane asked. 'Coming back soon, I hope?'

'She wasn't too good. She'll be in for a while yet. The doctors want to do tests. There's one or two things they're not happy about apparently.'

'Oh, that's a pity,' said Jane. 'Give her my best wishes.'

'I will,' Beryl said, 'Not that she'll appreciate it.' She closed the window and drove off.

The remaining days of Suzy's visit passed in a flash and Jane came as close to happiness as she had in a long time. The pain and grief would always be with her; she knew that, ebbing and flowing like the sea's tides. But she was learning to live with it, and even enjoy these moments of quiet joy without guilt. She couldn't wait to set off in her new car every morning and she didn't care where they went. They just drove anywhere the road took them, explored little villages and visited castles and ate out in pubs and laughed a great deal.

Peter rang every night, full of the conference and what a success it had been. 'Anything been happening back there?' he asked.

'Where do I start?' said Jane, deciding not to tell him about the new car. That surprise could wait till later. 'Well, Mrs Mortimer's in hospital. She had a fall, bashed her head. Her sister's staying next door to look after the cat. Totally different from Morticia. Blonde, loud and brassy...'

Suzy was rolling her eyes towards the door. Beryl Clarke had walked in without knocking. 'Coo-ee. It's only me.' she called. She obviously hadn't heard Jane's comments. 'Well, I've just been over to see our Peggy, but she was still groggy from the operation and couldn't talk.'

'Operation?' said Jane, having said a swift goodbye and see you tomorrow to Peter.

'Oh yes, they did a scan and found she had some sort of problem in her stomach. They operated straight away. A tumour, they said, but it was too soon to say if it's benign or not.'

Beryl had brought them fish and chips from Seahouses, spoiling Jane's plans for healthy veggie lasagne and salad. They sat with the greasy paper on their knees, eating with their fingers. Beryl finished hers before Jane and Suzy had got halfway through theirs. She wiped her fingers on a tea towel, then pulled a dog-eared photo album out of her bag. 'I thought you girls would like to see these pictures of me in my younger days.'

The photos dated from the nineteen seventies; the colours had faded and time had given them a hazy orange hue. 'That's me on holiday at Butlins. I won the beauty competition there three years in a row, you know.' Jane and Suzy peered over her shoulder at the images, trying to match the pert and slender girl in the swimsuit with the stout Beryl who now took up most of the sofa.

'Who's that standing next to you in this one?' Jane asked. 'That's not your sister, is it?'

'Oh yes, that's her, our Peg, looking a right sour-puss as usual,' said Beryl. 'She never liked having her picture taken. Poor dear. Plain, wasn't she?'

Jane said nothing, but she knew Suzy was thinking the same thing. Beryl had been pretty, but Peggy Mortimer when she was young was strikingly beautiful, with long black hair, high cheekbones and large dark eyes. 'I think she looks like Cher,' said Suzy.

'Oh do you think so?' Beryl said. 'I can't see it myself. Some people thought I bore a strong resemblance to Marilyn Monroe though. I always had lots of boyfriends chasing after me, but Peggy never had much success with the lads. Then she went and married that nasty piece of work Eric Mortimer, the first lad who paid her any attention, and she was absolutely besotted with him. Goodness knows why. Oh, he was good looking, I'll grant you, lots of long curly hair, big blue twinkly eyes, cheesy smile. But handsome is as handsome does I always say. She was well rid of him.'

It was after midnight before Beryl finally left, having finished off the last of Peter's gin.

Suzy left on Thursday morning. 'Are you sure you'll be OK?' she said.

'Yes, of course I will. Peter's back tonight, and we'll lock the door and pretend we can't hear if Beryl comes knocking.' What she really wanted to say was, 'Don't go, Suzy, stay a few days more.'

They hugged, promised to keep in touch. Jane would call her the moment they got back to town, and they would make plans for Christmas together. 'And after Christmas we'll go shopping for baby things,' said Jane. She had thought about offering Suzy all Angela's baby clothes, still in the nursery chest of drawers back at the flat. But she couldn't bear to part with them just yet, and anyway Suzy probably wouldn't want her little girl to wear things that were once worn by a child who had died.

Once Suzy's car had gone out of sight round the bend in the track, Jane felt her bright, optimistic mood start to drop away. As if echoing her feelings, the sky darkened, and the sea turned an odd dark purple-grey. Without Suzy there, the house felt too quiet, almost oppressive, as if all the light and warmth of the past few days had vanished. Jane found herself thinking about the little girl for the first time in days. Since the tapping on the door on Saturday and the realisation that there was nothing sinister going on next door, she had not given her a single thought. It was as if she'd disappeared completely, like the sea fret dissolving when the sun broke through. She should have felt relieved, but she didn't. What happened to her, and the reason for her appearances, would remain a mystery now, a phenomenon she would never be able to understand.

Her phone rang. It was Peter. 'Darling,' he said. 'Bad news I'm afraid. The fog here's absolutely awful. They've cancelled all flights till tomorrow.'

'Oh no, will you have to spend the night in the airport?'

'No, they're putting us up in a hotel close by. But all being well we should be able to get away tomorrow. Has Suzy gone? Will you be all right on your own tonight?'

'Yes, she's gone. But I shall be fine, don't worry. I've got the world's busiest busybody staying next door if there's any problems.'

'Ah yes, the sister. I'll look forward to making her acquaintance. Anyway darling, my phone's running out of juice, so see you tomorrow. Can't wait.'

'Nor me. Love you, Peter.'

'Love you too.'

Jane shivered. She hadn't once been cold in the house while Suzy had been there, but now the chill had returned. She suddenly felt alone. Even Beryl's company would have been better than this empty silence, but her car wasn't there so she must be out shopping or at the hospital. She'd relished the solitude for a short while after Peter had left, but now it was bringing back the loneliness she felt when she was a small girl. She couldn't remember the time when her mother was a proper parent, caring for her, playing with her, laughing and reading her bedtime stories. Nan had told her how her mother had tried her best to be a good parent, until she moved with little Jane to Leeds to be with Uncle Dennis, the latest in a long succession of disastrous boyfriends. But then everything went wrong. Dennis threw them out, and Jane's mother was on her own with a small child, jobless and away from Nan's steadying influence. That was when her mother discovered her only consolation was drinking.

Jane knew all about loneliness then. She spent long hours in her bedroom, reading and re-reading her story books, drawing pictures, while her mother was drinking or sleeping it off. Christmas and birthdays went by uncelebrated. Nobody came to school parents' evenings, or to see her in school plays and concerts. It was then her imaginary friend arrived. Sometimes she was Jane's sister, sometimes a close friend, but she sat beside Jane, chatting and playing games. Jane called her Judy. Judy had beautiful clean clothes, pretty golden hair. She would cheer Jane up, saying 'Never mind, it will be all right' and helping Jane with the chores like washing dishes and going to the shops. Like Beryl and her dolls, she knew Judy wasn't real, but she could imagine that she was and she could picture her in every detail. It was Judy who said to her one day, 'Jane, you must ring up Nan, ask her to come down. You can't look after Mammy on your own anymore.'

Thinking of those times now was taking Jane back down into a deep dark place again, a place she didn't want to visit. She must shake herself out of it, pull her socks up, as Nan always said, stop moping about the house, do something. She grabbed her coat, her sketch pad and her box of pastels. The tide was still quite far out but was on the turn, so she would take her mind off things, follow Suzy's advice, and go down the steps to the little patch of rock-strewn beach for a while to try to capture on paper the odd colour of the sea and the great billows of looming purple clouds above.

She made her way to the front of the house and the low stone wall. She paused at the top of the stone steps, looking down in the fading light at the beach with its scattering of pebbles and seaweed-covered rocks. In the small stretch of clear sand someone had scratched two words in large spidery letters. Jane couldn't quite make them out in the fading light of the November afternoon, but she knew what they would say. She left her sketch pad and pastels on the wall, hurried down the steps. The words were clearly visible now:

Dont leave.

She was back.

Jane looked along the shore for the little figure in red, but she wasn't there.

'Where are you? Who are you?' Jane's shout of frustration carried out to the open sea and sky. 'Why mustn't I leave? What do you want from me?'

There was no answer but the rumbling waves rolling over the pebbles and the forlorn cry of a seabird circling overhead.

'Show me. Please, show me what happened to you,' she called to the empty air.

'Coo-ee.' Oh no, it was Beryl, braying at her from the open window. 'Are you all right pet? I heard you shouting.'

'Yes, I'm fine, just – you know – letting off a bit of steam.'

Beryl gave her an odd look. 'Oh? It sounded like you were shouting at someone out at sea.' She emerged from the house, bustled up to the top of the steps where Jane was standing. 'I know how you feel though, I feel like yelling myself. You won't believe what Peggy's done. I've just went all the way to the hospital to visit her, but the nurse on her ward stopped me at the door, told me Peggy had asked them not to let me see her, said she didn't want to have any visitors. Then when I asked to speak to the doctor about her, they said Peggy had now made it very clear, insisted, she didn't want them discussing her test results or anything else with me. I mean, really, I told them, I'm her next of kin, I've a right to know. But they just went on about respecting patient confidentiality blah-blah-blah. Typical of our

Peggy, always has to be secretive about everything. I tell you, I've half a mind to go home, leave that cat of hers to fend for itself.'

'Oh dear. Well, as I said, I don't mind feeding the cat.'

'Thank you, dear, but I might just stay on a bit. The sea air's doing my bad chest a power of good. I tell you what though, I could murder a nice cup of tea right now.'

Ten minutes ago, Jane would have invited her in, anything to dispel the dismal silence in the cottage, but the writing in the sand had set her mind in turmoil again. 'Sorry, Beryl, another time maybe. I've got to go, there's things I need to do.' She turned and went back to the house. She paced around for a while, wondering whether to call Nigel. No, better not, he might still be feeling poorly. Suzy would be home by now, so maybe she could call her? Her fingers hovered over her phone. Then a thought slipped into her head. She would go down on to the beach before the tide came in and take a photo of the writing, then she could send it to Suzy and Nigel, see what they thought. She checked that Beryl was no longer lurking about, and rushed outside, looked over the wall.

The tide was already crawling in frothy waves up the little beach, covering the pebbles, swirling round the rocks. The words had gone.

Before she went to bed, Jane took two sleeping pills, prescribed months ago when she'd been suffering from night after night of insomnia. Now that the spirit child was here again, the expectation of hearing the slightest sound would have kept her wide awake and rigid with apprehension. As she went to draw the curtains, she gazed at the night sky. The brooding clouds of the afternoon had blown away and the sky was clear, sprinkled with millions of tiny stars, and a sliver of waxing crescent moon. It was so beautiful she would leave the curtains open so that she could look out at the scene as she fell asleep.

She must have slept soundly for some time, and the sleeping pills had clouded her brain, so when she suddenly awoke in the early hours it took her some moments to remember where she was and what was happening. It was a sound that had woken her. She was foggily aware of the patter of running feet outside the door, then the familiar *tap-tap-*

tap. Pause. *Tap-tap-tap.* She sat up, rigid. The tapping stopped. The room seemed filled with light, and she remembered she hadn't closed the curtains. But the odd thing was the eerie brightness, and she looked out to see a large full moon, a perfect creamy-gold circle, glowing in the night sky with an aura of light around it. Even in her drowsy state, she remembered it had been a thin crescent moon last night. Now it was full. It didn't make sense.

She pushed aside the bed covers, slowly opened the bedroom door, afraid of what might be there, but she had to see. The landing was deserted. And then she heard it.

Someone was downstairs. There was the quiet murmur of voices, footsteps, a tap turned on in the kitchen, a cupboard door being closed, the clattering of dishes in the sink. The snuffling, gulping sound of a child quietly crying.

CHAPTER 21

The child's voice rang out clearly: 'No Mummy, no, I don't want it. It tastes nasty.'

And a woman's brittle voice answered, 'Come on Emily. Drink it up. It's to help you sleep.'

Rooted to the spot. Jane thought, I'm dreaming, that's what's happening. Of course, hypnagogia, like Peter had said, she was experiencing a vivid waking dream. What else could it be? But the landing floorboards felt real and cold under her feet as she crept closer towards the top of the stairs. From here, she looked down into the living room. Everything there seemed the same as normal, but the side light was on, casting a soft glow over the room, and there were two suitcases in front of the fireplace, an unfamiliar coat slung over the back of a chair. Huddled on the sofa, in her Minnie Mouse pyjamas, lay the little girl. Standing over her was a tall woman with light brown hair, cropped very short. Her eyes looked like two dark hollows, her face expressionless.

Strangely, Jane felt no fear as she willed herself to take the first steps down the stairs. She kept repeating to herself, *This is just a dream, just a dream, nothing to be scared of, they're not really here. This is all in my head. All in my head.* And now she was so close she could see the glass tumbler in the woman's hand, the freckles on the child's face, her red pyjama top with the picture on it, Minnie Mouse with her curly cartoon eyelashes and a big spotted bow between the big round mouse ears.

The child took the glass from the woman and drank it down. She sniffed and shuddered, wiped tears from her eyes with the back of her hand, and Jane felt a sudden surge of pain around her heart. She wanted to run to that poor little girl, hold her, save her. Oh, she knew how she felt, because she'd been there too, alone, helpless and scared of the one person in the world she ought to trust. But she couldn't help her. Halfway down the stairs, it was as if an invisible solid wall stopped her from moving forward.

'I want to go back to Daddy's,' came the child's voice, half sob, half wail.

'Shut up about Daddy, will you.' The woman snatched the glass back from the child's hand, turned her back, then seemed to relent. She sat down next to the child, stroked her hair tenderly, whispered soothing words Jane couldn't quite make out. The child closed her eyes.

'I'm sorry, Emily, it's the only way. Go to sleep, go to sleep.'

And then she picked up the big red cushion and pressed it down hard over the little girl's face. She stood up, holding the cushion down with rigid arms, pressing, pressing. The child did not move.

Jane howled *NO!* Every fibre of her body screamed, but no sound came out of her mouth. She willed herself to move her legs, but they stayed rooted to the stair. The scene remained frozen for what seemed like several agonising minutes, the woman pressing down the cushion, grimacing with the effort.

I want to wake up! Jane shouted in a silent scream. Please, please, I don't want to dream this anymore.

And suddenly the woman flung the cushion to the floor and gathered the child up in her arms. She strode across the sitting room, to the lobby, and out through the door. Jane's legs freed themselves from paralysis and she stumbled down the stairs, across the room, out of the door. Outside the night air was freezing cold, the full moon making everything as clear as daylight, but bleached of colour to a uniform grey. Ahead of her, Jane saw the tall woman, the child's lolling head and dangling legs hanging from her arms, as she marched on up the path towards the cliff top, her posture almost mechanical in its slow, relentless strides. Jane followed, her bare feet in agony on the stony path. She stepped on the grass, not much better; it was hard with frost and sharp as glass.

STOP! Jane screamed. The woman was carrying the child towards the cliff edge. She couldn't see Jane, couldn't hear her. It was useless. *Please, let me wake up* Jane begged. This dream was unbearable now, and she was shivering violently in the bitter cold. Only a little way in front of her, the woman stood on the cliff's edge, not looking down, but straight ahead, the night breeze ruffling the child's fair hair. Jane shut her eyes, praying when she opened them, she would be back in the cottage, back in her warm bed. When she forced her eyes open, she was still on the cliff top, barefoot and in her night shirt. But the woman and the child had gone.

Jane gazed at the empty space where they had been, then out to the black sea with a shimmering silvery strip of the full moon's reflection leading to the far horizon. As a child, she'd loved the sight of moonlight on the sea, imagining herself running and skipping over the water on the shining pathway, which would take her to a better time, a better place. Now she felt only horror and despair.

'Oh, Emily. Now I know who you are,' she said to the frosty air. 'Now I know what happened to you.'

She walked to the edge of the cliff and looked down. It was high tide, the waves swirling and crashing over the rocks below. There was no sign of the woman and the child. She pictured their bodies being swept away in the undercurrent, far, far away and out into the open sea, the child gradually floating away from the embrace of her mother's arms, the two of them drifting apart forever.

Jane had no recollection of returning to the cottage or going back to the warmth and comfort of her bed. When she woke again it was eight thirty in the morning, and daylight.

Oh God, that dream, that terrible nightmare. She threw back the covers, put her feet on the bedside mat. She winced. The soles of her

183

feet felt sore, and she looked down to see blood streaks on the mat. Her toes, her soles, her heels were covered in little cuts and scratches.

And when she came out of the bedroom, on the landing there again were small, wet footprints.

'Nigel? Oh, thank heavens I've caught you.' Jane was on her phone, breathless. 'I had to tell you, I know what happened to Emily.'

Nigel sounded tired and still full of cold. 'Emily? Who's Emily?'

'The little girl. That's her name. Last night she showed me what happened. She was murdered, Nigel, murdered by her mother. Her mother took that cushion – that cushion Norman Bell sensed was choking him, remember? And she smothered her. Then she took her up to the cliff top in her arms and jumped off. That's what happened.'

'You saw this? How? Was it in a dream?'

'Yes. Well, no. I'm not sure. But it all makes sense now – the business with Norman Bell and the cushion. We laughed at him at the time, if you remember, but he could tell, he knew, something terrible had happened with it. And you remember, don't you, how someone or something took that cushion out of the house and threw it on the beach? Whoever or whatever did that knew what it had been used for.'

'Yes, but, Jane, what do you want me to do? We still have no idea who this Emily and her mother were, and even if we did find out there's not a lot we could do, is there?'

'I need to find Emily's father. I've been thinking it over and I'm sure from what I heard them say last night that Emily was somehow taken from her father's care, snatched against her will. There may be some way I can find out if she'd been reported missing. Or maybe he thinks his daughter and her mother have just moved away somewhere, doesn't realise she's been murdered. Either way, I think Emily wants me to know the truth so that I can tell her father.'

Nigel sighed wearily. 'Oh, I don't know, Jane. It was only a dream. I've had some pretty wild dreams in my time, too.'

Jane was disappointed. He clearly didn't want to help her. But she could at least ask him one thing. 'You may be right, maybe I did dream it, but could you do me one small favour? Could you contact Norman

Bell, ask him if he could come here again? Now that we know Emily's name, it might be easier for him to make contact with her. I feel so guilty we laughed at him last time. We should have believed him.'

'Well, all right. I can do that,' he said.

'Thanks. Oh, and, Nigel, sorry, I forgot to ask how you are. How's the cold?'

'On the way out, I think. It's been a stinker though, still feel a bit shabby. And all that business with poor Peggy hasn't helped. I rang the hospital to ask after her, but they said she'd asked for no information to be passed on and didn't want visitors.'

'So her sister informed me. Oh well, maybe she'll be home soon. It's funny, but now I know she's not a baby trafficker I quite miss her.'

When Jane rang off, she sat for a while, going over and over in her mind what she'd seen last night. Then she went to the living room. There was the red cushion on the sofa, looking just as usual. She picked it up, then quickly let it drop. It no longer felt cuddly or comforting. It was an object of horror and disgust. Holding it by one corner, she carried it to the kitchen, found a plastic bin liner under the sink, pushed the cushion in and tied a knot in the top. She went outside and flung it in the wheelie bin. It couldn't stay in the house. And even if it really had been used in a murder, any forensic evidence that might have been on it would have been destroyed when she washed it after finding it on the shore.

For the rest of the morning and early afternoon, Jane was on her laptop. She googled everything she could find about missing people. She scoured the information from the Police Missing Persons Unit. She could try contacting them but doubted they would pay much attention to something as vague as a dream. There were other sites, one listing bodies that had been found but not identified. It made sad reading, knowing there were so many nameless people who had nobody looking for them, nobody to care. But there was nothing, no accounts of bodies washed ashore to match the description of Emily and her mother. Other sites were run by charities, like Missing Kids

UK, but again, nothing. Most of the missing children listed were teenagers, and none were called Emily.

Was it really possible that this woman and her child had been swept out to sea, and nobody even knew they were missing?

Jane shut her eyes, trying to picture over and over again every detail of the dream – if that was what it was. Something was bugging her. Something about Emily's mother. But she just couldn't put her finger on it. If she could just find out their surname, that would help.

Late in the afternoon, she realised she hadn't eaten or had a drink all day. She went to the kitchen, filled the kettle, and looked up to see a car coming down the track. Peter was back. She hadn't made the bed, lit the fire, or got anything ready for their tea – she'd completely forgotten it was today he was coming home.

But now he was here. She waved from the window as he got out of the car and ran out to meet him as he took his case out of the boot. He dropped the case to enfold her in an embrace. They hugged and kissed. 'I've missed you,' he said.

'And I've missed you. I've got so much to tell you.'

'Have you got the kettle on? The coffee's great in the Netherlands, but you can't get a decent cup of tea.'

'Yes, I just put it on, your timing's perfect.'

Jane smiled. She could remember times in the early days of their marriage when Peter came home after being away, times when he'd hardly got through the door before they were pulling off each other's clothes, making love in the hallway, not able to wait to get to the bedroom. Now those days of passion and excitement had faded, and it was tea utmost on his mind. Oh well.

'Whose are the two cars parked outside?' Peter asked once settled in the kitchen with tea and digestive biscuits. 'I guess one of them must belong to Morticia's sister, but whose is the other one?'

'The red one is Beryl's. The white Suzuki is mine. I bought it last week – and don't worry Peter, I've not been raiding our joint account. I used my savings from Nan's will.'

'Well, you certainly have been busy while I've been away. What else have you been up to?'

Jane remembered Suzy's words. She must remember to focus on Peter sometimes, it wasn't all about her. 'Never mind about me, tell me about the conference. I want to hear everything.'

Peter reached out and took Jane's hand. 'Well, it was fantastic. My presentation went better than I could have hoped. I've met so many people, made so many contacts, learnt so much. My head's buzzing. I've already been asked to head a seminar in Boston next summer. Oh, and there's talk of a new science programme on Channel 4 I could be asked to take part in.'

She was longing to tell him about last night, but Peter was so full of the past few days in Utrecht, she let him talk while she prepared an omelette and salad supper. He looked like a changed man; vigorous, confident, and the dark shadows under his eyes and the deeply etched worry lines on his forehead seemed to have magically vanished.

'So,' he said at last, 'it's your turn to tell me the news. What did you do while Suzy was here, apart from buy a car? And how is poor old Morticia? Is she still in hospital?'

Jane gave him a rundown of Suzy's visit, told him about Mrs Mortimer's fall, Beryl's arrival, and finally, related the events and misunderstandings leading to the discovery of the fake babies.

Peter hooted with laughter. 'Good God. That's hilarious – and bizarre. Morticia playing with dolls. Who'd have thought it?

He was still chuckling while she was pouring him a coffee after the meal. Her phone rang. She picked it up from the kitchen worktop.

'Jane, it's Nigel. I've tried to get in touch with Norman Bell but apparently, he and his wife are in New Zealand visiting their son and won't be back until the New Year.'

'That's a pity,' she said, moving into the living room. She didn't want Peter to hear this conversation. 'I don't suppose you know any other mediums, do you?'

'Well, no, I don't really mix in those sort of circles. The only other medium I've ever met is Aunt Irene.'

'Of course. Your aunt. I'd like to meet her. Would that be possible, do you think?'

'Oh no Jane, not a good idea. She has dementia, I told you. And she's very old, very frail. Not long for this world we've been told.'

'Yes, I know, but sometimes they have moments of lucidity, don't they? I know it's a long shot, but she might be able to get through to Emily, give me something more to go on.'

'I very much doubt it. The last time I went to see her she just stared at the wall, said nothing. And when she's does talk, it's in gibberish. But if you really want to, I suppose—'

'Yes, please, I do want to,' Jane said. 'Thank you, Nigel. I've got to go now. Peter's back.'

'OK, I'll be in touch, and we'll arrange something.'

Jane turned to see Peter standing behind her.

'What's this are you setting up with Blackwood? Who's Emily? What's all this about mediums?' His tone was sharp, the buzzing, cheerful Peter had gone.

She remembered now how it felt, now he was home, having all her actions monitored, the cross-questioning, having to constantly justify herself. Although she'd missed Peter while he'd been away, she hadn't missed that. In fact, she'd relished the freedom she'd rediscovered, driving her own car, making her own decisions, taking charge of her own life, without having to answer to him all the time.

She sat down on the sofa. She knew how he would react, but she had to tell him.

'Last night,' she said, 'I saw a woman murder her own child. Here, on this sofa, where I'm sitting now.'

Sure enough, Peter closed his eyes, shook his head and sat down with a long, heavy sigh. 'Go on,' he said wearily.

So she told him everything. 'And so, you see, I know now what she wants me to do – find her daddy and tell him what happened to her, what her mother did.'

She'd expected Peter to be angry, but he just seemed suddenly incredibly tired and sad as he came over and put his arms around her.

'Look, I know it's been a horrible experience for you, seeing something like that, but you do know, don't you, it was just a vivid nightmare? That's all. You say you took two sleeping pills – they can sometimes have that side effect.'

'Then how do you explain this?' She kicked off her slippers and pointed at her bare feet, still scratched and bloodied from walking up the stony path to the cliff.

'Good grief. You poor darling. It's obvious, you were sleepwalking. Oh love, you could have sleepwalked over the cliff yourself. If only I'd been here – or Suzy – we could have stopped you, brought you safely back to bed.'

'Could you just this once, Peter, consider the possibility that what I saw was something that really happened here, in this house, sometime in the past?'

'OK, let's consider that. Say it happened years and years ago, what's the point of worrying about it now? Maybe when she was young, batty old Miss Blackwood had a child nobody knew about and did away with it? The child's father wouldn't even be alive anymore.'

'No, impossible. This didn't happen a long time ago. It happened recently. I saw them. Emily was wearing Minnie Mouse pyjamas and her mother was in modern clothes – jeans and a sweater – and the cottage looked much the same as it does now.'

'So, if it happened recently, why didn't anybody – your pal Nigel Blackwood, or Mrs Mortimer next door – wonder why the occupants of the cottage disappeared overnight? And didn't you say they'd left suitcases in here? That would have made them raise the alarm surely. If they'd just done a bunk, they wouldn't have left their luggage behind. Or their car, if that's how they arrived here. And another thing – it's very unusual for one body, let alone two, to get swept out to sea and never found. Sooner or later the tide would wash the bodies up on shore somewhere along the coast.'

Jane nodded. 'I suppose you must be right,' she said. What he said made sense – it had obviously been a dream. And yet...

'There were little footprints on the landing again, Peter. Like we saw before, remember? We never did work out an explanation for that, did we?'

Peter frowned. 'That was strange, I'll admit. But the more I think about it, the more I'm sure we were just mistaken. They could have been footprints – or more likely they were just smudges on the floorboards that happened to look like footprints.'

'I suppose so,' she said, although she was sure he was wrong.

'And you know, I thought of something else while I was away. Something you told me once that could explain everything.'

'Oh?'

'You told me about how your grandmother came to the rescue when you were living with your mother in Leeds. You said when you left, your mother clung to you and begged you not to leave.'

'So?'

'So those words, "don't leave" must have stuck somewhere in your subconscious mind. And you told me you had an invisible friend, and she became so real to you that when you were walking away with your grandmother you turned and thought you saw her looking out of the window.'

'Yes, I knew I didn't need her anymore. I could leave her behind.' Jane said.

'Well, I'm no psychoanalyst, but you don't have to be a genius to see how that could be manifesting itself now in your dreams and visions. Your imaginary friend come back, echoing your mother's words. They must have haunted you, those words, especially as your mother died so soon afterwards.'

'You mean I felt guilty? Maybe at the time, but not anymore, no. I was only a child. It wasn't my fault, her overdose. Nan made sure I understood all that, and I went over it all with the counsellor, came to terms with it.'

'Of course it wasn't your fault. I'm not suggesting that. It just seems a bit of a coincidence, that's all.'

'Well thanks for your insights, Doctor Freud.' Jane tried to keep her tone light-hearted, but his words had stirred up memories she didn't want to return to. That final visit hadn't been the only time Nan had come down. About once a year, she would turn up, sort out the mess in the house, tell Jane's mother to pull her socks up, and take Jane back to Durham for a few blissful days of good home-cooked food, clean clothes, love, and attention. And her mother always begged her to come back, swore she'd turned over a new leaf, welcomed her return with hugs and kisses and promises. But it never lasted. That final time she never went back, and soon after her mother was dead.

'Well, it's only a theory,' Peter said. 'Something for you to consider. Now, I'm pretty shattered. Let's go up to bed, shall we?'

Jane lay awake until the small hours, while Peter snored quietly beside her. She thought over what he had said. And the more she thought about it, the more sure she was that he was wrong; Emily was nothing like Judy, her imaginary childhood friend, and her mother's last words to her had no connection to Emily's pleas.

Once again, she went over in her mind the vivid details of what she'd witnessed downstairs and up on the cliff top. Emily's mother reminded her of someone she'd seen at some other time and place, but she just couldn't pin it down. Someone tall – she must have been at least six foot – with the same deep-set eyes, sharp features, the same brittle voice with an edge of hysteria to it.

This is going to drive me mad, she thought. I'm never going to remember. I may as well forget about it, like Peter says, try to get some sleep.

As soon as she turned over and settled her head into the pillow, she remembered.

CHAPTER 22

'I'm going into Alnwick, love, we need to do a supermarket shop. Want to come?' It was Saturday morning, and Peter was checking the fridge and the cupboards, seeing what they needed to buy.

'Do you mind if I don't?' Jane said. 'I've got a thumping headache. I think I need to go back to bed for a bit.'

She hadn't got a headache, but she did need to make a couple of phone calls without Peter hovering over her.

'Yes, you do that. I'm not surprised. You were tossing and turning in the night.'

'Was I? Sorry about that.'

Peter picked up his car keys and as soon as his car disappeared round the bend in the track, Jane was trawling through the contacts on her phone. She was looking for the name Nicola. When she'd been in hospital last July, Nicola was on the same ward, and they'd struck up a bit of a friendship, shared each other's stories at mealtimes and over coffee and group therapy sessions. Nicola was bipolar, and had been hospitalised after a suicide attempt, and like Jane, she'd experienced tragic loss. Her twin babies were stillborn. But with medication and therapy, she was turning the corner and she was discharged a couple of days before Jane. 'We must meet up some time,' she'd said to Jane, and scribbled down her phone number. Jane always meant to contact her, but somehow, once she was back home, she didn't really want to do anything that reminded her of being in the psychiatric ward.

'Nicola? Hi, it's Jane. Remember me, from St Nick's, four or five months ago, wasn't it?'

Nicola sounded pleased and surprised to hear from her. Jane told her a white lie that she'd mislaid her number, only just found it. They exchanged updates. Nicola said she was doing fine; the medication was keeping the lid on her depression, and they were thinking about trying for another baby. She sounded happy.

Jane said, 'Nicola, I'm staying in a cottage in Northumberland at the moment, but I'll be back in town before Christmas. We'll definitely have a get-together then. But listen, the other thing I rang you about – this may sound a bit weird – but I wonder if you remember that very tall woman who was on our ward? The one who never spoke to anyone?'

'Oh yes, she'd been sectioned, hadn't she? The rumour was she'd attacked her ex-husband with a carving knife.'

'That's her. Do you remember what her name was?'

'Something beginning with D, wasn't it? Dianne? Donna?'

'Deanna. Yes, that was it. Do you know what her surname was?'

'No, I'm afraid not. Why do you want to know?'

'Oh, it's just that I heard a bit of gossip, a rumour, that she'd disappeared, gone missing. She and her daughter, Emily, I think her name was.'

'I don't think that can be right. It's funny you should mention her, because I saw her quite recently.'

'When? Where? Did she have a little girl with her? Did you speak to her?'

Nicola was beginning to sound a bit wary. 'I saw her in Primark. It must have been about a week ago. From a distance. We didn't speak or anything. And I don't think she had anyone with her. I was a bit surprised they'd let her out, if it was true what she'd done. Jane, are you sure you're all right? Why is this so important?'

'Oh, no, it's just I was wondering – well, it really doesn't matter. I'll be in touch about that meet up. Bye, Nicola.'

Jane rang off. She felt like an idiot. Of course, Deanna wasn't Emily's mother. Deanna was walking around Newcastle, not floating in a watery grave somewhere out in the North Sea. And anyway, now she thought about it, Deanna had long blonde hair. The woman she'd seen suffocate her child had mousy brown hair, cut very short.

Next, she would ring Nigel. But just as she picked up her phone again, she heard the crunch of car tyres on the gravel. It was him. She waved and went out to speak to him. Was it her imagination, or did he look a bit apprehensive as she approached?

'Ah, morning, Jane. I was just going to pop in and speak to Beryl, see if she had any more news about Peggy Mortimer.'

'Oh, right? Could I have a quick word with you first?'

'Sure, I wanted to speak to you anyway,' he followed her into the house. He turned down her offer of coffee. 'I wanted to tell you I spoke to Hillfield House – that's the nursing home where Aunt Irene is – about a visit. They said that would be OK, but she's in failing health, very confused, bedridden and refusing to eat. They don't think she'll be with us for much longer. So yes, we should go and see her soon, but don't expect too much.'

'Oh dear. Well, that's all right, I'd still like to see her.'

Nigel nodded. He seemed in a hurry to go. Jane said, 'Before you go to Beryl's, can I just ask you something? How long ago did you say this cottage was refurbished?'

'Let me see now – it was at the end of the summer season last year, about September, October time. Why?'

'When I had that dream I told you about, the cottage looked just as it does now. The same pictures on the wall, the same furniture, the dark grey sofa.'

'Yes, that was bought brand new. Before that it was a battered old leather Chesterfield, with dark-brown velvet cushions. Very gloomy.'

'And the red cushion, that was definitely brand new as well?'

'That's right, I bought it same time as the new furniture. Look, Jane, what's this all leading up to?'

Jane was excited now. Why hadn't she thought of this before?

'It's obvious, Nigel. What I saw happening in this cottage—'

'In your dream?'

'Yes, if you like, in my dream, well, the cottage was just the same as it looks now. So that means Emily was murdered sometime between September last year and the time we arrived. Nigel, I need you to let me have a list of everyone who rented this cottage in that time, their addresses and phone numbers if possible.'

'Oh dear, sorry, I can't do that. It's out of the question. Data protection laws are very strict. I can't pass on any information like that.'

Jane was crestfallen. 'Are you sure you can't just bend the rules a bit? Just this once?'

'No, sorry. I could have a look in our records on your behalf, perhaps, see if anything fits. But I couldn't give you names or phone numbers.'

'That would be better than nothing, I suppose.' Jane's face lit up. She'd had an idea. 'I could narrow it down for you. I saw everything that happened on that cliff top so clearly because there was a big, bright full moon. I can look up the dates of the full moons over the past year and a bit, then all you'd have to do is check who was here on those dates.'

'If you like,' he said. Something had changed between them. The easy chat, the warmth of his smile had gone. Was she asking too many favours of him?

As he got up to go, she touched his arm. 'Nigel, is something wrong? You seem so tense. I'm being a massive nuisance, aren't I? Please tell me, and I won't bother you again, I promise.'

To her relief, he grinned. The old, twinkly smile. 'Yes, you're being a nuisance. But I don't mind. In fact, you can bother away as much as you like.' He leant forward and whispered in her ear. 'If only you knew how much I want to kiss you again. It's no wonder I look tense.' He winked, and left, heading for next door.

Not long after, Peter was back with the shopping. He thumped the bulging bags down on the worktop. 'Was that Mr Smarmy Pants' car I just passed on the track? What did he want?'

'If you mean Nigel Blackwood, yes it was. And he hadn't come to see me, he wanted to speak to Beryl about Mrs Mortimer.'

The atmosphere between them was strained all that weekend. Peter worked in his study upstairs, Jane spent hours on the internet, looking for information, any information that might help her search. Although Nicola had said she'd seen Deanna only recently, she could have been mistaken. It could have been someone who looked like her. Yes, the woman she saw with Emily didn't have Deanna's hair, but she could have changed it, had it cropped short and changed the colour. Without a surname she couldn't trace Deanna on any social media, so she searched local news sites for reports of a court case that might have arisen from the assault on her husband. But there was nothing. She wouldn't even try to contact the hospital; she knew they would never give out information about past patients.

On Sunday afternoon she told Peter she needed some fresh air and called in at the farm for a friendly chat with Mrs Armstrong, asked if she'd remembered any incidents of bodies washed up over the past year. 'There was one, I think. An old man who fell off the harbour wall at Craster, got washed up further down the coast. There have been a few shouts for the lifeboat, fishing boats in trouble, surfers and youngsters swept out on inflatables, walkers cut off by the tide, that sort of thing, but no drownings, thank goodness.'

Peter had taken Monday off to sort out stuff from the conference, so Jane drove to the village, reacquainted herself with the mouse lady in the post office. She told the same story. 'I hear plenty of rumours in here, hinny, and I always read the local paper cover to cover but can't remember anything about bodies getting washed ashore. A woman and child, you say? Tsk, I would've heard about something as tragic as that, I'm sure.'

She wandered round the overgrown churchyard, fighting her way through the waist-high brambles and nettles, reading the tombstones.

But the most recent graves there dated from the early nineteen fifties, and there was no Emily.

It all seemed hopeless, and puzzling. Now she must pin her hopes on Nigel coming up with some information about the occupants of the cottage. Either that or Miss Blackwood bringing a message from Emily from beyond the grave. When she got home, instead of going back inside, she went up on the windy cliff top, begged out loud for Emily to find a way to tell her what more she could do. There was no answer.

As she came home and neared the cottage, Beryl's braying voice called out, and she waddled over.

'Eee, I've just been chatting to your father. What a nice man,' she said.

'My father? I don't think so, Beryl. I don't even know who my father is.'

'Oops, have a put my foot in it?'

'No, it's an understandable mistake. Peter – my husband – he is twenty-four years older than me.'

'Oh, he's your husband? Well, I never. I just popped in to tell him they're letting Peggy come home on Wednesday, so I'll most likely be leaving then. I'll offer to stay a bit and look after Peggy, but I know what she'll say.'

'That's good news – about her coming home, I mean. She must be better.'

'I wouldn't know, dear. Peggy still won't let me visit and the hospital tell me nowt, apart from the fact she's being discharged.'

So, Mrs Mortimer was coming back. Once again, Jane felt a wave of sympathy for this woman, an unwanted child, unloved by her parents, abused and deserted by her husband, with only a cat and baby dolls to care about.

The day passed with little conversation between her and Peter, and when they did talk it was on a superficial level, what the weather was doing, what to have for supper. It was a relief when Tuesday came, and Peter was back at work. Jane had spent much of the previous evening researching the twelve full moon dates since September last year. She rang Nigel.

'I've done that list of dates,' she said. 'The full moons. Shall I email them to you?

'No, it's all right. Can you print them off and I'll pop down today and you can give them to me then?' That seemed a bit odd. Why come out of his way to visit when she could just send him the list? Maybe there was some reason he wanted to see her face to face.

When he arrived, he seemed edgy again, not his old, relaxed self. This time he accepted her offer of coffee, but wouldn't sit down, walking up and down by the window, gazing out at the autumn fret rolling in like smoke from the sea.

'I've spoken to Hillfield House again. We can go and see Irene tomorrow morning, if that suits you,' he said, still looking out of the window as if trying to avoid Jane's eye.

'Yes, great, suits me fine.'

'I should warn you though, they say she doesn't speak much to visitors anymore, although she does spend a lot of time having long conversations and arguments with an empty chair.'

'Who does she think she is talking to? Do they know?'

'Mrs Thatcher mostly, I think.' He laughed.

'Mrs Thatcher – as in Margaret Thatcher, the ex-Prime Minister?'

'Oh yes. She was Aunty Irene's arch-enemy, the devil incarnate, according to her. Granddad was a staunch Tory, but Irene went the other way. She was always a religious fanatic, but she became a fervent socialist too as she got older. During the miners' strike she was often down on the picket lines, waving a banner. That's when she wasn't standing on a soap box in the middle of town, either shouting about hell and damnation or denouncing the government.'

'She sounds like an interesting woman, your aunt.'

'Yes, but you know, she was never the same after the strike. I think it tipped her mind over the edge when it ended in failure. Poor old soul, she went from being an absent-minded eccentric to – well, you'll see tomorrow.'

Nigel put down his coffee mug and walked over to where Jane sat. He coughed nervously.

'What's the matter, Nigel? It seems like you want to say something.'

He sat down next to her, looking down at his hands. 'Yes. But can I just ask you a question first? A rather personal one? And please tell me to mind my own business if you want, I'll understand.'

'Go on.'

'How are things between you and the Prof? Your marriage, I mean? From what you've told me, it hasn't been too good.'

'No, it hasn't. We've had our ups and downs. Mostly downs, to be honest. Especially since we lost Angela, and now everything that's happened since we came here. Getting my own car made me realise how much I'd been depending on him, how suffocating and controlling he can be. Sometimes he feels more like my father than my husband. He can be very kind and loving too, of course, but...' Her voice trailed off. She didn't know what else to say, or where this conversation was leading. She didn't want to tell him about their sporadic sex life, the lack of intimacy they once shared.

'OK, so I'll just say this, and then, no pressure, you needn't say anything. I'll leave it with you to think about. If you do ever decide your marriage is over, remember I'm here for you. I've tried to fight these feelings I have for you, but I can't. That's all I've got to say.'

He got up abruptly, picked up the list of dates Jane had printed out for him, and headed for the door. Jane followed him, her mind in turmoil. 'Nigel, wait—'

'I'll pick you up tomorrow,' he said, just before he stepped into his car. 'We'll go in my car. It's right out in the middle of nowhere, the nursing home.'

And then he was gone. She stood for a long while at the door, looking out over the field with its yellowing clumps of rough grass and thistles. 'Did that just happen? Is Nigel Blackwood really in love with me?' Her heart banged in her chest; her stomach was churning. She wondered how it was possible to feel excited and elated but terrified and confused at the same time. This could change everything.

****

Mrs Mortimer sat up in her hospital bed, looking at the tray in front of her and the congealing brown mess of lumps that was supposed to be vegetable soup. Only one more day of this to endure before she could be home, back with Whisky, and the sound of the sea that had lulled her to sleep for over forty years and become part of her, like breathing in and breathing out. It was impossible to sleep in this place, with all the snoring and coughing and moaning that went on.

She'd said no to the chemotherapy. Why would she want to prolong things, keep having to come back here, suffer all those unpleasant side-effects and lose her hair into the bargain? Absolutely not. She'd been in control of her own life since Eric departed, and that's the way it would continue, right to the end.

They couldn't tell her exactly when that end would be. 'We can't predict that I'm afraid,' the oncologist had told her at that morning's meeting. 'We could be looking at a matter of weeks, or, especially if we opt for chemotherapy, as long as two years.'

She knew it wasn't going to be good news when they asked if she wanted anyone with her at the consultation. She didn't, of course. She'd been wheeled to a side room, and the nurse stayed with her. The nurse was overweight, Mrs Mortimer observed, like a lot of the nurses seemed to be, their great bosoms and bottoms straining against the material of the shapeless blue tunic tops and trousers they had now, not like the smart uniforms they used to wear, with starched white aprons and caps, looking trim and neat, like proper nurses.

The specialist was speaking to her in that gentle, quiet way. She could see his lips moving but the words floated over her head. That didn't matter because she could pick out a few words and phrases that told her all she needed to know:

'Sorry to have to tell you…stage four. …metastasis…extensive secondary tumours…inoperable…spread to the liver…palliative care…making you comfortable…'

The nurse went to put her arm round her shoulders but stopped when she flinched away. 'Is there anyone we can call for you, Peggy?'

That was another thing she didn't care for. She liked to be addressed as Mrs Mortimer, even by people she knew. Only Beryl called her Peggy.

'No thank you,' she said. And no, she didn't have any questions.

It was all right. She could accept it. And strangely enough, the morphine and anti-sickness drugs they'd given her made her feel better than she had for a long time. The floaty wrapped-in-warmth feeling the morphine gave her was a sensation she imagined was something like what people described as happiness. She really didn't care about anything much at all, even dying.

All she wanted to do now was get home. There were a number of important things she needed to sort out there before she left it all behind.

CHAPTER 23

Hillfield Nursing Home was an ivy-covered Victorian house at the end of a long driveway surrounded by trees. It stood among the foothills of the Cheviots, near Wooler, overlooking a sweep of fields and moorland.

'We were really lucky to get her in here,' Nigel said as they drove up to the imposing entrance. 'It's a beautiful place, and the care's been brilliant. It's very unusual for someone with her condition to live so long. Mind, it's not cheap, but Granddad saw to it she was left well provided for.'

Inside the wood-panelled hall they were met by a smiling member of staff. The tag she wore pinned to her tunic told them she was Alison Fairbairn, assistant manager.

'Ah yes, Mr Blackwood and friend. You've come to see Irene. I'll take you along. She's hasn't been very well lately, I'm afraid. Although, this morning she's been quite lively, chatting away to one of her invisible visitors, laughing her head off.'

'Not Mrs Thatcher this time then?' Nigel said.

'Ha, no, we know when it's Mrs T by the angry shouting.'

They followed Alison down a long thickly carpeted corridor. The place was stuffily overheated and smelt of lavender furniture polish and disinfectant. From behind the closed doors, came the occasional shouts and wails of the demented. For all the quietly comfortable surroundings, Jane imagined that if there was such a thing as Hell, this must be what the entrance was like, far too hot and filled with lost souls whose cries went unnoticed. As they turned a corner, an elderly man shuffled towards them, mumbling and cursing, smartly dressed in a shirt, jacket and tie, but completely naked below the waist.

'Geoffrey, go and put your trousers on sweetheart.' Alison steered him gently back in the direction of his room.

At the end of the corridor, she pushed open a door. They could hear someone chattering away inside in a sing-song quavery voice.

'Yes, yes, let's play on the beach after tea. We can look for crabs in the rock pools. Come on, John, hold my hand, good boy.'

'Irene, visitors for you,' Alison said, adding in a whisper to Nigel and Jane, 'She probably won't talk to you.'

Irene Blackwood had once been an imposing woman, Jane could tell. But now the old lady's flesh was shrunken away, leaving only a bent and skeletal frame. She lay propped up on pillows in her bed facing the tall sash window. Her gaunt face, with its prominent sharp nose and thin purple lips, did not turn to acknowledge their entrance. She was staring steadfastly at the empty armchair at the end of the bed.

'I've told you, Jennifer, that's my tuck box. If you touch it again, I'll tell Matron. Oh, what a beastly thing to say. Go away, you're mean. I'm not your best friend anymore.' Her voice had become surprisingly loud and strident coming from such a feeble body.

'She thinks she's back in boarding school,' Nigel whispered to Jane. He bent over the bed, took her claw-like hand. 'Hello, Aunty, it's me, Nigel. And this is my friend Jane, come to see you."

She frowned, turned to look at him. Her eyes were like two jet black stones, sunken and red-rimmed, but surprisingly bright.

'Daddy, have you come to take me home? Is it the hols now?'

'No, Irene, I'm Nigel, your brother John's son. You remember John? I think you were talking to him just before we came in, weren't you?'

No response. Jane could see this was not going to be easy, but the least she could do was try. She sat on the chair beside the bed. Nigel stayed standing. She leant towards the old woman.

'Miss Blackwood, I'm Jane. What a lovely view you've got from your window, right over the garden. Look at those dahlias, such bright colours.'

'Nice flowers,' she said, smiling and nodding.

'Wow,' Nigel said. 'She must like you, Jane. That's the first sensible response I've heard her make in years.'

Jane was just as surprised. Irene was now studying her intently with those piercing black eyes, a puzzled frown on her face.

'Miss Blackwood, I'm living in the house where you used to live. Two Chimneys. So close to the sea. Next door to Mrs Mortimer. Do you remember her, Peggy Mortimer, with all the cats?' The eyes were still fixed on Jane, but she didn't respond. Jane pressed on. 'I know you can see and speak to people in the spirit world, is that right?'

The old woman suddenly grabbed Jane's hand. 'Is she dead?' she barked.

'Is who dead? Do you mean Mrs Mortimer? No, she's not.'

'No, no, Margaret Thatcher. Is she dead?'

'Yes, she is, she died some years ago,' Jane said.

'Of course, she is. She was here again today. I told her she was wrong, what she did. But she wouldn't have it. Stubborn woman.'

'Miss Blackwood,' Jane persisted. 'Can you help me? I need to speak to a child in the spirit world. A little girl called Emily. I believe she was murdered, in the house where you used to live.'

The old woman let Jane's hand go and sunk back against her pillows, her eyes closed. She appeared to have fallen asleep. Jane and Nigel exchanged anxious glances.

'Aunty? Are you all right? Aunty?' Nigel shook her shoulder gently.

Irene Blackwood's eyes snapped open, fixing on Jane again.

'Oh yes, murdered. I remember. She killed them, you know,' she said.

Jane jolted upright in her chair. She clasped Irene's hands. 'Who was she, Miss Blackwood? Who did she kill? Please, tell us, who did she kill? Who are you talking about?'

Irene pulled her hands away, scowling. After a maddeningly long pause, she turned her gaze back to Jane. 'That woman. Margaret Thatcher. She finished them off, the mines. Killed them, destroyed them all. Not one left.'

Nigel shot Jane a 'what did I tell you?' look. There was another long pause. The old woman was plucking at her bed covers in an agitated fashion.

'It was a terrible thing, terrible. I tried my best, I did what I could to help, you know,' Irene said, a look of infinite sadness crossing her sunken face.

'Aye, I know you did Aunty,' Nigel said gently. 'You were down on the picket line at Ellington, weren't you, handing round all those sandwiches you made, and raising money for the welfare fund? You did your bit.'

More silence. Jane wondered how she could steer the conversation back to Emily but was already realising it would be a fruitless exercise.

Irene spoke again. 'It was very hard work, digging away down into the earth in the dark. It was horrible, dirty.' She shuddered.

'It was, Aunty,' Nigel said. 'A miner's life was tough, that's for sure. Probably a good thing it's in the past.'

Irene Blackwood's eyes had closed and her head, with its cobwebby strands of white hair, had dropped to her chest.

'I think she's asleep,' Nigel whispered to Jane. 'Perhaps now might be a good moment to make our exit. I think we've got as far as we're ever going to get.'

Jane nodded sadly and started to rise from her chair. And at that moment, the old woman's eyes snapped open, and her hand shot out and grabbed Jane's arm. Her nails dug into her wrist, and she pulled Jane towards her, so their faces were almost touching each other. The black eyes bored into Jane's.

'Who did you say you are?' she rasped.

'I'm Jane. Jane Eagle. I'm staying in your old house.'

A bony finger poked hard in Jane's shoulder. 'You – you have the gift,' she said. 'I can tell. You can see them, can't you? It's a rare thing, the gift. I have it too. Yes, you have the gift. You must use it for good, not evil. Renounce the devil and all his works, the vain pomp and glory of this world and the carnal desires of the flesh…' Her voice trailed off and she released Jane's arm and turned away, staring steadfastly at the chair at the foot of the bed. 'Yes, what do you want?' she snapped, addressing the empty chair. She nodded, seemingly listening to the words of the invisible visitor. 'I see, yes, yes, I will tell her.'

'Is it her? Is it Emily?' Jane leant forward expectantly.

Irene Blackwood turned her head to Jane, wagging her forefinger towards the empty chair. 'That woman there in the blue coat says to tell you everything will be all right. She says you must pull your socks up, leave the past behind, and look to the future. "Look to the future, Flower", she says, "and everything will be all right." '

'That's Nan.' Jane gasped, jumping to her feet. 'Oh, Nigel, she called me Flower – that's what Nan called me. She always called me Flower.' She sat down heavily, too shocked to say more.

The old woman looked exhausted now. She flopped back against the pillows, her eyes closed, her head dropping down. There was so much more Jane wanted to ask her, but Nigel said, 'Come on, I think she's had enough. She's said more to us today than she's said the last dozen times I've visited, and some of it even made sense.' He bent to kiss his aunt's cheek. 'See you again soon, Aunty,' he said.

Miss Blackwood didn't open her eyes, but as they left, they heard her mumble, 'Bye bye, Daddy. Bye bye, Mummy.'

As they drove back, Nigel said; 'Sorry, that wasn't exactly what you wanted, was it?'

'Well, not as far as getting through to Emily, no. But maybe I could call on her again?'

'No, Jane.' Nigel's tone was sharp. 'Poor old Irene. She needs to be left in peace now. Believe it or not, that was a good day. When she was talking about the hard life of the miners, that was almost a proper conversation we had there for a while. I'm amazed.'

'Sorry, I was being insensitive. Thank you for bringing me anyway. It was disappointing about Emily, but hearing Nan talking to me through Irene was wonderful. I feel like Nan's here with me, looking out for me.'

'She must have loved you a lot, your nan,' Nigel said.

'She did. I was all she had. She was widowed young. Oh, she was quite strict, a bit old-fashioned. But she was the wisest, kindest person in the world. And she helped me understand about my mother too, made me see that my mother really did love me. Although unfortunately in the end she loved the booze more. Nan helped me come to terms with that and move on.'

They were quiet for a while. Jane could tell Nigel was plucking up the courage to say something. As they neared the turn off to the cottage, he said, 'So, have you thought about what I said the other day? About your marriage, about my feelings for you?'

'I have – a bit.' Jane felt her cheeks flush. 'I'll admit I've tried to push it to the back of my mind. I need more time, Nigel. It's a big decision to make, whether to end my marriage. And to be honest, I've been concentrating on finding out more about Emily.'

'I understand,' he said as they pulled up outside the house. 'The last thing you need is any more pressure from me. Anyway, I've got that information you wanted about the people staying here on that list of dates you gave me. I can go through them now if you like.'

'Wonderful. Yes, come in, and I'll put the kettle on.'

Beryl's car was parked on the gravel outside Mrs Mortimer's door. 'Peggy must be home from hospital already,' Nigel said. 'And that reminds me, I've got some flowers for her in the boot. I'll just leave them on her doorstep. Don't want to disturb her if she's settling back in.'

Nigel had bought a huge bouquet of red and gold autumn blooms that almost obscured his face as he carried them to the doorstep. Jane watched him as he laid them carefully on the step. She felt a tender, almost painful, sensation in her heart. But was it love?

****

Whisky was pleased she was home. Like most cats, he was largely indifferent to human comings and goings, but he had missed her, she was sure of that. As soon as she'd got settled in her chair, he leapt into her lap, purring loudly and rubbing his head against her hand.

Beryl, as usual, was prattling away, fussing about getting the heating on, sorting out the supplies she'd bought to stock up the fridge and freezer. 'You'll be all right for the next week or two, Peg. Now, how about some tea, eh? A decent cuppa, not that stewed hospital brew.'

Peggy Mortimer wished her sister would go away. She was home now. She just wanted to be left alone. She hadn't even wanted Beryl to collect her from hospital. She'd much rather it had been an ambulance or a taxi, but Beryl insisted. And on the way back she'd been cross-questioning her. What exactly had the doctors said? Was she quite better now? Was it a malignant tumour they'd taken out? Did they manage to get it all? Peggy had said nothing, but Beryl wouldn't stop badgering her for information, and in the end, Peggy had snapped,

'I'm champion, Beryl man. There's nowt wrong with me, so stop asking.'

As she made the tea, Beryl saw Nigel Blackwood's car draw up.

'Oooh, Peg, it's Mr Blackwood come to see you. Oh, and he's got Jane from next door with him.'

'Huh, so that's still going on, is it?' Peggy muttered. 'I don't want to speak to them, Beryl. If they knock, tell them I'm resting.'

'Don't worry, looks like they're going into hers. But I think he's left something at the door. I'll go and look.'

Beryl came back in with her arms full of flowers. 'Look, Peg, aren't they lovely? What a kind thought.' She ripped open the little envelope addressed to Mrs Mortimer. 'It says, With best wishes for a speedy recovery, Nigel Blackwood. Ah, isn't that nice. Where do you keep your vases? I'll arrange them for you. shall I?'

Peggy never cared much for flowers, especially not cut ones. You had all the bother of finding the right vase for them, and trimming the stems, and in a few days the water was slimy and stinking, and the flowers were dying and dropping their messy petals all over the place.

'No, just leave them. I'll see to them later. And don't bother with the tea,' she said. 'I shall be perfectly all right now. You don't have to stay any longer.'

Once Beryl had gone, and if the operation stitches weren't too painful, she would take the flowers up to the field and dump them.

CHAPTER 24

Nigel had his laptop propped open on the coffee table and sat down next to Jane. His closeness, the subtle scent of his aftershave, were starting to stir her senses so she had to force herself to ignore the messages her body was giving her, the hot ache inside, even though all she wanted to do at that moment was reach over and hold him. But no, she must concentrate, keep her mind on the matter in hand. This was important. This could be the vital clue to finding out about Emily.

'Right. Here's what we've got,' Nigel said, brisk and business-like. 'We completed the refurbishment of the house during the last week of September last year. The first tenants in after that were here for two weeks including the full moon date. David and Simon, they've been before. Nice fellas. David writes books, Simon's a birder, so they love it here. That takes us to the next date on your list, in October. A women's group had it for four days for some sort of training event, four of them stayed overnight, the others just came in the daytime. I called in for a chat. No kids with them.'

'You've just got initials next to the dates, Nigel. How can you remember who they are?'

'I told you. Data protection. Mrs Mortimer has the full name and contact details of whoever made the booking on her computer, and we hold the same information at the office, but you know I can't show you that. We don't keep a record of who the additional occupants were. But I can remember just about everyone, at least the recent ones, because Mrs M, bless her, always gives me a rundown on them when I call her to check and see if everything is all right.'

'Oh dear, what did she say about us?'

'She said you'd be no trouble. She got that wrong, didn't she?' He grinned, giving Jane a playful nudge. 'Anyhow, let's press on, shall we? November, GD. Oh yes, I remember Gemma, she was a lady in her forties, I'd say. Getting married again, stayed here with three of her pals for a hen weekend. Mrs Mortimer said they were a noisy lot, drinking and shouting and laughing till the early hours. Several bag loads of empty bottles she had to clear out, tab ends all over the place even though we ask people not to smoke indoors. Definitely no kids with them. December, another rowdy crew, a couple with two teenage boys were in here for Christmas. Apparently, a whole gang of their family and mates descended for a massive party. Mrs M was not amused. They left the place in a right state too. We had to replace a ruined mattress, a broken door and more than a few smashed glasses. Charged them for it of course.'

'What about January? There's no initials next to that full moon date.'

'No, there was nobody in. January's usually a quiet month, after new year. And it gives Mrs M a chance to give the place a good clean-through, and us to organise any repairs and replacements and things like that.'

'Would it have been remotely possible for anyone to get in while it's empty?'

'What, you mean like a squatter? Not a chance. Mrs M watches the place like a hawk. That's why it's so good having someone like her here all the time. We've got security alarms on most of our other properties, but we don't need them here. Which now brings us to February. We'd had no bookings, so that's the date when I let Laura and Sarah have a long weekend here for a bit of a break.'

'Laura and Sarah?'

'My ex-wife and her partner. Laura did have our two youngest with her, but they're both lads and, not surprisingly, neither are called Emily.'

'What about Sarah? Does she have children?'

'No, and what's more, she is very much alive and well, as is Laura. At least, they were when I called on them and the kids last week. OK, so that brings us to March. A couple running a yoga and aromatherapy workshop. They didn't stay the night, just had it for the day. No kids. The cottage smelt beautiful after they'd left, mind. April, oh, David and Simon again. They just can't keep away. Then in May, quite an elderly German Herr and Frau, touring the north-east, just the two of them. Lovely people.'

'I'm not too interested in the summer months. When I saw the murder happen, Nigel, there was a sharp frost, and it was bitterly cold. I know that can sometimes happen in June, but it's quite unusual.'

'Right, well anyway, June and July were the American couple I told you about, the ones that come every summer, and August a group of four astronomers had it for a bit of star gazing, all fellas. September, this was the last date before you and the Prof arrived. A couple and their daughter. The daughter was in her early twenties, not a child, had quite severe learning disabilities, so they needed somewhere quiet and out of the way for her.'

'And then it was us.'

'And then it was you.' He shut his laptop. 'And my life was never the same.'

'Nor mine,' she said. 'Oh well, I suppose that's it then. The end of the line. Unless…'

'Unless what?'

'Unless I've got it wrong. The cottage looked just as it looks now when I saw the murder happen, the same sofa, the same decor. And the red cushion. But maybe the events I saw happened some time before that, two or three years back, even longer. What if the vision I had just showed me Emily and the woman, their actions, but the background and surroundings were as they are in the present?'

212

Nigel squeezed his eyes shut, rubbed the bridge of his nose between thumb and forefinger. 'Can I be honest with you? I think you should let it lie now. I really can't go back over all the past ten years' worth of bookings. We've deleted all our records from before that. I haven't got the time to spare, and anyway, I'm not sure the results would be that different. Obviously, I can't remember every single tenant that's ever stayed here, but of the ones I met and can recall I don't think there was anyone matching your description. A tall woman with cropped hair and a blonde-haired child of about seven, I think you said? It doesn't ring any bells at all I'm afraid. We could ask Mrs Mortimer, I suppose…'

'No, it's all right.' Jane sighed. A sense of the hopelessness of it all swept over her. 'Thanks anyway. I need to think about all this now, sort it out in my head.'

He stood, gathering up his laptop and car keys. 'And – that other thing we talked about? You'll think about that too?'

She nodded. 'Yes, I will.'

She watched him get into his car, start the engine, drive off, only for him to reverse to allow another car coming down the track to pass. It was Peter. He was home early.

Jane's heart sank. She knew the interrogation that was coming, and she wasn't wrong.

He didn't seem angry when he came in, just stony-faced and somehow older and more hunched than usual. 'I trust you've had a pleasant day with Mr Blackwood,' he said, addressing her back as she rinsed out coffee mugs in the sink.

Jane turned to face him. It was time to set the record straight – not about her feelings for Nigel or his for her but assuring him of the true fact they'd never been lovers. 'Peter, whatever you think is going on between Nigel and me, you're wrong. We've become friends, yes, but that's all. He took me to see his aunt in her nursing home. I was hoping she would give me a message from Emily, now that I know her name.'

'And did she?'

'Sadly, no, but – oh, Peter – she gave me a message from Nan. I know it was really her, she said she was wearing her blue coat, and she called me Flower, and told me to pull my socks up. She said I must put the past behind me and look to the future.'

'Well, whether it came from beyond the grave or not, that was a very sensible piece of advice. Isn't that what I've been telling you all along? We can't turn back the clock, change the past, whether it's losing Angela or that child murder you say you saw, if it really did happen. We've just got to put it behind us and focus on what lies ahead.'

Jane nodded. She knew he was right, but how could she push those memories out of her mind? They were there when she woke up every morning, and the last thing she thought of before sleep. Memories of Angela. Memories of the cushion pressing down, and the lifeless child carried up to the cliff top. Memories of Nigel's lips on hers, his arms enfolding her. They all swirled together in a powerful brew of torment and confusion.

She made cheese on toast, and Peter lit the log burner. The darkness was coming on earlier and earlier as the year drew towards its final month. They sat in silence. Jane reached for the remote to turn on the TV, but Peter said, 'Hang on a minute. There's something I want to talk to you about.'

'I've already told you, Nigel and me—'

'No, it's not about him. It's about us. I got a call from Dr Tan today. They've bought a house in Darras Hall. They want to move in there straight away, so they'll be leaving the flat earlier than expected. So if we want, we can go back to our own place next week.'

'As soon as that? But we've paid the rent till the seventeenth.'

'Yes, but look.' He swept his arm towards the window and the blackness outside. 'Winter's coming. Nothing but cold, darkness, and gloom. And I'm getting sick of the drive to town and back here every night. The traffic crawling up the A1. The filthy weather. I think it's what you need too, darling. You need to be back among people, bright lights, friends, places to go, city life. I thought peace and quiet was what you needed, but I was wrong. Let's go back.'

Yet another decision to make. At that moment Jane just wanted to crawl into bed, pull the covers over her head and escape into sleep. But Peter was looking at her expectantly. 'Jane? What do you think?'

'I'm not sure I can leave. That's the one thing Emily doesn't want me to do. I need a little longer, I need to speak to Miss Blackwood again, see if she can—'

'No.' Peter jumped to his feet, knocking his half-eaten plate of cheese on toast to the floor. 'I'm done with tiptoeing round this, trying not to upset you. For the last time, Emily doesn't exist. She never did. Staying here, look what it's done to you – this non-existent spook kid scaring you witless.'

Jane shouted back, 'But she doesn't scare me, not anymore. She's only a little girl, a sad, frightened little girl. She can't hurt me. She only wants me to help, but I don't know why, and I don't know how.'

Peter sat down heavily on the chair opposite. 'OK, have it your own way. You're your own woman. I can't make you do anything against your will. But I'm telling you this, Jane. I'm packing up my things and I'm leaving here next week to go back to town, with or without you. You can stay here chasing ghosts with lover boy Blackwood if you like.'

So that's it, Jane thought. This wasn't just about Emily, it was about him getting her away from Nigel, back where he could keep an eye on her.

'So, let me get this straight,' she said quietly. 'Are you asking me to choose between helping Emily and our marriage?'

'If you want to put it that way, yes. Yes, I am. Us, our marriage, or this so-called ghost. Now I've got some work to do. I'll be sleeping in my work room tonight.'

He stomped upstairs.

****

Them next door had been shouting again last night. She heard them through the wall. But Mrs Mortimer wasn't bothered about that. They wouldn't be here much longer, and thanks to the morphine, she really didn't care what they were up to anymore. She had fallen asleep listening to the familiar ebb and flow of the sea and slept soundly. She was warm and for the moment pain-free and Whisky was curled up on the end of the bed, purring.

It was seven o'clock and still dark when she got up and went into the kitchen, Whisky padding after her. Out of the window she saw Mr Eagle getting in his car, setting off for work. She could have gone back to bed, rested some more, but there were things she had to do, and the sooner she got them over with, the better.

For a start, she was going to put the bairns up for sale on eBay, Arabella, Lily, Aidan, and Serena. And all their lovely clothes, their cots, and the pram. It was sad, and she would miss them, but she didn't want Beryl getting her hands on them after she'd gone. They were her bairns, and she'd rather they went to a stranger than have her sister touching them, dressing them, holding them. She'd kept the boxes they arrived in, so it would be an easy job packing them all up again, and she'd ring the farm, ask one of the Armstrong lads to pick up the packages and take them to the post office for her.

Then there was her will to check over. She'd made it some time ago. There wasn't much to leave, but she had a bit put by. Although they'd always made it all too obvious they favoured Beryl over her, her parents had been fair when it came to treating both their daughters equally in their will, and she'd kept it in a secret account where Eric couldn't touch it. Peggy Mortimer had long ago decided that all her assets would go to the Cats Protection charity. She wasn't having a penny going to Beryl, whose late husband had left her very well off, and certainly not to those two lazy slob nephews.

She didn't want a funeral. And anyway, who would come? Beryl, perhaps, and maybe Mr Blackwood. So, no fuss, no hymns and prayers, no eulogies. Just a cremation and her ashes scattered in the sea.

But then there was Whisky. What would become of him? She didn't think Blackwood's would put a new caretaker in her house; they would want to turn it into another holiday let, another money-spinner. This had always been Whisky's home. He would hate to be anywhere else.

So, she would write a note and add it to her will. On her death, she wanted Whisky humanely put to sleep, cremated, and his ashes scattered in the sea with hers to join all those poor little kittens Eric had murdered. She didn't trust Beryl to follow her wishes, so she would address the note to Mr Blackwood. He had gone down in her estimation, carrying on with Her Next Door, but despite that he was still a good man, as men go.

Once that was out of the way, she'd think about writing that other letter. The one she really didn't want to write but knew she must.

CHAPTER 25

'I'm so sorry, Irene isn't having any visitors at the moment.' Alison Fairbairn was talking to Jane in the hallway of Hillfield House. 'I'm afraid she's deteriorated in the last few hours, and she's sleeping most of the time now. I don't think she has very much longer, so we're keeping her quiet and comfortable.'

This was it then, her last attempt at finding an answer slipping away from her. Jane had jumped in her car that morning and headed for the nursing home, despite what Nigel had said about leaving her in peace. Now she realised she should have rung first and saved herself the trip.

Goodbye, Miss Blackwood, she thought. Give Nan and Angela a hug from me when you get to the other side. If there is another side.

Now the whole day stretched ahead of her, cold, damp and grey. She didn't want to go back to the cottage. She had a lot of thinking to do.

She drove round aimlessly for a while. The early morning drizzle had eased off, so she headed north. She parked the car at Bamburgh, under the shadow of the brooding castle, and started to walk over the dunes back towards Seahouses. A feeble late autumn sun emerged from behind the clouds. She found a high hollowed out spot among the spiky marram grass and sat down, hugging her coat round her, gazing out to sea.

Miss Blackwood was dying and could tell her no more. There was no trace of anyone matching Emily and her mother, either having stayed at the cottage or their bodies being found. No record that she could find of them being reported missing either. It seemed like the end of the road. And gradually, a realisation dawned: there was only one conclusion. Peter was right. Emily did not exist. The little girl, her mother, the murder – none of it was real.

Her thoughts went back to the meeting she and Peter had with the consultant psychiatrist last summer at the hospital. He'd spent a long time explaining about the schizophrenia diagnosis, drawing little spidery diagrams of the brain, talking about delusions and hallucinations, neurotransmitters and synapses. She wasn't really listening to any of it, because she was looking at the picture of the doctor with his wife and children on the shelf near his desk. The little girl on his knee in the photograph looked a bit like Angela. But Peter was hanging on his every word, bombarding him with questions, and soon the doctor was addressing everything he said to Peter, and Jane just looked out of the window at the birds swooping across a blue summer sky. Only one thing she remembered clearly from that meeting was the consultant saying, 'Your brain is basically just a three-pound blob sitting inside your skull, but it's the most complex organ in the body. It controls everything, every voluntary and involuntary move you make, all the sensory impressions you receive, all the emotions you feel. So, it's not surprising that sometimes the electrochemical balance goes out of kilter.'

Now the penny finally dropped with a sickening clunk, and she realised that the faulty wiring, the misfiring neurons and synapses in her three-pound blob had created Emily and the whole scenario. Made them seem real. It was the blob had made her sleepwalk and write the message on the sketch pad and in the sand, and probably throw the cushion into the sea. But what about the message from Nan? That was real, wasn't it? Miss Blackwood had told her she had the gift, but maybe it wasn't a gift, or a curse come to that. It was just the blob that was her broken, messed-up brain.

And then there was Nigel. Jane stared out at the pearly grey sea, searching for an answer. Nigel had come along at a time when she'd really needed him. He was understanding, kind. He made her feel like an attractive, desirable woman again, and there was no doubt the physical attraction between them was a powerful thing. She loved the way he treated her as an equal, never made her feel like a fragile, dependent child as Peter so often did. But did she really know him? They'd only met a few weeks ago. She and Peter had been together for over eight years.

Nigel understood her emotions over the death of Angela. That was true. But Peter had shared them, been through the same grief. Angela was his child too, but Jane hadn't really considered that before. She thought back to Suzy's words, how Peter hadn't been able to grieve over Angela because he was too focused on supporting her. It was true, she'd been trapped in her own little bubble of anger and sadness when she should have let Peter in, should have let them grieve together, support each other.

Until recently, she'd gone over and over that terrible night they lost Angela so many times in her mind, and only in the last few weeks had been able to bury it away to a place deep inside, where it would always remain. But she no longer felt the need to keep re-visiting those agonising memories. Until now.

She got to her feet, wrapping her coat firmly round her against the sea breeze, and as she marched on over the soft sand of the dunes she was there again with Peter, holding his hand as they sat side by side in the poky waiting room in A&E while across the corridor the doctors were crowded round their precious daughter, fighting to save her. She could picture the red plastic chairs, the rain crawling down the windowpane, the bright strip light above and the dark night outside, the coffee machine with its stack of polystyrene cups. She breathed in again the hot stuffy hospital smell and felt the fear and panic move in her stomach.

'Peter, I'm going to be sick.' And hurtling through the swing doors and down the corridor to the toilets. And after she'd thrown up, she splashed her face with cold water, and instead of going back to A&E went outside and stood on the hospital steps in the rain, staring up at the night sky and prayed to a God she didn't really believe in, but might, just might, be there. 'Dear God, please, please, please let her be all right.'

And when she came back to the ward, there was one of the doctors talking quietly to Peter in the corridor. The doctor hadn't seen Jane approaching and as he walked away, Peter slumped back against the wall and she saw his knees give way as he slithered down to the floor, crouching in a ball with his head in his hands, his shoulders heaving. He was crying, and that could only mean one thing. But instead of going to him, holding him, so they could cry together, she walked past him, ignored him, running after the doctor, calling out to him 'What's happened?'

She remembered feeling angry with Peter. He should be the one to tell her the unbearable news, so why was he huddled there on the floor? How could he fall apart, let her down, when she needed him to be her strong, firm rock, holding her up as this tsunami of grief swept over her?

But of course, the tidal wave had come crashing down just as hard on him. How could she have been so selfish, so blind? And was it too late now to tell him she was sorry?

She walked on, up and down the sand dunes, going over and over everything about her life with Peter, remembering the moment she first saw him, striding across the campus with a wodge of books and papers under his arm. As soon as she saw him she thought, *It's him, it's Mr Rochester. Jane Eyre* was her favourite book of all time; one she'd read over and over again. She identified completely with that plain little misfit, and not just because her name was Jane too, but because of the way she overcame her bleak childhood and won the heart of the granite-featured Mr Rochester. And there he was. Mr Rochester made real, walking towards her. She saw him, just as Charlotte Bronte described him, the great dark eyes, the stern features, the heavy brow, the thick, dark hair streaked with grey – it was him. She rushed back to the office and asked Suzy and the other women who he was.

221

'Oh, that sounds like Professor Eagle,' they said. 'The students call him Prof Beaky.'

'Professor Eagle – it suits him. And his nose isn't beaky – it's noble, majestic.'

They'd laughed. 'Forget it, Jane. He's much too old for you, and he's a crusty old bachelor.'

But Suzy said, 'He's a lovely man, Jane. Everybody who knows him likes him.'

And then, not long after, the miracle happened. He told her afterwards that he noticed her, one warm summer day, sitting alone on the University steps opposite the Haymarket, reading a book, and fell in love with her at once. 'You looked just like a pre-Raphaelite painting, with your flowing auburn hair and your long skirt,' he said. He sat down beside her, asked her what she was reading. It was *Jane Eyre,* of course, and they'd had a long conversation about the Brontes. He asked her if she'd ever been to the Parsonage at Haworth, and when she said she hadn't, he promised he'd take her there.

While Jane's contemporaries were out clubbing and drinking, she and Peter had their first date at the Laing Art Gallery, to see the pre-Raphaelites. And a few weeks later, he took her to Haworth, and they stayed the night at a country hotel. Lying in his arms that night she felt safe and loved for the first time since Nan died.

'Sorry, I'm a bit rusty at this,' Peter had said. He'd had a number of relationships with women, but they never lasted long because, before Jane, his first love was always his work. But Jane laughed, kissed him and said, 'If that was you being rusty, I can't wait till we've polished the rust away.'

Peter came from a different background from Jane's – a comfortably-off, stable and affectionate academic family, a home full of books and music and dogs, conversation and laughter, a private education and no discernible hang-ups or baggage. He was older, of course, set in his ways, and beginning to edge towards that grumpy, intolerant persona that seemed to be so common in men once they reached middle-age. But Jane was sure she could change that, and in return he could teach her so much. He was the most brilliant person she'd ever met; his knowledge was amazing, not just about physics, maths and the scientific world, but art and literature and music, philosophy, history and politics. He opened Jane's eyes, literally showing her a whole new universe when he sat by her side as she looked through his telescope at the night sky. He was her mentor, her teacher, her guide, and most of all, her lover, husband and a tender and devoted father to Angela.

How could she ever have considered leaving him?

Jane had been walking and thinking for hours, and now the light was fading, and she would have to get back to Bamburgh. The walk back seemed to take twice as long; her legs ached by the time she reached her car. Before she drove back to the cottage, she must ring Nigel. She knew it would be difficult to tell him her decision, so the sooner she got it over with the better. She was more than a little relieved when she heard his recorded voice: Nigel Blackwood here. Sorry I can't take your call at the moment. Please leave a message and I'll get back to you.

This would be so much easier, no conversation, no explanations. 'Hi, it's me, Jane. Just wanted to let you know that Peter and I will be vacating the cottage earlier than planned next week and returning to Newcastle – together. Sorry. I think – I know – you'll understand. Hope you'll always be my friend. Goodbye, and thanks for everything.'

Then for some reason she couldn't explain she started to sob. Whether it was relief or whether it was sadness, she couldn't tell. Maybe a combination of both. But as Nan would say, it was time to pull her socks up. She blew her nose, wiped her tears, and turned the ignition key.

****

For Mrs Mortimer the day had been satisfactory. The morphine had kept the worst of the pain at bay and made her pleasantly sleepy. In the morning, she'd taken photographs of the bairns, arranging them in their best outfits, and posted them on eBay, and in a matter of hours she'd had a string of bids for all of them. She'd slept for three solid hours in the afternoon, only woken by the phone ringing. It was the hospital, asking her to come in for another appointment. She wouldn't go. She'd told them plain enough she didn't want chemotherapy, so why trek all that way in an expensive taxi just to have the same discussion?

They'd talked about her having a nurse call regularly to make sure she was comfortable, but that was for further down the line. She told them no. For the moment, she was better off on her own. And if the morphine stopped being enough to deal with the pain, she'd already made the decision. She would go for a long walk into the sea and let the waves close over her. She had never learned to swim, so it would be quick.

She settled down with a cup of tea at the kitchen table with a sheet of paper, an envelope, and a pen. On the envelope she wrote: To be opened only after my death.

She had just written today's date at the top of the paper when there was a knock at the door, and there was Mr Eagle, looking distracted, clutching his phone, running his fingers through his hair. 'Mrs Mortimer, sorry to disturb you, but I've just got home, and my wife isn't there, nor is her car. It's dark and I'm worried. I've tried ringing her, but I can't get a signal on my phone. Did you happen to notice when she went out?'

'I did see her leave, yes, about eleven thirty this morning, I believe.'

'Was she on her own?'

'Yes, she was. You could try walking up the track a little way. The phone signal down here is very unpredictable. It's because of the house being situated in a dip.'

She watched as he followed her advice and stood up the track, fiddling with his phone. He came back. 'It's no good, nothing's working,' he said. 'Mrs Mortimer, you have a landline in your house, don't you? Could I try that? If I can't get through to Jane, I'll have to ring the police, you see. She's not been in a good state recently, and we – well, we've been having some disagreements. I'm very concerned she might do something silly.'

Mrs Mortimer did not like having anyone in her house, apart from Mr Blackwood of course, but he never stayed too long. She was still furious with Beryl, letting Her Next Door and her friend come in, showing them the bairns. But poor Mr Eagle, he really did look distraught, although it was her opinion the only silly thing his wife was likely to be doing at that moment was cosying up somewhere with Mr Blackwood. Just as she reluctantly opened her door for him to come in, car headlights appeared coming down the track.

'Oh, thank God. It's her,' he shouted. 'Thanks, Mrs Mortimer, sorry to have bothered you.'

'Don't mention it, I'm sure,' she said, shutting the door.

What a relief.

****

Jane was in his arms the moment she stepped out of the car. Peter hugged her.

'Oh love, I was so worried, I was just on the verge of ringing the police. Where have you been? Are you all right?'

'Of course I am,' she said. 'Honestly, Peter, there's no need to make a fuss. It's only six o'clock, not the middle of the night.' She'd expected him to be angry, accusing, but he just seemed relieved. 'I've just been walking - and thinking.'

'What about?'

'Oh everything. You. Me. Emily. My brain. Us leaving here. Jane Eyre.'

'Jane Eyre?'

'I spent so long looking for my Mr Rochester, and then I found him.' She took his face between her hands, kissed him. 'So I'm not letting him go now. Even if he does decide to shove his mad wife up in the attic.'

'I haven't got a mad wife. Just a beautiful, young, talented wife. And I don't want you in the attic. I want you in my bed, next to me.' He stroked her hair, pressed his face against her shoulder. 'I've been so terrified of losing you. I've been going over in my head what I was going to say to you tonight. I was going to say that I'll never try to tie you down or control you again, and if you wanted to leave me for Nigel Blackwood, then I wouldn't try to stop you. But all I want to say to you now is please, Jane, please don't leave me. I'll be no good without you. I need you.'

He needed her? That was a revelation. Jane had always thought she was the needy one. They went back into the house. In the kitchen, they kissed.

'I've been a self-absorbed cow, haven't I?' she said. 'Suzy told me what you told her, that you hadn't felt able to grieve for Angela because you were so wrapped up in coping with me.'

'Did she say that? She shouldn't have, although it's true. I used to go off for long walks over the Town Moor, those early days after she died, just so I could howl my eyes out without you seeing.'

'You did all the supporting. We should have been supporting each other. I'm sorry. And that night at the hospital, when I walked past you, I shouldn't—'

He put his finger against her lips. 'Don't say any more. I understand. We weren't in our right minds. Neither of us will ever forget that time, but let's not dwell on it. It's gone, it's past.' They stood holding each other close for a while. Then Peter said, 'Shall we go out tonight? Find a pub and have dinner?'

'No, let's stay in. There's a chicken curry in the freezer I can defrost.'

'OK, but not just yet,' he said, drawing her close again. They went upstairs.

Later, as they shared their supper, he said, 'So what about those other decisions you made while you were walking? About Emily, for instance?'

'I think – she doesn't exist. She never did. I have schizophrenia, and I'll take the medication. I'll deal with it.'

He nodded. 'And what about us vacating the cottage next week? Will you be coming with me?'

'Yes, of course,' she said, kissing him again. 'Let's go home.'

****

Mrs Mortimer picked up the pen. She had never been much good at expressing herself, but this had to be done. She must set the record straight. She didn't think Katie Harris's parents would still be alive, but if they were, they must still wonder every single day what happened to their daughter. And as for Eric's nasty old witch of a mother, she was almost certainly dead, but there were his brothers and a sister who she'd not spoken to in years. They deserved to know.

Slowly and carefully, she wrote: In April 1985, I shot and killed my husband, Eric Mortimer, and his lover, Katie Harris. Their bodies are buried in the field about ten yards from the rear of the house. I acted alone, and no other person was involved.

She signed her name at the bottom, folded the paper in half, and put it inside the envelope. She propped it up against her tea mug, wondering who would open it, and when, and what they would think.

After a few moments, she picked the envelope up and took it to the empty sink. She held it by a corner, struck a match and let the flame lick and curl up the paper, and when it was well alight, dropped it in the sink until it was just flakes of ash, turned on the tap, and washed it down the plug hole.

Because it wasn't true. It was a lie. That wasn't what happened.

CHAPTER 26

Despite the medication, Peggy Mortimer had not slept well. She lay staring at the ceiling most of the night, wondering if she should write another letter, only this time it would be the truth. But what was the truth? It had been so long ago, and she had, over the years, deliberately pushed thoughts of it out of her mind whenever they threatened to intrude. Some events of that terrible day were still clear, but others had faded. It was painful, but she must try to remember, get it right, if she was to leave an accurate account of what really happened.

Of course, she knew about Eric and Katie Harris. Men were such fools, thinking a woman doesn't notice things like the smell of unfamiliar perfume on his clothes, or the receipts for jewellery and restaurant meals found in his trouser pockets when she checked before putting them in the wash. It hurt, but she'd choose to ignore it, like she had all the other times, and it would blow over soon enough.

Keeping busy helped keep her mind off it. She was out most days, on her bike, pedalling up and down the country lanes, cleaning holiday cottages for John Blackwood. At that time, they only had half a dozen properties, not like now. And she'd taken on an unpaid job too; looking after Irene Blackwood next door. Her neighbour was only in her mid-fifties, but she'd been getting more and more forgetful and muddled, neglecting herself and letting the house get in a dirty and disorganised mess. Peggy Mortimer took to calling in on her every day, giving the place a bit of a clean and tidy up, making Miss Blackwood cups of tea and sandwiches, doing her laundry. She didn't even mind having to listen to her increasingly deranged ranting about religion and politics, subjects which held not the slightest interest for her.

It was the defeat of the miners and the end of the strike in March that year which seemed to trigger Miss Blackwood's rapid decline. Peggy Mortimer would go in to find she'd put her shoes in the fridge or left the oven on all night with nothing in it. Another time, she nearly set fire to the house, after knocking over a candle and letting it burn away half the curtains. At night she could be heard through the wall, shouting and raging, especially if Mrs Thatcher was on the TV.

It was a Thursday night in April – she couldn't remember the exact date – when Eric came home from work and announced, quite casually, 'I'm leaving tomorrow, Peg. Gannin' to London.'

'Why? How long for?'

She could picture him now, slouching at the kitchen table, still in his work boots, tab dangling from his lips. 'There's a gadgie I know down there says there's plenty of gardening work going in the London parks. Reckon I could make a lot more money than working at the Hall.'

'Will you be sending for me once you've found a place for us then?' she asked.

He gave her a sneering grin. 'Nah. You'll not be coming, Peg. When I said I'm leaving, I meant I'm leaving you. For good. So you'd better get used to the idea.'

'But, what about your job? This house? Your garden?'

'I've packed the job in. You'll have to get out of the house. You'll never manage the rent on what you earn. Blackwood will hoy you out.'

She remembered the feeling of utter despair that swept over her. She hated the man, but she supposed she loved him too, although she wasn't sure what love meant. She just knew she needed him, craved even the rough and brutish encounters that passed for lovemaking. She couldn't imagine life without him, for all he made that life a misery.

'Don't leave, Eric. You can carry on seeing Katie Harris, I won't mind. Just don't leave.'

'Tough. Me and Katie, we're off tomorrow. So you can stay here till they chuck you out, you and that fucking cat.' He laughed, threw his tab end on the floor and ground it out with the heel of his boot. 'And look after that garden of mine while you're still here. I just put the seed tatties in, so you'll get a good crop come the summer. If Blackwood hasn't kicked you out by then.'

Next morning, as usual, she went to see to Miss Blackwood. She was wandering aimlessly round the house, wearing a summer dress that looked like it dated from the nineteen fifties over a dirty pair of tracksuit bottoms.

'Miss Blackwood, I might not be able to come in and help you for much longer.' She explained as simply as she could what Eric had said.

'How dare he? Wickedness, wickedness.' Miss Blackwood exploded. 'The man is a monster. I know how he treats you, my dear, I can hear what goes on through the wall. You will be well rid of him, but you shouldn't lose your home. I shall see to it you don't. You are not to worry. I will speak to my brother, make sure he lets you stay in the house. After all, you do work for him. And what would I do without you? I need you here.'

Then followed a long tirade about the evils of fornication, how sinners would meet their just deserts in hell. 'Leviticus, Chapter Twenty, dear – the adulterer and the adulteress shall surely be put to death.'

Eric had left the house early, but his things were still lying around, so she guessed he must be going to pick up the wages he was owed at the Hall and would be back later to pack his bags. Friday was Peggy's busiest day, the day holidaymakers usually left, and she had to get the properties clean and ship-shape for the next arrivals. That Friday was no different, so she expected to be out all day. Feeling desolate and sick at heart, despite Miss Blackwood's promise to help, she got on her bike and pedalled off to work.

It was only when she'd finished the second cottage on the list that she realised that with all the shock and upset, she'd forgotten to bring her usual sandwiches. Now it was two o'clock and her stomach was rumbling with hunger. She had felt too churned up to eat any breakfast. The next cottage on the list was in Embleton, not too far from home, so she would go back home and make herself a quick snack.

It was a beautiful day, she remembered, bright and sunny, the birds singing and the first buds of spring beginning to show in the bare hedgerows. She rattled down the track on her bike, being careful to avoid the deep ruts. She was halfway down the track when she heard two sharp cracks. Bird scarer? Surely not, there was no crop growing nearby. Or was Eric out in the field shooting rabbits again? She hoped he wasn't there. She really didn't want to see him. There were two more loud cracks. And then, as she swung round the bend, she saw Eric's car, the Morris Traveller, parked outside, and the back door of the house wide open. She stopped, half intending to turn round and just press on to the next job.

But at that moment, Miss Blackwood appeared at the back door, her long grey hair hanging unpinned and straggly. She was holding Eric's shotgun and looking dazed.

'What have you done? What have you done?' Mrs Mortimer remembered shouting as she flung the bike to one side and pushed past her. 'Where's Eric?'

'They're upstairs,' Miss Blackwood said. Then she added, 'I think they may be dead.'

Peggy flew up the seven steps to the one little bedroom. There on the bed was Eric, her husband, face down and naked except for the jeans and underpants crumpled around his ankles. She remembered thinking how pale his buttocks looked in contrast to his muscular back, tanned brown from working shirtless in the sun. The back of his head, with that lovely shoulder length curly hair, was a smashed and matted mess of blood. And underneath him lay Katie, her plump white legs spread wide either side of Eric's body, and the top of her head, just visible under Eric's shoulder, blown away and slowly pulsing out thick red spurts over the white pillow.

The moments after that were a blur to her now. She remembered running to the bathroom, retching up bile over the toilet, and Miss

Blackwood standing beside her, still clutching the gun, saying, 'Oh dear, are you all right? Was it something you ate, do you think?'

'Something I ate? Miss Blackwood, you've killed my husband.'

The horror of what she'd done must have come home to Irene Blackwood then, because she let the gun clatter to the floor. 'I did it for you, dear. You are so good to me, so kind. And they were fornicating, defiling your marriage bed with their filthy lust. I couldn't allow it to go on, could I? The adulterer and the adulteress must surely be put to death.'

'I shall have to ring the police.'

'No.' Miss Blackwood wailed, clutching Peggy's hands. 'No, not the police. They're the agents of State, the oppressors, the enemies of the people, they'll throw me in prison. Please, don't let them take me, dear Mrs Mortimer, please.'

'You won't go to prison. You weren't in your right mind, Miss Blackwood. You'll be sent to a mental hospital I expect.'

'I won't go. I shall shoot myself.' She went to grab the gun, but Peggy managed to snatch it first.

'I think we must sit down calmly now, think about what we are going to do.' She felt as if she was in the middle of a mad nightmare, but she'd never been one to give in to hysterics or shows of emotion. So she calmly put the gun aside, filled the kettle, and they sat down at the kitchen table, just as if they were having a friendly chat over afternoon tea. 'You'd better tell me exactly what happened,' she said.

Miss Blackwood told her how she'd seen Eric and Katie arrive at the cottage at lunchtime. She'd watched them running around in the field together, Eric showing off, shooting at birds, jokily pointing the gun at Katie, and laughing when she shrieked. They'd gone in the house, Eric coming out later with a couple of suitcases which he put in the back of the Morris Traveller. Then Katie came out and they leant against the side of the car.

'She had her hands all over him, and his hands were up her skirt. Oh it was disgusting, horrible. And then they went back into the house, still pawing at each other. I knew then I had to do God's will. I only meant to come round here and give them a piece of my mind. But then I heard Almighty God's voice, commanding me to tell them they must repent their evil-doing and be saved.'

'But he didn't tell you to murder them, did he?' Panic and nausea began to churn in Peggy Mortimer's stomach again.

'I don't know. I just knew I had to make it stop, those terrible noises. When I came into the house, I could hear them. Bestial sounds, him grunting like a pig, her squealing, the bed rattling against the wall. I had to put an end to it, don't you see? And I saw the gun propped up against the kitchen table here, and an open box of cartridges on the table. I know how to handle a shotgun, you know. Daddy used to take me clay pigeon shooting when I was still just a child, and when I was older let me join the shooting parties up at the Hall, so I developed quite a skill at it. I was a good shot, Daddy said.'

'Never mind about that, tell me what happened next.' Peggy's hand was shaking violently as she poured out the tea.

It must be the shock setting in, she thought.

'I slid a couple of cartridges in the barrels, went upstairs. I saw him on top of her, his nasty little rump pounding away, such a revolting sight, I couldn't stand it. She saw me over his shoulder, started screaming, "Eric! Eric!", but he didn't look round. Filthy beast, he laughed, he must have thought she was screaming with pleasure. I aimed at the back of his head and pulled the trigger. She was screaming even louder then, trying to push him off her, so I shot her too, but she was still moaning and twitching, so I went down and reloaded and came back up to finish them off.' She stared at Peggy, her mouth dropping open, suddenly aghast. 'I've done a very wrong thing, haven't I?'

What they talked about after that, Peggy Mortimer couldn't recall. At some point, it had dawned on her that the police, if she called them, might think she'd killed them. She had more of a motive than Miss Blackwood. She was the wronged wife, and it was common knowledge in the village that Eric was violent and abusive towards her. She'd started wearing heavy make-up early on in her marriage to disguise the bruises, but a black eye and swollen lip were harder to cover up. And even if Miss Blackwood admitted to the murder, would they believe her?

Miss Blackwood was getting agitated now, realising what she'd done, so to calm her down Peggy said, 'It's all right, don't worry. I won't call the police. Eric and Katie were going away together, so if they disappear, nobody will be surprised. So all we have to do is dispose of their bodies.'

They discussed various options. Rolling them over the cliff top was dismissed as the bodies would surely come to light sooner or later and they didn't have access to a boat that would allow them to dump the bodies far out at sea. The possibility of opening the hatch to the septic tank at the top of the field near the farm and dropping them in there was considered, and again discounted. The septic tank was in clear sight of the farm so they might be spotted, or else the bodies would be found when the tank was emptied.

'I think we'll have to bury them,' Peggy said. Miss Blackwood had an ancient and very battered white van which she'd owned for years, but rarely drove now since being banned for a year for dangerous driving following an incident with her van and a tractor. They could put the bodies in the back and take them somewhere miles away, to Kielder Forest perhaps. Northumberland had so many large areas of wild woodland and forest. But it would be a risky business, always a chance they might be seen, and they would need to spend a long time digging a deep enough grave to hold two bodies.

It was then that an idea came to her. Eric had built a little water feature next to his vegetable plot, a smaller version of the one he had constructed in the garden of the Hall. He'd made a rockery, dug a pond, rigged up a fountain to trickle down the rockery into it. It had taken him months, and he was very proud of it. He'd stocked the pond with water lilies and nicked a few goldfish from the Hall to put in it. But over the winter, the pond lining cracked, and the water gradually seeped away, so that now it was just a pit with a puddle of muddy water at the bottom.

It couldn't have been more convenient, and it struck Peggy then it was rather fitting that Eric Mortimer had dug his own grave.

But until they could put the bodies in it, there was a lot of work to be done. Gritting herself, she went upstairs again, this time with a roll of black plastic sacks, scissors, baling twine and duct tape. 'Come and help me, Miss Blackwood,' she called. In the bedroom, Coco the cat was sitting on the bed, just inches from the entwined bodies. She was curled up in a neat ball, blinking sleepily. She would never go anywhere near Eric when he was alive. She already had a belly full of kittens again, so maybe she realised that this time she was going to keep them.

The two women heaved and tugged, prising apart the dead lovers, Miss Blackwood insisting that Peggy pull up Eric's trousers, the sight of his exposed genitals being more repellent to her than his exploded skull. They wrapped the bodies in several layers of black plastic and bound them up securely with the tape, so that they looked like two Egyptian mummies lying side by side.

Peggy folded the blood-soaked bedspread tightly around them both, parcelled them up as one with baling twine and together they pushed, pulled and rolled them off the bed, bumped them down the stairs into the kitchen. It was hard and heavy work, even though Miss Blackwood was a physically fit and wiry woman, and Peggy, not yet thirty, was strong as an athlete from all the bicycling and cleaning she did. They rested for a while. It was late afternoon now, and Peggy was hoping and praying no one would come down the track and see what was going on. There was no time to rest any more, they would have to be quick.

She went to the door, intending to go and inspect the state of the empty pond, but it was then that she saw Eric's car, the Morris Traveller, still parked outside. How would she explain that? Eric and Katie had disappeared, but the car was still there. They could have gone to London on the train or the coach, of course, but they would have driven the car to the railway station, or the bus station. A taxi?

No, Katie's parents might take it in their heads to ask around, find out if any taxi driver remembered them.

Miss Blackwood could drive the car to Alnmouth station, perhaps, leave it in the car park? It would soon be discovered there, of course. Where could they dump it where it wouldn't be found, at least for some time? It was Miss Blackwood who came up with the idea to abandon it near the airport. 'They could have caught the plane to Heathrow. There's a lot of open countryside surrounding the airport where we can leave the car,' she said.

'Right. We need to do that tonight, while it's dark and there's hardly anyone around. We can't leave them two on the kitchen floor like that. We'll have to put them in the back of your van, Miss Blackwood. You drive ahead of me, and I'll follow in the Traveller. Then you can drive us back here.'

There was a snag with that; Peggy Mortimer couldn't drive. Eric had given her two or three lessons earlier in their marriage, but they always ended in arguments, so she'd not pursued it. Oh well, she'd just have to do her best, and hope that there was nothing else on the road, especially not a police car.

While they waited for night fall, Peggy went up and stripped the bed of all the bloodstained sheets and pillows. The blood had soaked through to the mattress, and there were blood splashes up the wall. She bundled up the soiled linen and bagged it and scrubbed away any traces of blood she could find on the wall and floor. She picked up the spent cartridges and threw them in the bin. Eric's denim jacket was slung over the back of the chair. She would have to dispose of all his clothes, but that could wait. She checked the pockets of his jacket and found his wallet. In it was a bundle of twenty-pound notes, twenty-five of them. That was about all they had in their joint bank account. He must have cleared it out, leaving her nothing. She stuffed the money in her pocket. Good, she would use it to add to the secret account she had in her name, the one where she'd put her parents' legacy.

As darkness fell, they dragged the dead weight of the gruesome parcel slowly, inch by inch, thumping and bumping out of the house, over the gravel, out and into the back of Miss Blackwood's van. It was a painful struggle, with much heaving and pushing, leaving them gasping for breath, but they managed it. They covered the wrapped bodies with a large tarpaulin and locked the doors. It was decided they would wait until two in the morning before embarking on the trip to the airport.

It would take them under an hour, Miss Blackwood thought. There was no question of getting any sleep, although they were both exhausted emotionally and physically, so they went back to Miss Blackwood's house. Peggy made them cocoa, and they sat in her gloomy parlour, waiting for the hours to pass.

Eric and Katie's cases were still in the back of the Traveller. Peggy took them out, stashed them away in a cupboard, and cleared out other bits and pieces from the glove compartment. Another thing to deal with later. At two a.m. they set off, Peggy crunching the gears and kangaroo hopping to start with, but she soon got into the swing of it and once they got a clear run on the A1 she could keep it in fourth gear and it was easy, just a case of keeping her foot steady on the accelerator. Apart from the occasional lorry, the roads were deserted, and at the Ponteland turning they headed right towards the airport, down dark and empty lanes. About half a mile before the roundabout where they'd have turned left for the airport, Miss Blackwood signalled a right turn and Peggy followed the van into the entrance to a large, ploughed field, ringed with trees and thick hedges. They bumped slowly down the rough ground at the side of the field until a particularly deep rut caused the steering wheel to lurch out of Peggy's grasp and the Traveller rolled down into a ditch, almost lying on its side, with the exhaust hanging off. Miss Blackwood helped her scramble out, shaken but unharmed. 'My dear, you've done splendidly,' she said. 'They won't find it for a while, it's almost hidden by the undergrowth. Now, hop in the van and let's get back. And you're not to think of staying in your house tonight. You must stay with me.'

Peggy remembered the journey back as being the most frightening part of the whole nightmarish day. Miss Blackwood drove as if pursued by demons, much too fast, so that the bodies in the back rolled and thumped against the sides of the van as they slewed round corners. 'We'll leave them until the morning,' Miss Blackwood said, almost cheerily. Peggy sat rigid and speechless, terrified that she was going to die at any minute.

Strange that now she was really staring death in the face, she wasn't in the least afraid.

CHAPTER 27

'Good Lord, whatever is Morticia up to?'

Peter was making them tea and toast in the kitchen. He was leaving later today; his first tutorial wasn't until eleven thirty. Jane joined him at the window. They could see Mrs Mortimer making her way over the steep uphill slope of the field holding an armful of flowers.

'Those were the flowers Nigel left for her,' Jane said. 'Obviously, she doesn't like them.'

'She doesn't look at all well, does she?' Peter said. 'Very tottery. Do you think she's OK?'

'Well, she hasn't been out of hospital long, and according to her sister she did have quite a big operation.'

They watched as she stopped at a point in the middle of the field where the ground levelled out and there was a slightly raised hump, covered in tufts of grass and brambles. She flung the flowers down, and turned back, treading cautiously over the uneven ground.

Peter was going to take next week off, packing up his boxes full of books and papers, his computer, printer, and the telescope over the coming weekend, and returning to the flat on Monday. He would sort things out in the flat ready for Jane's return, and Jane would stay in the cottage for a couple of days to pack up her things and give the place a thorough clean.

'We don't want Morticia to have to do it, with her still convalescing,' Peter said. 'I'm sure Blackwood could arrange for another cleaner to come in and do it, but I can't imagine she'd like

239

that. She's very proprietary about this cottage, isn't she? It's her patch.'

Once Peter had gone, she checked her phone. There was a text from Nigel:

Jane, thanks for the message. Sincerely wishing you and the Prof all the best. Yes, friends it is then, and remember I'm always here for you, if you need me for anything, any time. Not goodbye, but au revoir. Nigel. P.S. Hillfield House rang me this morning. Aunt Irene passed away peacefully in her sleep during the night.

There was another message, from Sheila Wetherall, inviting Jane to an Art Group meeting at the village hall next Thursday. She'd forgotten all about them. She tapped out a brief reply, thanking her and saying she'd have loved to come, but she was going home next Wednesday. Maybe she would come up again next year, if they had another exhibition.

****

Peggy Mortimer was glad she'd got rid of those flowers. They were starting to wither, and the sight of them depressed her. She wasn't sure what had prompted her to leave them on the grave. For all these years she'd done her best to block it out of her mind, never going anywhere near it, but thinking about writing down the true facts of what happened had forced her to focus her mind on it again. She'd just sat down, wondering where to begin, when the phone rang. It was Mr Blackwood, to tell her that his aunt had died.

'I'm sorry to hear that, I'm sure,' she said.

'Yes, she was a remarkable lady, wasn't she? You'll be welcome to come to the funeral, of course,' he said. 'The family won't forget how good you were to her for all those years. It must have been difficult. My father was very grateful to you.'

'Thank you, but I don't care for funerals,' she said.

So that was that then. And suddenly there didn't seem any point in writing down the truth. She tore up the blank sheet of paper in front of her. The truth could go with her to the crematorium flames. Why destroy Mr Blackwood's memory of his aunt? Let him remember her as that remarkable lady, not a murderer.

She began to think about those days after they'd dumped the car. She'd inspected the ditch that had been Eric's pond and concluded that it wasn't deep enough. She would have to dig out more earth, and Miss Blackwood readily agreed to do what she could to help her. They would do it at night, in the dark, when nobody was likely to be coming down to the cottage. They set to with their shovels by the flickering light of two hurricane lamps, and luckily the weather kept dry. It took them three nights, but at last Peggy said, 'Right, Miss Blackwood. I think that's deep enough. Let's get them in there.' They were weak from the toil and lack of sleep, but eventually, working together, they dragged the parcel of bodies, already beginning to reek the odour of decay, from the back of the van and rolled it laboriously uphill, over and over the grass, and finally tumbling down into the yawning hole. Then came the hard task of filling it in, first using the rocks and boulders from the rockery, heaving them in one at a time, each one landing with a heavy thud. Then they worked with their shovels, refilling the hole from the mound of earth they'd dug out, forming a small hump over the grave. The two women pressed the earth firmly in place, stamping up and down in their wellington boots, as if performing some macabre tribal dance.

Miss Blackwood stood beside the grave and started to recite lines from the burial service, 'We therefore commit their bodies to the ground, earth to earth, ashes to ashes...' but Peggy shut her up, told her to go indoors. The sun was rising, it was nearly dawn, and her work was not yet finished.

Using her bare hands as well as a garden spade, she ripped up or stamped down every plant growing in Eric's Garden. With her last remnants of strength, she pulled apart the water feature, smashed the spade down again and again on the little greenhouse, till all that was left was a pile of broken glass and bent metal. It utterly exhausted her, but she felt triumphant, empowered. 'So what do you think of your precious garden now, Eric?' she said, looking around at the devastation. After five years of being in constant fear of the man, she'd got her own back at last.

Yet despite everything, she had loved him once and part of her still grieved for him, or at least for the man he had been when they first met. He had been different then; loving, attentive, exciting. That first time he'd put her on the back of his motor bike, and away they'd flown, out of the town, and then they were in each other's arms, tumbling and rolling in a field of ripe corn in the warm summer night and afterwards he said, 'You're my lass now, Peg.' Strange, too, how gentle he could be, cupping tender seedlings in his hands, showing her how to plant them, carefully pressing down the earth with his bare fingers. 'See, you have to mind not to damage the roots, Peg.' He could drown a kitten or break a rabbit's neck with a flick of his wrist, but she'd seen him carefully wash and wrap a prize leek and carry it cradled in his arms like a baby to the village produce show.

But all that was in the past now. In a month or two, nature would do its work and the grass, nettles and thistles would obliterate all signs of this night's work. And she would cease to grieve and be free of him forever.

There was no way she could sleep on that bloodstained bed, but she refused Miss Blackwood's offer to stay with her. She washed the mud and dirt from her hands, put her dirty clothes in the washer, collected pillows and a blanket, lay down on the sofa in her sitting room, and slept, dreamlessly, until noon next day.

Later that same day, she and Miss Blackwood started to build a bonfire on the field, close to where the bodies were buried. All of Eric's clothes, shoes, personal belongings and papers, the suitcases Eric and Katie had packed, everything he owned, even his stash of pornography she found in the back of the wardrobe – it all went into cardboard boxes leftover from when they'd moved in. Miss Blackwood contributed some of the old broken furniture still cluttering up her part of the house, old newspapers and bundles of firewood from the woodshed. They carried all the bagged up bloodstained bed linen out, and last of all, the bed, the mattress and then the divan base.

'Destroy it all, my dear. Miss Blackwood commanded, splashing petrol from a can over the towering pyre. She was almost dancing with excitement, as if she was relishing it all. 'It is tainted with sin.'

The blaze roared up quickly, devouring everything, sending up spirals of pungent smoke. It wasn't long before Farmer Armstrong and his son appeared, thinking the cottage must be on fire. Well, what did it matter if everyone knew she'd destroyed Eric's stuff? She didn't even care if this, like the news of Eric and Katie's disappearance, was flying round the village gossip circles, as it surely was. She was just relieved that every last trace of Eric was gone. The fire continued to burn all day and late into the night, and by the morning all that was left was a smouldering heap of ashes and the blackened metal bedsprings.

There was just one of Eric's possessions left – his shotgun. She decided not to replace it back in the locked cupboard under the stairs where it was usually kept in a metal box. She didn't want to see it ever again. So, she wiped it clean and put it, in its box, up in the little narrow loft above Miss Blackwood's house. And just to make sure Miss Blackwood never got her hands on it again, she removed the loft ladder and stashed it in her own outhouse.

As soon as all these jobs were completed, her new bed bought and delivered and the bedroom carpet and remaining furniture thoroughly scrubbed and the walls repainted, Peggy said to Miss Blackwood, 'It's all sorted now, it's all over, so we must never speak of any of this again. And you must not say anything, to anybody, ever. Do you understand, Miss Blackwood? Never say anything, or we would both be in serious trouble. Promise me,'

'I promise, dear. It'll be as if it never happened. As the Lord is my witness, I will keep my promise. And in return, will you promise me something?'

'What?'

'I know my mind is going the same way as my poor mother's. I forget things, muddle things, I don't know what I'm doing or why I'm doing it half the time, and it will only get worse. Will you look after me, my dear Mrs Mortimer? Please don't ever let them take me away, put me in one of those dreadful homes. Do you promise?'

Peggy didn't have much choice. 'All right, I promise. I'll do my best.'

So for the next ten years, she did. And neither of them ever mentioned the killings of Eric and Katie again. As Irene Blackwood's brain slowly unravelled, it seemed, to Peggy's relief, as if she'd completely forgotten what she'd done.

Miss Blackwood had also forgotten her promise to speak to her brother about letting Mrs Mortimer stay on. But that didn't matter, as John Blackwood came to see her, assured her there was no question of evicting her from the cottage, and if she would agree to care for his poor sister Irene, and continue her holiday cottage cleaning work, she could stay on rent-free as long as she wished.

It was a good four or five weeks after the killings that police came to Mrs Mortimer's door. The car had been found, and they'd traced it back to Mr Eric Mortimer of this address. Mrs Mortimer stayed very calm as she explained to the young officer that he had gone, and nobody knew where he was. No, she couldn't shed any light on why he had abandoned the car there, other than it was about fourteen years old and riddled with rust. 'Only fit for scrap,' she told him. He seemed happy with that explanation, and the police never bothered her again.

If there was gossip in the village, Peggy didn't hear about it because, apart from going out to work, she rarely ventured out much anymore, just getting the bus to Alnwick to do her shopping once a week. But about six months later, in the autumn, there was a knock at her door and there stood Jim Harris, Katie's father. She was shocked, not just to see him there, but at his appearance. The jovial, stocky pub landlord she remembered seemed to have shrunk and aged into a grey shadow of a man.

He was sorry to bother her, didn't want to intrude or ask difficult personal questions, but he and his wife were worried sick, he said, about their daughter.

'Mrs Mortimer, we were dead against this thing she had going on with your husband. We tried to stop it, but once she turned eighteen – well, she could do what she wanted, she said. But you know, we would have forgiven her in the end. She knew that. She was our only one, after all. And you see, it's been six months now, and we haven't heard a word. We've no idea where they could be. We can't understand why she hasn't been in touch, let us know she's all right.'

'I don't know how I can help you, Mr Harris.'

'We just wondered if you'd heard from Eric at all? We thought he might have been in touch about getting a divorce or something?'

'I've heard nothing at all from my husband,' she replied, starting to close the door to indicate she wished the conversation to end.

'I heard they found his car, you know, near the airport,' he persisted. 'Katie's note said they were going to London, but we managed to contact Eric's mate down there, and he said he was expecting them, but they never turned up. We think they may have gone abroad. I often heard him sounding off in the pub about how he wanted to go somewhere warm and sunny one day, open his own bar. We wondered if you knew if Eric had taken his passport when he left?'

'As far as I am aware, Eric didn't have a passport. He may have got himself one without my knowledge, of course. Now if you'll excuse me—'

Jim Harris wasn't going to let this go. He stopped the door from shutting with the flat of his hand.

'Sorry to press you on this Mrs Mortimer, but our worst fear is that something terrible has happened to her. I don't want to raise this subject, it must be painful for you, but do you think your Eric could have…' He paused, looking as if he might break down in tears at any moment. 'Was he the kind of man who could have harmed our Katie, or God forbid worse, do you think? We do remember more than a few times we saw you, Mrs Mortimer, with a black eye, or a cut lip, and that time your arm was in plaster—'

'I had several mishaps, falling from my bicycle,' she snapped. 'I am quite sure Eric has not harmed your daughter.'

'Are you?' He looked doubtful. 'Well, please, you will let us know if you ever do hear anything from Eric? Or have any thoughts on where they might be? My wife is so upset. The bairn must have arrived by now. And we would forgive Katie anything if we could only just see the baby, our grandchild.'

Peggy was astounded. 'A baby? What baby?'

'Oh aye,' Jim Harris said, his voice beginning to break. 'Katie was in the family way. My wife knew. Well, women do notice these things, don't they? I think that's why Katie decided to run away. She thought we'd make her give up the baby I expect, but we wouldn't have done that.'

The man's shoulders were shaking. He put his head in his hand, stifling a sob. Mrs Mortimer didn't want that kind of scene on her doorstep. 'I will most certainly inform you if I hear of anything, Mr Harris. But I very much doubt I will.' And with that she shut the door with a firm click. She had got rid of him, and without actually telling a single untruth. Apart from the one about falling off her bike.

So Katie Harris was expecting. That was an upsetting thing to hear, and surprising too. Eric always said he didn't like children, hated babies, never wanted any. So Miss Blackwood had destroyed the lives of three, not two. Still, the child had probably been spared a terrible upbringing, with a flighty teenage mother and a sadistic bully for a father. She would never let Miss Blackwood know that she'd killed an unborn bairn. She had strong views on abortion, the massacre of the innocents, she called it.

It was a good thing, Peggy thought, that Miss Blackwood didn't know about the two terminations Eric forced her to have. 'Get rid of it, or I'll knock it out of you,' he'd said, both times, pressing his clenched fist under her chin.

The years went by, and she kept her promise to care for the old lady. But she knew she couldn't carry on when she saw Miss Blackwood late one night, stark naked, standing in the field, shouting and pacing up and down at the spot where the bodies were buried. She then tottered up the path to the cliff top as if the hounds of hell were behind her and would have jumped over the edge if Mrs Mortimer hadn't grabbed her, wrapped a blanket around her, and taken her home. 'They were rising up, Mrs Mortimer, coming to seek their revenge.' she said, shivering with fear and cold.

'Who was rising up?' Peggy asked her, dreading to hear the answer.

Miss Blackwood's gaunt face crumpled into an expression of utter confusion and distress. 'I don't know. I can't remember. But it's to do with something bad, very bad,' she wailed. 'Somebody died. There was blood. We buried them. Was it you killed them? Or was it me?'

Next morning, Mrs Mortimer rang Mr Blackwood and told him she couldn't care for his sister anymore.

Peggy stayed inside the house when they came. Miss Blackwood was probably too far gone to realise that Mrs Mortimer hadn't kept her promise, but nevertheless, she didn't want to see her face as they took her away.

They didn't expect her to live much longer, John Blackwood told her. The longest time a dementia sufferer survived after the onset was usually between eight and twelve years. But somehow, Miss Blackwood defied the odds, resisting death for more than another twenty-five years.

But now the old lady was gone. Sitting at her kitchen table, Mrs Mortimer decided she wouldn't think about the past anymore. It all seemed like a bad, distant nightmare anyway, so best let it go.

In another fifty years or so this cottage might well have tumbled into the sea, and in time, the waves would begin to claim the field behind. And maybe then the grave and its secrets would be revealed as the earth crumbled away. But what did it matter? She would be long gone by then, along with everyone who remembered that Eric and Katie ever existed.

CHAPTER 28

Peter was all packed up and ready to go. It was eight in the morning and looked as if it would be a bright and sunny day for late November, the sea a deep and calm Mediterranean blue. As the weather had been good, they'd spent their last weekend out and about, discovering a couple of little hidden bays to walk along, as well as a pub with views across wide fields to the distant hills.

'We'll come back up this way again,' Peter promised. 'But not for quite so long next time.'

Jane came out to see him off, assuring him, yes, she would be fine on her own, and yes, she could manage to pack up all the remaining stuff.

Just before he set off, he hugged her and said, 'You know, I was thinking. I was wrong to overrule you about the inscription on Angela's memorial stone. If you want, I can arrange to have those words you wanted put on it. You know, the *love you lots like jelly tots* thing.'

'It's all right,' she said. 'It doesn't make any difference now what's on it. She knew we loved her when she was with us, that's all that matters.'

'Yes, I suppose so.' They both stood silent for a moment, remembering Angela.

'Peter—'

'What?'

'Why did it happen to us? Why was it our daughter that had to die?'

'Jane, I don't know. Ask me why the stars shine, why water is fluid, why the sky's blue, what we are made of, what black holes are, and why the universe is expanding. I can answer those questions. But there are some things I can't answer, nobody can answer.'

'Yes, I know,' she said. 'I suppose the answer is that there isn't an answer.' She kissed him. 'See you on Wednesday then.'

Once he was gone, she got busy with a mop and bucket and cleaned all the floors downstairs. She took the rugs outside and gave them a good shake. She dusted the ornaments, the shelves, the dresser, brushed and straightened the curtains, cleaned the windows and windowsills. Now to tackle upstairs. She picked up the bucket and mop. As she took the first step, she heard a quiet little voice above her say, *Don't leave.*

Emily was standing on the landing at the top of the stairs, looking directly at Jane.

Jane stared back, her heart pounding. 'Please go away, Emily,' she said shakily. 'You aren't there, you don't exist.'

As if to prove her right, the girl evaporated, disappeared in an instant, like a popped bubble.

She went upstairs, into the bedroom, stripped the bed. She was just bundling all the bed linen together when the bedroom door slammed shut with a loud bang. That was odd, it wasn't a windy day. She dropped the sheets, went to open the door. It wouldn't open. She pushed, rattled the handle, shouted, 'Let me out, Emily, let me out.', her breath was coming in quick panicky gasps. She heard footsteps running up and down outside on the landing, down the stairs. How had her mind made up a locked door? Then suddenly the door flew open again. She ran out. Emily was there, facing her, on the landing at the top of the stairs. *Don't leave*, she said in her high, shrill child's voice.

'Why do you keep saying that? I am leaving. I can't take any notice of you. You aren't there. It's just the blob in my head making you up.'

Pop – she vanished again. As Jane came to the top of the stairs, Emily appeared again at the bottom, staring up at her with a desperate, pleading look in her eyes. Jane had to look away, squeeze her eyes shut. 'Go away. You're not real, you're not real, you're not real,' she kept repeating. And when she opened her eyes again, Emily had gone.

Jane embarked on a frenzy of cleaning, dreading the reappearance at any moment of the girl who wasn't real. She filled the washing machine with sheets and towels, scrubbed the bathroom till everything shone, cleaned the kitchen, the oven and hob, emptied the fridge and washed it. All was quiet. Too quiet. She would put the radio on, listen to some undemanding music. It was playing a thumping, catchy little pop song she didn't recognise, and she began to relax, bob about in time to it, as she wiped over the worktops. Then the music stopped abruptly. The radio began making a buzzing noise, like static, and that high, plaintive child's voice came loud and clear out of the radio.

Don't leave. Don't leave. Don't leave. Don't—' She pressed the off switch. She would have to get out of the house.

She threw on her coat, began walking up the path towards the cliff top. There, she paced up and down, looking out to the tranquil sea and the gently rolling waves, breathing deeply, trying to calm herself. For a while she watched a black cormorant, diving arrow-straight into the sea, emerging from the waves, then diving once more. And then she looked down and there she was again, the little girl, standing among the rocks. She lifted her head and her voice wafted up from below: *Don't leave.*

'Emily. Go away,' she shouted back. 'Leave me alone. You're in my head. You're not real. And even if you are a ghost, I can't help you. I can't bring you back to life. You're dead. But I'm alive, I'm real. Do you hear me, Emily? I'm real. You're not.'

She turned back to the house, her hands shaking as she made herself some tea, toast and Marmite, comforting food that helped to calm her, reminding her of cosy winter tea-times beside the fire with Nan. For the rest of the day, she carried on with the cleaning and tidying, dried and ironed the bed linen, then made a start on packing her things. Emily didn't appear again. Whoever or whatever she was, it seemed to Jane that she had got the message. Emily had gone.

Peter rang. 'Everything OK, darling?'

Jane said it was. No point in worrying him. Peter told her everything in the flat was good too, and ready for her return. The doctors had left everything spic and span, he said.

Jane said, 'Peter, is it OK if I come home tomorrow, instead of Wednesday? I've got the cottage looking presentable and done most of my packing. There doesn't seem much point in me hanging around for an extra day.'

'Yes, all right. That would be great. I'm missing you already.'

Later, she lit the fire, making a mental note that she would have to clean it out tomorrow. She rang Suzy, and they had a long chat about Christmas plans, and Suzy's baby news.

'The bump's getting huge, and she keeps me awake all night kicking,' Suzy said. And Jane felt a little pang, remembering how she would take Peter's hand and put it on her belly so he could feel Angela's hard little heel pressing against it.

Before she went to bed, Jane took all her clothes off their hangers in the wardrobe, folded and packed them. She emptied the chest of drawers and packed those things too. Now she only had to put her night clothes, wash bag and hairbrush in tomorrow. She fell asleep quickly, thinking about being back in the flat and how good that would feel. She would miss the sound of the sea though. She had grown used to it.

An hour later, she was wide awake. It was dark, and someone was in the room. She could hear scuffling sounds coming from the wardrobe, the wire coat hangers rattling inside, drawers being slid open, slammed shut, then a rustling noise from somewhere on the other side of the room. She lay frozen, surrounded by darkness.

'Emily?' she whispered. 'Is that you? I told you to go away.'

Dreading what she might see, she snapped on the bedside light. There didn't seem to be anyone there. But the wardrobe door was wide open, and all the clothes she'd packed away were inside, back on their hangers. The two suitcases she'd packed and closed were still on the floor, but their lids were thrown open, and they were empty. She got up, looked in the chest of drawers, and they too had been refilled with all her things. What could it mean? Surely her brain wasn't imagining this? Or had she been sleepwalking again? Yes, that must be the answer. She must have unpacked everything in her sleep. But why?

She got back into bed, turned out the light, and fell asleep. It was a restless uneasy sleep, filled with dreams of Emily. Emily running over the rocks on the beach. Emily on the stairs. Emily at the window, tapping. Emily, frantic and screaming over and over, *Don't leave, don't leave, don't leave.*

In the morning, she hurriedly packed all her things again, stripped her bed and made it up with the clean sheets. She couldn't wait to get out now, get away. The remains of the fire were still smouldering in the log burner, so she would have to leave that, and the sheets she'd slept in last night. She wheeled out her cases to put in her car. There was a plastic carrier bag on the doorstep. Inside was a flat bubble-wrapped parcel. She took it back indoors and read the Post-it Note attached: 'Dear Jane, we thought you might like this as a gift, to remind you of your stay. We hope to see you up this way again sometime, sincerely, Tim and Sheila Wetherall.' She unwrapped it. It was the oil painting of the cottage, with the field of poppies.

And the little figure was there once again. Not crumbs, not a squashed insect, but tiny painted brushstrokes, a child with blonde hair, dressed in red, standing in the field near the cottage. Only this time the face wasn't featureless. Its mouth was a dark round dot, a mouth open wide in a silent scream.

Why on earth would Sheila Wetherall have painted that on? Was it some kind of bizarre joke? Or was her brain imagining this too? Anyway, there was no way she would keep the picture. She never wanted to look at it again. She would leave it in the cottage.

She left it face down on the coffee table, had a quick look round to see everything was looking clean and tidy. Then she locked the door behind her, put the key in an envelope, wrote Mrs Mortimer on the front, adding the words thank you as an afterthought – although she didn't really think she had much to thank her for. Luckily, Mrs Mortimer wasn't in the kitchen to spot her as she pushed the envelope through her door.

She got in the car, breathing a sigh of relief, and turned the key. She would be home in forty-five minutes or so, if the roads were clear. She bumped up the track and just as she rounded the bend, there she was again. Emily was standing right in front of the car in the middle of the track, in her red pyjamas, arms spread wide like the Angel of the North, still and staring. Instinctively, Jane stamped on the brake.

What am I doing? she thought. I can't run over a hallucination. She's not real. She's not there.

Then – poof! – the figure disappeared. Releasing her breath, Jane started up again, jolting over the ruts towards the road. She had intended to stop off at the farm to say a quick goodbye to the Armstrongs, but now she just wanted to press on, put as much distance as she could between herself and the cottage.

As she reached a short distance from the end of the track, there was Emily again, standing right in the centre near the junction with the road. No, she wouldn't stop this time. She would drive straight at her. She pressed her foot down, and the engine roared as she came closer and closer, the little girl's face looming nearer and nearer. She was so close now, she could see Minnie Mouse's spidery eyelashes, the freckles on the girl's nose, and she shouted out loud, 'You're not there.', pushed the accelerator hard to the floor and then … nothing. No thump, no scream. She wasn't there. Never had been.

Thank God that's over, Jane thought.

At the junction, Jane slowed down to check for traffic. She looked left, and as she turned her head to the right – oh God. Emily reared up, tapping hard at her side window, closer than she'd ever been before. *Tap-tap-tap.*

Jane was angry now. She wound down the window. 'What do you want? Why won't you leave me alone?' and Emily shouted back, right in her face, *Don't leeeeeeave* drawing that last word out into a long, anguished howl.

Jane was frantic to get away now, close to tears, her heart banging in her chest. She remembered what Suzy had said. Was she staring at some version of herself she'd created in her messed-up brain, a lost and lonely child, desperate for help? Or, as she had once thought, some spirit of a murdered child, come from her watery grave under the sea? Whatever she was, Jane couldn't help her. 'I'm sorry Emily. I'm sorry if I've let you down, but I have to leave,' she said, her voice breaking into a sob. But Emily had gone.

She turned left into the road and headed for home. When she looked in her rear-view mirror, there was no sign of Emily.

****

Mrs Mortimer was pleasantly surprised. They had gone now, earlier than expected, and that was very convenient. It gave her a lot more time, nearly three weeks, to give the cottage a proper clean before the next occupant arrived. She was feeling more and more tired, so it was good she didn't have to rush at it. Mr Blackwood had called on her, told her on no account was she to do any cleaning until she was better. He would get the girls on the cleaning team to come down. But Mrs Mortimer had insisted she could do it, she wanted to do it. It was her job.

But now she was in, she saw that Her Next Door had left it spotless, even changed the bedding, so there wasn't too much to do, just the wood burner to clean out and a couple of sheets and pillowcases to wash. They'd replaced the carriage clock on the mantelpiece that had got smashed, and even left a new painting of the cottage. She was no judge of art, but it looked quite pretty with all those bright red poppies. Some sort of goodbye gift, she supposed. Anyway, it was a nice gesture, and she would find a suitable wall to hang it on.

One thing she noticed hadn't been done, and that was emptying the rubbish bin in the kitchen, but that wouldn't take a minute to do. She lifted out the plastic liner, tied up the top and carried it out to the wheelie bin which was due to be collected tomorrow. As she stuffed it in, she noticed the corner of something red poking out of a black sack at the bottom of the wheelie bin. That looked familiar. She pulled it out, untied the knot, and looked inside. It was the red cushion from the sofa. She took it out of the bag and inspected it. It was a bit smelly from being in with the rubbish, but otherwise there was nothing wrong with it. No stains or rips. Why on earth had Mrs Eagle – and she was sure it was her – done such a peculiar thing and thrown away a perfectly good cushion? It provided such a nice cheery splash of colour on the grey sofa. Well, no problem, she would wash it and put it back where it belonged.

CHAPTER 29

Winter had arrived. Jane opened her curtains that morning to see the bare branches of the tree outside edged with white frost. Strange, but until she went to live up the coast, she never really noticed the seasons of the year as one gradually merged into another, and how the subtle changes in the weather were reflected in the sky and the sea, the sounds and the scents.

She'd been back in town three weeks now, and already the cottage by the sea and all that had happened there were beginning to seem like a distant dream. Today, she had a doctor's appointment and afterwards she was calling in to the office to see everyone there. The students had all gone home, so they weren't busy and the whole campus was peaceful and quiet. She had a gossipy, happy lunch with Suzy, then did a bit of Christmas shopping. She wondered how she could ever have felt overwhelmed by the bustling crowds and the dazzling decorations. She loved it now, and for the first time since Angela died, she was looking forward to Christmas.

On the way home she called in at the chemist's and collected her prescription. She'd been to the doctor, who agreed to put her back on medication. She really didn't want to slip back into that dark place again. And this time there had been no pressure from Peter, who now seemed to be making a supreme effort not to be controlling or overbearing. 'Darling, it's your decision. You do what you think best,' he kept saying.

So now, back in the flat, among all the old familiar things, she took the blister pack of tablets out of the box and looked at it. Then she slid it back, closed the flap. She was feeling well, there'd been no hallucinations, no voices, no sleepwalking. It wouldn't hurt to wait a while, put the medication away, see how things went. And then there was something else, something really important, she had to check out. She lifted another little box she'd got at the chemist's out of her bag and took it to the bathroom.

****

Mrs Mortimer shivered when she opened her door. It was bitterly cold, the east wind spitting little needles of freezing rain in her face, each breath out forming a white cloud. The new occupant was due to arrive that afternoon, so she wanted to make sure the heating was on for them. She didn't know anything about them, only that it was a Mrs Bailey who had made the booking. She hoped she wouldn't have to wait too long. She was getting more tired and weak now, needing to rest every afternoon. The nurse had been to see her about stepping up her pain medication and talked about a stay at the hospice to sort that out. Now that prospect was beginning to look more inviting than a walk into the icy waters of the North Sea.

She'd just given the cottage a last flick over with a duster when she heard a car coming down the track.

Mrs Bailey was youngish, and on her own. That was unusual, Mrs Mortimer thought, and she looked the nervy type, fiddling with her car keys as she followed her into the cottage.

'I think you'll find everything you need here,' Mrs Mortimer said. The woman seemed distracted, not really taking in what Mrs Mortimer was saying as she explained the intricacies of the central heating controls and the washing machine. 'The cottage is very well equipped, very comfortable, as you can see.'

'Yes, yes, it all seems very nice.'

'I feel I should warn you, though, it can be a little isolated and quiet, you know. Especially now winter's here. The last couple who were here…well, it didn't suit her in particular, being here all day on her own.'

'Oh, I'm not on my own. My daughter will be with me. And it'll suit us just fine. To be honest with you, isolation is exactly what we need. I've just been through a very messy divorce, you see.'

'I'm sorry to hear that, I'm sure. And will your daughter be joining you later?'

'Oh no, she's with me now, still in the car. I'm afraid she's being a bit difficult today. She didn't want to get out.'

Mrs Mortimer looked out of the kitchen window to where the car was parked, and she could see now a child with fair hair in the back seat.

'I'll fetch her,' the woman said, striding out to the car. Mrs Mortimer noticed how tall Mrs Bailey was. She would have to warn her to watch her head coming in through the low doorway. Now Mrs Bailey was flinging open the rear door where the child sat with her head down, her arms folded defiantly.

'Get out of the car now.' the woman commanded.

'I don't want to. I want to go back to Daddy's. I don't like it here.' The girl's voice was shrill and insistent.

'Don't be silly. You haven't even seen it yet. It's lovely, and so close to the sea we'll feel like we're on a ship. Come and see.'

The child unfastened her seat belt and slithered reluctantly out of the car. Reading other people's emotions from their expression or body language wasn't one of Mrs Mortimer's skills, but when the child glanced over to her, she recognised at once the fear in her eyes.

The mother took hold of the little girl's hand. 'That's right. Now come along inside, Emily, before you get cold.'

Mrs Mortimer couldn't seem to settle to anything when she was back in her house. She felt uneasy. She could hear the child next door crying. Something didn't feel right about Mrs Bailey and the little girl.

****

Jane perched on the edge of the bath, staring at the small white stick in her hand. She'd been so nervous, waiting to see the result, she'd had a quick shower to distract herself, and now, wrapped in a towel, she picked up the stick and saw the two vertical blue lines. *Positive.*

So how did she feel about this? Excited? Yes. Elated? Yes. Terrified? Yes, yes, yes. But then she heard Nan's voice in her head, clear as a bell. 'Everything will be all right this time, Flower.' Yes, of course it would.

At four thirty, it was already dark outside. Peter was away for the day, taking Christmas presents to his sister and her family in Edinburgh. He wouldn't be back till later in the evening. Jane opened the bathroom window to let out the steam. The cold air was a shock to her warm, bare shoulders. As she looked up at the night sky, an almost full moon sailed into view from behind the wisps of cloud, a halo of bright light surrounding it. In another few hours it would be a perfect golden circle.

And as it shone down, filling the bathroom with its brilliance, so a sudden illumination flooded into Jane's mind, and everything became clear. Of course. Why hadn't she realised before? If spirits could come from the past, they could come from that other dimension too.

The future.

Nan had tried to tell her. 'Look to the future, Flower, look to the future,' came Nan's voice again. She couldn't change the past, but maybe – just maybe - she could change the future. The frosty night, the full moon. It would be tonight. And she knew now what she had to do.

She placed the pregnancy test carefully back on the shelf. That news could wait for now. As she quickly dressed, she considered whether she should phone someone. This couldn't wait till Peter's return. Nigel? No, this was something she had to do on her own. But there was someone else who could help. She prayed Peter had jotted down the number in his address book, not just kept it on his phone.

****

Mrs Mortimer was trying to doze, but she could hear the child still crying next door and it was making her very anxious. Her phone rang.

'Mrs Mortimer? It's Jane Eagle.' Her voice sounded breathless, excited.

What on earth could she want? 'Yes?'

'Look, has the new occupant next door arrived? Is she a tall woman with a young fair-haired girl?'

'That's correct. Mrs Bailey and her daughter.' Mrs Mortimer was wary. How did she know about them?

'Deanna Bailey, of course. Look, I know it sounds odd, but I know that woman. She is seriously disturbed, and I think – I know – the child is in terrible danger.'

'I see. Well, the bairn does seem upset. What should I do, Mrs Eagle? Should I ring the police?'

'No, not yet. I'm on my way. I wonder, could you possibly go round there, Mrs Mortimer, keep her talking until I get there? Make sure the child is safe, even find some excuse to take her back to your place if her mother will let you?'

'Keep her talking?' Mrs Mortimer was not sure what she would talk about. 'I suppose I could show her how to light the log burner.'

'Yes, anything. Just don't let Emily out of your sight. Thank you, Mrs Mortimer, thank you.'

'And what will you do when you get here?'

'I shall talk to her – the woman. She may remember me – we were in hospital together. She's mentally ill, Mrs Mortimer, and I know what that's like, I understand her torment. But the really important thing is we stop her harming herself – and Emily.'

'We?'

'Yes, we can do this if we work together, you and me. Will you help?'

There was a long silence. 'Mrs Mortimer?'

Mrs Mortimer stood motionless, staring into the middle distance. A dull ache from the pit of her stomach was creeping its way slowly through her body. It wasn't the cancer pain; it was something different, a deeper, darker pain that had been buried away for so long that she didn't recognise what it was at first. Then she understood. The forced abortions. The killing of Eric and Katie Harris and the innocent baby growing inside her belly. Even the poor kittens. Guilt. Grief. Anger. Helplessness. She couldn't do anything then. But she could do something now. Death and sorrow had cast enough shadows over this place. It was time to make amends.

Quietly, and with just the slightest tremble in her voice, she spoke: 'Very well. I will go round there now.'

Mrs Mortimer put down the phone and went to fetch her coat.

****

Jane scribbled a quick note for Peter, grabbed her car keys.

She would drive – as fast as she safely could now, she had another life beside her own to take care of – back up the A1, along the moonlit back lanes towards the sea and the cottage with the two chimneys.

'I'm coming, Emily,' she said. 'It's going to be all right.'

CHAPTER 30

The room was dim, the only light coming from the flickering flames of the log burner, and the creamy yellow full moon shining through a crack in the drawn curtains. Mrs Mortimer sat stiffly on the edge of the sofa, pain twisting her guts, and desperately hoping Mrs Eagle would hurry up. She wasn't sure how much longer she could carry on this conversation.

'You really don't have to stay with us,' Mrs Bailey said, her voice so flat and low Mrs Mortimer could barely hear it. 'Now the fire's alight and you've shown me how it works. I'm sure you have things to be getting on with. I know I do.'

She was an odd-looking woman, Mrs Mortimer thought, standing there in the kitchen doorway, so tall and rigid, with her short spiky hair, and her face almost skull-like in the half-light, with high cheekbones and little brown eyes set deep in dark sockets, constantly watching the child. The poor little girl was curled up on the floor next to the fire, hugging her knees, and only occasionally lifting her head to peep nervously back at her mother.

There was a long silence. Mrs Mortimer couldn't think what to say. Really, she wasn't any good at conversation at the best of times. But then she had an idea. 'Oh, before I go, I wonder if you were perhaps planning to put up some Christmas decorations? Some of our visitors like to bring their own, but if not I have a very nice artificial tree and a box of decorations I can fetch for you.'

'No, thank you.' Mrs Bailey said over her shoulder as she went into the kitchen. Mrs Mortimer could hear her rummaging in the cutlery drawer.

'Oh but you must have a tree for the bairn. She can come next door with me and help choose what decorations she'd like from the box. There's all sorts, lights, silver balls, tinsel. And I think a number of different fairies to go on the top.' She looked directly at the little girl. 'I think you'd like to choose which one you'd like best, wouldn't you?'

The child nodded. Her cheeks were wet with tears. Mrs Mortimer felt an odd emotion filling the area around her heart, a sensation she wasn't accustomed to. It must be what they called compassion.

She stood up and held out her hand to the girl. 'Howay then, come with me.' She bent her head towards her, and in what she hoped was an urgent but kindly tone whispered in her ear, 'You'll be safe with me. Come on, pet, quick. While your mammy's in the kitchen.' The little girl's hand was so small and warm and damp in her hand. She'd never held a real child's hand before.

Then they were in the lobby, at the door, about to open it, but Mrs Bailey was suddenly behind them. "No." she barked. Mrs Mortimer swung round to face her, pushing Emily behind her, shielding her. Mrs Bailey loomed over them, backing them trapped against the door. She stepped forwards and something flashed bright in her hand, something long, sharp, steely. She was clutching a carving knife, waving it inches from Mrs Mortimer's face. 'Don't you dare take my child away. If you take her away from me, I'll kill you, do you hear? I'll kill you,' she hissed.

Mrs Mortimer groped desperately behind her back for the door handle, praying it wasn't locked. If she could just open the door a little way, she could urge the child to run. But just as her fingers closed around the handle, she felt the cold sharpness of the knife point pressed against her neck. Emily shrieked and clutched the back of Mrs Mortimer's coat.

'I assure you, Mrs Bailey, killing me poses no threat,' Mrs Mortimer said, keeping her voice calm and steady. 'I am dying anyway, so the doctors say, so you would actually be doing me something of a favour, hastening the process. But really, think what witnessing such a thing would do to your poor bairn. Not to mention the consequences for you.'

'I don't care. Emily and I won't be in this world much longer anyway. We'll be together, forever. In Heaven.'

Mrs Mortimer felt the knife point release its pressure, saw the other woman's arm drawing back slowly, ready to strike. And then, there were headlights. A car door slamming. Running footsteps. Mrs Bailey looked up, startled. The door flew open, bringing in a blast of freezing air. Jane Eagle stood there, breathing hard. She lunged forward, grabbed Mrs Mortimer's arm with one hand, Emily's arm with the other, pushed them out of the door, shouting, 'Run. Both of you. Run!'

As they hurtled together towards the light and safety of Mrs Mortimer's door, Jane called after them, 'Ring the police, Mrs Mortimer. Tell them she's got a knife.'

****

'Deanna, it's all right. It's me. Jane Eagle. Remember me? We were in hospital together.' The woman stood opposite her, staring blankly, saying nothing, her fingers nervously clenching and unclenching around the knife handle. 'No, I don't suppose you do remember. We were both in a pretty bad state at the time. I just want to help you – you and Emily – so you don't need that knife, do you?'

More silence, more staring. Then Deanna Bailey said, 'She's taken my daughter. I've lost her, haven't I? Her knees folded beneath her, and she slithered down to the floor, slumped with her back against the wall. She turned the knife towards her own chest, the point pressing against her skin. 'I don't want to live any more. Not without Emily.'

Jane sat down beside her on the floor. She spoke quietly, urgently. 'Listen, Deanna, I know what it feels like, not wanting to live without your child, the one person you love most in the world. I understand that. Because I lost my daughter too, only I lost her forever and can never see her or hold her in my arms again, because she died. I won't ever see her grow up, become a young woman, be there when she graduates, or follows her chosen career, or even has children of her own. But Emily is alive, she can do all those things. Would you really want to rob her of that life, that future? And you can be a mother to her again, once you're well. You can beat this mental illness thing. It's a struggle, and heaven knows I've struggled too, but with the right help you can get better. And help is on its way soon. So put that knife down, please.'

There was no reply. But then Jane heard a deep sob, and the knife clattered to the floor as Deanna let it drop. A cold hand reached out and touched Jane's fingers. 'Will you stay with me?'

Jane took her hand in hers and held it. 'Of course, I will,' she said.

****

'Whisky likes you, I think. That's unusual for him. He doesn't normally like strangers.' Mrs Mortimer had finished making the phone call, and now stood in her tiny sitting room, watching the little girl huddled on the sofa. Whisky had jumped straight on to her lap, and settled down there. Emily froze with fear at first, but then began gently to stroke the cat's soft fur. Whisky purred under her touch. 'Shall I make you a drink? Hot chocolate perhaps?' Mrs Mortimer said. But Emily hung her head and didn't speak. 'Don't be scared. Everything will be all right, I'm sure.' Even as she said the words, Mrs Mortimer realised she was trying to reassure herself as well. There was no sound at all from next door, and that wasn't necessarily a good sign.

Mrs Mortimer spoke again. 'If you don't want to talk to me, perhaps you can talk to Whisky? Cats understand more than folk think they can. And I can tell you what Whisky would say to you, if cats could speak.'

The little girl nodded. She spoke at last. 'Whisky, is my daddy coming to take me home?'

Mrs Mortimer put her head on one side, as if listening to the cat's low purr. 'He says, yes. Mrs Mortimer – that's me – just rang the police. Your daddy has told them you were missing, and they've been trying to find you. They're on their way.'

'Will Mummy be all right? Are they going to take her away to the hospital again?'

'Yes, I expect they'll take your mammy somewhere safe, look after her.'

'And the other lady? I think her name is Jane?'

'Yes, I'm sure she'll be all right as well. You know her, do you?'

'Oh yes. I've seen her lots of times. At night, in my flying dreams. I tried to tell her.'

'Your flying dreams?'

'I came here. I saw her. I saw the cushion. It was over my face. And then we were in the dark, and under the water, and it was cold, so cold…' The child covered her face with her hands and her shoulders were trembling. Mrs Mortimer had no idea what the child was talking about, and she didn't know how to comfort her. So she sat down beside her and laid a hand on her shoulder.

The room filled with the beam of car headlights coming down the track. 'They're here, hinny. You're safe now,' she said.

EPILOGUE

It was a beautiful September morning. Rays of sunlight danced in sparkling bursts on the sea's smooth surface under a cloudless blue sky.

'Do you know, it must be almost exactly a year to the day we first arrived here.' Peter said. He and Jane were walking down the track towards the cottage, having parked the car at the top next to the farm gate. Maxim, just three weeks old, was asleep in the sling, his tiny head lolling against Peter's chest, a slight breeze ruffling the fluffy tufts of auburn baby hair.

'Don't suppose much has changed,' said Jane. She had been quite happy about coming back, but as they rounded the bend, she felt again the cold uneasy feeling she remembered from that first arrival a year ago. Peter noticed her sudden shudder. 'Are you all right?' he said, looking at her in the way he often did since the events of last December, a look of concern, but mingled with a tinge of something else – fear, perhaps? Or was it more a kind of puzzled wonderment, as if he was trying to figure out something about her that he knew he never could?

'Yes, yes, fine,' she said, and as the cottage came into view she laughed. 'Oh, I was wrong, looks like things have changed a bit.'

The cottage was surrounded with scaffolding and ladders and building materials – piles of stones and lengths of timber – heaped around, the grass churned up with mud.

'Blackwood will be knocking down the dividing wall and turning it back into one large property, I expect. Room for more holidaymakers, lots more cash in the kitty,' said Peter. Jane smiled to herself. He never had warmed to Nigel.

They looked up to the cliff top where they'd all agreed to meet. There was Nigel, large and jovial as ever, holding a cardboard box in his arms. Mr and Mrs Armstrong from the farm were there too. They gathered round Jane and Peter as they approached, focussing on baby Maxim, *oohing* and *aahing* in the expected fashion at his small perfection.

'It's a pity,' said Brian Armstrong, 'There's not many of us here to say goodbye to poor Peggy.'

'Well,' Nigel said, nodding towards the cardboard box he held. 'It's what she wanted. No fuss, no funeral. I would have thought her sister might have turned up, but apparently, she's away on a Caribbean cruise.'

'But looks like someone else is coming,' Jane said, pointing to a car just drawing up at the cottage. And when the occupants got out, she saw who it was. Emily had grown taller, filled out, and looked altogether less frail, less waif-like than Jane remembered. Her long blonde hair was a little darker and had been cut in a neat bob. Holding her hand was James Bailey, her father, bearded, fair-haired, smiling.

'I had to come today,' he explained. 'We owe a lot to that lady's courage, and yours, of course Jane. I didn't really think Emily should come. I thought it might stir up too many traumatic memories for her, but you insisted, didn't you, Em?'

She smiled shyly and squeezed her father's hand.

'Well, there's a few more of us now to see her off,' Nigel said. 'And we've done everything she asked. Except for one thing, eh, Emily?'

'Whisky,' the girl said, brightening up. 'He's my cat now.'

'Peggy left written instructions he was to be put to sleep when she went,' Nigel explained. 'But Emily and that cat took a shine to each other so, well, it seemed obvious she should have him. I spoke to

Peggy about it just before she went into the hospice, and she was happy with that.'

'Well, let's get on with the job in hand,' Nigel said, lifting a bulging plastic bag out of the box. 'I know it doesn't look quite proper, but Peggy wouldn't have wanted money wasted on some fancy urn. So, here she is. Let's take her to the cliff edge, shall we?'

As they walked across the rough grassy slope, Jane spoke to Emily's father. 'How is Deanna? I did go to see her a few times in the hospital, but last time I went they said she'd been discharged, and – with the baby and everything – I've been a bit busy these last few weeks.'

'Oh, I know you have, and I'm really grateful, the way you befriended her. It helped her a lot, I think. She's way better now they've sorted out the right meds; she hasn't had one of her episodes in months, and she's living down in Sussex with her parents. Emily gets to Zoom call her regularly. And maybe we'll try a visit when she's ready for it. Supervised, of course.'

Jane wanted to ask more, but Nigel handed the plastic bag to her and said, 'I think you should do this, Jane.'

The bag was surprisingly full and heavy and difficult to handle as she tilted it over the cliff edge and shook out the contents. The coarse gritty ashes dribbled out in a rush, too quickly, but a sudden sea breeze caught them and held them in a dense grey cloud for a moment before they scattered and floated down to the foaming waves below.

'Goodbye, Mrs Mortimer,' Jane said. 'Rest in peace, wherever you are.' Where and what Peggy was, where and what Angela was, and Nan, she didn't know, and would never know. But that was all right. Perhaps there were just some things none of us were meant to understand.

Maxim had woken up and his thin wails joined the cries of the gulls wheeling overhead. Jane felt the sting of milk filling her breasts.

'Now that's over, are you coming up to the farm for a brew and some cake?' Mrs Armstrong said.

'We'd love to but no, thanks,' Jane said. 'The baby needs feeding. Better get home.'

Peter and Jane walked back up the track. Just before the bend, Jane paused to turn and take a last look at the cottage.

Standing still as statues in the middle of the field and facing towards her were two people. A man, muscular, bare-chested, long shaggy hair, and a young woman, plump, with yellow hair, wearing a short denim skirt. There was something about their stillness and the hazy mist surrounding them that seemed odd. They were staring straight at her. As she stared back, the man slowly raised his hand, as if in greeting.

Peter had walked on some way ahead. She turned and called out to him: 'Peter.'

'What's the matter?'

But when she looked again, nobody was there. There was nothing in the field but the grass and weeds and a couple of grazing sheep.

Maxim's wails were becoming more persistent now.

'Oh, it's all right, I just thought…it's nothing,' she said, hurrying to catch Peter and the baby up.

She decided she wouldn't tell him what she'd seen. And she wouldn't look back at the cottage again.

Acknowledgements

A big thank you to the following, without whom this story would never have seen the light of day:

Conrad Jones and the team at Red Dragon Publishing.

Top thriller writer L.J Ross and the Lindisfarne Prize team for selecting Don't Leave as the 2020 winner.

Literary editor and author Cressida Downing, who as part of my prize provided me with some invaluable advice and suggestions.

My fellow Northumbrian novelist Marrisse Whittaker, for her encouragement, support and advice.

My long-standing writing buddies, Deb Court, Helen Snaith and Bill Durey, with special thanks to Helen for her suggestion for a different, more positive and better ending to the story than the one I had planned, and for the bird-watching information.

Last but not least, to Colin Heathcote and our daughters Selina and Anna Heathcote, for their unwavering support, eagle-eyed proof reading and helpful suggestions. Particular thanks go to Anna for ideas and practical help with all things techie.

Printed in Great Britain
by Amazon

87074514R00160